# Servicing the Target

# Also from Cherise Sinclair

*Masters of the Shadowlands (contemporary)*
Club Shadowlands
Dark Citadel
Breaking Free
Lean on Me
Make Me, Sir
To Command and Collar
This Is Who I Am
If Only
Show Me, Baby
Servicing the Target

*Mountain Masters and Dark Haven (contemporary)*
Master of the Mountain
Simon Says: Mine (novella)
Master of the Abyss
Master of the Dark Side (novella)
My Liege of Dark Haven
Edge of the Enforcer
Master of Freedom

*The Wild Hunt Legacy (paranormal)*
Hour of the Lion
Winter of the Wolf

*Standalone books*
The Starlight Rite (Sci-Fi Romance)
The Dom's Dungeon (contemporary)

# Servicing the Target

## A Masters of the Shadowlands Novel

## By Cherise Sinclair

EVIL EYE
CONCEPTS

Servicing the Target
A Masters of the Shadowlands Novel
By Cherise Sinclair

Copyright 2015 Cherise Sinclair
ISBN: 978-1-940887-92-0

Published by Evil Eye Concepts, Incorporated

# Acknowledgments

As always, my gratitude to Fiona Archer, Monette Michaels, and Bianca Sommerland, my crit partners. *mwah!*

A big shout-out this time goes to my News & Discussion peeps (AKA the Shadowkittens) who've had their little paws in quite a bit of this book, from finding Anne's pictures to baby name suggestions. And the fun with Master Z and Jessica's scenes? Oh, yes, my kittens, you were definitely of use.

My readers on Facebook helped out with suggestions for sensuous music while I write—so if you find the sex scenes even hotter this time, pat yourselves on the back.

A huge thank you to Liz Berry and M.J. Rose from Evil Eye Concepts for taking charge of the publishing details and, even more, for getting the word out about this book. Y'all are awesome.

Finally, when I got stuck on some of the military details, Kennedy Layne, author of the wonderfully action-packed CSA Case Files and Red Star series, lent me her Marine. Top Griz, thank you so, so much for helping out with this book.

This book's title, *Servicing the Target*, is a military term, used in the past to denote bombing the enemy, but is now occasionally used by snipers. To our people serving in the military, past and present, I am humbled by your courage. *May the burden of your memories lie lightly on your shoulders, and may happiness and peace walk with you on your journey.*

# Author's Note

To *my readers,*

The *books I write are fiction, not reality, and as in most romantic fiction, the romance is compressed into a very, very short time period.*

You, *my darlings, live in the real world, and I want you to take a little more time in your relationships. Good Doms don't grow on trees, and there are some strange people out there. So while you're looking for that special Dom, please, be careful.*

When *you find him, realize he can't read your mind. Yes, frightening as it might be, you're going to have to open up and talk to him. And you listen to him, in return. Share your hopes and fears, what you want from him, what scares you spitless. Okay, he may try to push your boundaries a little—he's a Dom, after all— but you will have your safe word. You will have a safe word, am I clear? Use protection. Have a backup person. Communicate.*

Remember: *safe, sane, and consensual.*

Know *that I'm hoping you find that special, loving person who will understand your needs and hold you close.*

And *while you're looking or even if you have already found your dearheart, come and hang out with the Masters of the Shadowlands.*

Love,
*Cherise*

Sign up for the 1001 Dark Nights Newsletter
and be entered to win a Tiffany Lock necklace.

There's a contest every quarter!

Go to www.1001DarkNights.com to subscribe.

As a bonus, all subscribers will receive a free
1001 Dark Nights story
*The First Night*
by Lexi Blake & M.J. Rose

# Chapter One

Bloody hell, she hurt.

Anne patted the wrought iron doorknocker on its snarling lion nose and pushed the door open. Damn thing seemed a lot heavier tonight.

She stalked into the foyer of the Shadowlands BDSM club—well, she tried to stalk—a Mistress had her pride, after all, but the limp must have destroyed the effect.

Damn her cousin anyway. Grandstanding plays belonged on the baseball diamond, not during an operation with armed felons.

As the door closed behind her, the Shadowlands security guard looked up. Scowled. He rounded the desk. A good six feet five, shoulders as wide as a football field, the goliath could have taken Schwarzenegger's role in the *Terminator*. "What the *hell* happened to you?" he barked.

Huh? She hadn't known he could raise his voice. He seemed such a sweetheart that, until recently, she'd wondered why Z had hired him for security. Then again, he looked rather like a Rottweiler—big-boned, oversized, and battered—and maybe he'd never needed to put his skills to the test.

He loomed over her, brows pulling together. "Are you all right?" His faded New York accent thickened, turning the *all right* to *ahrite*.

"Hello, Ben."

"Mistress Anne..." His voice came out a low rumble, and she lifted an eyebrow. The guard dog had a growl after all.

"I'm fine." She patted his arm and found rock-hard muscles beneath his loose, button-up shirt. She had to—quite inappropriately—

wonder at what else lay under all that fabric.

"Were you in an accident? Should I call someone?"

She laughed—and halted quickly as her right side blazed with pain. It felt as if someone had jammed a fiery spear between her ribs. *Don't laugh, stupid.* She put her hand over the ache, pleased that her over-the-dress bustier served as adequate support for a bruised ribcage. "The only *accident* was the need to rescue an inadequate member of my team." Because her cousin had located the fugitive and tried to apprehend the man himself without waiting for backup. Because the idiot had gotten the pistol kicked out of his hand. Because she'd had to jump in before the felon smashed Robert's head in with his baseball bat. "He got in a couple of good blows"—and a kick to her thigh—"before I took him down."

The narrowing of Ben's eyes made him look impressively menacing.

But after a second, he shook his head and returned to his position, leaving the air in his wake unsettled, as if a thunderstorm had moved through. He braced a hand on his desk and frowned at her. "Picking up fugitives is dangerous. Maybe you should…" He trailed off, frozen to silence by her icy stare.

Her father and uncles possessed an identical belief, and she gave his comment the same careful consideration she accorded theirs. *None.*

"Benjamin," she said softly. She met his gaze. Held his gaze. "When I want your opinion about my occupation, I'll beat it out of you."

He sat down slowly—and she gave him props for that, since a lot of boys went weak-kneed. But this was a man. She'd have said a very vanilla man, but heat flushed his cheeks and lips. And the concern in his eyes had changed to an edgy arousal.

*Interesting.*

But she shook her head. She didn't do vanilla.

And she certainly wouldn't mess with an employee of Z's.

Lifting a hand, she sauntered—with a damn limp—into the main clubroom. Into gut-wrenching screams, flickering sconces, and the scents of sex and sweat and pain.

*Home sweet home.*

\* \* \* \*

Three hours later, she'd assessed the various scenes being conducted, chosen a nice quiet caning, and eased down into a leather armchair outside the roped-off area. *Done, done, done.* Her stint as dungeon monitor was complete, and her leg throbbed as if a dwarf logger was using an ax on it. Galen and Vance were out of town, leaving the Masters short-handed, or else she'd have called to tell Z she couldn't make it tonight.

But she'd performed her duty.

"Mistress Anne, may I fetch you something to drink?"

She eyed the young man. Dressed in running shorts and nothing else, the blond actually vibrated with his need to please. He must be one of the new ones.

After eliminating the trainee positions, the club owner, Z, had tried professional waitstaff, been displeased with the results, and now offered his submissive members discounted dues if they served drinks a certain number of hours a month.

"What's your name?" Anne asked.

"Apple, Mistress Anne."

"Apple, as in take a bite out of you?" She watched him quiver.

"Yes, Mistress Anne. Any time the Mistress wishes."

"That's good to know, Apple." He was a very pretty lad—and she couldn't summon up an ounce of interest. She put a boot up on the long, dark wood table. "Right now, all I want is my second drink. Tell Master Cullen it's for Mistress Anne, please."

"Yes, Ma'am." His look of disappointment was so intense, she felt like patting him on the cheek and saying, "There, there."

But that would require moving.

Instead, she leaned her head back, closed her eyes, and listened to Seraphim Shock's "After Dark," the sinister music punctuated by the staccato sounds of the nearby caning. When she heard the thump of a glass on the end table, she held her hand out, palm up, and waggled her fingers. "In my hand, boy."

He set the drink in her hand.

"Thank you." One sip told her that Cullen had worked his usual magic. The silky smoothness of a perfectly chilled Manhattan eased her dry throat.

The chair beside her squeaked.

*Excuse me?* A slave dared sit in her presence? "Listen, boy…" She opened her eyes and met those of the owner of the Shadowlands.

"Good evening, Anne." Gray eyes alight with amusement, he leaned back and set a foot next to hers on the coffee table.

Since he'd been nice enough to bring her a drink, she drank more of it. *Lovely.* "Sorry, Z. I thought you were someone named *Apple*."

His lips twitched at the emphasis she gave to the name. "Did you have a craving to peel and core him?"

"Not even close. Today you could parade a few dozen eager submissives in front of me, and I still wouldn't be motivated to move." In fact, her limbs felt as if they were sinking into the furniture. "Actually, I'm not particularly interested in anyone these days."

"Are you missing Joey?"

Joey had been her latest slave; the one she'd kept for the longest period. They'd had so much fun together...and then not so much fun. "Not really. Not anymore."

"You never did tell me what happened." Damn psychologist waited silently.

His tricks didn't work on her. "No, I didn't, did I?"

He huffed an easy laugh. "All right, Anne." In the dim light of the wall sconces, his lean face showed only mild concern. "If your lack of interest in the available submissives isn't due to your breakup, then have your interests changed?"

*Changed.* She rather despised that word. "Of course not." Her eyes closed again. "The puppies just don't seem particularly satisfying." And some of them wanted more than she wanted to give.

"I see. Perhaps a different type of submissive might suit you better."

*Doubtful.* She glanced at her watch. "I didn't see you earlier. Did you just get here?"

"I'm running late, yes. Jessica worked overtime and was overtired when she arrived home."

*Oh, not good.* Z's wife was very, very pregnant. "Is she having problems?"

"She's fine. I gave her a backrub and tucked her in." He shook his head. "She's the only person I know who finds enjoyment in IRS forms."

Relieved, Anne relaxed. "Well, she *is* an accountant." And due to deliver sometime in the next couple of weeks. Sooner would be good since Anne had picked a March date and "girl" in the Shadowlands' betting pool.

"Indeed. A less dangerous job than some...like picking up bail fugitives." He regarded her. "Ben said you were hurting."

"Not so much at the moment." Probably because she'd downed two pain pills an hour earlier. She lifted her glass and drained it. "Does your guard dog report everything?"

He tilted his head. "Actually, he acted more like *your* guard dog. He was worried about you, Anne."

"Oh." Why that should stop her brain for a second, she didn't know. Then again, her brain wasn't processing well. And the glass she held seemed exceedingly heavy.

Z rose and plucked it from her fingers.

"Hey."

To her surprise, he sat down beside her on the couch and tilted her head. "Look at me, please."

The command—that of a Dom—held a punch she could resist fairly easily. But his politeness? She couldn't ever be rude to him. She met his gaze.

He studied her for a minute. "What did you take?"

"You're such a psychologist. I took a couple of pain pills. *After* I finished monitoring."

"Anne, I never doubted otherwise." His easy agreement let her relax. "However, you're in no shape to drive home."

"Not your decision." Planning to push his hand away, she lifted her arm…and felt as if she was moving through Jell-O. "Oh hell. I hate when you're right."

"It does get annoying, doesn't it?"

"Would you have someone call a taxi, please?"

"No. But I will have someone drive you home…and escort you safely into your house."

She eyed him. "Jessica has to put up with your overprotectiveness. I don't."

"Actually"—he turned her head to one side and examined the graze on her cheekbone— "this time you do."

\* \* \* \*

Ben Haugen had been to Anne's house before when he chauffeured her and her friends to a bachelorette party last winter. It was on the barrier island of Clearwater Beach and down a quiet cul-de-sac.

As Ben walked around his car, he could see past Anne's cottage-style house to the ocean beyond. How could she afford a beach house on a bounty hunter's salary?

When he opened the passenger door, the interior light showed she was still asleep in the tipped-back seat. She'd miscalculated the effect of alcohol on pain pills, Z had said. Ben had made that mistake a time or two.

Her dark brown hair, which she'd worn braided back in a severe style, had come undone. The loose tendrils softened her aristocratic face. She wasn't a small woman—maybe five-eight—but beautifully formed, with small breasts and a tight, rounded ass. A darkening bruise marred the sculpted beauty of her right cheekbone.

God fucking dammit, he'd never seen anyone so beautiful.

"Mistress Anne." He unfastened her seatbelt. Hell, she wasn't budging. With a grunt of exasperation, he checked the purse that Z had retrieved from her locker. Her house keys were clipped to the strap. "I hope you don't have a dog, woman, or you'll have a real bouncy ride." He set the purse in her lap and plucked her off the seat.

She was heavier than he expected. Undoubtedly had more muscles than the last woman he'd lifted. He kicked the car door shut and carried her up to the cottage.

After unlocking the door, he opened it cautiously. No dog. Anne snoozed against his shoulder as he walked through the foyer, took a guess, and headed up the stairs. An opened door revealed the master bedroom—or would that be called the mistress bedroom? Using his elbow, he flipped on the light switch.

A chandelier came to life revealing icy blue walls. A glass-fronted fireplace with an ornate mirror over the mantel. A canopied bed with a ruffled floral bedspread. A white couch with fancy legs in front of a wall of windows. All blue and white, like an airy summer garden, it was the most feminine room he'd ever seen.

But not a plant anywhere. Everything in place. As spotless as if a drill sergeant was due for inspection.

She roused when he laid her on the bed, and damned if Ms. Feminine didn't try to punch him.

The candle-shaped lights overhead provided crappy illumination— and hell, she probably only saw a hulking monster over her. He caught her delicate fist in his oversized palm. "Easy, Ma'am."

Her finely arched brows drew together as she tried to sit up. He didn't miss the way her hand grabbed her ribs. Damn foolish woman.

"It's Ben. From the Shadowlands. I brought you home."

"Ah. Ben." She gingerly relaxed back on the mattress. "Thanks for the ride. Please tell Z I said so."

"You're welcome, Mistress Anne." He shifted his weight, uncomfortable as hell. But the garment she wore seemed to be some combination of a corset and a dress. It had obvious ribbing and was way too tight. She couldn't sleep in it. "Uh…you need to get out of that contraption."

He was standing over her—one big ugly guy. She was flat on her back and totally unconcerned. "Do I now?"

The edge of warning in her voice made his cock stir.

"Yes, Ma'am." The honorific came easily to his lips. She reminded him of the elegant Army Ranger Captain during Ben's first deployment. The guy was always in control and, even when covered with blood and filth, still refined.

He smiled. "How about you order me to give you some help?"

Her snort of exasperation sounded like a kitten's sneeze. "Benjamin, if a subbie tells me to order him to do something, then who's in charge?"

"Got me there." And damned if he would leave without making her more comfortable. "You going to punch me if I help you strip down?"

She eyed him. Her pupils were still smaller than normal, turning her eyes more blue than gray. "I never appreciated how stubborn you are."

"Yes, Ma'am." Odd how much he liked saying that to her.

Her voice held a note of frustration. "Assist me out of this, then."

And he had a win. *Sergeant, Bravo Zulu.* He reached for the front and realized her ribbed long dress had no buttons. Stalling, he moved down to remove her thigh-high boots, which had lacing front straps. When he pulled them off, he heard her sigh of relief.

Damn, her pretty legs had a sexy golden tan. High-arched feet. Her toenails were a pale pink with white stripes. Amazing what women did for fun. Her mutant black dress was next. Thinking to salvage her modesty, he picked up the frilly knitted throw from the foot of the bed and draped it over her lower legs.

*Next.* He'd have been more comfortable walking into a firefight.

Her fucking dress had toothpick-sized metal studs down the front that poked through metal grommets. Only way to get it off would be to stick his fingers inside and draw the edges together to release each fucking stud. Her breasts were in there. Jesus, he couldn't do this.

Her lips curved in a wicked smile. "Don't stop now, Benjamin."

"Having fun are we, Mistress?" he muttered and slid his big fingers inside the top.

"Mmmhmm."

She was warm, her skin silky on the backs of his knuckles. And he was harder than a rock. He worked open the corset part of the dress, and it came undone, catch-by-catch. But the thing was damn tight over her ribs, and she made a sound of pain.

He stopped. How the fuck could he do this if he hurt her? "Anne?"

"Go on." Her hands were fisted, her fingernails digging into her palms. But her gaze was clear and level. "You're right—I would have had difficulty getting out of this. I'm not moving as well as I was earlier."

"What kind of damage are we looking at?" His jaw was tight as he continued as ordered. Prong after prong.

Although she controlled her face, she couldn't control the involuntary flinches and tightening of her belly.

"Bruised ribs. Nothing broken." Her voice sounded strained, but finally he was past the most constricted section.

He undid the looser part over her lower stomach and worked his way...down. As he flipped the dress open, he tried not to look.

Bullshit, he totally looked.

His gaze traveled from her thong-covered pussy, up a softly rounded belly, to her sweet, high breasts. Rosy-brown nipples perked up in the cool night air. Her scent was almost edible—like tangerines accompanied by the light musk of a female.

*Act like the gentleman you weren't raised as, Haugen.* He drew the blanket over her. Turning his gaze away—so he wouldn't see how he hurt her—he slid an arm under her back. Shit, her skin there was soft as well. Carefully, he lifted her far enough to slide her dress out.

Now she wore only a thong and a blanket.

The room had grown too damn warm.

"Thank you, Ben. That feels much better."

"I bet." He dared greatly and moved the covering to expose her legs. Her right thigh had a bruise almost the width of his fist. He glanced at her, eyebrows raised. "Boot?"

"The bail fugitive had an overly protective big brother."

What a fucking job. No wonder she often came into the Shadowlands with bruises and gashes. "Wouldn't you rather do something...safer?"

Her blue gaze turned chill as the arctic north. "No."

"Sorry, Ma'am."

"You do say that quite nicely, you know," she murmured. She had dimples, something he hadn't noticed until he'd seen her laughing during Gabi's bachelorette party.

"I do what?" He needed to leave or he was going to strip that blanket off her again. Find every bruise and kiss them all better.

"*Ma'am.* I thought you were vanilla, Ben."

"I am." And if he'd been daydreaming about her setting a sharp stiletto on his chest, he'd keep those thoughts to himself. "Did a bit of service, is all."

"Ah." She eyed him slowly, still not quite returned to her usual frightening brilliance. "Can I pay you for the time and gas to bring me all the way out here?"

"Yes, Ma'am." He paused a second. Hopefully, she'd never share Ben's request with Z—he'd get his ass fired on the spot. "I think I deserve a kiss from the Mistress."

Her eyebrows lifted. "You are just full of surprises tonight."

Her husky voice always sounded like a morning after raw sex, but when it dropped to that throaty tone, he could see why men crawled on their knees in her wake.

He waited while she thought. He'd wait all night—fuck knew, looking at her wasn't a chore.

Rather than answering, she held her arms up.

*God loves me.* He sat beside her hip, leaned down as she put her hands behind his neck. *More.* He carefully slid a hand under her shoulders. Her satin skin stretched over smooth feminine muscles. He opened his other hand behind her head to enjoy the thick mass of silky fine hair. He was used to visual delights—she was a tactile symphony.

He lifted slightly, just enough to draw her against his chest, so her breasts would press against him. Warm and firm and soft.

*Bless Z.*

When he gazed into her face, he could read her surprise at his daring, and then her eyes started to narrow. If he didn't move, he'd lose his treat. So he bent his head and brushed his lips against hers.

*Softness.* Damned if he'd hurry. He settled his mouth over hers and walked empty-handed into the fire zone.

The guard dog had moves.

His lips were firm and far more competent than his quiet demeanor had promised. His massive size and strength made her feel delicate.

Feminine.

He'd leashed all that power because of her. For her. The knowledge was heady.

Her fingers curled into his thick hair, and she traced a line over his lips with her tongue. "*More.*"

"Yes, ma'am." He tilted his head and turned the kiss hot and wet, driving into her mouth with an expert thrust of his tongue, then teasing again.

Despite the pain and meds, she felt heat sliding through her veins.

Her breasts were crushed against his rock-hard pectorals.

He gave a low growl and deepened the kiss.

And...she couldn't have that. She curved her fingers, digging her fingernails lightly into his scalp in warning.

To her surprise, he broke off, laying her down with disconcerting gentleness.

She ran her hand over his jaw, feeling the scratch of harsh stubble. Several scars stood out, white against the deep tan, on his right cheek, his heavy jaw, his neck. Sun creases fanned out from his eyes. More lines bracketed his mouth. But, his shoulder-length caramel-colored hair was pulled straight back in his usual tied-back style. She realized the streaks hid a few strands of gray in front of his ears.

She hadn't ever really looked at him, had she? "How old are you?"

"Older than you, Mistress," he muttered.

"That is not what I asked, Benjamin."

He was sitting on the side of the bed, hip against hers, leaning over with his weight supported on the arm next to her waist. His free hand, she realized, was toying with her hair. Somehow, she couldn't summon the proper indignation.

"Got a couple of years on you. Thirty-six."

Well, he wasn't as young as she'd thought. Of course, guard dogs rarely showed their ages, did they? He was certainly different from her usual choices. Her brows drew together. And he knew he was older than her thirty-four? "How did you know my age?"

"The Shadowlands member files include a copy of your driver's license so we know who signs in is the right person. You have a birthday coming up in April." He hesitated. "No need to worry. All the guards sign confidentiality agreements."

"Of course." Z was nothing if not protective of his members. A second or so later, her hazy mind registered how he watched his finger stroking her cheek. "Ben?"

"You are so fucking gorgeous." The bed creaked as he rose. He walked into the bathroom and returned to set a glass of water on her bedside table. He placed her purse next to it. "Is your phone in there?"

She nodded.

"Is there anything else I can do for you before I leave?"

She bit down on her lips to keep from laughing. He was a demon submissive, fiercely determined to be sweet. "No, I think you've covered the bases."

He said under his breath, "Didn't get close to running the bases."

She gave him a reproving look, and to her delight, he actually flushed.

"Thank you for the ride…and the care, Benjamin." And the kiss.

He nodded, paused, and his heavy brows came together. "Ma'am? Stay in bed tomorrow and get healed up."

A bossy submissive. Why couldn't she summon the appropriate amount of annoyance? Her standards must be slipping, she thought as the bed rose up to enfold her and sleep carried her away.

# Chapter Two

At the end of his three miles, Ben slowed to a jog and then walked the final block. Not that he'd cool down much in the humid Florida morning. It was only March, but the heat had already moved in. Growing up in New York, he'd often frozen his ass off in the mornings. At times, he missed those days.

Didn't particularly miss the snow, though.

Once inside his warehouse, he pulled off his tank top, using it to wipe himself down as he trotted up the stairs to his living quarters and hit the fridge for a bottle of vitamin water. Designer shit, but didn't taste too bad.

After an hour of weights in his home gym and a shower, he grabbed a fast-food breakfast in the car. He reached Sawgrass Lake Park as the afternoon sunlight slanted through the incoming storm clouds over the swamp.

Perfect.

Once his tripod was set up, he snapped a few shots of a graceful Little Blue Heron. Amazing how it managed to be both small and dignified—a lot like Anne.

All too soon the pelting rain began. Ben edged into a picnic shelter and took a final picture. Something, some movement, sparked a memory of peering through a scope, taking up the slack in the trigger, the world fading as he became hyperaware of the winds and light. Slow, steady pressure on the trigger, releasing a breath and pausing at the bottom of the exhale. Kill shot.

*No.*

As Z had taught him, he breathed through the flashback and let it dissipate.

*Gone.*

*Thank you, Z.* He owed the man more than he could say.

After tucking his camera in its waterproof bag, he settled down on the concrete bench in the shelter.

Owed the man for the treat last night as well.

Fuck, but the woman had a beauty like the morning after a New York blizzard. Hair the color of dark walnut, eyes the gray-blue of a winter sky. Stark and striking enough to stop a man's heart.

Her smallest smile would delineate her sharp cheekbones, but her real smile showed her dimples and changed her entire appearance. Made her human. A woman. And one he wanted so bad he could taste it.

Wind gusted into the shelter, whipping his hair around his face. The world flashed with a lightning strike. Five seconds later, he heard the crack of thunder announcing an approaching storm cell filled with fury. He loved Florida thunderstorms, even if they occasionally set off the messed-up storage program in his head. PTSD—and what idiot psych-tender came up with that phrase?

The lightning reminded him of the first time he'd heard Anne's low laugh. It'd been the night of the bachelorette party when he'd actually seen her without her Mistress *armor*. When everything that was her had sizzled into him and stopped his heart.

Not an hour later, she'd seen one of her friends being harassed and had been willing to step up to the plate and take on the assholes.

That's when he'd known he was in serious trouble.

*Anne.* She had a pretty name. Short. Terse. Much like the woman herself. She was completely different from the last woman he'd dated, who babbled at the drop of a hat. Or if a hat didn't drop. Or if the sun rose. Or set. Or if she was breathing. *Jesus.* Wouldn't have been so bad if she'd been interested in anything besides what she was babbling.

But the Mistress didn't babble. And she not only listened, she listened with all her attention.

That, right there, could steal a man's breath.

*But.*

She was a *Mistress*. There was where the problem came in. The woman had a rep. Not only was she a Domme, but also a fucking sadist. And although she played with quite a variety of submissives, the ones she kept around tended to be a type: mid-twenties, slender, model-gorgeous. The club members called them Anne's "pretty boys."

Settling down with his back against a shelter post, he put a boot on the bench and propped his arm on his knee. Scars ran down his muscular forearm, more across his thick knuckles. Even as a teen, he hadn't been "pretty."

Lotta hard miles since then. In fact, he'd scared more than a few females.

But he hadn't scared Anne.

He grinned. She was a take-no-prisoners, never-back-down, bossy woman. And fuck, he got off on that. Before last night, he'd hoped that if he had a taste of her, got a little closer, his curiosity would be satisfied. Instead, like the first shot of a fine whiskey, she'd teased his appetite.

Now he'd set his sights on the woman.

And—as his team in the Rangers had witnessed—he never missed.

\* \* \* \*

"...a cane works well for that," Anne said to Olivia as she walked into the Shadowlands. They'd been arguing over their favorite discipline methods on the walk in from the parking lot. "Check this one out." Anne held up the extra-long black cane which she'd chosen to embellish her Maleficent costume.

"Jesus, woman, I thought I told you to stay in bed." The growling voice came from her left.

The other Domme's eyes widened.

Anne's spine snapped straight, and she turned to look at Z's security guard.

Rising from his seat, Ben scowled at her. "You shouldn't be here. You're—"

She lifted her chin.

He stared at her, muttered, "Fuck," and dropped into his chair. Still scowling, but silent.

*Interesting.*

She was even more intrigued at his, "Sorry, Mistress."

He didn't know better, didn't know that he should call her Mistress Anne, rather than Mistress, as if he belonged to her.

She wasn't finding herself annoyed.

Unable to resist, she pushed back her black cape, walked behind the oversized desk, and stopped in front of him. When he tried to stand, she set her hand on his shoulder to halt him. She took a second to appreciate the bunching muscles before resting her fingertips on his cheek.

He was so tall his gaze didn't have far to lift to meet hers.

"Benjamin. I value your concern, but if you speak so disrespectfully to me again, I'll put you in the stocks and whip your ass."

Emotion imbued his dark tan with a lovely reddish tone. His golden-brown eyes studied her a careful minute, and then, to her surprise, he rumbled out, emphasizing each word, "Jesus, woman, I thought I told you to stay in bed."

As she stared at him, his head cocked slightly to one side. The gauntlet had been thrown.

Her first reaction was anger—but she wasn't a baby Domme to let a subbie unsettle her emotions. She studied his eyes, his expression. He wasn't being defiant as much as...challenging.

In fact, he'd asked for what he wanted in the only way that someone like him would. He wasn't an insecure submissive who'd beg.

A spark of interest flamed. Not a *boy*. Under her fingers, his jaw was scratchy with a heavy five-o'clock shadow. He was a man. And a challenge. She felt her lips tilting up and enjoyed the way his gaze shifted to take that in.

"Benjamin," she said, "you're just full of surprises." She held his eyes. "If I ask Z to take you off the door for an hour, what would you say?"

A corner of his mouth twitched up. "Thank you, Mistress?"

Amusement slid in to mix with her interest. "Good answer." She squeezed his shoulder—it was like patting a brick wall. "I'll see you later."

He leaned back in his chair. "Mistress, I look forward to that."

The look in his eyes, assessing and intrigued, sent a trickle of heat to her nether regions. Enough that second thoughts would be wise.

She didn't feel like being wise.

When she rejoined Olivia, the other Domme was frowning.

As the door to the main room closed behind Anne, all that was the Shadowlands washed across her. The scents of sex and leather with a hint of citrus cleanser. Perfume. The sharp tang of alcohol wipes indicating someone doing needle play.

On the dance floor to the right, submissives in school costumes danced with ghoulish figures to Athamay's "Restrict and Obey." Master Z had told the submissives to wear "student" clothing and that any not attired properly would be caned.

Then he'd instructed the Dominants that they were to dress as monsters—he didn't care what kind.

Two newer subs entered behind Anne and Olivia. Pigtails, short plaid skirts, knee-highs. Just inside the door, they came to a sudden halt. Obviously, the young women had expected to see professor-attired

Doms who would match their schoolgirl outfits.

What they got were nightmares. One made an "eeping" sound.

Anne glanced around the room. Holt was attired as Freddy Krueger.

Master Raoul as King Kong had his hands all over his slave Kim.

Seated at the bar was Marcus—an elegant Imhotep from the Mummy—being served by Wolfman Cullen. What looked like blood stained Cullen's ripped shirt.

Worried whispers came from the submissives.

*Lovely effect, Z.* Anne exchanged a smile with Olivia.

Cullen noticed Anne and Olivia at the entrance and lifted a bottle in an acknowledgment and welcome.

God, she loved this place. Here, the Mistresses were considered equal to the Masters. Competence, skill, power—those qualities were required for the Shadowlands title. Genitalia weren't a factor.

As she started forward, Olivia grasped her arm. "Did I seriously hear you say you'll punish Ben? Have you gone stark-raving bonkers?"

Everyone loved Z's guard dog.

Anne pursed her lips. "Possibly. But life's been boring lately."

"Boring?" Olivia's disapproving look could have been patented by Anne's mother. "I'd say you've had enough fun recently since you're moving like my aged grandmother. You have a limp—and a bruise on your face."

Well, hell, she'd thought she was walking quite nicely. Then again, an experienced Domme's powers of observation matched a superhero's, and Olivia had well earned her Mistress title. Anne shrugged. "Just a few leftovers from work."

"Right." Olivia fell into step with a vampirish smile enhanced by the long plastic fangs. "Are you going to let me watch Z shred you into confetti for touching his security guard?"

"He'll do no such thing." *I hope.* "Go find your sweetie and play."

"Spoilsport." Olivia looked around and headed for her sub-of-the-month, a pretty redhead seated with some of the Masters' submissives.

Anne reached the bar, slid onto a barstool, and suppressed her groan at the pull on her sore ribs. As she watched Cullen mix up some involved girly drink, she realized Ben was just about the same height—a good six-five or so. Both men were big-boned and rough-hewn. Cullen'd probably score high in a *Good Looks* contest.

But Ben would unquestionably win in the *More Deadly* one, something she'd first grasped when seeing a girl harassed at Gabi's bachelorette party. That night, he'd looked quite capable of ripping someone's throat out—and wasn't it perverse of her to find that incredibly hot.

*"Did a bit of service,"* Ben had said. It really, really showed.

"Nice Maleficent—you've sure got the required cheekbones." Cullen stopped in front of Anne. Before she could give him her order, he put down a delicate ice-filled crystal glass and filled it from a bottle of sparkling water.

Anne stared. "Water?"

His mouth thinned. "If you ever imbibe on top of pain medications again, I'll never serve you another drink."

Z had shared.

Anne tapped her fingernails on the bar top. Unfortunately, she'd earned the reprimand. Cullen was compulsive about the no-impairment Shadowlands rules; he'd cut people off after one drink if they appeared affected. He'd have blamed himself if she'd come to harm.

So rather than taking offense, she answered mildly, "Fair enough."

"And here I thought I'd need a crotch-guard to protect my pride 'n' joys from your snips."

A chuckle came from Marcus.

Cullen poured the remainder of the water into a beer mug and *clinked* it against her glass before drinking. "You scared me last night, love."

"Sorry, my friend. I hadn't realized how potent the pills were." She sipped the strawberry-flavored bubbly water. Not bad.

"You okay?"

"I'm just sore today. And my drug of choice this evening is only ibuprofen." She'd never make the mistake of taking pain meds unless she intended to stay home. And maybe not then either. Cullen wasn't the only one who'd been scared.

"Z took you off dungeon monitor duties tonight."

"Z's such a mother."

"Nah, we've got it covered. The Feds are back in Tampa."

Although Galen had resigned from the FBI, his partner Vance had stayed in—and both were out of town so often that they didn't go on the roster. But when home, the two Masters enjoyed filling in. "In that case, it's nice to have a break."

"Are you fixin' to play tonight?" Marcus asked in his deep, Southern-accented voice.

She hadn't planned to because of her soreness, although she'd taken the time to dress up. A girl had to have standards, after all. "Play? There's a chance I just might." She felt herself smiling.

"Aye? And what lucky boy gets the Mistress tonight?" Cullen asked. "Been a while since I saw you look interested."

"Indeed, I would have to agree." A snifter was set on the bar top, and Z took the seat to her right. His intent gaze swept over her in a Dom's automatic assessment.

She sighed, unable to summon any annoyance. Z did the same to all of the club members, submissive or Dominant, male, female, or gender-fluid. In his opinion, he was responsible for them all.

"Z. You're just the person I needed to see," she said. "I'd like to steal your security guard for an hour."

Z looked taken aback for a moment.

Cullen choked on his water. "Ben? Ben's the guard tonight. You want *Ben?*"

Z rubbed his lips, obviously smothering a smile at Cullen's reaction. Then his gray gaze landed on Anne. His brows drew together. "He's always insisted he was vanilla. Did he indicate he wanted a scene?"

"In an *I'm-too-macho-to-ask-for-what-I-want* way, yes. Most definitely."

"You're not one to misread a man's intention." Z's calm response was gratifying. "I'll send someone out for an hour while Ben takes a break. Would twenty-three hundred suit you?"

Eleven at night. Her favored time to have a session. Early enough that the ambiance in the room would still hold an edge. Late enough that the gung-ho players would have finished and not be impatiently waiting at a roped-off area for a turn. She'd be able to take her time during the scene. "Perfect. Thank you."

"You're welcome. Just don't break my guard, please."

"Not a problem." She hadn't felt like breaking a man in a while, at least not in the same way she had before.

And lightweight or not, the guard dog would be fun to play with.

\* \* \* \*

That night, Ben answered the thumping on the locked door and let his buddy Ghost into the Shadowlands. "Hey."

"Got called in to relieve you. The boss says you want to *play.*" Vocal cord damage during an early battle had given Ghost a hoarse voice more suited to telling horror stories—and sounding horrified, as well. "Seriously?"

"Yep." Ben grinned. "I figured it was time to liven up my life."

"I guess it can't be worse than getting shot at." The gray-haired vet should know. As Special Forces, he'd been in and out of every active shithole over the last twenty years. Dressed in black jeans and a button-up shirt—Z's minimum dress code—he crossed the room without a limp despite his leg prosthesis and tossed a crossword puzzle on the desk.

"It's quiet tonight." Ben tapped the membership list. "Mark off the members as they leave. If you're not sure someone is stable—or if any combo of people feels hinky, call Z."

"Roger that."

A month ago Ben had cut back his hours, recommended Ghost, then given him the token training needed. The position required a miniscule amount of paperwork, a closed mouth, good fighting skills, and even more common sense. Z said if his security guard had to fight, he'd already failed.

Ghost settled into the chair and leaned back. "I do appreciate the job though. It's interesting—and I was hell of bored."

"I know that one." Soldiers didn't do retirement well.

Ben entered the club, feeling his anticipation rising. He'd been told to report to the dungeon in the back. As he crossed the main room, he gave it a careful study.

Wall sconces were dim in the shadowy room, except near the well-lit equipment along the walls and the center bar. To the left was a munchie area with food, tables, and chairs. On the right was the dance floor. Farther back, planters offered privacy for scattered sitting groups. BDSM scenes were held in roped-off sections, and more seating had been provided for the viewers.

Even this late, people were dancing, and the scene areas were busy.

He had to say, the Shadowlands was damned sinister this evening. Innocent-looking schoolgirls—and boys—were wandering about at the mercy of some fucking ugly creatures. The place looked like a movie set for "Slaughter at Metropolis High."

He'd been inside a few times, but always to report in to Z about something. Never as a spectator. The clubroom looked and sounded different now that he was to be a...a participant.

Not that he hadn't paid attention when he'd been in here. Nah, he knew what he'd volunteered for. Had even seen Mistress Anne working over some poor schmuck before.

Now he'd be that poor bastard. Once again, he was being an idiot—like when he'd voluntarily taken the SERE course. Survival, Evasion, Resistance, and Escape—yeah, he'd accepted he was going to get hurt. At the time, the knowledge had been a lead weight of determination in his gut.

Tonight was much the same. One lead weight…along with a full-fledged cockstand. Mistress Anne would take one look at him and know precisely what he wanted.

*Maybe.* He wasn't exactly sure himself.

On the way through the room, he passed various scenes. Flogging. One where a zombie Dom was dumping wax on a woman's tits—although she did seem very onboard with the idea.

Not for him. Safe, sane, and consensual or not, he'd never be down with hurting a woman, which was why he'd known he wasn't any Dom type. Why he'd confidently told Z he was "vanilla."

He'd never given a thought to a gorgeous female hurting *him*.

Totally different mindset.

A scream made him stop. Tied to a post, little Uzuri was trying to evade a man caning her. "Red," she shouted, but the dumb fuck was too caught up to understand she'd safeworded.

Ben walked right in and trapped the swinging cane in his palm. Hurt like a son of a bitch. He yanked the stick away. "She said *red*." His voice came out threatening enough that the Dom paled and jerked back.

"Thanks, Ben." Vance Buchanan slapped his shoulder and tugged the cane from his hand. Dressed as Frankenstein's monster, he wore the gold-banded vest that marked a dungeon monitor.

"Not a problem." Good to know that if he hadn't been present, a DM would've rescued the pretty black submissive. Olivia slipped past him and tucked an arm around Uzuri, untying her with the other hand.

"Hey, I didn't hear her," the asshole protested and took a step toward the little trainee, who cringed back. "Listen, Uzuri, I—"

"Stay put, please." Vance gripped the Dom's arm hard enough to silence him, then lifted a quizzical brow at Ben. "I didn't know you provided security in here too."

Looked as if Buchanan had shit under control. "I don't." Ben waved a couple of fingers near his forehead and headed for the back.

Mistress Anne rested on a stone corner bench in the dungeon room, her back against the wall with her left leg outstretched. She'd pulled part of her hair up, spiking it into two horn-like shapes. A black, ankle-length robe covered a my-mouth-went-dry latex catsuit that clung to every one of her sweet curves. A long zipper ran down the front and he wanted to pull it down more than he wanted his next breath.

And his fucking jeans were way too tight.

She watched him walk in, her light eyes unreadable…until her gaze reached his crotch.

He could swear he saw a dimple appear. Yeah, she was sadistic.

After bending her left knee to lean against the wall, she patted the bench between her legs. "Sit here, please."

Good start. He sat where she indicated, feeling her left leg behind him, a pressure on his ass. To his pleasure, she set her right leg across his lap, close enough that the inside of her knee pressed on his dick.

He stared straight ahead and considered the merits of icy mountain streams, glaciers, and igloos. Didn't relieve shit.

"Now, Ben, first, this is just a scene for the next hour or so. Nothing more. I don't know how much you know about BDSM, but I'm not taking you on as a slave. I'm just going to give you a taste and perhaps help you put a curb on that tongue of yours.

In other words, she was warning him not to get his expectations up. They'd play and then she'd toss him back where she found him. He kept his face impassive and nodded. "I understand."

"Good. Then let's discuss your limits. What will you absolutely not do? What are you unsure about? And do you have any medical—or emotional—problems I should know about?"

Knowing he wouldn't be able to think worth shit with her leg rubbing his cock, he turned slightly toward her as if paying attention— which angled him enough to avoid the full-on pressure. *Limits. All right.*

"No permanent damage. No scarring. And I'd prefer not to talk in a falsetto." He considered. "I don't know you well enough for whips or anal shit."

"Well reasoned. Bondage?"

*Oh hell.* He could feel his muscles tense.

In the low lighting, her eyes seemed more gray than blue. "That looks like definitely no restraints."

After a second, he nodded. "I'd probably not do well if you put me in something I couldn't get loose from."

"That's good to know." She leaned forward and took his hands in hers. Her callused palms were a jarring contrast to her delicate fingers. "How about pain? You seemed rather…interested…in getting your ass whipped."

"Mistress, if pain pleases you, I'm willing to give it a try." He heard his words hang in the air. Fuck, had he said that to her? But yeah, he had. And meant it too.

The surprised pleasure in her eyes and the way she squeezed his fingers was as satisfying as the timeless moment of a perfect shot.

"All right, we'll keep it within those limits and see what happens," she said.

He had to say, he got off on her quick decisiveness. No waffling back and forth. No *"Are you sure you want to?"* or expecting him to read her mind and know what she wanted. She told him right up front how she felt and what she expected of him. Fucking relief.

As if to emphasize that, she reached up and removed the elastic band holding his hair back. "If I want your hair tied back," she said gently, "I'll do it." She tucked the band into his jeans pocket. "Now go over to the St. Andrew's cross"—she pointed to the seven-feet-high X-shaped device—"and remove your clothes. You can leave on your underwear if you're uncomfortable."

"That'd be a break...if I wore any."

Her eyes lit with laughter. "In that case, I get a treat, don't I?"

The soft grunt of pain she gave when she tried to move her leg from his lap reminded him of her sore ribs. Crazy woman. He put a hand under her calf and eased her foot down.

He straightened and realized she'd braced herself on his shoulder. Her mouth was only an inch from his, and her breath was scented with strawberries. Hell, he'd already won a punishment. What was one more? He closed the distance and brushed his lips against hers. *Oh yeah.*

Before he could take more, she'd gripped his hair and pulled his head back. "Ben," she chided. "I think you know you're overstepping your bounds."

"Mmm." Damn, she had soft lips. And a strong hand—her hold on his hair was damn tight. "Perhaps you'd better lay out the rules of engagement, Ma'am."

"All right. First, we're not a D/s couple, so these rules are only for the dungeon."

His swift regret at the limitation was surprising.

"You employ the proper terms of respect already. Remember to speak only when asked—or if there is a matter affecting your safety. No touching unless given permission. The safeword here is *red*, which means the scene stops completely. Use *yellow* if you need something but don't want a complete halt."

*Forget that halt shit.* "I suppose it's *green* for all systems go?"

"That's right. I should ask if you have a problem with my hands—or anything else—on your cock and balls."

*I'd have a problem if you didn't touch me.* A sense of caution amended the words to a polite, "No problem at all, Mistress."

"Excellent. Now do as I said."

A stint in the military pretty much wiped out modesty and his sojourn in a hospital had eliminated the rest. In front of the St.

Andrew's cross, Ben stripped down. He had a massive erection, but he figured the good Mistress might've been annoyed if he hadn't been aroused.

A black suede overnight-sized bag sat nearby. She'd have her so-called *toys* in it. His anticipation grew.

Hips swinging gently, she sauntered over and his mouth watered. She was slender, but her curvy ass would fill his big paws nicely.

In turn, she was looking at him with...enjoyment. Unlike some Masters he'd seen, she wasn't impassive, but openly showed that she appreciated what she saw.

*No, idiot, you can't flex your muscles for her.*

Her hand ran down his chest, ruffled the hair, and traced a puckered scar on his right side. "Bullet?"

Luckily, the insurgent had only hit him with a high-velocity ball or he'd bear a fist-sized exit wound. "Yes, Ma'am."

Her fingers pressed deeper. "It fractured your rib, I see." Without waiting for his reply, she continued. Soft hands over his belly, around his back and shoulders. Down his arms. His legs. She found all his scars and every bone he'd ever busted. Hell, his doctors had never checked him over so thoroughly.

"Spread your legs." She tugged on his pubic hair. Cupped his balls and massaged lightly. Her hand closed around his cock—his docs had never done *that*—and it took every single piece of control not to shoot his wad.

Her fingers clamped down in warning. "Don't come without permission, Benjamin."

"Understood, Ma'am." His voice probably sounded like a rooster being strangled. But, oddly enough, her command let him back away from the edge. His hands, which had clenched, eased open.

And she saw. Her gaze met his, straightforward, no games. "You please me, Ben."

*You fucking please me too, woman.* Wisely, he also kept those words shut down.

"Face the cross and hold onto those pegs over your head."

Each upright bar had an iron peg sticking out. He closed his fingers around them, which put his arms in an upraised V shape. In the pause between one heartbeat and another, he realized the music had changed to the ominous "Let Me Break You" by London after Midnight. The music's effect in this dark, cold dungeon was far more threatening than in his well-lit entry.

He could hear a woman sobbing and the snap of something—like a whip. His gut tightened, and he pulled in a slow inhalation.

"Your orders are to hold onto those pegs and not let go. No matter what I do. Can I trust you to do that for me, Ben?" Anne's husky voice drew him back, as stabilizing as the wooden frame supporting his body.

"You can, Mistress." He gripped harder. He'd die before he let one go.

"I'm going to hurt you, Ben—because this is what I told you I'd do. And because this is what you obviously want me to do."

Actually, he'd have agreed to anything that would gain him her attention and touch. Pain would be nothing new to him.

"But, because you please me, because this is your first time"—her furry voice touched his ears and stroked over his skin like a many-times-washed fleece—"and because I feel like giving you a lesson, I'm going to give you so much more than mere pain."

Talk about making him sit up and take notice. Hell, his body was already well past reveille, as if the cells had downed a gallon of coffee. As her fingertips brushed over his ass—which she hadn't touched before, he realized—his muscles twitched. She pressed her finger deeper, then gave him sweet, sweet pats, like a splattering of rain.

He huffed a laugh. That was a beating?

And he'd been worried?

"Is that Ben?" The almost inaudible voice came from behind him. Sounded shocked. More whispers drifted over his ears. He disliked having his back to the door, but fuck, this was the Shadowlands. He knew all the people here.

And, oddly enough, he trusted that the slender bounty hunter could probably take out nine-tenths of the members without breaking a sweat.

The rhythm of her patting hands on his ass paused for a second. He could imagine the gossips' expressions when she turned to look at them and undoubtedly gave them one of her ice-through-the-heart stares. The voices sure stopped, leaving only the music and the sound of someone moaning.

The Mistress slapped his ass more forcefully, and a pleasant heat grew, like the mildest of sunburns.

And then she stepped closer and leaned against him, full-body, her breasts providing increased pressure on his upper back. *Sweet.* He could feel her warmth all up and down with a tight burn where she pressed against his stinging butt.

And then she reached around and grasped his cock.

Startled, he jerked, and his hands almost slipped off the pegs. He recovered quickly.

Her fingers gave him a painful, admonishing squeeze. "Don't move, Benjamin."

"No, Mistress." He heard the growl in his voice.

She laughed. Squeezed again. "You move, and I'll hold your balls instead of your cock next time."

Fuck. Those strong little fingers of hers could do some serious damage.

But right now, she was stroking him, up and down, soft and sweet, and he hadn't thought it possible, but his dick lengthened even more. If she didn't let him finish, he'd have to jerk himself off in the bathroom before he could return to work.

He felt her breath between his shoulder blades. A butterfly kiss to one deltoid and the other. She stepped back and slapped his ass a couple of times firmly. Such little hands.

A pause.

And then something smacked him harder than shit.

*Jesus.*

His body went taut.

Before he could even process the pain, more blows hit his buttocks—and not leaving any mild stinging behind this time. His skin felt like a wildfire was burning it to ash. His hands tightened on the pegs; he bowed his head and took it.

She stopped and laid a paddle on the floor beside his feet.

This time when she leaned into him, her breasts still felt sweet as ice cream sundaes. And his ass felt raw as hell. She deliberately rubbed the stinging flesh with hers. "What color are you, Ben?"

When her hand closed on his cock, her fingers were far cooler than his straining erection—and, rather than deflating with the pain, he was even more achingly hard. She stroked him lightly.

He swallowed. Sadist. He was playing with a sadist. *Remember that, asshole.* "Green, Ma'am."

"Brave soldier. Now, do you regret challenging me in the entry?"

His ass sure would tomorrow. "No, Ma'am. I'd take a lot more to have your hands on me."

Silence.

"Did I ask for you to expand on that question?" Her voice had sharpened, and, fuck him, her fingers moved to cup his very, very exposed balls.

"No, Ma'am. But I heard that honesty was good between a top and bottom." He wasn't sure what defined Mistress and sub, but had a feeling that giving himself that designation might not be wise.

Wasn't sure if he wanted to call himself submissive or slave anyway.

"You're quite daring. So, I'll give you a choice. Would you like three blows done with all my might—or lighter ones until I tire?" Her thumbs rubbed the front of his cupped balls; her fingertips pressed upward almost to his asshole. Each movement sent such intense electrical arcs to his cock that he could almost hear the sizzle.

Choices, choices. And then he knew the right answer. "Whatever the Mistress pleases." Odd, just saying that sounded right. No choices, giving her all the control.

Her forehead was against his back. Her sigh made a circle of heat against one scapula. And then she stepped away.

He tensed. Prepared to take it.

She reached around him again, and her cold, slick hand circled his dick. Moved up and down. Her fingers, coated in lube, stroked him so fucking knowledgably that she had him at go within a minute.

His teeth ground together. "Mistress… I need to—"

"Five more strokes, Benjamin. Hold on until I say."

He could only grunt his answer.

"One. Two." She gripped him mercilessly, slid from the root to the tip—and her thumb circled the head.

*Jesus.* He'd never been so hard. His balls felt as if they'd compressed right into his groin. His entire spinal column was flattening with the pressure.

"Three. Four." Slower. Sliding over every fucking inch with a wrench-tight grip.

"Five." She drew it out and starbursts were flickering before his eyes.

"*Come* for me, Ben," she snapped out. One hand gripped his nuts and squeezed, her body rubbed on his burning ass to light up the skin like wildfire, and her hot fist jackhammered his shaft up and down.

He came. Jesus fucking Christ, he came, spurting all over her fingers, spasm after spasm, until he could swear he'd exhausted his load and started on blood.

He sagged against the cross, wishing it was a real cross so he'd have a place to lean his forehead.

Her hand still slid over his cock, ever so gently, letting him ride out the last clench. "Very nice, Ben. Stay there a minute."

To his bottomless regret, she moved away. Cool air wafted over his sweaty back and felt like heaven on his raw ass.

And then she put an arm around his waist. "Step back. Let's see how well your legs are working."

"As if you could hold me up."

The sharp smack on his ass almost made him yelp.

He snorted and grinned. She reminded him of his favorite drill sergeant. "Sorry, Ma'am." His legs held just fine as she guided him to the bench where she'd tossed a towel.

"Sit on that."

He sat and gritted his teeth, feeling every abrasive strand in the damn towel. She set a cleansing wipe on his thigh, the coolness startling against his hot skin.

"You may clean yourself, Benjamin."

She'd already wiped off her hands, he noticed as he gave himself a swiping.

"Very good." Standing right in front of him, she stroked his hair, and damn, he could smell her—pure sexy woman. Her steel blue gaze studied him for a moment before she handed him a bottle of water, the top already removed. "Drink all of this."

He drank some while he considered. How far could he push?

How far did he want to push?

"Thank you, Ma'am. I enjoyed this."

She sat beside him, her thigh warm against his. Her small hand took his jaw and turned his face to hers. He seized the moment to tip his lips into her palm and kiss lightly. That won him a quirk of her lips in a stifled smile as well as a cautionary flex of her fingers—he had no doubt she'd leave bruises if he didn't heed her warning.

"Did you enjoy the pain, Ben?"

Shit, she would ask about that. Extending his legs, he leaned back against the wall and chugged the water, trying to get his answer in order. "I'm pretty sure I don't get off on just pain. But when it's mixed with…"

"Arousal? In a sexual situation?"

"That. Yeah." When her hand rubbed his jaw, he could hear the *scritching* of the stubble. How would she feel about an abrasively heavy five-o'clock shadow between her silky thighs? "Haven't come that hard in years."

"I see." A moment of silence. "I suppose that gives you something to think about."

Hell, she was withdrawing. The sense of disappointment was keen and a bit ridiculous. Had he expected her to fall all over him, this Domme who could have any man she wanted at her feet?

Nonetheless, she needed to know he…wanted more. Turning, he faced her, placed his hand over hers to hold it in place. "Mistress Anne, can I perform any service for you in return?"

Her pupils dilated slightly, and he heard her catch her breath. She knew just what he was offering. Then her lips twisted in a slight smile that showed a single dimple. "I should have you wash my car."

"That wasn't what I meant, Ma'am." He made the reproach in his voice clear.

Laughter danced in her eyes. And here he'd always thought she was so serious. "You really are delightful, Ben. But I need nothing." Her hand moved from his face despite his attempt to keep her there. "You've finished the water. How do you feel?"

"Fine, Ma'am."

"Then I want you to get dressed and clean the equipment which you flooded."

Her gaze trapped his—to see if he'd react.

As if anyone who'd put in barracks time would be embarrassed by jism...anywhere? "Yes, Ma'am."

Her chuckle was low and pleased. "Not much upsets you, does it?"

"RPGs and IEDs, those are upsetting. Anything less—not so much."

"You're quite a guy, guard dog." She ran her hand down his arm, tracing the muscles of his biceps, in that way that women did—much the same way that a man would enjoy a woman's breasts. She liked his body. Liked him.

And was still stepping back. *Fuck. That.*

He dared much and touched her hair. It felt as smooth as his mother's prized silk shawl. If Anne were on top, that mass of hair would flow over his shoulders like a cool caress of water.

"Just so you know, Mistress, I'm calling my offer a rain check. You let me know when you want to cash it in. There's no expiration date."

Not only no expiration, but if she didn't take him up on his proposal, well, there were always numerous approaches available to achieve a target. She was worth taking the time to do it right.

# Chapter Three

Four days later, Anne picked through the Keurig pods to find a fudge-flavored coffee. It looked to be a long night, and she'd need all the caffeine she could get.

Hopefully her insides could handle the brew. After being sick since Sunday morning, she'd finally been able to keep food down today. At least she knew the origins of her illness—from babysitting her niece and nephew last week when they'd been home with a stomach bug.

More like a stomach demon.

After the machine finished hissing and thrumming, she carried her coffee out to the deck, snuggled into her favorite wicker chair, and checked out the view.

Apparently the weather report warning of a tropical storm had been accurate for a change. A high wall of black clouds in the west gave her normally white beach a gray cast. The wind whipped at the nearby palms as if trying to bend them in half, and white caps topped the choppy Gulf water. *Wonderful.* Should she call off the fugitive recovery team for the night?

No, skips often holed up during a storm, making it an excellent time to rout them out.

From the mansion beyond Harrison's house on the left came laughter; her nieces and nephews must be visiting her parents. On the right were the sounds of her brother Travis mowing his lawn.

She tipped her head back, drawing in the salt air, feeling blessed. Her mother's grandparents had bought up almost two acres on Clearwater Beach Island back when land was cheap. When her mother inherited, she'd resisted the pressure to sell to condo developers.

Instead, her parents had gifted Anne and her two brothers with a half-acre and house.

*Best present ever.* She made good money as a fugitive recovery agent, but not enough for a house right on the shore.

Ben had seen her house. She took a slow sip of her coffee and frowned. Did he think she was rich? Was that why he'd pushed her to top him last weekend? The idea cast an ugly light over what had been a beautiful scene.

But, no. She was way off base. Maybe they'd never spoken other than a good evening, but she'd "known" Ben for years. As had Z. The owner of the Shadowlands was not only far too empathic for anyone's peace of mind, but was also a psychologist. Ben wouldn't hold that position if he wasn't trustworthy.

She wrinkled her nose. So much for that weak excuse to devalue the scene. And all because she was unsettled about what she'd done. About Ben.

Because she'd felt a real thrill when he'd obeyed her, and another thrill when he'd come. They'd both been caught up in the moment and in each other. She'd sensed his every flinch, every breath, every tensing of his muscles.

And the man had muscles. Warmth stole into her core as she remembered. When his arms had been raised, his grip on the pegs had made his forearms rigid, the veins noticeable and begging to be traced with her tongue. His trapezius muscles had bunched, his lats had widened, the long muscles beside his spine had been like solid pillars of concrete.

And he had a simply gorgeous cock, completely proportional to his massive body.

Sex with him would be comparable to drinking strong coffee with chocolate—a definite kick with a mouthwatering extra.

Wasn't it odd how she'd been satisfied with such a lightweight scene? She hadn't done a session with so little pain provided in…in years. And yet she'd been perfectly content.

But, even if he were interested in more, she was finished. She didn't play with newbies to the lifestyle, especially ones like him who had no clue what was involved. The man was vanilla. And he was Z's employee—not someone to turn into her slave.

Besides, her emotions around him were uncomfortable. She didn't *do* uncomfortable.

Aside from not having a slave at the moment, her life was exactly the way she wanted it. Her job with its flexible hours was great. Her house, great. And when she found a young man to take as a slave, everything would be good.

Thinking of work, she needed to get moving.

She spent most of her daytime work hours doing searches on the computer and phone, knocking on doors, and picking up skips during the day. But often apprehending the more elusive fugitives meant going out at night. Tonight the team's quarry was a low-life dealer who tended to move between houses up in the Land O' Lakes district. The team would split up and do some simultaneous visits to his closest buddies who might have offered him shelter.

She eyed the dark clouds and sighed.

\* \* \* \*

That night, drenched to the skin and getting grumpier by the minute, Anne knocked on the fugitive's door. Covert body armor when soaked? Really heavy.

The gray-haired woman who opened the door saw Anne's dark green polo shirt with "THE BROTHERS BAIL BONDS" logo and the weapons belt with the .38 S&W and Taser. Dismay filled her face.

Pushing her wet hair out of her face, Anne spoke loudly to be heard over the rolling thunder and noise of the wind and rain. It was doubtful the fugitive would be out partying in this mess. "Ma'am, I'm sorry to report that your son missed his court date. Is he here?"

"Ah. No. No, he isn't."

The poor woman. Mrs. Wheeler was caught in an impossible situation. No matter how much a mother wanted to protect her offspring, some children made that almost impossible.

The lady was also a really poor liar.

Pity softened Anne's voice even as her hand behind her back motioned for her team to get positioned. "Mrs. Wheeler, you put your house up as collateral for your son's bail. I'm so sorry, but if I don't take Edward in, you will lose this place."

The woman's face paled. "I can't afford to lose..."

God, this was the saddest part of the job—seeing the trauma that a criminal inflicted on his own family. "You tried your best." Anne upped the dominance in her tone, the one that had her slaves kneeling without a thought. "Let us in now, Ma'am."

The woman stepped back.

Anne's pulse increased. The skip had a history of violence, one reason she'd called in the team instead of picking him up herself.

Mitchell had already disappeared around the back to watch the rear and south side of the house. Dude stationed himself to guard the front and north side. They sounded off in her walkie-talkie headset.

Exits secured, Anne entered.

Aaron, a retired cop from Texas, followed her in. A good man; a good teammate.

A second later, her cousin, Robert, swaggered in, hand on his holstered firearm. The same weapon that a fugitive had kicked out of his hand last week.

If Anne were given the choice, the idiot wouldn't be issued anything deadlier than a squirt gun. He sure wouldn't be on this team that she'd built. But her uncles—the owners of the bail company—had, as usual, caved in to his whining.

The distinctive click and thud of someone playing pool came from a room to the left. At least one person was in there.

Anne glanced right and noted what appeared to be a couple of bedrooms and a bathroom. "Robert, check the rooms to the right, please, and remain on guard here. Call if you find the skip. Aaron, let's go left."

Robert puffed up, mouth turning mulish. "But, I want to—"

"Do it now." Anne's cold stare reminded him that she was in charge.

He stomped off, his "fucking bitch" quite audible.

She exchanged exasperated glances with Aaron, then led the way across the faded carpet to where the dining room had been turned into a game room. That poor mother.

A quick glance showed a man playing a solitary game of pool.

Anne mentally checked his appearance against the arrest record photo she'd obtained during preparation. One hundred percent match.

She walked into the room. "Mr. Edward Wheeler, I'm with The Brothers Bail Bonds and here to pick you up. There is a bench warrant out for your failure to appear at your court date."

"Hell with that." Starting toward the kitchen door, he glanced out the window and spotted Mitchell in the middle of the backyard. Escape route blocked, Wheeler spun—and charged Anne.

*Fun.* Smiling slightly, she stepped out of his way, caught his arm on the way past, and redirected him into the doorframe.

He hit with a pleasant thud—but hey, she'd avoided sending him into the wall where the mother's pictures might be damaged.

Aaron tackled him.

On his stomach, Wheeler kicked and cursed, but couldn't get

enough leverage to struggle effectively.

*What a jerk.* Making his mother risk her house because he chose to sell meth to children.

Anne pulled her cuffs off her belt and secured his left wrist as he swore at her, using the f-word as a verb, adjective, and adverb.

"Young men today lack originality," Aaron complained. Then again, he'd married a history professor who could curse for hours without using a four-letter word.

"There he is!" Robert charged through the door, thumping into her as he tried to grab the perp's free arm. "Give me your wrist, you asshole."

Anne scowled, easily pinned the skip's tattooed arm, and finished cuffing him. "Get back to your post, Ro—"

A roar came from the doorway.

Anne caught movement from the corner of her eye and flung herself sideways. The boot aimed for her head slammed into her hip. Pain blasted into her. The kick knocked her into the pool table, and her head hit with a nasty crack.

Ears ringing, she shook her head, trying to clear her vision. *Son of a bitch.* Apparently Wheeler had a buddy.

Footsteps thudded as he stomped toward her.

*Move!* She rolled, kicked, and nailed his knee. The asshole buddy went down like a felled bull.

Head still spinning, she pushed to her feet, tested that her leg would hold her weight—her hip screamed a protest—and delivered a carefully placed kick into his testicles that would eliminate further attacks until after they'd left.

Holding his head, Aaron staggered to his feet. Apparently the bull had got him on the way to her.

Robert stood beside the fugitive. Doing nothing.

She eyed him. "Way to back up your teammates, Robert."

He flushed. "I secured the perp."

"Anne had already cuffed him," Aaron pointed out.

Anne glanced at the downed bull and saw the remnants of shaving lotion on his cheeks and jaw. Hair wet. Shirtless. "You didn't check the bathroom, did you, Robert? And if you'd stayed on guard as ordered, he wouldn't have gotten through."

Robert's lips twisted in a sneer. "You gonna cry because you got hurt?"

Oh, honestly. The station where she'd once been assigned as a cop had been famous for its misogynistic attitudes. And now she had to deal with it here.

Insecure men who were threatened by competent women were a pain in the ass.

But the stupid bullshit they spouted no longer made her furious. Now, the feeble yapping of men like her cousin was merely irritating, similar to the buzzing of a persistent fly.

"Actually, Robert, I'll simply note in the report that you disobeyed orders and were out of position which resulted in unnecessary violence and injury during a pickup. I'll also add that you sat on your ass while your teammates were fighting." She motioned to the fugitive. "Grab him, please, Aaron. I'll call Dude and Mitchell in."

Robert glared, muttered, "Cunt," and stalked out of the room.

She shook her head, frustration simmering in her gut. His insolence could be ignored, but his incompetence and inability to work as part of the team put everyone at risk.

As Aaron led Wheeler out to the van, Anne called in Mitchell and Dude, receiving "Good going, boss," from Mitchell, and "Rock on," from Dude.

"Miss, please." On the porch steps, the mother intercepted Anne. "My house? Since Eddie fought back, does that mean my house will be lost?"

Anne took her hands and spoke gently. "No, Mrs. Wheeler. As soon as the jail takes custody of him, the collateral papers are no longer in force." She squeezed the trembling fingers. "Your home is safe."

As she walked out into the downpour and wind, she glanced at her watch. Still fairly early. She might as well dispatch Mitchell to deliver the fugitive to the jail and fill out the Statement of Surrender form. The rest of them would see if any other skips had decided to stay home in the storm.

\* \* \* \*

The wall sconces in Z's lanai cast enough light that Ben could see the rain pouring down. Drops slammed against the sidewalk violently enough to bounce. Pools of water were streaming through the tropical landscaping.

His buddies stopped behind him in the open screen door.

Lightning seared his eyes followed by an ear-splitting clap. As the cool air turned hot and arid, filled with the grit of a sandstorm, Ben froze. *All around the team, flashes from artillery shells lit the night with cracks like thunder.*

No.

*Slowly inhale. In. Out.* He was in Florida. It was raining. He growled, half under his breath, "Damned thunderstorms."

"No shit," Digger's eyes met his in complete understanding. "Sounds too fucking much like an aerial bombardment."

Z walked up behind them and set his hand on Ben's shoulder. Warmth and reassurance flowed from the strong grip. After a second, he asked, "Can you stay a moment?"

"I'm okay."

"You are, indeed." Z squeezed his shoulder before releasing him. "This is another matter."

What would that be? "Yes, sir."

Z turned his attention to the others. "Gentlemen, I'll see you next month."

"Later, Dr. Grayson. Later, Haugen," Digger said, starting a chorus of good-byes.

Ben lifted his hand as the men headed out.

Guided by the rain-dimmed solar lights, they dashed for the fence gate and the Shadowlands parking lot.

A long zigzag of lightning lit the night as Ben returned to the screened and covered lanai. Z had resumed his seat on the dark-red cushioned, oak-and-iron chair.

"What's up?" Ben asked, sidestepping a hanging planter. A chill breeze rustled the trailing blooms and carried the scent of ocean and tropical flowers.

"Can you sit for a minute, please?"

Hell, that didn't sound good. Ben hadn't had any problems recently—nothing he couldn't handle, so he doubted Dr. Zachary Grayson, psychologist, had called him back to assess his PTSD. More likely, he was dealing with Z, the owner of the Shadowlands, who was one of the most protective motherfuckers Ben had ever met.

And stubborn as hell. Refusal was futile.

Ben scowled. "If you're planning to grill me for more than five minutes, I want a beer." Since two of the veterans were recovering alcoholics, the psychologist didn't serve anything stronger than sodas during the sessions.

Z gave him a relaxed grin. "Fair enough."

Against the wall, the fridge was filled with junk food, healthy snacks, juices—and alcohol of all kinds. As in the Shadowlands, Z made a point of stocking people's favorite drinks. Ben looked for a green label and found a Brooklyn Lager. Thinking of the strain in Z's face, he also splashed a shot of Glenlivet into a glass.

He handed Z the glass of scotch, then dropped into a facing chair and set his feet up on the heavy oak coffee table. He had to appreciate a décor designed for living as well as style. "What's on your mind, boss? Problems?"

"Not exactly problems." Z eyed his drink and took a sip. "Although I see you for group sessions and serve as your employer, I also consider you a friend."

Well, damn. Didn't that give him a fucking fine glow? Unable to come up with a suitable response—he didn't have Z's diplomatic vocabulary—he muttered, "Same here." He tipped the bottle back and drank down a good third to get his balance back.

Heartwarming words or not, he had a feeling he should've escaped with the others. "Sounds as if you're leading up to something."

"That's a very good guess." Z swirled his scotch and pinned Ben with a gray gaze. "By relieving you for an hour last Saturday, I essentially gave Mistress Anne permission to play with you. Did I make a mistake?"

Yep, his guess had been spot on. Unfortunately, he didn't have an easy yes or no answer since anything he said could cause problems for Anne. Ben selected his words with the exact brevity and care he'd give to an interrogator. "No mistake. I liked the scene."

Amusement showed in Z's expression before he set the glass down. *Oh shit.*


Zachary studied the man sitting across from him. Muscles slightly tensed, eyes level but wary, face blanked of expression. Protective posture. Protective thoughts. For Anne.

*Of course.*

Benjamin had grown up on New York streets, caring for his mother and sisters. He'd joined the U.S. Army to protect his country and moved into the Rangers to do an even better job. Anne might be the Dominant, but this soldier operated under his own priorities.

Zachary did the same.

"Should I sign you up for membership in the club?" he asked in a flanking maneuver.

"Shit." Benjamin choked on his beer and coughed. "Ah, no. That'd be like pulling the trigger before aiming."

"I see." What he could also see was that Benjamin had, indeed, enjoyed the session and wanted more.

As the Domme, Anne had the next move. She'd apparently not made one.

These weren't two people he'd have predicted to be a good match, but their scene on Saturday had held tremendous energy and chemistry. They'd been caught up in each other.

Normally a good thing. But…

Z regarded his glass, seeing the reflection of the lightning in the amber liquid. Although the scene in the Shadowlands had shown that Benjamin was sexually submissive, he didn't possess a slave's mentality, and it was doubtful the man could adapt to that lifestyle.

He doubted if Anne would even allow Ben to try.

"Spit it out, Z."

Z looked up. "Mistress Anne is one of the finest Dominants I've ever met. She is also exceptionally reserved. Her slaves don't live with her. Her control when she is with them is absolute. She picks her 'boys' carefully and they worship the ground she walks on. I'm not sure—"

"I'm not her type. I knew that." Ben's jaw was firm. "And you delivered your warning."

"I'm not finished. If a submissive isn't her slave, she might play with him in the club. Once or twice."

"Right."

"She's also a sadist."

"I do know that"—Ben held up his hand—"*and* I know she went lightly on me last week."

As thunder boomed, the wind picked up, sending cold, moist air across the lanai. The scones on the wall flickered.

Uneasy, Zachary glanced at the steps leading to the third floor, the private quarters. He'd left Jessica on the couch, Galahad on her lap, both contentedly watching an old *Die Hard* movie. He checked his cell phone. No, she hadn't messaged.

"Is Jessica all right?" Benjamin rose. "I'll get out of your way so you can check on her."

"Nice try, Benjamin, but I'm doing that now. Remotely." Zachary half-smiled. "She gets grumpy if she thinks I'm 'babysitting' her." So he texted, *"I'll be up in a few minutes. Can I bring you something?"*

*"Shhh. This is the best part of the movie!"*

Damn, he loved his woman. "She's fine." He sat back and continued with the topic. "If Mistress Anne doesn't call you, will you be comfortable with that? With seeing her pick up a new slave?"

He got a frown. "Z, we shared a scene, not a marriage." Unfortunately, the words weren't echoed by Benjamin's emotions, which were primarily regret and disappointment.

"D/s sessions can unsettle submissives, especially new ones. When you trust someone to care for you—and they do well for you—then a bond develops. It's easy to confuse that tie with other feelings."

"Good to know." Benjamin finished off his beer. "My friend and counselor," he said in a lightly ironic tone, "what happens between me and the women in my life—whether the woman is Dominant or vanilla—stays with me. All respect to you, Z, but butt out."

There were reasons he'd always respected the big Ranger. "Sergeant, you know I won't do that."

"You're fucking stubborn."

"Indeed. Since you enjoyed the scene, should I match you up with other Dommes?"

"*No.*" Benjamin stood. "Time for me to be going." He touched his forefinger to his forehead in a half-salute and turned toward the door.

Zachary saw the determined jaw, the set of his shoulders. The sergeant had listened…and now would go his own way. Fair enough.

Lightning struck so close that he could almost hear the sizzle.

The power went out.

In the sudden darkness, Zachary rose and paused to orient himself. "I need to get to Jessica." The club floors had low-level battery-operated emergency lights as required, but he'd never extended them to his private quarters. He usually appreciated the lull a power outage created in his busy life.

He'd never thought about having a pregnant wife and no power.

A chair creaked and Benjamin said, "I'll hang out down here for a bit in case you need help with anything."

"Thank you." Using his cell for light, Zachary ran up the stairs to the third floor entry. A kitchen drawer yielded two flashlights. "Jessica, where are you?"

"Living room."

She was still on the couch, the cat on her lap, and a delightful pout on her face. "The power cut out right when McClane was having a shootout. That's so not fair."

Damn, she delighted him. He crouched in front of her, running his palms over her round belly. His child was growing in there, surrounded by the woman he loved. "I'll have a word with the storm and register your complaint. How are you doing?"

"My back hurts. And I have to pee *again*, but Galahad says he doesn't want to move."

She had a soft spot for the battle-scarred cat. Ruthlessly, Zachary picked the feline up and set him on the floor, winning an impertinent flick of the tail.

He put his hands under Jessica's arms and stood, lifting her to her feet. So tiny to hold. Such a resilient, sturdy personality. She awed him at times. He kissed the top of her head. "Let's go, little one."

In the bathroom, as he lit the candles she kept around the bathtub, Jessica disappeared into the toilet stall. Her moan of relief made him laugh.

"Call when you're done so I can walk back with you, pet." Giving her the privacy she preferred, he stepped into the master bedroom.

A minute later, the sound she made wasn't his name. More like a groan or whimper.

"Jessica?"

"Um." He heard her whisper, "Oh, God," and concern tensed his gut.

He was in front of the stall before she had a chance to step out. In the flickering candlelight, he couldn't read her face, but her emotions were all over the place. Worry uppermost. And pain. "Tell me."

She bit her lip. "Well, I'm in labor. I thought so before, but I'm positive now since"—her skin darkened—"my water just broke."

He exhaled slowly and shut down his first instinct—a thorough scolding for not telling him sooner. "I see." With an arm around her, he guided her out of the bathroom. "How long would you estimate you've been in labor?"

"Weeell."

*Hell.*

"At first, I thought the contractions were just those Braxton-Hicks. They didn't really hurt and were far apart. Only the contractions haven't stopped. And really, I was going to tell you, only you had the group session today, and I didn't want to mess that up."

"Jessica, I'd have rescheduled."

"They're our soldiers. They deserve priority."

His stubborn, big-hearted submissive; she'd be the death of him. "Did you happen to time any of the last pains?"

"They're close to five minutes apart. I called the midwife right before the lights went out. She said to head for the birthing center now since the rain would slow us down. She'll leave now as well."

"Indeed. In that case, you've ruined the lecture I was planning."

Her wavy blonde hair glinted in the candlelight as she grinned up, looking like a roguish fairy. "There's good news."

He captured her face between his hands and kissed her, slow and sweet. "I love you, Jessica."

"That's a relief,"—she went on tiptoes to press a light kiss to his chin—"since we're going to have a baby."

\* \* \* \*

Anne parked her car in the Shadowlands parking lot, turned off the headlights, and stared through the pouring rain at the very dark, three-story, stone mansion. No lights were on. Tonight, of all nights, Z and Jessica weren't home?

No, wait. Z never left the entire house unlit. Now that she thought about it, she hadn't seen any house lights in miles. The power must be out in the area.

Through the rain and dark, she glimpsed flickering lights in the third story windows. It'd be worth checking. If the place was empty, she could sack out in the back of her vehicle. She'd slept in her SUV a time or two before, although what'd been cool in her twenties wasn't so much fun a decade later.

What a mess of a night. The second fugitive had fallen easily into their hands. But not the third. They'd knocked on doors of his closest friends and family, searched his favorite hangouts, and gotten drenched for nothing.

Then, after her team had called it a night, Anne had detoured to check out another skip's home. No joy there.

To top off the crap night, she'd been blocked by a traffic jam on the Suncoast Parkway where the rain had caused a multi-multi-car pileup. So she'd made her way by back roads to the Shadowlands. A good night's rest in her bed was obviously out of the question.

She grabbed her spare overnight bag and a flashlight and made a dash for the back garden gate. *I'm already wet—why am I running?*

She ran through the garden, opened the door, and stepped into the lanai. Her soaked hair flopped in her face, and with a huff of annoyance, she pushed the strands away.

Something huge moved on the dark patio. She turned the flashlight that way. Huge was right. A man—*Ben.*

He growled, "Stop right there and identify yourself." His threatening voice was sexy as hell.

With a chuckle, she closed her eyes and pointed the light at herself. "It's me, Ben."

"Fuck me, what are you doing out in the rain, Anne?"

"I—"

The door above them opened, and Z called down, "Benjamin, may I impose upon you to drive us to the hospital? Jessica's in labor."

"Be my pleasure, Z. Let me get—"

"Wait." Anne lifted her voice. "Z, the Suncoast is backed up with a multi-car accident. The news says a rig tipped over and is lying across the entire road. Other cars smashed into it and skidded into the oncoming lanes as well. Because the traffic jam goes in both directions, rescue vehicles haven't been able to get to the location to clear the mess."

Ben started, "We can take—"

"You can't even get to Gunn. The roads are flooding. I barely made it with my Ford Escape—and the water's still rising. I doubt any vehicle can get through now."

There was a long silence from above. She could feel Z's concern. Finally he said, "I'm glad you arrived when you did, Anne. At least we won't be trapped on the road."

"Delivering a baby in a car. Not my idea of fun," Ben muttered.

"Apparently, we'll have a home birth tonight. The midwife lives locally. Hopefully she can get here." Z's flashlight moved as he pulled out his cell phone. "Come on up, you two. The door's open."

A baby coming. A storm. No power. A chill crept up Anne's spine.

Thankfully, Jessica was strong and healthy.

Anne glanced at the dark bulk that was Ben. "Let's get up there and see if we can help."

"Yes, Ma'am." Ben put a hand behind her back to guide her toward the steps. His palm was warm through her wet clothing. And far too comforting.

After drying off and donning clothes from her go-pack, Anne talked with Z, then headed into the master bedroom. A myriad of candles lit the room, showing arched windows, pale walls, and dark furniture.

On the king-sized bed, Jessica sat with her back against the headboard, hands laced over her belly, eyes closed. The grimace on her face said she was in the middle of a contraction.

First babies never came quickly. Anne's experience wasn't extensive, but she'd been her sister-in-law's birthing partner twice while Harrison was in Iraq.

By tomorrow, Jessica would have a baby to show for the pain. Anne knew her friend wouldn't begrudge the work in the least.

After a half minute, Jessica relaxed and opened her eyes. "Anne. Hey."

Anne took a seat on the bed. "I came to keep you company while Z tries to reach the midwife before she gets stuck in the traffic jam. He hasn't had an answer yet. She's probably in a poor reception area."

A flash of worry crossed Jessica's face. "There are pockets of dead zones all around here."

A diversion was indicated. "So, did you change your mind about knowing whether you're carrying a girl or boy?"

"Nope." Jessica smiled wryly. "Although Z probably bribed the doctor to tell him."

"Ah." Oh, he undoubtedly had. "Possibly."

Jessica shifted, obviously uncomfortable, even without a contraction.

"Girl, there's no reason why you have to stay in here...not until you're closer to the big moment. Would you like to move into the living room?"

Jessica's eyes lit. "Can I? I feel as if I've been stuffed into a cave and forgotten."

"Then let's get that sorted. Couch or recliner? And let me grab some towels."

"Couch. There are old towels on the linen closet's bottom shelf. In the bathroom."

"Perfect. Stay put for a minute.

Anne set things up, added a sheet for comfort, and returned.

Jessica was sweating slightly, but eager to move.

Anne helped her up, out to the living room, and hesitated. "You know, as long as you have someone beside you, you can walk around."

"Really? Awesome." She gave Anne a rueful look. "Since it's tax season, I missed some birthing classes. Z and I had hoped to make them up this week."

"You're such an accountant. I'm surprised Z didn't insist on the classes."

"I got kind of hysterical, and he caved. Probably because I pointed out that I'd worry more if I had to file tax return extensions for every one of my clients."

Anne grinned as she steered her friend around the room. Jessica was one of her favorite people, but totally numbers crazy.

"Well—oh God, not again." Jessica swiftly sat on the couch and held her hardening belly. Through gritted teeth, she added, "The pains are down to every two or three minutes."

Anne pulled up her memory of when she'd helped with her niece and nephew's births. Such frequent contractions meant active labor, right? Time for the midwife to get here.

She took the blonde's hands in a firm grip and added a touch of command to her voice. "Look at me." When Jessica's eyes met hers, she said, "Inhale in through your nose, out through your mouth."

As the pain increased, Anne said, "Light breathing now. In and out."

Z's subbie followed orders well.

After a long minute, Jessica sagged. "If Z wants another baby, he's going to have to carry it."

Anne smiled. Not much kept Jessica's sense of humor down.

"It's better with someone to help. Thank you." Jessica gave her fingers a squeeze.

"My pleasure."

"Uh, not really, right?" Jessica looked as if she were searching for the right diplomatic words. "We're friends—and you don't—won't—enjoy watching me hurt, will you?"

"No." Anne snorted. "First, although I've topped female submissives when needed, I don't find any thrill from seeing a woman in pain. At all."

"Well. That's good. If that was first, is there a second?"

Anne frowned. She had put it like that, hadn't she? Because there was more, she just wasn't sure what. Exactly. "Do me a favor and don't share this with your snoopy Master."

"Girl stuff doesn't get shared. He's down with that."

Girl stuff. Anne rarely thought of herself as a girl, but in all reality, she was only about five years older than Jessica. "I've noticed that inflicting pain isn't as…satisfying…as it used to be."

"Huh. Does that mean you need to hurt someone worse to get enjoyment out of it?"

"Actually, less. Which doesn't make sense. Sadists usually escalate."

"That's why you broke up with Joey, isn't it?"

Joey—her last slave and a masochist—had wanted more pain from her than she'd wanted to dispense. She'd given him what he needed, but ultimately that difference in their needs had been a major reason for their breakup. "You're as perceptive as your Master, subbie," Anne said lightly.

"Well." Jessica stopped and groaned.

They breathed through another contraction.

After recovering, the blonde frowned. "If you want less—and for only one gender—then maybe it wasn't the actual pain you enjoyed. Could it be you just have a taste for turning males into gelatin?"

"Undoubtedly." Anne gave her a half-grin. Z loved how logical Jessica was. But...she might have a point. Perhaps that was why once she began to care for a slave, hurting him—for just pain's sake, became more difficult.

Zachary found his control tested to its limits as he took Anne's place on the couch.

The midwife, Fay, had arrived a few minutes before, just in time for what Anne said was the transitional stage. Personally, Zachary considered this level a form of hell. Seeing Jessica in that much pain—pain he couldn't relieve—made him want to kill something. The contractions were coming every two to three minutes and lasting...he could swear, forever.

For the first time, he was grateful his previous wife had borne their two sons by C-section.

*God, Jessica.*

He could see the moment when she wasn't sure she could endure more—even before she announced, "I'm done now. I quit."

"There is no quitting," he murmured. "But each contraction gets you closer to the end."

She actually glared at him. "That's not helping. Damn you, you have children. Why'd you want more?"

"Jessica, *you* wanted children."

"You're so fucking wrong. I never—" The next contraction hit.

"Breathe, little one."

"You breathe, you dickhead. How could you do this to me? You told me you weren't a sadist, you fucking liar." She dug her little fingernails into his forearm deep enough to draw blood. "You like pain? Does that feel good?"

Behind him, he heard a snort of laughter from Ben. "She's gonna regret that later."

Returning from the bedroom she'd been setting up, the midwife said with a smile, "Nope. Zachary agreed—as do all my clients—that what is said or done during the transitional stage is forgiven. No ifs, ands, or buts."

Zachary pried his wife's finger loose and didn't give a damn if he was bleeding. She was shaking and shivering, and all he wanted to do was pull her into his arms.

"Don't touch me." She batted his hands away. "I hate you."

He winced at the anger and pain filling her to bursting, and felt completely, horribly helpless as she groaned her way through another contraction.

"Easy, Z," Anne murmured and squeezed his shoulder, then passed a cooled hand towel to the midwife.

Fay set the cloth on Jessica's forehead. "Do you want your husband to massage your back, honey? Or do you want to go onto all fours?"

"No, dammit, I just want it over." Her voice lifted in a half-scream. "God fucking, cock-sucking shit damn piss."

Even as Z's shoulders tensed in sympathy, he couldn't suppress the huff of laughter. He'd never heard her use such language.

"You...piss-ant shithead. This. Is. Not. Funny." She went limp, gasping for air, sweat making her skin glow. Her emerald-sharp glare could have sliced through steel. "Your cock ever comes near me again and I'll cut it off."

"Now that's just mean," Ben muttered. "I think you're getting competition in the cock torture department, Mistress Anne."

Jessica, a formerly sweet wife turned demon, turned her glower toward the corner where Ben stood. "You...I liked you. I was wrong."

The bulky shadow that was Ben seemed to shrink into the wall. He cleared his throat. "I'm going to just go...check on how the rain is falling and, yeah..."

As he left, Zachary glanced around. Anne had stayed. She gave him a firm nod that said she'd be available as needed. Her presence helped, but nothing could ease his fear. If anything went wrong, there would be no ambulance in time.

Jessica was already starting another contraction.

*So much pain.* Zachary curled his hand around hers, trying with all his might to lend her his strength.

When Jessica finally, finally, relaxed again, Fay asked, "You need to push, don't you?"

Jessica nodded.

Fay said, "Let me assess how dilated you are. Then we'll move to the bedroom where everything is set up."

The examination resulted in more cursing from Jessica.

Fay announced, "You've reached ten centimeters. Let's go." She rose, taking Jessica's underpants with her.

"Hey, I want my briefs on." Jessica held her hand out.

"It's time to leave them off, honey."

"No. Put them *back*." When Fay didn't move, his beloved kitten turned her scowl to Zachary. "She's being mean. Hurt her."

"Easy, sweetheart. This will be over soon." His sympathy earned him more fingernails digging into his wrist.

Fay grinned. "Now, Jessica, we both know you've gone without underwear before—or you wouldn't need my services today."

Damned if he didn't feel guilty himself about his part in getting her pregnant. Before Jessica could respond, he swept her up. "To the bedroom."

Even as he carried her, she went into another contraction, and he could feel her bearing down. "She's pushing, Fay."

"Good. It should go fast now."

"God, this hurts!"

"I know, kitten, I know," Zachary murmured.

Through a clenched jaw, she gritted out, "I know Masters are conceited, but by no stretch of the imagination are—you—God."

He didn't smother his chuckle adequately, and, as he set her on the bed, he barely managed to dodge her punch.

An hour later, having called Anne in to hold Jessica's hands and support her shoulders, Zachary caught his baby as she exited the womb.

Blood-streaked with white vernix patches, her fair skin mottled, and a few wisps of blonde hair, she was the most beautiful little girl in the world.

As the midwife dealt with the umbilical cord, he could only stand and hold his child. So tiny and fragile. He'd forgotten how little they were upon arrival. How miraculous.

"Zachary?" Jessica called.

He had to blink the wetness from his eyes before he could carry his baby to her mother. "We have a girl, kitten. A perfect little girl." Carefully, he set the baby in her arms and stole a kiss from his love. "Thank you for our daughter, Jessica."

Her lips curved under his, and she whispered, "You're very welcome, Master."

A second later, the baby managed to find Jessica's nipple, and she jerked slightly as the little girl latched on. "Whoa, and I thought nipple clamps were bad."

\* \* \* \*

"We have a girl." Completely, thoroughly exhausted, Anne dropped down on the other end of the couch from Ben. She'd slipped out of the bedroom to give Z time with his newly enlarged family.

"Halleluiah," Ben said quietly. "I'm glad you were here to help them."

"Actually, so am I." She half-grinned. "I think Marcus won the betting pool though."

"I was way off, by a good two weeks." To her surprise, Ben handed her a scone and a glass of milk. "I raided the kitchen and grabbed these for you. Consider it breakfast."

She glanced at the windows and realized the sun was well up. "I had no idea. Thank you, Ben." When she took the first bite, her hunger wakened, and she finished it all.

Smiling, he took the plate and glass, set it on the coffee table. "I checked on the roads. Everything is open again." He pulled Anne's legs onto his lap and started kneading her bare feet.

*Heaven.* She'd had her feet massaged by her slaves, sometimes one male per foot, but this was the first time a man had simply done it without being directed. He used firm, powerful pressure, nothing like the tentative touch of the boys.

And she was turning into a happy puddle. She slid down farther on the couch. "You'll never know how good that feels."

In the bright morning light, his forbidding features softened. Her approval apparently meant something to him, even outside of the dungeon. "Don't know why you women wear fucked-up shoes that make your feet hurt."

Not the words she usually heard from her slaves. Head on the armrest, Anne smiled at the ceiling. "Perhaps it's because we enjoy the way you males stare at us when we do." Her smile widened. "Considering Z gave you charge of determining whether a submissive's footwear is sexy enough for the club or she goes barefoot, I'd say you already lost this argument."

He snorted. "Point to you, Ma'am. And you do walk in them more gracefully than anyone I've ever seen." His fingers pulled gently on her toes, a plucking motion that sang along her nerves all the way to her breasts. Those big hands of his were incredibly sexy. "You wore boots today though."

"Can't chase a fugitive if I'm wearing stilettos, although the heels do make an excellent weapon."

He squeezed her foot painfully. "You go out to round up crooks at *night?*"

Z's overprotective guard dog. "Yes, Ben. Picking up fugitives is easier when there are less people around and more people in bed."

"Jesus," he muttered. His measuring gaze was much like that of her parents, her brothers, and the cops at her station. All considered her too delicate, too pretty, too...female to deal with anything physically dangerous.

With a sour taste in her mouth, she swung her feet down and sat up. As she pulled on her boots, she let her disgusted silence fill the room, a talent that any Domme worth her whip could employ.

"Stepped in it, didn't I," he said. "I'm sorry, Anne. It's a knee-jerk reaction."

"Of course." He was only being protective. He hadn't said anything rude, simply acted like a typical male. Normally, she could ignore other peoples' opinions, but Ben's disapproval had hurt. "No problem."

Her boots were on. She rose. Time to head home.

He reached up and yanked her down, right into his lap, arms tight around her.

Rigid with annoyance, she gave him a look.

His arms loosened, but he didn't release her.

"Anne."

"What?" He had the most beautiful brown eyes she'd ever seen— amber rays shooting out from the pupil, circled by a yellow line, then a darker brown ring. And those eyes showed repentance.

"I'd prefer your kicking my balls over the goal post to seeing you unhappy. Or pissed at me. Can you maybe forgive me instead of just saying the words?"

"Well." He was right.

As she touched his lean cheek with her fingertips, she felt his pleasure so strongly that it was almost her own. "No submissive has reprimanded me and begged forgiveness in the same sentence. Quite interesting."

"Interesting enough to win a kiss of absolution?"

This was not a man to be underestimated. Give him an inch and he'd take the entire county. And yet, the challenge in his gaze was so, so delightful.

She bent and kissed him.

Men had such different mouths. His lips were firm and competent, his tongue canny without being aggressive or sloppy. He tasted of the mocha coffee she'd made earlier—chocolate and coffee and man. *Mmm.*

All man. Yet, when she took control, holding his face between her hands, slanting her mouth for a deeper kiss, he didn't move, simply accepted and made a sound of enjoyment.

An alpha male…except with her.

Under her buttocks, he lengthened and thickened.

What kind of a challenge would he present? Arousal seeped into her blood.

Farther away, a door opened and closed. Anne looked up.

Z came into the living room, a neutral gaze on her and Ben. Anne finally interpreted it as neither approval nor disapproval. He was reserving judgment. "Anne. Benjamin. Would you care to pay a visit to our new daughter?"

"Of course." Anne stood, took Ben's hand, and yanked him to his feet.

As they walked to the bedroom, Ben eyed her thoughtfully. "You pack a lot of muscle in that little body."

He really was just begging to be hurt.

Z made a sound, far too much like a muffled laugh.

*Men.*

Jessica was propped up in the bed on pillows. In her arms, the sleeping baby was wrapped in a pink blanket.

"She looks just like Jessica." Ben touched the baby's fair-skinned cheek with a finger as big as the infant's arm. "Sorry, Z, you lost out there."

Z's gaze was on his mate. "I can't think of anything more perfect."

Eyes filling, Jessica gave him a tremulous smile. After a second, she looked up at Anne. "Do you want to hold Miss Sophia Grayson?"

"I would love to." Anne took the tiny bundle, snuggled her close, and kissed the wispy blonde hair. What was there about holding a baby that filled something needy inside?

*I want a child.* The longing had grown—and been ignored—over the past year. She pressed a kiss to the little head, and Sophia's rosebud lips made a smacking sound. "She's beautiful, Jessica. Fine work, Z."

She realized Ben had leaned against a wall, arms crossed—a common posture with him—and his whiskey brown eyes were studying her, probably coming to the correct conclusion: Mistress Anne was a sucker for babies.

"Well, I need to get home." With a sense of loss, she gave the baby back to Jessica, added a quick hug for the new mother, and nodded at Z.

Ben followed her out.

In the living room, Z walked over. "We have bedrooms for both of you. Why don't you stay and catch some sleep?"

"That's a kind offer, but I'll sleep better in my own bed," she said.

"I see." Z set a warm hand on her shoulder. "Jessica and I appreciate your assistance last night."

"Actually, I should be thanking you for letting me be part of a miracle. Sophia is lovely."

"She is, isn't she?" Z's quick smile faded. "Please be cautious on the drive home. Our country roads can be hazardous after a storm." He hesitated and glanced at Ben.

Anne picked up her bag. "I'll take care. You better try to catch a little sleep, Z, since it'll be in short supply from now on."

A smile softened his hard face.

She added, "And call me when you need a break. I'm good with babies."

# Chapter Four

Ben pulled his SUV into Anne's drive, parked off to the side, and jumped out. Hands in his pockets, he regarded the area. He'd never seen her home in the daylight. Hell of a place.

The two-story house was dark green with white trim and raised high enough to provide a slightly sunken carport beneath—not a bad idea considering how close to the shore this was. From this angle, he could see a shoulder-high deck extended toward the water. She'd had a balcony off the master bedroom, hadn't she? With beach houses, it was all about the ocean view.

As Anne watched him walk up the steps, her pissed-off expression made him long for a groin protector. He was in for it now.

"Choice *A*. You're stalking me," she said bluntly. "Choice *B*. Mama Z told you to shadow me home."

He grinned. No flies on this woman. "*B*. Although I wouldn't mind *A*, if it wouldn't get me filled with bullet holes."

His answer didn't diminish the steam he could almost see coming from her ears. Damn, she was gorgeous when her color was up.

"Oh, honestly, Ben. That's simply—"

"He knows you can take care of yourself in a fight. But you can't lift a palm tree, and I doubt you carry a chainsaw in your trunk."

"A chainsaw? Seriously?" She glanced at his Jeep Grand Cherokee.

"I'm in the wilderness a lot. Comes in handy."

"Well." She didn't...quite...growl. "Right. Thank you then. This is a long way to come when you haven't had any sleep."

"You're welcome, Anne." He smiled slowly, thinking of Patton's favorite quote, *"Audacity, audacity, always audacity."* All right then. "I wouldn't mind a cup of coffee if it wouldn't be too much trouble."

Considering they'd passed a myriad of stores and coffee shops, she knew he could find his own. His request was for something else, and being the woman she was, she knew that.

She crossed her arms and looked him over like a side of beef.

It took some work, but he stood his ground.

And then she smiled. "You are the pushiest submissive I've ever met. Why am I enjoying that?" She motioned him into her house. "Come on in."

Submissive. The word—applied to him—made him pause, but only a second. And then he was right on her heels.

Inside, he caught a glimpse of her living room that seemed all sunlight and windows. She stopped in the foyer to remove her boots and went barefoot up the stairs.

After doing the same, he followed her. Three steps up, he paused to adjust himself. His jeans felt as if they were shrinking around his cock. Wasn't it nice that he didn't have to wonder how she'd react to a man's hard-on? He'd never met any woman so straightforward about sex.

"You're thinking too much, Benjamin." Halfway up, she stripped off her shirt and tossed it down.

He caught the garment before it landed on his head—barely. His gaze had been occupied with the sight of her bare back. How her hips started to widen before being covered by her jeans. How her skin was so smooth and golden.

He took the steps three at a time and followed her into the bedroom. "Ma'am, I'd be delighted to serve, to help you"—*strip naked*—"with disrobing."

"Aren't you the generous one?" A dimple flashed in her right cheek, always the first one to show.

He intended to see both dimples displayed before the hour was over.

"Yes, Ma'am. That's me." He stepped closer and ran his hands up and down her arms, feeling the firm muscle beneath all that soft skin.

The slight tilt of her head told him to stop while he was ahead. She looked up at him, her eyes a clear blue-gray, like a sunlit mountain lake. "I think we'll take turns disrobing, so neither of us misses out on the fun." And she proceeded to yank off his Hard Rock T-shirt.

"Mmm." Her husky voice held only approval as she ran her hands over his pectorals, ruffling his chest hair before tracing the narrow line down his belly to where it disappeared under his jeans.

And fuck, the sizzle from her touch continued all the way to his dick. His cock surged upward, trying to burst from its confines. His shirt might be off, but he was radiating so much heat that he'd probably scorch her exquisite skin.

Smiling, she pushed one strap of her bra over her shoulder and smiled at him. Giving him permission.

The universe was looking favorably on him today.

With one finger, he teased her other strap off, and his pulse skipped a beat when her bra lowered far enough that he could see the edges of her pink-brown nipples. He might get eyestrain if he didn't get her uncovered soon.

"I thought you were beautiful in the Shadowlands," he managed to say. "In full daylight, you're even more gorgeous."

Her eyes lit. "You know, I think of you as Z's guard dog, not one of my boys, so when you say something like that, it's surprising and very effective." She gripped his upper arms and rose onto tiptoes to kiss him, a generous, sweet kiss with tongue. "Thank you."

*My fucking pleasure.* She was near enough he could reach around her, unfasten her bra, and slide it off. Her breasts were high and full—a man's finest fantasy, up close and touchable.

Touch he did, filling his palms. Her breasts were probably about the same weight as navel oranges, and yet that was like comparing the satisfaction in playing tennis or fucking. Nothing in the world could feel as sweet as her breasts.

She made an approving sound as he rubbed his thumbs over her nipples. When he squeezed slightly and then tugged lightly on the peaks, he felt her quiver.

He needed more.

But, with desperate control, he lowered his hands, forcing himself to let her take the next step. She could lead him wherever her heart desired.

Her eyebrows rose. "You keep surprising me." To his delight, she undid his jeans and released him.

As the cool air from an open window hit his overheated cock, he drew in a steadying breath.

"Yes, you're just as magnificent as I remembered," she murmured.

The sheer satisfaction at hearing that was almost as fantastic as the way her hands gripped him, as the way she varied her hold from a firm stroke at the base to a feather-light grazing of the head.

She shoved his jeans down until they tangled at his ankles. "Part your legs as far as you can."

Setting a hand on her shoulder for balance, he moved his feet apart.

Her free hand cupped his balls, pulling and teasing, while her other hand played with his dick. With uncanny skill, she drove him up until he was too damn close to coming.

"Mistress." The sound emerged despite his clenched jaw. "I'd rather—" *fuck you.*

Her gaze was a laser beam of incandescent blue light. "I'd rather too, for that matter. And it *is* your turn for the disrobing, isn't it?" She stepped back. "On your knees, please."

He went down on one knee, leaning forward to kiss her bare stomach. Kneeling didn't bother him—not if he got to remove her clothes. Hell, he'd even use his teeth if that were what she wanted. He wouldn't have minded one fucking bit. With careful fingers, he unbuttoned her jeans.

Setting a hand on his shoulder, she lifted her foot.

Her skin was distractingly smooth as he pushed the material off her calves and feet. His gaze ran up. Curvy calves, long sweet thighs that led to... Yeah, he was going to die. Last time he'd been here, he'd thought...maybe...that she shaved. Now he knew.

Her pussy was completely bare of hair. Damn, that was sexy.

She made a sound and he realized his fingers had tightened around her ankles. He managed to loosen them for a second, but with one inhalation, he was lost. First, the scent of something spicy—like cinnamon and cloves, then a lightly delicate feminine musk.

Her hand smacked the top of his head, breaking the spell. Painfully.

He released her, seeing the marks of his hands on her ankles.

"Benjamin, you're not just back from the wars—and I doubt this is the first time you've seen a woman."

He cleared his throat. "Not a woman like you, Ma'am." There'd never been a woman like her in his entire, fairly exhaustive experience. He stayed where he was and dared to run his hand up and down her legs, wanting nothing more than to bury his face between her thighs. "Ma'am. May I—"

Her eyes narrowed. "No, I don't think so." One finger, the elegant nail with a white flower on pink polish, pointed to the bed. "Put yourself there. On your back, so I can sample the wares at my pleasure."

He wasn't sure whether to protest, to grab her, or to cheer. Sampling meant she'd touch. He was down with that. And even if he hadn't been, the oddest satisfaction came from obeying her orders. Maybe he could overpower her physically, but in matters of the spirit, she had a will that might be stronger than his own. "Yes'm."

Now that was one of the finest sights she'd ever seen, Anne thought as Ben ducked under the canopy and stretched out on her king-sized bed. The ultimate in darkly tanned masculinity provided a startling contrast to her feminine floral bedspread. His shoulders were wide and strong, his chest hugely muscled, his stomach ridged. His cock sprang up, thick and long, from a nest of light brown curls. His thighs showed the long divide between the muscles.

She sauntered over, his gaze on her like a scorching sun. He made her feel beautiful, which was always nice. Nicer than normal because she…respected him and valued his opinion.

With a shake of her head to dislodge stray thoughts, she leaned over the bed. "And what have we here? This seems to be quite the odd protuberance." She grasped his cock with a firm hand and twisted just enough to lift his head off the pillow with a gasp. The shaft palpably thickened.

His eyes burned golden.

"You have tiger's eyes." They reminded her of one of her favorite bracelets. "Are you going to lie there and take what I do to you?" she asked softly.

The pulse of desire and dominance rippled through her, heightening her senses. She could taste his lust, hear his need, not only for sex, but also for her control. The challenge of trying to obey her added to his arousal.

"I'm all yours, Mistress." His answer held determination—and his anticipation was like a dollop of whipped cream in her chocolate.

He'd experienced some of what she might do, and he wanted more.

She considered blindfolding him, but she really did appreciate the way he focused on her. Her eyes, her mouth, her muscles. Every jiggle of her breasts was noted.

Her nipples ached with anticipation.

Why not? She straddled him with a quick movement, avoiding his cock, and settling her ass on his stomach. Bending, she took his lips. Firm and enthusiastic. She controlled the kiss, taking what she wanted, and when she sat back, he let out a faint groan. Until she positioned herself to give him a nipple.

He'd been good until then, but now one hand gripped her ass, the other behind her back, pulling her down so he could suckle and lick vigorously. His mouth was hot, his lips soft, his tongue like a lash.

Desire spiraled up her center until he could undoubtedly feel her dampness on his belly.

The second she pulled against his hold, he released her. And looked up so hopefully that she gave him her other breast.

"Mmm. You're good at that, Benjamin." Each suck of his mouth zinged straight to her clit. She found his flat male nipples, circled them with a fingertip until they jutted out, then pinched them cruelly enough his body went rigid beneath her.

Her body trembled in response. She needed...needed to move, to take him. Maintaining her control was more difficult than anything she'd ever felt before.

His tanned face was darkened with lust when she sat back to study him. She'd never met anyone more...unreservedly masculine, all steely planes and craggy features and solidly packed muscles. She ran a finger down his large nose, feeling the bump where it'd been broken in the past.

"Please. Mistress. I'd like to taste more." His gaze slid down her torso. "More."

So well said. She did appreciate a man who could be frank without being coarse. And he'd sent need churning in her veins with just a look and a few words.

"In a bit." He deserved a little attention for himself...and, God, she wanted to explore all those muscles for herself.

After releasing his hair, she slowly kissed his scarred cheek, moving down. His jaw and neck held the light tang of sweat. A night's worth of beard stubble rasped over her tongue, making her anticipate feeling that scratch elsewhere. Over his wide chest, his springy hair was the same tawny color as his hair. The way his thick pectorals were rock hard made her stomach flutter in a primal reaction.

As she tongued and nipped his flat nipples, she twisted and gripped his cock, enjoying the jerk and surge.

The man openly liked everything she did, and his enjoyment added to her restless hunger.

When her breasts dragged across his chest, his hips rose under her, adding another layer of anticipation.

She used her legs to push his apart and settled between his knees. The coarse hair of his thighs rubbed against her hips as if to emphasize the differences between them, to make her feel more silkily female.

A man's smoothly waxed skin was nice. Somehow, she'd forgotten the textural pleasures of a more natural look.

When she bit his lean belly, he inhaled sharply and his erection pulsed. She soothed the spot with her tongue, licked the soft crease at the top of his thigh, and felt him quiver with his restraint.

Everything she did to him made him hotter—and did the same to her, like a tide coming in, rising higher with every set of waves. And yet, controlling him, the way he followed her directions, was a roaring storm of pleasure putting the whitecaps on the breakers, lashing her with need.

The head of his cock was velvet, the shaft was satin, and the tortuous veins bulged with blood. He had a lovely musky scent—totally intoxicating.

As she moved down and nipped his thigh, she could feel his struggle to not release. In fact, if she administered sharp pain right now, he'd come whether he wanted to or not. So tempting. She really, really fancied seeing him come again.

But she shouldn't short herself this time. She had needs…and he'd expressed a desire to *taste*.

Wasn't he lucky that she felt like granting his wish?

"All right, Benjamin. Let's see how well you use that mouth and tongue."

His brown eyes lit with anticipation, turning golden in the bright sunlight from the window. "Thank you, Jesus."

"I prefer Goddess," she said primly. Her whole body was humming with its own eagerness as she moved off him and onto her back.

His laugh was a guttural rumble, and he was over her before she could blink. So gorgeously virile, he simmered with heat.

As his powerful hands closed on her thighs, he paused. "I thought Dommes always sat on their guys' faces."

She rolled her eyes. "Sitting takes effort; I've been up all night." She waved her fingers. "You work. I rest."

"Yes, Ma'am." His grip on her legs clamped down as if he feared she'd escape.

Would this giant of a man require instruction in the fine art of—?

His tongue touched her clit ever so delicately.

No instruction needed.

He maneuvered his way lower between her legs, opened her carefully, and ran his tongue over her clit, around, under, over. Teasing. Gradually increasing the force. Reading her body as sweetly as any slave she'd ever had.

Her pussy throbbed, demanding attention, sending needy demands. There were occasionally times she liked being teased; this wasn't one of them. She fisted his hair. "Go for it, Benjamin. Mouth only—but get me off in the next ten minutes or you get sent home."

Excellent threat. His hands clenched hard enough to bruise, and then he went to work, teasing her clit, around the hood, the sides, the top.

*Amazing.* Her breathing slipped out of her control at the full, hot sensation as her pussy engorged with blood, as pressure coiled in her depths.

He took her clit in his mouth, engulfing it in heat and wet, and her need grew. Her fingers in his hair pulled him forcefully against her— and he laughed.

She tugged again, more painfully.

His only reaction was to fit his lips around her more tightly—and then he sucked. Relentless, pulsing sucks. Stopped to flicker his tongue over her before sucking again.

Her muscles went taut under his hand as the coil in her core tightened, as her hips tried to lift, and then he flattened his tongue, rubbing determinedly right on the top.

The wildfire battering her senses roared out of control, whipped by the winds of need. Her hips bucked against his hold as the pressure grew, grew, grew...and detonated. Searing sensation scorched across her nerves, flaming outward in pulsing streams of pleasure.

Past the bruising hammering of her heart, she could feel his hands gliding up and down her thighs. Eventually, she opened her eyes, saw his grin, and...the softness in his eyes. Her pulse skipped. She could barely control her voice—and all she could think about was the overwhelming desire to have him inside her. "Benjamin. You're amazing."

He didn't answer for a second, just stared at her. "Did you know you're abso-fucking-lutely gorgeous when you come?"

Her heart warmed. Oh yes, she really, really wanted him. "Muss me up, then, Benjamin."

The flare of heat in his gaze could have seared the planet.

She yanked his hair, the implacable demand clawing at her required action. "Move, subbie. *Now.*"

"Fuck, *yes*, Ma'am." He was over her in an instant and thrust in, powerful and fast.

*Holy fucking Jes—Goddess.* The top of Ben's head almost shot off. Anne was hot and slick—and tight enough to make him almost come on entry. With a rigid grip on his control, he managed to stop before full penetration to let her adjust to his size.

Some women couldn't ever take him to the hilt.

But Anne? Face still flushed from her climax, she was smiling with pleasure. At his lack of movement, she opened her eyes and the heat in them burned his skin. "Guard dog, did you stop for a reason? Now, now, *now.*"

She sure didn't need to tell him twice.

As he pressed in, his hands dug into her hips as he struggled for control. Jesus, she felt good. With a groan, he tried to slow, fought to keep from hurting her. He felt the resistance as her cunt stretched around him, and then he was… "*Fuck!*"

He pulled out, appalled at himself. "Need protection, Ma'am."

Her eyes widened, and her expression held the same shock as his.

"I fucked up." Tensely, he waited for her to rake him over the coals. Deservedly, too. It was a man's job to protect the woman. Always.

"Well, I haven't forgotten that essential since I was in college." She met his eyes. "I'm sorry—and I can see you are as well. We both messed up." She rubbed his shoulder. "I'm on birth control pills."

Per Shadowlands requirements, she'd also be tested routinely for STDs. He offered his own reassurance. "I get tested right along with the members. I'm clean."

"Good enough." With a wave of her hand, she indicated the left. "Bedside drawer."

That was it? No yelling? Both of them were slaphappy with lack of sleep, but he should be thumped for screwing up. Only…he had to appreciate her calmness and how she'd shouldered part of the blame herself. She was as classy down deep as she was on the surface.

Reaching over, he yanked the bedside table drawer out, finding condoms as well as toys that—if he hadn't thought she'd hurt him— he'd have explored further. Instead, he grabbed a packet, ripped it open, and covered himself. "Let's try this again."

He stroked her hips with his hand, ran a finger through her folds…still drenched for him and damn he liked that bare look. Parting her gently, he established his landing zone—and took her with one aggressive assault. Sheathed or not, his cock was in heaven.

She inhaled fast, and he could feel her cunt around him, throbbing, gripping him in a mercilessly slick fist.

He'd wanted her for so long—he wasn't going to last long. Grinding his teeth, he paused. Should he be doing something—anything else?

Her eyes opened. One dimple showed. "Mmm, lovely." Her words were so throaty she could make a man come with her voice alone. "Did you stop for a reason?"

Damn, she was something. "Um. Aside from hammering you into the bed, can I do anything else?"

Amusement danced in her eyes. "No, Benjamin. That will be sufficient." She'd sound elegant even in the middle of a firefight.

And he had a go order. *Oh, yeah.* He pulled back, pressed in, feeling the *nothing-equals-this* slide of his cock inside a tight cunt. His next thrust was harder, his next one harder still.

Her eyes closed. Her lips curved, making her cheekbones sharper. She was obviously enjoying his size—and wasn't that a hell of a turn-on?

"Okay, Mistress, I got you," he muttered. With deep, driving thrusts, he took her, filled her, and joined them together. And she gave back, running her hands over his shoulders, curling a leg behind his ass and lifting herself to him.

He took her soft lips, tilted his pelvis enough to graze her clit, and felt her fingers clutch his arms and her hips push up to meet him. Her face flushed a deeper red.

And then she came, the beauty of it such that he lost himself and realized far too late that his cock had a mind of its own. The buffeting spasms around his shaft sent him spiraling out of control, and then the pile driver of his own climax slammed into him, pulsing in her welcoming heat with searing bolts of pleasure.

Bending his neck, he kissed her shoulder and reveled in the sensations.

"Well." A while later, she ran her fingers through his hair, pushing it back from his face. Her lips were swollen, her cheeks pink, her skin slightly damp. She wasn't the cool Mistress at the moment. "That was an excellent way to celebrate a new birth." Her voice was as deep as Lauren Bacall's throaty contralto. "Thank you, Ben."

She was damned welcome. And she'd called him Ben. He liked the sound of it—just as much as he enjoyed when she drew all three syllables out.

"I'm available to celebrate new births any time you want. Or for birthdays too. You got a birthday this week, right?"

Her eyes narrowed.

Women sure did hate their birthdays, didn't they?

"I do."

"You look as if a birthday's equivalent to a murder trial. You're still a baby, darlin'."

Her glare was gorgeous. "The last subbie who gave me grief cleaned my toilet with a toothbrush."

"Did that in basic," Ben commented.

"And did you also hold an enema in…with the toilet seat chained down until after the room passed inspection." She gave him a slight smile. "It's amazing how much faster a room gets scrubbed with a little incentive."

"Jesus fuck, you got a mean side, woman."

She laughed. "So be grateful you're not mine."

He'd be hers; damned if he wouldn't. She had no clue how determined a Ranger could be to complete a mission successfully. "Sorry, Anne, but truth is truth. You're only going to be thirty-five."

"Thirty-five," she muttered in disgust. She scooped her hair back off her face.

He ran his fingers through it. Soft and silky, with almost a sandalwood fragrance. A few glints of red and lighter brown showed in the sun-kissed brunette strands. And he could see some gray in front of her ears. Bet that pissed her off. "Does getting older bother you?"

"You know, I hadn't thought it would, but it's not as much my age, but…" She pursed her lips. "I love what I do, love where I live. But, now my mind is asking what comes next."

"What's wrong with that?"

"I don't want there to be a next. I want to be happy with where I'm at." She scowled. "I don't like things changing. Ever."

His laugh died. Because she was serious. "I'll try to remember that." As he nuzzled her temple, he tasted the slight trace of salt from her damp skin. Her hair brushed over his cheek like a fragrant breeze.

Lifting up, he looked down at her. Even as his cock softened within her, he was ready to start over.

But he needed more. Would she ask him to spend the night? Defenses were lowered during sleep and subtle links were created. He wanted those ties…with her.

He leaned down to take her lips again.


Ben could kiss…really, really kiss. Anne let him, feeling the low hum of her satiated body, the almost shocking pleasure of being pressed into the mattress by his huge frame. Why was that so sexy?

He teased her lips, kissed her cheek and jaw, and the rough scrape of his beard against her skin tantalized her senses.

She set her hand behind his head, holding him as she savored the way he still filled her deep inside. "More," she said.

With a low growl, he angled his mouth over hers, taking her deeper. Yummier.

When he lifted his head, her arms were around his neck with her forearms resting on his thick shoulder muscles. The man was seriously built, and his body radiated a furnace-like heat.

She kissed his corded neck, tasting the slight salty tang, before nipping the long muscle angling from his chest to his jaw.

Should she make him stay for a long nap and then another wonderful interlude? Reward him with supper? He'd relish her cooking—and feeding him up would be a delight.

She'd like to spend some more time with him. During the interminable hours of waiting, she'd found that—with encouragement—he not only talked, but also had an intriguingly wry sense of humor.

"Ben," she started.

And then he looked down at her and...her soft mood stumbled to a halt, tripped over the curb, and crashed into the pavement.

Because his gaze held more than the lazy aftermath of sex, more than the usual awe and reverence from her slaves. He looked at her as if he wanted more from her. As if he "liked" her and wanted a, *heaven help her*, relationship.

*No. No, no, no.*

As her smile slipped, she slapped it back on, making his eyes narrow as he registered the difference he couldn't understand.

"Well, that was definitely pleasant," she said. "But, I have work to do tonight and I need to catch some sleep before that."

He angled his head, his demeanor firming. His eyes grew intent. "I make a big, but huggable teddy bear."

She pressed a hand on his shoulder, telling him silently to remove himself. "That's a nice offer, Benjamin, but..." Hurting someone...hurt. And so did the guilt that swamped her now. She should never have invited him in.

He shifted his weight and pulled out slowly. The loss created an emptiness that extended further than just her core. As he swung his legs over, he helped her up so they sat side-by-side.

She frowned, realizing he'd sat beside her, not at her feet.

Without permission, he curled his fingers around her hand. "What's wrong?"

"I'm sorry. I intended this as a simple way to pass time, nothing more." She squeezed his hand with her free one and tugged free. "I think you might have more kink than either of us suspected, but, Ben, you're not a slave."

His gaze stayed on her face. "And?"

"And for anything other than a…well, a non-involved one-time-only, I confine myself to experienced slaves who know what it's all about."

"Warning understood. What if I want another…non-involved…time?"

She rose, instinctively needing to be higher than him, to influence him to listen. He needed to hear her now. She set her hand on his shoulder to keep him in place. When she cupped his jaw, the rigidity of his muscles confirmed her worries. She should be whipped for forgetting how easily newbies could think the bond created during a D/s scene meant…more.

She knew better. Early in her Domme days, she'd made the mistake of thinking a submissive was equivalent to a slave. But although both types might give up control, a slave wanted to surrender…everything. As a Mistress, she wanted it all.

Being unable to meet her needs had hurt those submissives—and hurting them had damaged her as well. She wouldn't do that again.

"I'm sorry, Ben, but another time wouldn't be wise." Feeling his flinch, she had to force herself to stay the course. She pulled him to his feet. "There's a bathroom across the hall."

"Got it." His eyes showed his unhappiness as he grabbed his jeans.

Silently, Anne rose and dressed. How could she have been so foolish? She'd wounded this amazing man in a way she'd never intended.

He was gone within ten minutes. She gave him a "nice" kiss at the front door, one that permitted her lips but held none of "her," and she could see he knew the difference.

Didn't like the difference.

She didn't like the difference either. She headed back up the stairs, feeling weariness tugging at her as if she were still wearing the heavy weapons belt and body armor. In trying not to wound him…she'd still hurt him. She felt as if she'd kicked a puppy.

But, what was the alternative? She didn't do relationships—not "emotional" ones, anyway. Long and long ago, she'd learned that she wasn't the type of person who did well with the *love* stuff. It was even more risky than friendships.

As she moved toward the bed, she realized she smelled of sex and a faint hint of Ben's woodsy soap. Turning, she went into her huge master bath, stripped, and flicked on the rain shower.

The water poured down over her, but nothing could wash away her feeling of guilt.

Nonetheless, no matter how awful she felt now, the greater crime would be allowing Z's man to fall for someone who couldn't return the emotion.

# Chapter Five

That weekend, Ben sat at his desk in the Shadowlands entry...and planned.

Anne hadn't been in last night...but she was here now. He had a chance.

In that one afternoon with him, Anne had gone from a warm, willing woman to one wearing more armor over her emotions than a soldier wore to protect his guts.

Okay, he understood the slave versus submissive stuff to a degree. But...she'd sure seemed to be enjoying herself while they were interacting. And fuck knew, he had. Then she'd totally shut down.

His best guess was that her exhaustion—and the exhilaration of Sophia's birth—had lowered her defenses, and she'd let him get too close. Over the past years, he'd watched her with her slaves, and she'd always been in control. Always reserved. Emotions always guarded.

Just as Z had said.

Hell, when she'd come in tonight, unfortunately with a crowd of other members, she'd smiled at him politely. As if he didn't know what she felt like beneath him, how she tasted, how her coolness hid passion and...sweetness.

Yeah, Ben wanted the woman—and the Mistress—beneath those barriers. He'd seen her, held her, made love to her.

He'd analyzed his target. Studied that fucking armor of hers, evaluated her strength and her reserves, considered her possible choices for action. Unfortunately, he'd have to operate on her terrain, the Shadowlands. But he had a tentative plan for tonight, initiating movement and making a personal reconnaissance.

After talking Holt into babysitting his guard station, Ben strolled through the main clubroom and watched for her, his slender brunette with a body to die for and sleek curves that hid the muscles beneath.

He saw Mistress Olivia with a new submissive, a woman close to her own age—an executive type with classically styled hair, carefully applied makeup, and a beautiful, expensive leather dress. Since she'd worn the prettiest stilettos he'd ever seen, he'd allowed her to keep them on.

When he located Mistress Anne, he'd have to point them out.

If he ever found the woman.

He spotted Galen, Vance, and Sally watching a wax play scene. "Have you seen Mistress Anne?"

"You want *Anne*?" Vance's eyebrows lifted.

Ben nodded.

"Sorry, Ben. I haven't seen her," Galen said with a frown.

Their reaction made him wonder if they disliked the thought of someone so big and ugly playing with their pretty Mistress. Too bad.

He headed for the bar. Cullen would probably know where Anne was.

The bartender was moving fast, swamped with the crowd around his long oval bar. The only empty barstool was beside the barmaid station. Uzuri stood there, waiting with her tray and a list of orders.

Ben studied her. When she'd come in at the start of the night, she'd seemed…off. Her coloring tonight was more gray than brown, and she moved as if she was exhausted. It wasn't his job to babysit the submissives, but maybe he'd give one of the Masters a heads-up.

All of the other Shadowlands trainees had found their Doms, leaving the little prankster behind. The single Doms had tried their hardest to win her over though. And she was damned pretty. With her wide-set dark brown eyes, skin the color of lightened coffee, and high cheekbones, she reminded him of Brandy in the Cinderella musical.

Z had said he didn't know if she had it in her to pick a Dom—that she might not be willing to take the risk. Ben hadn't understood his reasoning at the time.

But last winter an altercation had occurred at a bachelorette party. Whereas Rainie had been upset about her obnoxious friends, Uzuri had been terrified at the potential for violence. She must have some ugly shit in her past.

In the years Ben had worked here, he'd discovered how often abusers preyed upon submissives. Those unfamiliar with BDSM didn't always realize that dominance and submission wasn't a competition—it was a waltz. One person got to lead. But if the other partner was being trampled, then it sure as hell wasn't a dance.

Uzuri looked up as he slid onto a stool beside her. "Ben, what are you doing in here?"

"Lookin' for Mistress Anne. Have you seen her?"

Her eyes grew wide. "I didn't believe them when they said you and she were... Ben, that's not a good idea. Sure, she's pretty, but she's also a—"

"I know." Fuck, there was no end.

Cullen came over and damned if his mouth didn't thin at the sight of Ben. "Tell me you're not here looking for Anne."

Well, hell. He'd thought he and Cullen were friends. They went drinking now and then. Had shared job horror stories—Cullen from being a cop and firefighter, Ben from the military. After imbibing more alcohol, they'd even ventured into uglier tales—how Cullen had lost his fiancée to a fire, how Ben had been dumped by his wife when deployed.

Ben gave him a level stare. "I'm telling you I'm looking for Anne."

"Buddy, listen—"

"Nope." Ben rose and then hesitated. "Rather than worrying about a woman fully capable of caring for herself, you might check out the trainee who obviously can't."

He glanced at the little submissive to show who he meant, then turned his back on both of them and continued scouting.


Well, honestly. Why did Ben have to sic a Master on her? Uzuri frowned after the big security guard, then—keeping her gaze down—pushed the drink tickets toward Master Cullen. "All these and Master Sam's Linda wants a glass of white wine."

Ben and Cullen were equally huge—and in some ways, they both made her nervous. Some people preferred big guys. In fact, her fellow Shadowkittens sometimes teased their Doms saying, "Size really does matter."

Maybe a bigger cock was a good thing—she didn't particularly care—but when it came to men in general? She'd far rather have a smaller one.

A punch from a smaller man didn't break bones.

"Uzuri, eyes on me." Master Cullen's gaze felt like the pressure change before a storm moved in.

*Bollocks*, as Mistress Olivia might say. She looked up obediently.

"You do look tired. Stressed." His heavy brows drew together.

"What's going on, love?"

"Work stress." Almost an honest answer. She'd been moving up the corporate ladder so life was never stress-free. The trouble was...work wasn't the problem.

"Look, Cullen. I found a bar ornament for you." At the far end, a Dom dumped a submissive on the bar top. "She's already gagged."

Master Cullen held up a hand in a wait gesture before frowning at Uzuri.

His sub Andrea thought he resembled Boromir in Lord of the Rings. Unfortunately, Boromir now looked as frustrated and pissed off as when Elrond refused to hand over the ring. "When your serving time is over, you find me. We're going to chat about stress."

"Yes, Sir." As he moved toward his new bar ornament, Uzuri relaxed. She could talk about stress all day. Other things, no.

Anne pulled off the Shadowlands' dungeon monitor vest and stuffed it in her locker. Hands over her head, she stretched upward, removing the knots. Her duty was over. Now, she could head home, or coax Sam and Linda into going out for a drink, or maybe find someone here to play with.

Option three might be a good choice.

Find a good boy. Work him over until he was shaking, not able to tell the difference between pain and pleasure. Maybe reward him with a trip upstairs to let him touch her. Have some no-strings-attached sex.

She damn well needed something to erase the memories of Ben in her bed. All those steel-hard muscles. The weight of him on top of her—the feeling of being penetrated by his heavy shaft.

The way his eyes lit as if he held sunshine in his soul.

And then she'd been cruel. Shot down his hopes and wounded his spirit.

The small hurt then had been necessary to prevent a larger one. She sighed, losing the urge to play at all. She just didn't have the heart to chance flattening another subbie's desires.

And wasn't that just pitiful?

One of these days, the sadist police would show up to take her membership card away.

Instead, she'd just get a drink here and forget about playing with anyone. As she walked out of the locker room, she growled low. Cullen had better have gotten over being pissy about her mixing pain meds and alcohol. If he gave her another sparkling water, she'd dump it on his head, even if she had to stand on a barstool to reach the right height.

"Mistress Anne," Sally called from where she sat between her two Masters. She jumped up and ran over.

Anne had to smile—a common reaction at seeing the vibrant submissive. "You look very happy; marriage agrees with you."

"I'd given up hope of finding one Dom and here I am with two. It still seems like a dream." The brunette's nose wrinkled. "Unless I'm in trouble. Then it's a nightmare."

Punishment at the hands of Galen and Vance? Having watched the two Doms co-top, Anne knew a sub wouldn't have a chance. "Hopefully you'll learn to stay out of trouble," she said, spouting the Dominants' party line.

"But it's a submissive's duty to keep her Doms on their toes and well exercised." Sally grinned. "Anyway, the guys are going to be gone part of next week, and I'd really appreciate some company. Can you come over on Thursday? It'll just be me and maybe Beth or Gabi. The house still gets scary when my men aren't home."

Thursday? That was her birthday. But Anne couldn't say no. She understood loneliness. And Sally had been attacked in that house; being alone was probably still difficult. "Of course, I'll come."

"Awesome. Thank you!" Sally squeezed her hand and hurried away.

Anne continued toward the bar.

Adjusting her long latex gown, she eased onto a barstool next to Sam and Raoul, two of the other Shadowlands Masters. Glancing around, she saw they'd left their women in the subbie area, Raoul even going so far as to chain his slave, Kim, marking her as unavailable.

Wasn't it odd that Anne had never chained up any of her slaves? Maybe because she'd never felt particularly territorial.

Then again, she hadn't loved any of them—not in the way that Raoul loved Kim.

"Anne," Sam said. The dim lighting around the bar gave the sadist's face a sinister cast and glinted off his silvered hair.

"You look lovely tonight." Raoul's light accent showed why Spanish was considered one of the romance languages.

"Hi, lads." She twisted to check out the available submissives in the sitting area.

There was a nice assortment of male and female, including two appealing men in their mid-twenties. They were conversing while watching the rest of the room. Anne had done a scene with the firefighter in the past. He'd been fun, but a lightweight when it came to pain. She no longer wanted a hard-core masochist, but surely a little endurance wasn't too much to ask.

The other male she hadn't yet met. Pleasingly lean shape. About her height. Buzz-cut blonde hair. He wore only a pair of dark-red biker shorts.

When he saw her looking at him, he flushed from his upper chest to his forehead. His gaze dropped.

*Very nice.*

"Good to see you getting back to normal," Raoul said in approval.

"Really," she said, adding a hint of ice.

Sam chuckled. Unlike Raoul, he tended to mind his own business. She'd always liked the old rancher.

"I heard rumors that you'd played with Ben, and I was worried." Raoul's dark brown eyes met hers. "I know firsthand how disastrous it can be when a Master takes on someone who isn't a real slave."

Her irritation died under his obvious worry. "You don't need to—"

"Anne." Cullen's usually easygoing tone was chilled. "Ben is looking for you."

She straightened. "Is that right?"

"Aye." Cullen leaned an arm on the bar, getting in her face. "Everyone likes Ben, you know."

"This is true." And she had no plans of playing with him again. "Listen, Cullen—"

"My friend, the man is vanilla," Raoul said.

He made it sound as if she'd gone after a virginal eighteen-year-old, not an ex-soldier in his mid-thirties. She kept her tone reasonable. "I think the operative word here is *man*."

"Seems to me the operative word is *sadist* —which you are," Cullen said as if he didn't trust her not to damage a submissive who didn't want it. To know if a man was vanilla or not.

That hurt. She could battle it out with them, but what would that prove? Especially since she'd already ended matters with Ben.

She slid off the barstool.

Sam's eyes met hers and the corner of his mouth lifted. He understood. Sadists had a rep.

She nodded at him, took a step back, and bumped into someone.

From the size of the hands steadying her, she recognized Ben even before he spoke. "Mistress Anne?"

Ignoring the way Cullen and Raoul stiffened, she turned. "Ben, what can I do for you?" Even as she told herself to be cold, the sight of him lifted her spirits and filled unacknowledged hollows.

Hands at his sides, he smiled down at her. "Ma'am, if you're available, could I ask you for another scene?"

She tsk-tsked. "I think you know that submissives don't push themselves forward in this way."

The hint of challenge in his gaze sent a current of electricity running between them. "Ma'am, since I'm not a member of the club, I didn't think Z would let me sit over there"—he motioned to the subbie area—"and make cow eyes at you in hopes you'd favor me."

She choked. The blond young man in the area was doing exactly that. "I...see." Then, deciding to toss her fellow Masters under the train, she nodded toward Cullen and Raoul. "Your friends informed me that you're vanilla and shouldn't do scenes. Are you vanilla...pet?"

He straightened, as if he'd needed to add another inch to his height. Without a glance at the Doms, he snorted. "I didn't realize I had to ask anyone's permission but yours."

"I believe that is correct," she said gravely.

To her surprise, he sank down onto one knee. Yet, he was still so large that he simply exuded menace. "Mistress Anne. Please?"

The singing in her blood wasn't new. It was pulled from the depths of her spirit, a weft across the mundane world into the very different one of dominance and submission—and was a celebration of the moment a submissive gifted her with his power as a man might hand over his cloak. Of the moment he entrusted her with his body and mind and soul.

She'd been a Domme for years and yet the wonder never diminished.

Leaning forward, she laid her palm along his face. The smooth skin meant he'd shaved before coming. This wasn't a sudden request; he'd intended to play.

His clothing confirmed her supposition. Although he'd balk at the skimpy attire some male slaves favored, he'd removed his shoes and socks in compliance with Z's "submissives go barefoot" decree. His fairly new jeans were admirably tight. His form-fitting gray tank clung to the heavy slabs of pectoral muscle.

His gaze met hers—*such a bad submissive*—and she could see the plea. The need. He wanted her to take the control from him.

But...under all that, she could see something else. The desire and need that he'd shown her in her bed. The pull that she must resist.

Because Raoul was right. This submissive wasn't a slave. And his heart needed to be guarded, even if her protection was against her own self.

She closed her eyes against his appeal, and then bent and gripped his arms, pulling him back to his feet. "I'm sorry, guard dog. But we've had our fun, you and me." She lowered her voice, wanting to hold him, to soften the blow. "I explained my reasons, Ben. They haven't changed."

His jaw went rigid, but she shook her head when his mouth opened. And turning on her heel, she walked away.

# Chapter Six

"Anne, you made it!" Sally swung the door wide.

"I did. How are you doing? Are your Doms due back soon?" Anne smiled at the short brunette, pleased to see her looking so content. Sally had searched for the right Dom for years and despaired of finding one as smart as she was, one who could keep up with her mischievous nature, one who she could trust with everything she was.

Watching Vance and Galen take her under command—and fall in love with her—had been incredibly heartwarming.

"They're not gone for long," Sally said. "Come on in. I found some good stuff to watch."

Anne followed her through the beautiful foyer, past the game room with every toy known to man, and to the great room in the back, which was dark. "Weren't Beth and Gabi able to come?"

"Oh…they were," Sally said and flipped the light switch.

"Happy Birthday!"

Anne dropped into a fighting stance at the roar of sound. Women…everywhere. On the long sectional, on chairs, sitting on the floor. All members of the Shadowlands. All grinning at her.

"Wh-what?" Anne actually stammered.

Gabi and Uzuri exchanged high-fives.

"Girl, is this your first surprise party?" Sally slung an arm around her and pulled her forward. "Happy birthday!"

A birthday party. The feeling was like stepping off an unnoticed curb, feeling the ground drop away, being disorientated, stumbling.

Aside from family gatherings, she hadn't had a birthday party since she was ten.

"I… This is lovely." She looked around. Gabi, Kim, Uzuri, Linda, Beth, and Jessica were lounging on the U-shaped sectional. Andrea and Rainie had chairs. Cat, Olivia, and Kari were seated on the floor. Shadowkittens and Dommes. Quite the mixture.

"It's about time you arrived," Olivia said from the floor. "We're critiquing porn techniques."

Anne glanced at the wide-screen television where a fairly studly male was bending over a naked female. She frowned. "He's going to kill the woman tying her like that."

"See?" Andrea waved her hand at Kim. "That's what *I* said. Scarves get too thin and dig in too much and are impossible to unknot."

"True enough," Kim answered, "And he's doing it wrong. But I still think scarves are hot."

"The bondage is bad enough." Gabi tugged at her blue-streaked strand of hair. "But the dialogue? That's seriously lame."

"Birthday cake soon," Sally announced to the room. "What are you drinking, Anne? I have margaritas, beer, wine, and sodas."

*Margaritas?* Anne's mouth almost watered. *Dammit.* "I'd love a margarita, but I can't. An informant called, so I scheduled my bail bond recovery team to get together at four a.m. We're almost out of time before forfeiture of the bond, so we have to get the skip now—which means no alcohol for me." She couldn't afford to be impaired.

"Aww, that's too bad." Sally gave her a sympathetic hug. "Diet Coke then?"

"'Fraid so." *Mistresses don't pout.* She totally wanted to sulk.

"Sit over here, Anne." Olivia patted the floor beside her.

Anne navigated her way across the room, getting hugs and hand squeezes from everyone. By the time she sat down between Olivia and Kari, a warm candle of happiness glowed in her chest. *Friends. A birthday party. Who knew?*

"Oh, baby. Take me." On the television, the actor pushed the actress's legs apart with little finesse, accompanied by groaning—from the Shadowkittens.

Jessica joined the actor in another groan of *"Oh, baby,"* before throwing a potato chip at the television. "Gag me. They need better script writers."

"It must be difficult to write sex dialogue, don't you think?" Linda was around forty and often served as the voice of reason, even when well hammered. "I mean, how many of your men talk during the…act? I'd have to admit, Sam isn't exactly chatty."

Anne sputtered a laugh. Linda's silver-haired rancher had terse down to a science—and he'd totally whip his submissive's ass if he knew she'd shared. Not that anyone was about to tell him.

Ben wasn't exactly talkative during sex either, although when he did speak... *"Please. Mistress. I'd like to taste more." "Did you know you're abso-fucking-lutely gorgeous when you come?"* Anne felt her bones begin to melt at just the memory. Too many memories, actually. She'd heard his rough voice in her dreams, felt his hands, his mouth—

Hooting laughter broke into her thoughts.

"How about if Studly Dumbass says something like this?" Gabi hit MUTE on the remote and turned to Kim, beside her on the sectional. "Cum-bucket, brace yourself."

Kim blinked and leaned away. "What?"

Gabi pretended to unzip her jeans and withdraw an obviously massive cock. The waggle she gave her pretend erection was truly obscene. In a deep voice, she announced, "My ginormous slit-eyed demon's gonna invade your pretty pink fortress. Oh yeah, my cunt thumper's gonna penetrate that cocksocket."

Cheers filled the room even as Kim made a barfing noise. "You call that better?"

"Well, yeah. Far more imaginative than *'Ugh, grunt. Ugh. Oh, baby,'* like a caveman." Gabi punched Kim in the arm. "So, nay-sayer, you're the female in the bed. See if you can do better."

Kim studied the television where the actor was stroking his cock, preparing to do some serious work. "Right." She pressed her hands to her cheeks. "Oh, oh, oh, look at you. My goodness, your Puff, the One-eyed Dragon is so tall and straight. I am overwhelmed with my womanly lust. My meat curtains are soaked. Fuck my love canal, *now.*"

The moans around the room almost matched those starting on the screen.

"Meat curtains?" Farther down the sectional, Linda stared at Kim in disbelief, turned to Sally. "*Wooman,* I need a really big drink." She waved a hand a Gabi. "One that's bigger than that cock."

Shoulders shaking, Sally headed for the kitchen. "Coming right up."


Several hours later, butt still on the floor, Anne leaned her shoulders back against the couch. The noise level hadn't abated, although fewer guests were in the room. Jessica and Kari had gone home to their children. Andrea had a cleaning job to see to; Cat had to go to work early. Jake had picked up Rainie and Gabi, leaving only

Uzuri, Sally, Kim, Beth, Olivia, and Linda.

Laughter and conversation flowed around her, as cheerful as the bright helium balloons bopping on the high ceiling.

What a wonderful way to survive turning thirty-five. And how cleverly Sally had laid the trap. No wonder Galen and Vance were always half-complaining, half-boasting about how sneaky their fun-loving submissive was.

Anne rubbed her arm against Olivia's, happiness a glow inside her as she glanced around the room. At one time, she hadn't thought she could be friends with submissives. But, somehow, with these women, the Mistress-submissive dynamic had eroded over the years. She smiled. The last reserves had disappeared as she taught the Shadowkittens self-defense. Who could maintain a distance when delivering victory whoops for a subbie who'd finally succeeded in tossing the Mistress on her ass?

Yet—although she'd attended her friends' birthday parties—she'd never thought they'd throw one for her. But they had.

She wrapped her arms around herself, so filled with the warm 'n' fuzzy feelings—as Gabi would say—that she had trouble containing them all.

"Hold'em up, ladies. Who's empty?" Sally emerged from the kitchen. Holding a pitcher of margaritas, she topped off any needy glass on her way through. "I have another Coke for you, Anne."

"Thank you, Sally." She pushed herself up to accept the can, heard an "ooof" from Olivia who sat beside her, and realized her support was the Domme's stomach. "Oops. Sorry."

"If you were a subbie, I'd make you regret that. I think you took out my liver—despite the ample padding I have around it," Olivia said in her crisp voice. Her gaze swept over Anne. "I don't know how you stay so slender."

"I still can't believe she's thirty-five," Sally said. "I've always wanted a body like yours, Anne. We probably weigh the same and I'm four inches shorter."

"Try getting a job where you have to keep up with walking, talking testosterone-factories." Anne held up an arm and flexed her biceps. "But see? I have muscles."

"Oooo's" and "aaaaahhhh's" filled the room.

Her mock-indignant glare had no effect. "I'll have you know it takes work to maintain all that is me." She gestured to her lean, mean fighting machine...and earned a barrage of popcorn. "But honestly? It's only because being slower or weaker would put my teammates at risk."

"I hate sweating. I think I'd rather have a few extra dimples around my hips. Besides, Galen appreciates them." Smiling, Sally turned toward the massive U-shaped sectional. "Anyone else?"

On the right end of the sectional, Uzuri pointed at the television screen. "I keep forgetting to drink. Just look at that man."

After the arrival of "meat curtains," and the competition for worst penis slang, porn had been supplanted by classic chick flicks. Anne turned to see Patrick Swayze showing Jennifer Grey how to dance. *Mmm-mmm-mmm.* "Now that is one yummy boy. Makes me want to get out my cuffs and collar."

Dominating someone with that bottomless self-confidence would probably be similar to doing a scene with Ben…and was incredibly tempting.

Next to Uzuri, Sally heaved a lusty sigh. "I bet Swayze could've taught even me to dance."

"Doubtful," Kim said judiciously, "although, at least, you'd have enjoyed failing."

"Oh, rude!" Uzuri threw a kernel of popcorn at her.

"Hey, no throwing the popcorn." Sally shook her head at the floor, littered with popcorn, chips, and colorful pillows. "Galen's going to kill me when he sees this mess."

"You shouldn't have put on that really bad movie if you didn't want popcorn thrown at the screen," Kim said in a righteous tone.

"You diss *my* porn, foolish woman? I'm going to tell your Master Raoul what you called his cock." Sally hummed *"Puff, the Magic Dragon."*

Linda choked on her drink. Uzuri snorted. Anne and Olivia laughed.

Kim's mouth dropped open. "You *wouldn't.*"

Sally hummed louder.

"Hey, it's my turn to make Anne a toast." Beth put down the recliner section of the couch and struggled to her feet, swaying slightly.

"I don't know what you're going to toast to, Beth." Anne smiled up at the slender redhead—one of the most courageous women she knew. Actually, she was proud to call each and every one of the women in the room a friend. "So far, I've been wished a long life, wealth, happiness and"—she grinned at Sally—"and great, inventive sex, at which, just so you know, I'm already superb."

Sally threw a popcorn at her.

"You threw popcorn!" Uzuri eyed Sally narrowly. "I'm going to tell your Masters. They'll have you cleaning the place on your hands and knees."

"Naked," Olivia contributed.

"Oh yes. Definitely naked." Kim waggled her eyebrows. "Master R has a very...aggressive...reaction if I get naked to scrub the floors."

"Really?" Sally's response was so intrigued, everyone laughed.

"Ahem." Beth lifted her glass. "To Anne. May you find your ultimate man and may his needs match what you want to give, and vice versa."

*"Man?"* Kim grinned at Beth. "Girlfriend, haven't you noticed Anne prefers pretty boys?"

When Beth hesitated, Anne said warmly, "That was a lovely blessing. Thank you."

Beth dropped onto the couch with a bounce and put her feet back up. "Nolan said Anne played with Ben, and he's sure not a boy."

*No, he certainly isn't.*

"I'm still surprised that Z didn't kill you for messing with his guard," Olivia said. "But, since he didn't, will you be taking Ben on as a slave?"

Sally planted herself on the arm of the sectional beside Uzuri, looking expectant. Linda leaned forward.

"What a nosy bunch. I should string you all up to a cross and beat on your butts for a while."

She only got grins back along with a muttered, "Just try it, chickie," from Olivia.

"There's no respect left in the world for over-the-hill Mistresses," Anne said mournfully. Then again, she'd listened to all of *their* stories, had lent a shoulder for tears, had given advice.

She just wasn't used to sharing her own.

Military brats made casual friends at the drop of a hat—and learned how much it hurt to lose the close ones. She hadn't had a girlfriend since she was ten. But she had several now. And friendship was a two-way street, wasn't it?

She still had to draw in some air before she could speak. "No, I won't take Ben on. Olivia, you were right. Messing with Z's guard dog isn't a smart move."

"Does he not suit you?" Linda asked in her beautifully melodic voice. "I saw some of your scene and you both looked...complete."

The sweet remark and the memory of the sheer...rightness...of the scene silenced Anne for a moment.

Kim grinned. "Cullen talked to Raoul about it. He was all worried you'd squish Ben's balls or something."

"He was?" Anne winced, the hurt as unexpected as a paper cut. Surely, Cullen knew she'd never give a submissive more than he wanted—and sometimes not even that.

"Ohh, squish the balls. Please!" Sally bounced on the sectional. "You know how Ben's so picky about our shoes. Almost nothing is good enough, so then you get the growl. *'Take those shoes off.'* But once Anne finishes torturing his manly bits, he'll sound like this"—she pitched her voice to a high falsetto—"Take dos shoes oooff."

As the women broke out in laughter, Anne choked on her drink and grinned. She'd have to tell Ben what Sally had said.

Or not. Distance would be best.

How pitiful that just hearing his name had sped up her pulse. She still remembered the feel of his callused hands caressing her breasts. And wouldn't she just love to tie him to a cross, so she could run her own hands all over him.

*Stop. Now. Stay in the real world, not fantasyland.* "You do realize, if a subbie could still talk, I'd feel as if I fell down on the job."

"Oooh, poor Ben," Sally said, doing a mime where a speechless Ben motioned to Uzuri to remove her shoes.

Uzuri blinked her imaginary confusion and pretended to hand Ben her thong instead.

Sally gaped and flung the thong from her in mortification.

"Oh, that's too realistic." Linda clapped. "Isn't it cute how poor Ben still becomes embarrassed?"

"He blushes beautifully. I must say, he's quite the hunk, if you prefer the masculine gender. And, from what I saw when Anne had him, he has a lot to squish." Olivia's cupped hands showed *poor Ben* had watermelon-sized testicles.

*Poor Ben* had better never hear how the women discussed him or he'd be blushing for a month.

Olivia continued, "I also noticed you didn't push the pain when you scened with him. Did he make that a hard limit?"

"No." Anne took a sip and studied the color of her drink. "I just didn't have any urge to make him scream. I haven't needed that in a while."

Silence.

"But you were with Joey, and he's a total pain-slut." Sally yelped when Uzuri elbowed her in the ribs.

"You're being impolite," Uzuri scolded. Despite being a covert prankster, she was also the most respectful and courteous of the Shadowkittens.

"Sorry. I shouldn't—"

"It's all right, Sally," Anne said. "I'm over Joey." Although she had to admit his absence had created an aching void in her life. But, no matter how delightful he'd been, Joey's dependence had become exhausting. "He wanted a full-time Mistress and, as you said, a higher level of pain."

Olivia tilted her head. "I've noticed when your scenes contain more dominance than sadism, you appear most satisfied."

"If your scenes are changing, are you changing as well?" Linda asked softly.

*Changing.* The foul word chilled Anne's skin like the spray from a sleet storm. On the screen, Jennifer Grey was confronting her father for the first time. "Baby" was growing up, becoming a woman. *I'm already a woman. Way past all that.*

"You know, I really hate that word—change." Anne's voice came out thin. Small.

"Oh, Anne." Linda slid from the couch to sit on Anne's right, close enough that their shoulders rubbed as she said softly, "The earth is all about change. The seasons move from summer to winter. The continental plates push up mountains that the weather slowly grinds back down. On this planet, in this universe, nothing stands still."

*Change.* Just the thought set up a queasiness inside. "Some of us prefer to stay in summer." She managed a half a smile. "And prefer that our scenes don't shift under our feet."

"Sam said part of the power in your scenes came from anger, and you chose slaves who fed off that anger and the pain." Linda stopped, letting her silence ask the question—*is that what changed?*

"That's the problem." Anne swallowed the rest of her drink, wishing it were alcohol-laden. "I'm not all that angry at men. Not any longer."

"How come you were so mad?" Uzuri asked. "Did something happen that…" Her dusky skin darkened with her flush, and she turned her gaze to the television.

Anne twisted around to study her uneasily. The girl was going to have to talk about what had happened in her past one of these days. Z's patience with the submissive's so-called hard limit on her history wouldn't last much longer. He'd given her a deadline, which was approaching fast.

But this wasn't the time. She softened her voice. "No, Uzuri. More like an accumulation of job and family frustrations."

"Family can sure mess with your head," Sally said under her breath, her mouth twisting with unhappiness.

Remembering what Sally had shared about her unloving father,

Anne squeezed her hand, hurting for her. "Hey. In the past, right?"

"In the past." Sally managed a slight smile. "So what did your family do?"

Needing to take the pain out of Sally's eyes, Anne offered up more than she would have normally. "My father was career military and totally old school. Dad believes girls are to be protected. They don't fight, and his baby certainly shouldn't be doing anything where she could get hurt."

"Bugger that." After a second, Olivia pointed her finger at Anne and smirked. "So, because your daddy wanted to protect you, you instantly signed up for danger. First as a Marine, then a cop."

Stunned, Anne stared at her. "I-I never quite thought of my career choices in that light, but"—she tossed Olivia a salute—"probably it was a part." Although the overprotective gene that ran rampant in her family probably also played a part.

"I knew you'd been a police officer, but you were a Marine too?" Uzuri's eyes were big.

"Tough jobs, you had," Kim said. "So, is bounty hunting more fun than being a cop?"

"Not really." Her brothers and Dan, a police officer in the Shadowlands, had discovered why she'd left law enforcement, but she'd never discussed it with anyone. But…here…*here*, she could share and receive only sympathy. The realization created a lump in her throat.

She cleared her voice, feeling as if she were uncovering an old wound. "I loved being a police officer, and I thought I'd like the people I was with. Unfortunately, in the station I got, if you didn't have balls, you were mostly an irritant." She imitated the lieutenant's whiny voice. "*Female cops put real cops' lives at risk and take up paying jobs needed by men supporting families.*' As far as the lieutenant was concerned, women officers were only good for fetching coffee or possibly retiring long-dead cases."

"Oh, that really sucks," Sally said.

"Men can really suck," Kim muttered.

"So you told them to sod off," Olivia said in approval.

"Did you tie their balls into pretzel shapes before you quit?" Linda asked and made the rest laugh.

"I might have felt better about everything if I had." But, over the years, apparently her frustrated resentment had eased. She knew who she was. What she could do. And had proven herself over and over.

"Did you like catching crooks? Is that why you're a bounty hunter now?" Uzuri asked.

"I enjoy the chase, yes. Although, I've got a PI license and take cases for a friend now and then, I prefer the straight-forwardness of tossing a bad guy in jail—whether I do it as a cop or a bail bond agent."

The main annoyance in the bail bond agent job—aside from Robert—was the way her uncles would have preferred to keep her in the office, not risking herself on the streets.

"The other people don't give you grief for being female?" Sally asked.

"Not the same way. I lead the fugitive recovery team." She grinned. "And, although I won't tolerate being treated as less competent than a male, I rarely have to punch someone to prove I am anymore."

Linda, mother of two grown children, smiled knowingly. "I bet you fought your way through grade school."

"I came home with more black eyes and bruises than my two brothers combined." Anne grinned. Looking back without the reddish lens of anger, she had to say, she'd had some fun.

"I don't like violence," Uzuri whispered, her eyes haunted.

Anne gentled her voice. *Share with us, Uzuri.* "Did you have to fight someone?"

"No. I don't know how." Uzuri shrank into the cushions.

Anne glanced at Olivia. Olivia tapped her watch...Uzuri's deadline was going to end soon and then they'd get to the bottom of this.

"I didn't fight at one time either," Beth wrapped an arm around Uzuri's shoulders. Beth's ex had left her with scars that would never fade. "But I learned how."

Sally bumped Uzuri's shoulder on the other side. "Are you ever going to join our self-defense classes? Jessica hasn't been able to come for a while, and Kari is hit-and-miss, because of baby Zane. One more person there would be good."

"Maybe," Uzuri said. But from the tone, maybe meant no.

Too softhearted to push, Sally changed the subject. "Speaking of which, you have baby duty tomorrow afternoon, right?"

Uzuri shook her head. "I have the day after."

"I have tomorrow," Anne said. Jessica's mother and aunt had shown up for a couple of days after Sophia's birth, then Z's mother. But Z wasn't the sort of man who wanted live-in help, especially doting grandmothers.

So the Shadowlands women had set up a schedule to drop by at a set time every afternoon to bring food and run errands for Jessica. Or babysit so Jessica could get out of the house.

Anne found the visits the perfect excuse to go and cuddle Sophia.

And every time Anne was there, the desire to have a child grew stronger. She'd never felt the need before, but somehow, she'd...changed—there was that damn word again—and now she wanted to open her life to a child.

It was terrifying to imagine being responsible for a little person, and yet, everything in her simply...yearned. When she left Jessica's house, her arms still felt as if they should be holding a baby. The lingering fragrance of baby powder and milk made her smile.

And babies seemed to be everywhere she looked.

But *wants* weren't *needs*...and a child was the last thing she needed right now.

# Chapter Seven

Ben tapped his fingers on the desk before glancing at the clock. *Fuck.* Saturday at ten p.m. It seemed pretty obvious that Anne was avoiding the Shadowlands this weekend.

Was avoiding him.

He scowled at the door. Dammit. He wasn't a pimple-faced teen to misread a woman's signals. He'd had his fair share of lovers, and he knew she'd fucking enjoyed everything they'd done.

She'd bailed out of what could have been something fine. He was tempted to call her a coward.

But no. She had a point. He wasn't a slave. Or…he didn't think he was. He could try—and would—to be with her, but would she even consider it? Had she ever tried to be with a man who wasn't, maybe, totally a slave?

Seemed to him that they should at least give it a shot and see where the path took them.

The phone rang. He picked it up. "Shadowlands."

"Ben, this is Uzuri. Can you tell Master Z that I won't be in tonight?"

"Sure." He hesitated. "He's going to want a reason, you know."

"Oh, it's nothing bad. Not really." She let out a frustrated sigh and then the deluge broke, her words coming faster and faster. "I was supposed to move into my new duplex all this week, and I'd arranged vacation days and everything, only the previous renters got messed up and ended up staying until today, and the landlords couldn't do much about it without taking them to court." She gulped air, and Ben was grinning as the speed of her speech increased as well as the unhappy whine. "So I only have tomorrow to pack and arrange for some movers, only at this point I might not be able to because it'll be Sunday, only I have to go out of town Monday and for a week and my lease is up and this is just a *mess*."

He'd have to agree. "I have an SUV and free time. I know a couple of guys with pickups. Want some help?"

Silence.

He worried for a moment that he'd scared the little submissive and then he heard a screech of glee. "Would you? Really—you could help? I can drive back and forth, but I can't get the big stuff. There's not that much but—really? You'd help?"

Fuck, she was cute. "Really. What time are you starting?"

"I can't get the keys until nine in the morning. But I can start loading boxes from my apartment, only maybe that's too early for—"

"I'll be there at eight," he said firmly.

"Oh, man. Thank you, Ben. Thank you!"

"Address?"

He took down all the information he'd need, shoved the paper in his pocket, texted Z about his missing trainee...and asked for permission to go a step further. The Shadowlands Masters essentially "owned" the little submissive. They'd pitch in.

He received an instant agreement. That was Master Z.

After pulling out the files of the Masters—and Mistresses—Ben started writing down numbers.

\* \* \* \*

"Ben." Anne squeezed her cell phone. Her heart had *not* just skipped a beat. Absolutely *not*. "Is anything wrong?"

Why else would he be calling her so late on a Saturday night?

"Yes and no. It's Uzuri. She needs to move and only has tomorrow to do it in. The previous tenants screwed her over and didn't vacate the place on time, so she's doing a rush move. For some reason, she didn't call on her buddies."

"I'm not surprised."

Independent and fun loving, Uzuri every now and then displayed behaviors—like this insecurity—that showed she had issues. Z should never have let her get away with putting her past traumas off-limits.

"A bunch of us are going over in the morning to get her moved," Ben said. "Any chance you want to help?"

"Of course." An edge of hurt eroded her pleasure at hearing Ben's voice. Why had no one else called to tell her what was going on? "As early as you need me."

"Perfect. Can you meet Uzuri at her new place and get the keys from her? We'll have trucks coming and going most of the day."

"Absolutely."

As Ben gave her the information, she jotted it down. He finished with, "I'll see you."

And yes, her heart had undeniably slid into a syncopated jazz beat. Whatever had happened to her proverbial control?

# Chapter Eight

Somewhere around noon in Uzuri's new place, Anne walked through the rooms, surveying the work being done. The off-white living room walls and dark blue tile floors were scoured clean. The small dining area likewise. Linda and Beth were washing down the windows and the white trim.

In the kitchen, she smiled at Andrea. "How's it going in here?"

Looking like an autumn day with her curly golden-brown hair, amber eyes, and darkly golden skin, Andrea was an inch or so taller than Anne's five-eight. Cullen called her his Amazon.

Andrea waved her hand at the three high school students in ratty jeans and ripped T-shirts. "I mustered my fastest workers. Cleaning here is done and ready for the unpackers, right, guys?"

The boys all grinned. "You bet." "Word." "*Sí.*"

Anne looked around and marveled at the gleaming blue tile counters, oven, and open cupboards. One boy was finishing up the refrigerator, which positively sparkled. "Amazing."

Earlier Anne had arrived to find Uzuri in tears. When management had handed over the duplex keys, they'd told her their cleaning service didn't work weekends. Not having a choice and hoping for the best, Uzuri had accepted the keys.

The best didn't happen. The place was a disaster. Even meth houses were cleaner. The rooms had garbage strewn everywhere, and the stench of rotting food from the kitchen, urine from the bathroom, and sheer filth was overwhelming. Uzuri's dark skin had taken on a green tint as she gagged.

Anne had firmly sent her friend back to finish packing up her old apartment, then had called and redirected half the gang to the new location for emergency cleaning.

One more call had successfully summoned Andrea, who'd planned to arrive later to help with the unpacking. But, the woman owned a *cleaning* business. At Anne's beseeching explanation, she'd come right away and brought along some part-timers.

"You are all wonder-workers," Anne told the lads. "I'm so glad you were available."

They gave her the wide-eyed looks of youths more accustomed to being cursed than complimented, then puffed up their skinny chests. So cute.

She exchanged smiles with Andrea before telling the boys, "Unfortunately, now I have to send you off to do the yucky bathroom." After smothering a grin at their groans, she added, "However, I ordered pizza to make up for the trauma. By the time you get done, food will be here. You'll definitely deserve a break."

"Awesome." Exchanging fist-bumps, the troop moved on to their next assignment.

"You're as good at motivating the young ones as you are at keeping your slaves in line," Andrea said. "By the way, Dan and Ben are outside with a load of kitchen stuff and living room furniture. Ben came in a minute ago with Starbuck's. One of the cups has your name on it."

"Does it now?" Her pulse pattered faster—only from the thought of getting some caffeine in her system. *No other reason. No.* In the long carton filled with cups, only one held a name. "*ANNE'S.*"

She picked it up and sipped. Mocha coffee. He'd remembered her choice of brew at Z's house. That was…impressive.

Of course, her slaves had all learned her preferences, but tended to wait for directions from her. Ben's combination of independence and thoughtfulness could easily grow addictive.

"Hey, Anne, where do you want us now?" Sally asked. Gabi appeared behind her, both women bedraggled. "The bedroom is clean and ready for furniture."

"Excellent timing. Sam and Holt are in route with the bedroom stuff." She pointed to the coffee carton. "Why don't you grab coffee while I get boxes hauled in here? You two can work on setting up the kitchen."

Gabi took a long look. "Wow, 'drea, your people did a great job. It looks completely different."

As Andrea beamed, Anne pulled out her phone and took some pictures. "For Uzuri's lease, I snapped a bunch of pictures when I came.

But now you can have before and after shots for your website."

"What a grand idea." Andrea smiled. "Thank you."

When Anne checked out the living room, she shook her head. The men had brought in a couch and chairs and arranged them in absurd locations.

Dan walked past and set down a chair against the wall—in the spot where the television should go.

"Honestly," Anne said under her breath. After a second of thinking, she rounded up Linda and asked her to direct the furniture placement. "Beth, when the bedroom truck comes, can you do the same?"

"Of course."

"Grab some coffee while you have a chance and—" Recognizing the footsteps, Anne turned.

Followed by a beautiful golden retriever, Ben carried a heavy armchair into the room all by himself. Every muscle in his upper half was so pumped up that his brown Merle Haggard T-shirt was straining over his chest.

Anne had a craving simply to bite into the curve of his biceps. *Yum.*

When his gaze hit her, he smiled slowly. "Anne."

"Ben." The growing heat in his eyes slid beneath her skin and deep into her core. Fighting the urge to pull him to her, she took a step back.

"Is this your dog? He's gorgeous." She held her hand out.

"Yep, that's Bronx."

With a well-loved dog's confidence, the retriever trotted over, tail waving gracefully. When the dog informed her that they were now best of buddies, she stole herself a quick snuggle.

Rising, she saw Ben watching her with a half-smile and a bit of envy. The man obviously wanted his own hug.

Anne cleared her throat. "Can you—"

"Eeeks!" Sally's shriek came from the kitchen.

Anne ran in, Ben behind her, close enough that when she jumped back, she hit his solid frame. A huge flying cockroach, half the size of her hand, was crawling across the counter. *Oh, God.* She tried to back up farther. *Get it away!*

"Ben." She pointed to the ghastly black palmetto bug with a shaky hand. "Please."

"Yes, Ma'am." He swung into action.

As he disposed of the creature, Anne retreated into the dining area.

Sally followed. "Christ on a cockroach, did you see the size of that monster?"

"Nothing that size should be allowed to have wings." Anne's heart rate hadn't slowed.

"I'm so sorry me and Uzuri and Rainie tried to scare you with fake bugs last spring." Sally put an arm around Anne's waist. "Talk about karmic justice. That thing almost gave me a heart attack."

"I know the feeling," Anne said in a dry voice. When she'd opened her locker at the Shadowlands and seen bugs everywhere... Well. It had taken her far too long to realize they were rubber.

A minute later, their defender returned. Hair pulled back in a rough tie, broad shoulders military straight, expression bland...and his tiger-colored eyes were dancing with laughter.

"Thank you, Ben," Anne said. "Nicely done."

"I swear, that's the only reason God put males on this earth—for bug disposal," Sally said.

Anne considered, her gaze still caught in Ben's. "They might have a...few...other reasons."

His eyes warmed.

"Yeah. I made the mistake of saying that to Vance and he told Galen and they spent an entire night demonstrating. Reason after reason after reason." Sally sounded positively disgruntled. "I couldn't even get out of bed the next morning."

Anne's lips twitched.

Being a clever lad, Ben didn't say anything, but his gaze stayed on Anne's in a way that said he'd be delighted to perform his own demonstration.

The temptation was far too appealing. She shook her head. "Ben, can you help Linda get the living room arranged, please?"

Rather than looking irritated, he came to token attention. "Be my pleasure, Ma'am."

Hearing Anne's request, Linda waved him into the room and pointed to a chair. "That chair should sit over there, Ben." She indicated the far corner. "And the media stand goes against that wall."

"Yeah," Ben muttered. "I told Dan that."

Anne grinned. He had a good eye—and Dan didn't. What a nice reminder that a person shouldn't be judged by outward appearance.

Her phone beeped and displayed a text from Nolan. She lifted her voice. "People, the old apartment is empty, and the last load is on the way."

Cheers came from the various rooms.

Anne checked on the bathroom crew. Although disgusted by the stench, the boys were working energetically.

One glanced at her. "And my mama said *my* room was a pigsty—she ain't seen nothing."

The next truck arrived, and Sam started bringing in the load. Silver-gray hair, pale blue eyes, darkly tanned, the rancher might be in his fifties, but he carried the oak dresser as if it weighed no more than a toothpick.

Ben would be as tough, no matter how old he got.

In the bedroom, Anne found Beth waiting and sipping her coffee.

As Sam set the dresser down, Anne told him, "Beth is in charge of this room. She'll tell you where to put the furniture."

Beth gave the notorious Shadowlands sadist a nervous look. She'd been married to a truly abusive sadist. Since meeting Nolan, she'd overcome many of her fears, but Anne had noticed that male sadists still made her a bit wary when her Dom wasn't present.

This would be an excellent time for her to work on that.

Sam's glance at Anne held amusement, but when he looked at Beth, his face was gentle. He said in his roughly graveled voice, "Didn't bring my whip, missy. Instruct away."

Neither one of them missed Beth's relieved sigh.

Good enough. Smiling, Anne headed to the kitchen, passing Holt on the way in with a bedside stand.

The kitchen was coming along nicely. Sally had the dish cupboards almost filled. Gabi was organizing the canned goods.

"You two move really fast," Anne said.

"Isn't this great?" Sally bounced on her toes. "Uzuri thought she'd have to rent a motel room for tonight."

"We're going to have everything done even before the others arrive," Gabi said.

"The others?" Anne tossed her coffee cup into the giant box labeled "garbage."

"The ones who couldn't get here early." Sally set a cup onto a shelf. "Master Z was going to come and maybe bring Jessica and Sophia, depending on how they felt."

Gabi said, "Cat's gone for the week. Jake and Rainie are buried in puppy and kitten season. Raoul is out of town, but Kim is coming. Marcus and Cullen will be here soon. Olivia was going to arrive this afternoon, too."

"My Galen is on the way. Vance is in Atlanta for another day," Sally said. She listened for a second. "Actually, it sounds as if Galen and Marcus are already here."

Anne glanced at the time on her phone. "My God, it's after lunch."

"Time flies when you're having fun." Sally grinned. "I'm really glad you came. At Uzuri's old place, there we were and no one was sure what to do. We were all getting in each other's way. You cut through the chaos like a hot knife through butter."

"Not surprising." Dan walked into the kitchen, followed by Ben. "Anne leads a team of the toughest sons-of-bitches you've ever seen. Directing a moving crew—even one with Sam and Nolan on it—is nothing."

"Well, no wonder then." Sally pushed the empty box to one side. "I didn't realize bounty hunters had teams."

"If the skip has a history of violence, it's safer for everyone—including him—if we use a team," Anne said.

"Sounds smart." Ben's gaze was speculative, as if he were putting pieces of her life together like a jigsaw puzzle.

"Hey, Ben," Gabi said as she closed a cupboard door. "You did a great job of rounding everyone up. I'm glad you realized Uzuri needed help, even if she didn't want to admit it."

"You arranged all this?" Anne asked him.

He shrugged. "I was the one who found out she had a problem, so I checked with Z and kicked it off. Mostly, I assigned people to notify other people." He stepped close enough that her shoulder brushed his chest.

Her skin tingled at just the slight contact with his body, and her quick breath brought her his clean, tangy scent. *Stop it.* She took a step back.

"I saved your call for myself though," he added.

No wonder no one else had called. But... "Why? Were you afraid I'd be rude if someone asked me for help?" She didn't have that bad of a reputation, did she?

"No, Ma'am." When he moved closer again, she frowned him into stopping.

Because touching him was just too tempting.

His gaze was steady on hers, and then he smiled. "I made the call because I get off on listening to your voice. Even when you're pissed off, you sound like Lauren Bacall."

"Excuse me?" She couldn't keep the frost from entering her voice.

"Yeah, like that." He grinned. "If you ever get tired of bounty hunting, you could have a great career in phone sex."

Gasps sounded in the kitchen. Ben got worried looks from her friends, who knew what she did to disrespectful males.

Anne set her hand on Ben's chest. His muscles were pumped up and rock hard, creating a deep valley between his pecs. A wave of heat consumed her.

Annoyed, she pushed lightly.

He instantly took a step back. His hand covered hers, holding it to his chest.

"You're deliberately being provoking, Benjamin. Do you want me to beat on you?" she asked, only half joking.

"Any day. Any time." The desire in his gaze couldn't be misinterpreted. "Please."

"Jesus, Ben, are you insane?" Cullen asked from behind Anne. "She'll turn your frank 'n' beans into ground-up sandwich spread."

Anne stiffened.

"Enough with the bullshit, O'Keefe," Ben growled.

The chill in Anne's heart melted like butter in the Florida sun.

And Cullen stepped back as if he'd been punched. "I—"

"Anne. Benjamin. It's good to see you both." As Z strolled in, the power in his smooth voice silenced everyone in the kitchen. He ran his hand down her bare arm in a deliberately affectionate greeting that finished her off.

She struggled to keep her voice level. "Z. Is Jessica here? And the baby?"

"Jessica wanted to come, but she's fighting off a cold. Kari's staying with her and Sophia, but she sent along a platter of her brownies. I also brought a cooler of beer and soft drinks."

"Brownies?" asked one of Andrea's high schoolers. When everyone looked at him, he flushed so deeply his ears turned red.

"Indeed. In the living room." Z chuckled when the boy disappeared. "I believe your pizza has arrived as well. I saw the delivery van looking for a parking spot."

"That's perfect timing. Excuse me." Anne hurried out—a complete retreat—to deal with the delivery.

A few minutes later, most of the helpers were sitting on the couch, chairs, and the floor, gobbling down pizza. After handing out napkins and drinks, then finding food for herself, Anne regarded the room with pleasure. They'd done well.

A car door slammed outside, and a minute later, Uzuri appeared in the doorway. She stared at the spotless room and the people filling it. "What are you..." She put her hands over her mouth. Tears filled her eyes and ran down her cheeks. She looked at Anne. "I didn't... Everyone is here."

Retriever at his feet, Ben was frozen in place, holding a framed picture.

Anne looked at him, expecting him to explain.

Instead, he looked appalled. And silent. *Tough guys and tears. So not a good mix.*

"Come here, baby." Anne set her food down and pulled Uzuri close as the meltdown started. "The minute Ben said you had a problem, everyone wanted to help."

Uzuri pressed her face into Anne's shoulder...and cried.

Anne simply held her and stroked her shoulders comfortingly. Nothing else to be done—sometimes a girl just had to cry.

Sam and Holt came out of the bedroom. Sam saw Uzuri and gave Anne an approving nod. There was one man who wasn't worried about tears.

Holt took a step toward them, concern in his eyes. After a second, he shook his head and glanced at Anne. "Bed is put together and ready to be made."

"Thank you." She surveyed the room for new additions to the crew. "Kim, when you're done, can you and Linda unpack the bedroom wardrobe and make the bed."

"Of course." Kim had tears in her eyes when she looked at Uzuri.

On the other side of the living room, Nolan strolled in the front door and nodded to Anne. "Truck's empty."

"Here, Sir." Beth rose from her chair and handed her Master pizza on a paper plate.

He took her place, opened his legs, and she settled between them on the floor. After leaning forward and taking a quick kiss, he accepted the bottle of Corona from her.

They really did look perfect together. Anne smiled slightly. Almost three years ago, she'd told Nolan that having a more permanent submissive was worth it. Since then, he'd found Beth—and she'd lost Joey. Now she was the lonely one. And wasn't that just pitiful?

In Anne's arms, Uzuri lifted her head.

"All right now?" Anne asked.

Uzuri nodded and whispered, "Thank you. I'm sorry."

"Not a problem."

"Come with me, girlfriend. There's still more work to be done and food to eat." Gabi tucked a handful of tissues into Uzuri's hand.

Sally slung an arm around her waist. "Come and see your kitchen. You won't recognize it."

The two dragged Uzuri away, setting her to laughing—and giving her time to recover her composure away from everyone else.

*Nicely done.*

After picking up her abandoned food, Anne settled into the chair Gabi had vacated.

To her surprise, Bronx dropped down at her feet. At the entreating look in his eyes, she plucked a piece of pepperoni off her pizza. His tail thumped the floor as he delicately accepted her gift.

At the sound of a familiar, hearty laugh, Anne looked up.

Laughing at a comment one of the boys made, Ben was choosing slices of the meatlover's pizza. His face fell at the sight of the empty brownie platter.

After looking around, he walked over and joined Bronx at her feet.

"Ben." Her voice held a warning he completely ignored.

He set his plate and Coke on the floor, turned sideways, and positioned her left foot on his thigh so he could edge between her legs. His left shoulder leaned on the couch cushion—almost on her pussy; her right leg was behind his back.

With a contented sigh, he picked up his drink.

Around the room were snorts of amusement and giggles.

*Pushy submissive.* Anne set her pizza down, put a hand on his shoulder, and fisted his hair, tilting his head back.

Heat flared in his eyes, and like a wolf facing its alpha, he exposed his neck even further.

She loved the way he responded to her. Nonetheless…

"Benjamin, did I ask you to sit at my feet." Her voice carried to his ears and none other.

"Ma'am, no." He gave her an easy smile and moved his plate before Bronx could get to it. He didn't lower his voice. "After that bullshit of Cullen's, I wanted to make a point." His brows drew together. "If you really don't want me here, I'll move."

Across the room, Cullen frowned. "Ben…"

"You know, Anne, he deserves to lose those balls," Dan called.

"What's going on?" one of the youngsters whispered to another.

"*Estúpidos babosos.*" Andrea slapped her Dom's arm before glaring at Dan. "My *workers* are here."

Cullen winced at the reminder.

Dan gave her a repentant chin lift.

"What's going on is that Cullen thinks I'm too pushy with this woman." Even as he offered Bronx a sausage tidbit, Ben grinned over at the boys, not uncomfortable at all. "You ever get that from your friends?"

Two of them turned to the third and started teasing him.

A perfect diversion. Anne gave Ben's hair a tiny tug of approval.

His shoulders loosened under her hand.

The young lads were nudging each other and trading insults, and she could see where boys that age could certainly turn a person's life upside-down. Yet, even in all their teenaged idiocy, they really were cute.

As the conversations floated around her, she finished her pizza and wiped her fingers on the napkin. Ben had already cleaned his plate.

"Good pizza, Ma'am," he said. "Thank you for feeding all of us."

"You're welcome." She picked up her other plate from the end table, knowing—*knowing*—she shouldn't give him any encouragement. Nonetheless, her heart wouldn't let her set the dessert back down. "Despite your extremely pushy behavior, I think you've earned a reward. You did a nice thing today for Uzuri." She uncovered the big chocolate-frosting covered brownie.

His gaze held the delight of a man getting a tasty treat as well as the pleasure that she'd thought of him when others were grabbing their food. "Thank you, Mistress." Before he took a bite, he paused. "Did you get some?"

"I know better. I've had Kari's brownies before. If I ate one, I'd have to run an extra mile tomorrow morning."

His eyes glinted golden. "I could be of service in working off calories."

Well, she knew that for a fact. And the desire to burn a few calories with him was growing overwhelming. "Well, in that case, maybe I should indulge." She leaned forward, letting her breast brush against his face as she grasped his wrist and pulled his brownie to her lips. She took a small bite.

"Oh, now, Ma'am, you know I'm good for more calories than that," he murmured.

She choked.

Her cell rang. *Saved by the bell.* She checked the display and answered. "This is Anne. What's up?"

"We have a pickup for you, if you have time," Loretta said. "Do you remember Jane? However, she sounds nearly hysterical. You probably should take some backup."

After getting the location, Anne frowned down at her phone. *Dammit, Jane. Why'd you go back to that asshole?*

A big hand closed over hers. "Problem?" Ben studied her, eyes concerned.

"I'm afraid so. I need to give someone a ride." But both her brothers were working today, and she didn't have any trained female friends she'd feel comfortable risking in a possibly dangerous situation.

"Just a ride wouldn't make you so worried. Can I help?"

"I…" Could he? He was ex-military. And Z did extensive background checks on anyone setting foot in his Shadowlands, so he'd be safe. Even better, as a guard in a BDSM club, he'd have seen and dealt with emotional meltdowns. "If you don't mind leaving now, I'd love some help."

"If Bronx can come too, I'm in."

\* \* \* \*

Anne was delivering a woman to a battered women's shelter? The woman had more facets than a diamond. Ben stared at her as she drove her Ford Escape to the designated pickup area. "Why aren't the cops providing transportation for the woman?"

"They do sometimes. But all too often, a woman won't call the police, so the shelter calls in volunteers."

"If a man has hit his wife, what keeps him from attacking a driver?"

She smiled. "It's not as dangerous as it sounds. We don't meet women at their work or houses, and we only do pickups from public areas."

Still didn't sound particularly safe. Ben sat back. At least he was here. "Do you know who we're fetching?"

"Actually, I do. Jane and her daughter, Paige, stayed at the shelter for a while, but when her husband agreed to counseling, she went back to him." She scowled.

"You don't approve of a guy getting a second chance?"

"Well, sometimes an abuser is shocked at his actions and realizes he's got a problem. He's the type that can learn." Her lips tightened. "I met Jane's husband. He's a manipulative bastard and sure not interested in amending his behavior. He used every trick in the book to get her to return to him."

Considering Anne's experience as a Domme, she had probably read him correctly. He sounded like a real bastard. "So she loved him and went back."

"Uh-uh. I think the love is long gone. I'd say she was afraid of being on her own and of having to turn her life upside-down. Of how much she'd have to *change*." Anne's fingers clenched and loosened on the steering wheel.

She'd spat that word out—*change*—as if it had a foul taste. Interesting.

"This is the place." Anne drove through a mall parking lot, pulled over to the curb in front of a department store, and turned the parking lights on. She jumped out.

Ben hand-signaled Bronx to stay put and joined her on the sidewalk. "Where do you want me?"

"Can you wait by the car?" Her lips curved. "You can be a scary lad at times."

Ben winced. Although he'd come to enjoy being a big guy, he didn't like that his face could terrify children.

She noticed and ran her hand up his arm. "It so happens that I appreciate scary lads, you know," she said in her husky voice.

When she looked at him as if he were a delectable treat, his ego expanded to fill all of Pinellas County. He cleared his throat. "I'll wait here." Unless there was a problem...then all bets were off.

She strode briskly into the store, and he'd known her long enough to read the tension in her body and the way she was alert to the people nearby. She'd tried to act as if the pickups weren't dangerous, but she was obviously ready for action.

A minute later, she walked out, her arm around a woman's waist, supporting her.

*Jesus.*

The limping woman had a black eye and a golf-ball-sized swelling on her cheek. A fat lip. Her stiff torso indicated her ribs were bruised or busted.

Anger roused and lifted its ugly head.

He took a step forward, then saw a young girl trailing after Anne. She couldn't be more than twelve. Tears streaked her dirty cheeks.

Ben throttled his rage back. She'd seen enough violence. Trying to look harmless, he opened the back seat door and stepped away.

As the women approached the SUV, a man shouted. "Found you, you bitch. Stop right there."

Like a terrified bird, Jane froze.

"Oh, honestly." With a huff of irritation, Anne glanced over her shoulder. "Jane, get in the car."

The woman didn't move.

Her husband headed toward them with the narrow-minded focus of a fanatical insurgent.

*So much for a safe pickup.* The asshole had white dust on his ragged jeans and sweat-marked T-shirt. He probably worked in construction. About six feet and well over two hundred pounds, the man was muscular with a good-sized beer gut.

His expression was…off, and Ben figured he was high on either drugs or alcohol or both.

"Incoming, Anne," Ben warned as she helped Jane to the side of the car. "May I take him out?"

"I'd rather do it myself."

*Fuck.* Ben suppressed the need to intervene. *Down, Haugen.* Anne wouldn't give up her toy easily, and he had to trust she knew what she was doing. "Figures."

Anne gave him a grim half-smile, released Jane, squeezed the kid's shoulder, and walked toward the store.

Ben stepped in front of Jane and the child to shield them from the sight of the abuser. "Get in the car, please, while Anne deals with" *the fucking shithead* "any problems."

After a blink, Jane focused on him and, if anything, looked even more frightened.

"I—" She actually started to retreat.

To Ben's relief, her daughter piped up. "Get in, Mom. We need to leave."

Good kid. Terrified, wide-eyed, dead white—and she still kept her head.

From behind Ben came the sound of the asshole's raised voice, then the smack of flesh on flesh.

*Anne can handle him. She can handle him.* Ben unclenched his jaw and snapped his fingers for Bronx to jump from the backseat to the front.

"Stay right here, kiddo," he said gently, making sure Paige was right beside the car.

He looked at the mother. "My name's Ben, Ma'am. I'm helping Anne drive." He assisted Jane into the backseat and carefully strapped her in.

One down. "Paige, get on in."

The girl shook her head. "We might have to help Anne." With fists clenched, she planted her feet, going nowhere.

Well, hell. Stymied, Ben set a light hand on her shoulder so he could keep track of her, then turned to watch the fight.

If Anne needed help, he intended to be right there. And if the bastard attempted to lay a hand on the kid, he'd draw back a bloody stump.

Unfortunately, Ben's assistance wasn't going to be required, which was a fucking shame.

The asshole was trying to hit Anne and was missing every time. The woman had some seriously fine footwork. She delivered a perfectly executed snap kick to a knee.

The bastard went down hard.

Concrete meets face—face loses. Ben laughed under his breath. And tried to make his woody go away.

Still in stance, Anne waited, obviously hoping the dumbass would stand up so she could knock him down again.

*Bad Domme.* "Ma'am, that was good to watch, but your chariot waits."

And the little bit had seen enough.

Anne frowned at Ben, fury still riding her shoulders, but when he glanced meaningfully down at the munchkin, she caught on immediately. "Right. Let's get moving then."

To Ben's surprise, Paige still didn't move. Her eyes held hatred as she stared at her father.

Fuck, that was just sad.

Ben cleared his throat. "Paige. Hop in now."

Before he could help, she ran around the car, opened the rear door, and stopped.

"Paige?"

"A dog."

Ben realized Bronx had stuck his head between the front seats, hoping someone would throw him some attention.

"You have a dog." The wonder in her voice made the retriever whine.

Ben smiled. Someone could use comforting, and he had just the dog to do it. "Want to ride in the front with Bronx?"

If the gates of heaven had opened, the child couldn't look more ecstatic. "Really?"

In answer, Ben pulled open the front passenger door, motioned Bronx to the floor, and stepped out of the way.

After Paige got in, Ben had to hold her back long enough to fasten the seat belt. Then she leaned forward, her arms went around the dog's neck, and she buried her face in his fur.

"Well," Anne said. "I think Bronx could be more popular than the firemen's beloved teddy bears."

Jane whispered, "Will the dog attack her? She's so upset..."

Ben squatted down beside the mother. "Bronx has a big heart, and he loves children. They're fine."

To his surprise, Anne handed him the car keys and jumped into the back. "Jane, I need to know how badly you're hurt."

*Ah.* Ben slid into the driver's seat, checked the girl, and snorted.

She was half-crying and half-laughing as Bronx gave little whines and tried to lick her tears away.

With Anne's directing from the back, Ben drove to the shelter and parked in the rear.

As he assisted Jane from the car, Anne slid out on the other side.

With an arm around Jane, she said, "Be right back." She helped Jane to the building and rang the bell. Some women opened the door.

As Paige gave Bronx a last hug, Ben leaned a hip against the SUV.

"Mister Ben?"

Ben looked down into bright blue eyes. "You don't need the Mister part—Ben is fine. You got a question for me?"

"You're a man. Aren't you supposed to protect Miss Anne?"

Having expected a question about Bronx, he took a moment to recover. "Yes. I'll always protect her. But she didn't need my help with the as—uh, with…today." He smiled slightly. "Did just fine on her own, didn't she?"

The child's eyes were swollen from crying, but very, very alert. "So even though she knocked my father down, you still like her?"

Ben simply laughed. "Damn straight."

"Paige." Anne stood a pace away. She gave Ben a glance filled with amusement. "Honey, you need to go on in now."

The child kissed Bronx's nose and hugged Anne. "You'll come and see me? Please?"

Ben could only stare as the most sadistic Mistress in the Shadowlands turned into jelly.

Yeah, he'd found his woman.

# Chapter Nine

As Ben drove Anne's vehicle back to Uzuri's, she regarded him. He seemed unfazed by Jane's tears and terror, the husband's anger, or the fight. His attention was on the traffic, his fingers keeping time with the radio's music.

Country-western, unfortunately. But, for him, she'd put up with the music.

For him, she'd put up with a lot.

She was still trying to get her head around the way he'd watched her take on Jane's husband. Her brother Travis would have argued and eventually have backed off. Harrison and her father—never.

But Ben hadn't tried to throw his weight around at all. He'd let her handle it; damn, he pleased her.

"You do that stuff often?" he asked. "Picking up women?"

"Now and then. I spend most of my volunteer time with the girls in the shelter. The teens, especially, are pretty angry and confused."

"I saw you with Andrea's crew. You're good with kids. But the shelter stuff—why that?" He gave her a concerned glance. "Did you have a violent husband or boyfriend in the past?"

After a second of feeling insulted, she realized his question arose out of concern. "No. But as a military brat, I saw a fair number of abusive husbands." Like her best friend's mama, who'd been married to a captain. The woman had concealed her black eyes and bruises with makeup. Had made excuses to her daughter and everyone else. *"I fell down." "I'm so clumsy." "I bumped my head on the cupboard."*

He winced. "Yeah. Seen that. I get you."

Anne had hated that captain with all her childish might. Had kicked him one day when he'd hit Tracy…and that had gotten her father involved. The captain had been drummed out of the service, but then Tracy and her mother had moved away.

The ache of losing someone never disappeared entirely.

Anne returned to the conversation. "As a police officer, well, I had to handle domestic violence calls." Those involving children still haunted her dreams. Babies should be protected.

"I thought you were a fugitive recovery agent. You're a cop?"

The surprise in his eyes was delightful. "I was. Olivia thinks that because my father tried so adamantly to shelter me, I naturally joined the Marines and then the police force."

"I can see that." His laughter filled the car, a heartening rough roar. Still grinning, he said, "In that case, I'm glad I stayed out of the fight."

She snorted. "Funny man. Really, I think my family has a protect-and-serve gene, even if my male relatives refuse to acknowledge its existence in the women."

"But you're not in law enforcement any longer? What happened?" His voice was casual, but his fingers tightened on the steering wheel.

"Nothing particularly ugly, Ben. I simply didn't appreciate the bigotry against female officers." Between the climate there and the domestic violence cases, she'd started to hate everyone with a dick.

She added, "Later, I discovered my station had a reputation for misogyny, and I should have transferred. Instead, I bailed into bail bonds."

He smiled at her feeble pun. "No husbands in the past? Serious men in your life?"

Snoopy submissive. But under his quiet interest, she didn't mind sharing. "No husbands. Nothing serious." She'd had a few guys in her younger days who…maybe…she might have loved. And in college, the man she'd loved had been vanilla, so that relationship had crashed and burned. And hurt.

She probably just didn't have it in her to love anyone deeply enough to sustain a real relationship.

In recent years, although she'd owned longer-term slaves whom she'd loved, she'd never been "in love" with them. "You?"

"One ex-wife."

He'd been married? Feeling the oddest sense of jealousy, Anne studied him. Yes, she could see him as a married man. He would tend to what was important to him with the same seriousness he gave to his other duties. His wife would have been a lucky woman. "What happened?"

"She divorced me when I was in the service. Couple of girlfriends since, not what I'd call serious-serious. Not sure how to explain that."

"There should be a scale of relationship gradients." When Ben paused for a red light, Anne's gaze landed on a gun shop. "Something to show how deadly love is." She considered. "A BB-gun denotes a casual first date. A .22 revolver for the first night of sex. A .38 semi-automatic for reaching the non-serious, exclusive stage."

"All right." He was smiling as he turned the corner. "An M24 SWS 'sniper weapon' for locking on to someone—getting engaged. And maybe a Carl Gustav for doing the deed—getting married."

She grinned, remembering that the Carl Gustav was an antitank weapon. "There's a cynical man. So what rating did your past flames get?"

"One girlfriend would have been a....38. The other a .44 magnum."

One step above exclusive, meaning he'd been serious about the woman. "I see."

He hesitated and asked, "What was Joey?"

As her spine stiffened, she bit back her first response—*none of your business*. But, perhaps it was. "I'd say a .38, because I don't go over a .38."

The tiny muscles beside his eyes tensed as if absorbing a blow. "Got it."

"I don't have typical man/woman relationships, Ben. You could call that a hard limit with me. I have slaves. I care for them—love them even—but never in a man-woman-love kind of way."

He nodded.

Time to change the subject. Past time. "You were good with Paige today." She turned to give Bronx a pat. "And so were you, baby."

Bronx responded with a delighted thumping of the tail and a sneaky finger lick.

"I've had practice with Marcus's crew," Ben said. "When he takes his martial arts teens out, he asks for volunteers to herd the pack."

"Ah. Well, you gave Paige something to think about." Thoughtlessly, she laid her hand on his thigh. The way his muscles went taut under her touch shifted the dynamic between them to something more sexual.

She was afraid that their dating score was rising rapidly from a nice .22 to something with more impact. What was she going to do about this?

"What do you mean?" he asked, derailing her thoughts.

"Her parents taught her that women are passive. That a man would never tolerate an assertive woman." She grinned. "Definitely not an aggressive one."

"Fucking stupid."

"Exactly. But now Paige has seen a woman fight back and heard a confident man say he enjoyed the show—and still likes said woman."

"I did like the show," he said.

"I noticed."

He snorted. "You did, huh?"

Paige hadn't noticed, but Anne had spotted the very large bulge in Ben's jeans. He deserved to be rewarded for such a lovely reaction, but it wouldn't be—

He put his hand over hers and slid it up to his groin. He was still semi-hard. "I get your limit, Ma'am. But lots of people have limits and still manage to have sex. Let's have sex."

Her body stilled at the surge of desire. And yet..."I don't want you to be hurt, Ben."

He glanced at her, his tawny tiger's eyes intent. "Anne, do you like it when people restrict your life because they're afraid you'll get hurt?"

His words were a light stinging to the face, waking her up.

His smile appeared...until she cupped his cock. "Well, Benjamin, we wouldn't want to worry about you getting hurt, now would we? Want to meet at my place?"

* * * *

Ben knew for a fact that he was going to have a fucking heart attack—fucking soon—and Mistress Anne would be stuck explaining why she had a naked dead man sprawled on his back in her bed.

Why there were finger dents in her headboard.

She nipped his cock.

"Jesus!" His head rose off the bed, and he glared at her.

The Mistress raised an eyebrow. "I'd suggest you stop thinking, Benjamin. Or else." Her fingers cupped one of his balls, then the other in a warm threat. When she squeezed, sweat broke out on his body.

As her fingernail scraped the sensitive spot just in front of his asshole, lights danced in his vision.

And when she released his junk, the blood flowed straight to his dick, which was already straining against the leather strands wrapped around it.

His head fell back on the pillow as every muscle in his body turned rigid.

He needed to come. So. Fucking. Bad.

When she smiled at him—hell, that was almost enough to get him off. She was magnificent, all naked, her skin a golden tan. High, full breasts with tight nipples. Heavy-lidded eyes. Mouth swollen from his kisses. She looked like one of those female sex demons—a succubus—the ones no man could resist.

As she bent closer, her hair spilled over his groin in silky sweetness and her sultry laugh stroked his skin with warmth. And then he felt...

Oh, Jesus, she wouldn't...

She did.

Her tongue traced over the head of his cock. The wet heat circled the slit and licked over the leather. His erection managed to engorge even further. The laces grew painfully tight as she teased him. Nipped the helmet. Sucked lightly.

His body started to shake. His clenched hands cramped around the oak spindles. The groan that escaped him couldn't have come from anything living.

"All right, Benjamin. I think you're ready, and I'll even give you a choice today. Do you want me to ride you or do you want the top?"

Could he talk without shouting? He breathed out—and swore he could still feel her fingernails on his nipples. "Top. Please. Mistress."

Her disconcertingly strong, delicate hands stroked up and down his thighs. "So be it. When I release the last strand and after I put a condom on you, you may let go of the headboard and jump me."

Her lips curved in an innocent smile, as if she'd just agreed he could have a cookie rather than permitting him to fuck her senseless. She was screwing with his mind as easily as she'd tormented his body. *Sadist.*

And he'd never been so hard in his damned life. What did that make him?

She, ever so slowly, unwound each leather strip, and he felt the blood rush back into his dick, like the ocean at high tide. His eyes strained as he watched her finally, unhurriedly undo the last strand.

She rolled a condom onto him, inch-by-fucking-inch.

Her gaze met his.

He was on her so fast she didn't have a chance in hell of resisting.

Like a mindless barbarian, he tossed her on her back, shoved her legs open, and speared her in one brutal move. As all that heat sheathed him, he froze, teetering on the edge.

He hadn't lost control like that since he'd been a teenager.

Snugged up tight to his groin, his balls throbbed with the pressure of an imminent explosion.

Sweating, he fought himself back. If she moved—moved at all—he'd go off.

She didn't move.

With a slow inhalation, he backed away from the precipice and opened his eyes.

Her rich brown hair tumbled gloriously over the pillow. Her face was flushed with heat. And her eyes were filled with approval as she smiled at him. "I'm impressed, guard dog."

"You should be," he growled. "I may never walk again."

At her laugh, her cunt constricted around him, and he sucked in air. *Not yet. Please.* Jesus, when he started thrusting, he wasn't going to last long at all. "I want you to come too. First. But—"

"Benjamin, if you didn't get off quickly now, I'd consider myself a failure." She grinned and picked up a remote control box from beside the pillow. "You probably didn't notice, but I'm going to help out here."

A small buzzing started, and he felt the vibration on his pubic bone. He lifted up slightly. Carefully. She wore some triangle thing that covered her clit and vibrated. Fucking awesome...but when had she put it on?

"Do I get the remote?" he asked hopefully.

She actually laughed. "No."

Damn, he liked a woman who knew her mind. And his.

As the vibrator worked its magic, he watched a flush creep up her chest, her neck, her face. Propping himself up with one hand, he used the other to enjoy her breasts. She filled his big hand just right—so firm and round. Her nipples were as rigid as small bullets. He plucked them, rolled them, making them lengthen, and enjoying the hell out of her soft sounds of enjoyment.

Her cunt tightened around him.

*Almost. Almost.*

"Can I get you to put your legs around my waist, Ma'am?" He totally wanted her elegant little heels thumping just above his ass when he started hammering into her.

She looked up at him in consideration. Still in control—the woman was superhuman.

Anne had to admit, it was getting difficult to think. She was damned close to coming with the butterfly vibrator on high and all that thickness of him inside her. The man was truly hung like a bull.

He'd asked her something—to move her legs. *Right.* She felt herself tightening, the pressure growing. She could give in to his request. To some extent. She cleared her throat. "If you hang onto the headboard with one hand, you may do anything you want with my legs."

His answer was a growl of appreciation. He yanked her left leg up to his waist and grabbed the headboard with his right hand. After moving his knees apart for better balance, he put his left arm under her right knee, lifting and spreading her, surging even deeper.

Her fingernails dug into his skin at the glorious sensation.

As he slid his cock out slowly, his jaw went tight. "I can still feel every wrap on my dick," he muttered, making her laugh.

His tanned face darkened with lust as he deliberately penetrated her, pulled back, thrust in faster. And ground his pelvis against the butterfly over her clit.

The last straw.

*Oh God.* The coiling pressure in her core clenched like a fist, encountered his heavy shaft, and exploded, battering across her senses with thunderous waves of pleasure.

Her hips bucked and even in the middle of her orgasm, she heard his, "Fucking hell." And then her leg was lifted higher, and he started hammering into her. Deep. Hard. Powerful. The entire bed rocked as he kept his grip on the headboard, as his huge body rammed into her.

With an ear-ringing rush, she went over again, the pleasure consuming her. God, she'd never felt anything like it.

As her vision cleared slightly, she nuzzled his neck, kissing the white scars, and then ran her fingernails down his chest to find—and pinch—his nipples.

He roared…and slammed into her, rocking the bed with each thrust.

Something cracked—and the bed tilted diagonally.

Growling, Ben pressed deep, deep into her, and his cock pulsed with his climax, sending more sizzling pleasure through her.

She managed to fumble the remote to OFF and simply went limp.

Eventually, when her heart rate slowed to a less painful gait, she opened her eyes. Head bowed, Ben was immobile, his wide chest expanding and contracting with his breathing. His face was flushed, the cords on his neck still taut.

Magnificent.

She rubbed her hands over his back, appreciating the solid feel of his muscles.

Holding the headboard with one hand—*good submissive*—he carefully let her leg down.

Still buried deep, his cock was giving small twitches. She grinned inwardly. His tool would remember her tomorrow.

"Ma'am?" His voice sounded as if he'd swallowed half of her sandy beach. "Are you…"

So sweet. She ran her hand over his strong face. "I'm fine, Benjamin." She paused. "But you broke my bed."

He didn't even look embarrassed. Instead, his eyes glinted as he smiled slowly. "Guess we'll have to move to the floor for the next round."

* * * *

A couple of hours later, Anne came out of the shower to the sound of someone pounding on her back door.

While she'd finished washing her hair, Ben had taken Bronx for a walk. Now the dog lay in the corner…and Ben was repairing the damage to her bed. "Bed's almost fixed."

He nodded toward the door. "Problems?" His long hair was disheveled, his five-o'clock shadow visible. He looked like a tousled, annoyed male, and she wanted to push him onto the pile of bed linens and muss him up some more.

"Probably not," she said. "But, unfortunately, since my car's here, my family knows I'm home. Whoever it is won't stop until I answer the door."

"I got firearms in my ride."

She grinned. "So do I, but shooting relatives is considered bad manners."

"True." He rose and ran his fingers over her face. "I can't get over how beautiful you are, no matter what you wear, what time of day."

Everything within her melted into a puddle. She gave him an exasperated look to cover that up, opened the window, and shouted, "I'll be down in a couple of minutes. Bestow yourself with patience."

She closed the window on Travis's X-rated answer. "Men," she said in a low voice and picked out clean underwear.

"Anne." Ben had squatted back beside the bed.

She braced, expecting a complaint about how she was neglecting him. Joey had been a good enough slave to be silent, but he'd certainly have pouted.

"I'll be done with this in a minute. Want me to stay up here or let myself out quietly?" he asked.

The tactfulness of the question staggered her. And reminded her not to judge this man by anyone else.

And…she realized she didn't want him sneaking away. "No, come on down and I'll fix you supper. My brother knows I have a personal life. He might tease me, but not you."

His face darkened. "He'd better not give you any grief."

Even though his protectiveness was oddly warming, her spine still stiffened. "Down, Benjamin. I can handle my own family."

After a second, he gave a jerk of his head. "Yes, Ma'am, I guess you could, at that."

The way he could be protective, yet trust her to look after herself, both warmed and delighted her—and she indulged herself in a long, decadent kiss.

On the way out, she stopped to pet Bronx. "You're such a good dog." His tail thumped the carpet.

Downstairs, she unlocked the back door that opened onto her high deck.

Travis sauntered in. "'Bout time. You're getting slow, sis." He tugged on her hair.

Jeans, ratty gray T-shirt, boots. His hair was the same rich brown as hers, although kept almost as short as in his military days. Dark blue eyes, classically handsome features, tall and muscular and tan. Like their mother, he was far more fun loving and sociable than she was.

If she'd had a favorite brother, he might have made the cut.

"I saw the extra vehicle outside." He headed straight to the kitchen. "Got a new man?"

"You are such a snoopy-pants." Despite the late afternoon time, she selected a caramel-flavored coffee pod and put it into the Keurig. "What are you doing over here?"

"No food in my fridge. Any chance you have lasagna left?" He gave her the appealing grin which worked so well on his women.

Sex appeal didn't work on a sister, poor lad.

"Maybe. And maybe I'd feed you *if* you mow my lawn." She took her cup from the machine and inserted a dark roast coffee pod for him, along with a clean mug.

"Deal. Can I get garlic bread too?"

"Fine." She pulled out the remains of a loaf of French bread and started to cut slices. A few minutes later, Ben and Bronx came down the stairs.

Travis's jaw dropped as he stared at Ben. "Jesus fuck, where'd she find you?"

The guard dog's shoulders stiffened.

Anne smacked the back of her brother's head. "Were you raised in a barn?" How could she explain to Ben that Travis hadn't meant his words as an insult?

"Ah, sorry, man. Didn't mean it that way," Travis said.

When Ben's gaze hit hers, comprehension showed on his face as he undoubtedly recalled her typically younger, more slender slaves.

"Ben, this is my brother, Travis. Travis, Ben."

"Good to meet you." Travis bent to let Bronx sniff his hand and then ruffled his fur. "Great-looking dog."

"Thanks."

Anne walked over to put an arm around Ben, to finish easing the awkwardness her brother had created. "Ben, Travis is here to mooch leftovers since I made lasagna a couple of days ago. If you hate Italian food, I have sandwich fixings." She pushed the basket holding the coffee pods toward him. "Pick a coffee if it's not too late for you. Or there's wine and beer in the fridge."

"If you have enough, lasagna sounds fantastic."

"I always make plenty." She buttered the bread, adding herbs and garlic, then tucked the tray under the broiler. The lasagna went into the microwave. "Travis, aren't you off work a little early?"

"Well, yeah. I didn't want to miss any of the fun." He took his cup from the machine, motioned to Ben to use it, and frowned at Anne. "Did you forget you'd planned a team exercise tonight?"

She froze. "That's on...oh, damn. I lost track. A friend needed a rush move today. That's where Ben and I were earlier."

"Yeah, Mom wondered why you weren't at Sunday dinner." Travis looked at her over his cup. "Is your buddy all moved or do you need more help?"

And that was why she loved her brothers. Hardasses, but with good hearts. "We got her all set up."

Ben was watching her, his gaze intent. "If you have work planned, sounds as if I need to get moving along."

Travis looked him over slowly, eyes speculative. "You ever shot a firearm?"

"A time or two." Ben's voice was...odd. Anne studied him, trying to read his body language. Assurance was there, but he'd tensed as well. His face had gone unreadable, eyes shuttered. But, as a soldier, he would have not only used weapons, but also killed.

"Military?" Travis always had to push. When Ben nodded, he frowned. "You've been out for a while to get your hair that long."

Ben grinned and relaxed. "'Bout five years now. You?"

"Only two. Marines."

"Army." Ben dumped an appalling amount of sugar into his cup and took a sip. "Do you want company tonight...Anne?" He would have used *Mistress* if they'd been alone.

To her, that hesitation meant he wanted her to make the decision if he should attend the team exercise. Should he?

The man wasn't a pushover. Although other fugitive recovery agents occasionally brought along friends or girlfriends, Anne hadn't ever taken her slaves. The other team members were overly testosteroned males. Takedowns could get a bit violent, and ex-military or not, security guard or not, Ben was as easygoing a man as she'd ever met. He might not enjoy the scenarios.

Then again, he was an adult. And a fighter. Rather than a housecat, he was more like a Siberian tiger, big and heavy—and deadly.

She'd invite him and then he could decide whether he could cut the mustard.

She smiled at him. "Most of us recovery agents are used to working alone, but recently I set up a team. The exercises improve how we work together. People take turns playing the fugitive, and we practice doing takedowns. It sometimes gets rough."

A smile spread over his craggy face. "Sounds like fun."

*Men.* Always eager for a little gratuitous violence. Then again, she enjoyed the games too. She nodded at her brother. "Your spare eye gear should fit Ben. Bring it along, please."

"Will do." Travis gave Ben a pleased look before smirking at her. "Glad you finally have someone worthy of his nuts."

*Jerk.* Rather than rewarding him with an insult, she mused, "I think I'll top the lasagna off with mushrooms for a good flavor."

"No," Travis said hurriedly. "Fuck, I'm sorry."

She gave Travis a *look,* and he almost whined. "Seriously, sis." He turned. "Ben, you don't want fungi on your lasagna, do you?"

Ben's golden eyes gleamed with laughter. "Ma'am, although mushrooms are low on my favorite list, I'll happily eat whatever you prepare."

She tilted her head in acknowledgment of his well-played card— letting her know his preferences while reaffirming he'd not question her choice.

To frighten Travis, she picked up the mushrooms and heard her brother moan.

But, in recognition of Ben's deference, she only added them to her portion of the lasagna.

His rough chuckle was her reward.

* * * *

The sun was setting as Ben waited in a small, ramshackle mobile home on a heavily wooded property near Curlew Creek. Another mobile home and a shed stood in a line next to the house. Outside, his "family members" were putting up plastic fencing.

Anne had explained that each exercise was designed to simulate typical takedown scenarios, usually with the fugitive holed up with family, possibly with more relatives or friends next door. The potted plants, yard equipment, and fencing were moved around to keep the crew from becoming complacent.

It brought back fond memories of Ranger combat scenarios.

In this case, Ben was roleplaying the enemy—the fugitive. Anne even snapped his picture with her phone to use to brief her agents. She'd told him to look mean since it was supposed to be his arrest photo.

He'd been laughing when she took it.

With his fake family, Ben sat down at the dining table as ordered. He wore no special costume, just jeans, a T-shirt, and eye-safety glasses.

Supposedly, he was a drug dealer, out on bail, staying with his brother, two children, and two women. Two more relatives waited in the building next door to start a fight if they got a chance. Ben's only goal was to escape. His family would attempt to hinder the bail agents from capturing him.

Although the training was deadly serious, the team and the part-timers like Travis approached the exercise in an atmosphere of fun. Or most of them did.

Travis had mentioned there was some friction in the group. A couple of men resented having a woman in charge; one wanted her position. Ben had noticed Anne's cousin Robert never lost an opportunity to make a derogatory comment.

A knock sounded on the door. A brawny, blond agent named Mitchell pushed his chair back and rose. "Who the hell is that?" Totally into his role as Ben's brother, he walked to the door grumbling loudly, "Try to get a good meal, and some asshole shows up and—"

He opened the door. "*What?*"

With game weaponry loaded in his belt, Travis stood in the door. "I apologize for bothering you at this late hour, sir, but I'm with The Brothers Bail Bonds. I'm sorry to report that your brother didn't show up in court today and..."

That was Ben's cue to get the hell out. He'd already assessed his possible escape routes and the surroundings. With limited choices, he'd decided to exit through the back bedroom window. Hopefully, the portable fence and potted shrubberies would partially shield him from view.

He assumed the team leader would've stationed people at all potential exits. Caution would be needed.

He didn't spot anyone as he slid out the glassless window. Landing as softly as possible, he bent his knees to present a smaller silhouette. The sun was just below the horizon, and the encroaching forest shadowed the area.

As he moved across the patchy lawn, he caught sight of someone coming around the side of the house to his right. Another person on the left blocked his chosen route. He broke into a run, automatically zigzagging, although Anne had said firearms were only used in case of life-threatening danger.

He headed toward the opening in the fence, veered at the last minute, and shouldered past the man who attempted to block him. Using a tree for an assist, he jumped the fence.

Someone yelled, "East side!"

A body hit him from the left in an unsuccessful tackle. While they grappled, Anne slammed into him from the rear, and he tripped over the other guy.

As he landed on his front, someone dropped onto his legs.

Still struggling, he felt a sharp sting on his back. *Shit.* He played dead.

"What the hell?" The man on his legs rolled off. "Hey, buddy, you okay? He just went limp, Anne."

She knelt. "Ben, are you all right?"

"Am I allowed to be alive now?"

"What do you mean?" Her hand was on his cheek, smelling of her floral bath soap.

"Someone shot me in the back. Aren't I supposed to die if that happens?"

In the dim light, he saw her perfectly curved brows draw together. "No one shot you."

"Yeah, someone did. At a guess, the shooter was fairly close."

Anne glanced at the two men who'd grappled with him.

Neither had weapons drawn.

Ben sat up as two more trotted over from the back of the house. Aaron and Robert.

"Which one of you shot him?" Anne snapped at them.

From the front of the house came more team members.

"I'm not carrying. Not enough pistols to go around," Aaron said with a slow Texas drawl. He turned his head and spit.

Everyone looked at Robert.

Anne's cousin stiffened and glared at Anne. "Fuck, I didn't shoot him. Your guy doesn't know what he's talking about."

*What an asshole.* "I've played Airsoft before and know how a pellet hit feels." Ben pulled off his threadbare T-shirt and turned toward the flashlight Travis was holding. "See for yourself—mid-back, right of the spine."

Anne touched the stinging spot. "That's a hit and a lethal one. Now we have a man dead in a non-life-threatening situation. The relatives were witnesses that he was unarmed and on the ground when shot." She fixed Robert with an aggravated gaze. "Lawsuit material. You know better, Robert."

The bastard looked her up and down and simply walked away.

Anne didn't react visibly, but Ben could feel her irritation—and dammit, there wasn't a thing he could do to help.

Aaron leaned down, offered Ben a hand, and yanked him to his feet. "Shit, man, you weigh a ton. Can't believe you can move so fast."

"Had practice." Since they had the best long-range spotting equipment, snipers did a whole lot of scouting. And sometimes a whole lot of retreating if a situation turned sour.

Anne walked over, carrying two bottled waters. She studied him as he pulled his T-shirt back on. "Any injuries, my tiger?" she asked softly.

*Tiger.* He could live with that, especially with the *my* tucked in front of it. "Nope. I'm good." He took a bottle and chugged it down. "You letting the twit get away with the disobedience?"

She pushed back her hair. "With anyone else, he'd be off my crew so quickly, his head would spin. But Robert is the son of one of the owners. Although I told them he's a lawsuit waiting to happen, I was forced to let him onto the team. He's quite good at manipulating his father."

"That sucks."

"It does. His incompetence and grandstanding are liable to get someone killed."

She had a clear assessment of the problem. And, aside from Robert, the men seemed to be stand-up guys.

"We'll start the next scenario as soon as we move the props around." She opened the other bottle and took a sip. "Would you prefer to play good guy or family member?"

"Fight or sit on my ass. What do you think?"

Her husky laugh made him harden to discomfort. "All right. Are you any good at hand-to-hand or—"

"Put me where you need me, Anne. I can hold my own."

"As you wish." She smiled. "The second scenario is done in full gear. Prepare to get sweaty."

\* \* \* \*

The end of the third scenario escalated into a total brawl. Grinning happily in the humid night air, Anne dodged a fist and counter-punched. Hers landed. Sweat trickled down her back. Her hair had come loose from the braid and was sticking to her damp face.

The final takedown had turned into a free-for-all. The fugitive—she'd assigned Robert as a punishment—had broken out of the house, along with his violent relatives who were determined not to let the agents take him. The team had surrounded the group in the backyard and moved in.

*So. Much. Fun.*

The ground was soft, and the filtered moonlight made opponents difficult to see. By tradition, the game used an honor system of light torso hits. If two blows landed, the receiver went down for a ten count.

Ben was amazing.

As Aaron had noted, the guard dog was surprisingly fast. He was also excellent at hand-to-hand. If he wasn't a black belt in a martial art, she'd eat her pistol. And he was obviously enjoying himself.

Even better, he'd fought beside her, and—rather than going all protective on her ass—he'd grinned as she flattened a bad guy. *"Bravo Zulu, Ma'am."*

She swiped an arm over her forehead and stepped back to assess the situation. Only two of the skip's relatives were still fighting. And the fugitive—

"You're all dead," Robert screamed and aimed at Anne with a pistol someone had dropped.

Her weapon was holstered. She heard the ping of a bead hitting cloth—and then multiple pellets hit her in the chest.

Robert, the repugnant rodent, had killed her. He'd also won, since the "death" of anyone stopped the play. The fact was acid in her gut.

"Stand down," Anne shouted. "Game over."

As the casualties regained their feet, Anne turned toward her brother. As the backup guy, he was to be standing off to one side, and available to use "lethal force" if needed. "Why aren't you in position?"

Travis shrugged. "I wanted to fight, so halfway through I traded assignments with Ben." He glanced at Ben. "Why didn't you shoot him?"

Ben smiled slightly. "I did. Before he pulled the trigger. He ignored it."

Anne stiffened. "Seriously?" The rodent had screwed up *again?* She raised her voice. "Robert, Ben says he shot you before you started shooting."

"Nah, he didn't. No one shot me. He must've missed."

She didn't doubt Ben's word at all. Anne glanced around at the rest of the players. "Did any of you see?"

No one had.

"There should be two marks on his sternum," Ben said, an amused glint in his eyes.

Anne studied him. She'd seen him angry once—at a bachelorette party when someone had harassed Rainie. Today? Despite having his word questioned twice, he wasn't even close to being upset. She turned back to Robert. "Lift up your shirt. Let's see."

"You want to look at my cock too, while you're at it?"

Oh, she'd had enough of that. Anne's foot impacted said cock—and balls as well—solidly enough to fold the idiot half over…although not nearly enough to have him puking for an hour.

Sometimes she hated showing restraint.

However, he was nicely bent over so she could grab his shirt's hem and yank the garment up and off.

He remained bent over, hiding his chest.

Still annoyed, she kicked his feet out from under him.

He landed on his back with a solid thud and made a pitiful whining sound.

Laughing under his breath, Travis shined his flashlight on Robert's pale white chest. Everyone could see two red marks within an inch of each other.

"You were dead already." Anne stared down at him in disbelief. "That makes twice you've cheated and lied."

He scrambled up. "Those marks were from when I ran into a tree.

You're just trying to make me look bad because I'm better than you are."

"In your dreams," she said.

"You won't lead this team for long, bitch." After yanking his shirt back on, he scooped up the weapon he'd lost. "I'm out of here."

His departure didn't bother her, but two men followed him. He'd created a schism in her team.

"Hey, Anne. I caught the ending. Hell of a finale." Her brother Harrison strolled across the grass, looking like a GQ model, quite the contrast to the bedraggled, muddy, sweating agents.

He offered Ben his hand. "Nice fighting and shooting. I don't go out in the field often, but I'd team up with you any day. Harrison Desmarais."

"Thanks. But I'm not on the crew. Just visiting Anne." Ben shook his hand. "Ben Haugen."

"That's too ba—Ben Haugen, as in a Ranger?"

Ben's face went blank. He nodded.

Frowning, Anne moved closer in case he needed her help.

"Jesus fuck. You're a legend, man. I'm proud to meet you." Harrison turned to Travis. "Bro, you're playing with an Army Ranger sniper."

*Well.* No wonder the man was so comfortable with team games.

Travis grinned. "And Robert tried to say you'd missed? What a dick."

"C'mon, let me treat you to a beer." Harrison slapped Ben on the back.

When Ben gave her an inquiring glance, she smiled and nodded. She needed to start debriefing the team on the latest exercise; he might as well go have a drink.

As Ben and Harrison headed toward the front yard and the cooler, Anne noticed her father in the parking area. He strolled up, shoulders still military straight, gray hair kept short, aware of everything around him. If a grizzly attacked, her father would probably put it down in speedy order.

"Hey, Dad," Travis said from beside her. "What brings you out?"

"I came with Harrison to watch the last game—or should I call it a brawl?" He smiled and slapped his son's shoulder. "Fine job with the old one-two-three."

Travis grinned. "I let a punch past that I should have blocked, but it was a good fight."

"Until the end," Anne's father said and turned to her.

Her hopes rose for one brief second. Since she'd kept an eye on the others, she knew her brother had skirmished well. She also knew her fighting had been as good, if not better than her brother's. Would her father say so?

"What the *H* were you doing out there in the fight?" her father snapped. "What Robert did was exactly what I worry about—that you'll get yourself killed. You shouldn't have been involved at all."

Her anticipation collapsed into bitter disappointment, and the backs of her eyes prickled. Why did she always set herself up this way? She knew—*knew*—he'd never praise her fighting. He'd been generous with approval when she was singing, cooking, painting, or doing school projects and homework.

But get a compliment from her father for something traditionally performed by a male? Never.

Her head knew he wouldn't ever change; for some stupid reason, her heart kept hoping.

"Maybe..." She evened out her voice. "Maybe someday, you'll realize you were a good teacher." He'd taught all his children to fight and shoot, although when Anne started taking martial arts seriously, he'd refused to teach her any longer. She'd paid for additional lessons with her own money—although her mother had quietly raised her allowance to help. "Now, if you'll excuse me, I need to gather my crew and start the analysis."

By the time she'd reached her group, he was already leaving. She shook her head. Wasn't it funny that a parent could shape who a person was—and then refuse to see them that way?

While Travis handed out sandwiches, beer, and cold drinks, the team sprawled out on blankets as Anne led the wrap-up and dissection of the scenarios. Everyone ignored the fact three team members were missing. The discussion was lively.

After dismissing the group, she waved a farewell to Travis and headed for the parking lot.

Ben waited patiently by the SUV where Bronx had been tied.

Anne glanced around and saw the retriever was hunting field mice in the grass.

"Time to go, buddy," Ben called before smiling at her. "You want to drive or want me to?"

"You can, if you don't mind," she said. "I'd love to be pampered."

He touched her cheek with gentle fingers. "It would be my pleasure to pamper you, Ma'am."

She laid her hand on his chest, feeling the warmth of his skin through the T-shirt. Somehow, being cared for by him felt...different...than from her slaves, yet his obvious delight in serving was the same. "Thank you."

The highway was dark and soon empty as the others turned off, going their various ways. Leaving the smaller road, Ben swung onto Highway 19, heading south.

After pulling a sparkling water from the cooler for her and handing him a Coke, Anne settled back against the seat cushions. "So. Army Rangers?"

"Been a few years now."

She took a sip of her drink and considered asking more questions. Something wasn't quite right with him, and she itched to explore further. To fix whatever was wrong. But, it wouldn't be fair to him. He wasn't her boy; he wasn't her job. "Okay. So what did you think of the team?"

He glanced at her. "You're not going to push for more information?"

Definitely a smart guy. "No. You're not my slave. I don't have the right."

The light from the dash showed how his lips pressed together. After a long pause, he said, "I was a sniper and good at it. Killed a lot of the enemy. I caught a bullet, was on medical leave. After thinking about it, I didn't re-up."

Short and terse, yet the words seemed drawn from the bottom of his soul. Something in there still bothered him.

And why was he telling her? Because he disagreed with the limits she'd placed on their...whatever this was?

"Being out of the service doesn't solve everything, or can even make things worse." She left the comment without following up with a question. It was up to him if he wanted to tell her more.

Lord knew, she wouldn't judge him weak. Although she hadn't had problems afterward, others she'd served with had struggled.

"No shit." A corner of his mouth tilted up. "That's how I met Z. Did you know he counsels vets now and then?"

Actually, she hadn't known.

"The VA is improving, but then—and now—a lot of us needed more. I was drowning; Z pulled me out. And still keeps an eye on me. On all of us. The night Jessica went into labor was a group session night."

"Ah." Anne was grateful he couldn't see her teary eyes. Z'd got him straightened out—and won himself the kind of loyalty that few men receive.

As she stroked her hand up and down Ben's arm, his taut muscles loosened. Apparently, he'd worried what she might think.

She was thinking that he'd shared something he considered very personal. Why?

After a second, she chuckled.

"What?"

"I know you didn't enjoy being outted by my brother, but I have to say that all by yourself, you made that slimeball Robert look bad. I appreciate it."

His grin transformed his face from Rottweiler to magnetic. "Had a few in my squad who had no judgment or had no guts. Your cousin lacks both." Then his smile faded. "Be careful, Anne. It's not wise to have a fuck-up at your back when you walk into danger."

He was not only serious…but his concern for her showed all too well.

"I will."

She was half-asleep when he pulled into her under-the-house carport.

With Bronx beside him, Ben helped her out of the car, then with a hand at her back, unlocked and opened the door…and waited.

Half-asleep she might be, but she knew that letting him stay the night would be a bad, bad idea, even if the thought of having his big body in her bed and those strong arms around her filled her with longing. They'd agreed on sex-only.

Sleeping together was more than that.

So she lifted up on tiptoes and gave him a brief, firm kiss. "Good night, Ben. Thank you for driving."

She could see the desire in his eyes, the urge to grab her and take a longer kiss, to haul her upstairs.

Bending, she gave the retriever a quick head rub. "Good night, Bronx."

"Can I talk you into a scene at the Shadowlands this weekend?" he asked.

She'd like nothing better, but he was as close to vanilla as a person could come. And he wanted to be more than a submissive, more than a slave—a real lover.

She only wanted a slave.

"No, Ben. But since you're an expert at burning off calories, I hope to do that again sometime."

"I see. Ma'am, I'm available whenever and however you desire."

She had no answer to that.

To her relief, he only tilted his head, kissed her cheek lightly, and trotted down the steps to his vehicle. Bronx whined his doggy disappointment, then followed.

She closed the door and stood with her hand on it, listening as the sound of the Jeep faded away. Her sigh came from deep inside because all she felt was regret.

Maybe, maybe someday, she could allow herself to see Ben again. Depending on how he reacted in future encounters, she might even treat them both to a shallow, sex-only marathon. Nothing more intimate would be wise.

Especially since she was feeling the same attraction as he was, which meant it would be too easy to create a different kind of bond.

She mustn't lead him on. He was an incredible man, one who deserved better than she could give him. One who had a lot of love to give.

But he wasn't a slave.

She turned and picked up her saxophone and carried it out to the deck. The moon was setting, leaving the glittering stars in command of the dark sky.

She blew a few tentative notes and settled into the old "Funky Blues."

Maybe she should have tried to explain to Ben. Tell him that just liking a person wasn't always enough. She'd learned the hard way.

True, she hadn't had very much experience with "love" relationships. She'd dated while in the Corp and been thoroughly unsatisfied...until a Domme had introduced her to the lifestyle. Her lips tilted up. The initial rush of discovery had been amazing.

Out of the service and in college, she'd fallen for a great guy—one who wasn't submissive. But vanilla simply didn't work for her, and as their relationship slowly failed, they'd both been hurt.

Lesson learned. To her, sex without being in control was like...like the desert. Dry and flat and barren. Sure, there were moments of beauty, but she was a tropics gal—she wanted the lush scenery and the changing violent weather of a D/s relationship.

Being a Mistress was who she was.

Like any new Dominant, she'd gradually worked out what she liked, testing out submissives and slaves, and found she preferred utter control.

The beauty of receiving everything.

She enjoyed the responsibility of caring for her slaves and making the decisions.

And she'd gone through a fair number of boys over the years.

At first, they'd lived with her, sometimes more than one. But then she'd moved into the beach house, owning her own home for the first time, and somehow hadn't wanted anyone else in her space.

So for the last two or three years, her slaves had been less than 24/7, which also let her demand strict protocol when they *were* with her. They asked permission to touch, to sit on the furniture, checked with her before doing anything.

In return for their devotion, she helped them grow, learn new skills, advance their careers, improve their social abilities, deepen their slavery. But before a slave grew too dependent on her, she'd find him a new Mistress.

She sighed. That was what had taught her that she didn't have much of a heart. She'd never had trouble breaking the attachment. When each slave left, she'd miss him for a bit—not long—and soon start the search for someone else.

Perhaps she wasn't a typical Mistress, but her ways worked for her—and who was to say her nay?

Ben wouldn't understand her limitations, that she could give only so much and not more. And since the thought of hurting him was intolerable, she'd simply keep her distance.

# Chapter Ten

On Thursday, the sultry evening was so humid with the approaching storm that moisture filmed Ben's arms as he walked the two blocks to his neighborhood tavern. He stepped inside, enjoying the blast of air-conditioned air. After nodding to the handful of regulars, he swung by the bar and bought a draft. Beer in hand, he took a small table by the window where he could enjoy the view.

The way the sunlight filtered through the heavy air made him wish he'd brought his camera.

On the sidewalk, people were hurrying home from work. Others strolled more leisurely as they took their dogs to the small block-long park. Maybe he should start a new series, focusing on humans rather than wildlife.

He'd always enjoyed watching people. In fact, back in the beginning, Z had given him grief about observing instead of participating.

But over the last few years, he'd returned to status quo, although he still took his time in making friends. Military friendships were a tough act to follow. He'd known his team would have his back, no matter what.

Seemed as if ties born in blood and pain went deeper. Maybe that was why he felt so close to Anne. He'd trusted her to take care of him, and she hadn't let him down.

At least not physically. Emotionally though?

He hadn't seen her since last weekend.

Staring out the window, he drank his beer and watched the darkness eat away the light. Watched the rain begin and trickle down the dirty glass.

Anne didn't trust him to guard her back, that was certain. She'd let him fuck her, but not know her.

His mouth twisted. What was his next move? A woman had the right to establish the boundaries of a relationship; a Mistress even more so. But where did that leave him?

"Yo, Longshot." Danvers crossed the bar. He was a short, tough guy, rather like a sawed-off redwood. Discharged a year before Ben, he'd found Ben the warehouse and helped convert it into a studio and living space.

"What's up?" Ben shoved a chair out in invitation.

His friend dropped down hard enough the chair let out a protesting groan. A glance at Ben's pale beer earned a sneer.

"Miss," Danvers said to the waitress who was wiping down a nearby table. "Can you bring me the darkest beer on tap?"

"Of course."

The tavern rotated the draft beers with the seasons, something the locals had come to enjoy.

As Danvers slouched in his chair, Ben frowned. "You look like hell. You okay?"

"Fuck, no." The vet scowled out the window. "You haven't heard?"

At the flatness of his voice, Ben felt his gut twist. "Heard what?"

"The team. Walked into an ambush. Lost…" he swallowed. "Three gone. Most were wounded."

Ben's mouth tasted like sand and blood. As he lifted his drink, beer sloshed over the rim onto his fingers. His hand was shaking. "Who?"

"Wrench. Petrousky. And Mouse. Mouse didn't make it." Danvers rubbed his face. "Fuck, I'm sorry, bro."

The blow cracked Ben's soul open, slashing a gap in the fabric of his world. The whole fucking room darkened. He and Mouse had been sniper and spotter, closer than some marriages. Under fire together. Bled together. Saved each other's ass more than once. Could almost read each other's mind.

But when Ben didn't re-up, Mouse'd been pissed. Yeah, his friend had tried to understand, but killing insurgents didn't eat at him as it did Ben. Mouse's world was black and white. Us and them. Good and bad. Rangers and enemy. The spotter didn't think of the enemy as men who were also someone's father, son, brother. Men who loved and laughed and lived.

Still…Mouse'd talked about getting out after his term was up. Ben would've been there to help ease the transition. Would've...

*Fuck. Just fuck.*

He set his beer down. His throat was too tight to swallow anything. Or to speak.

Rising, he clapped a hand on Danver's shoulder and walked out into the black night and drizzling rain.

# Chapter Eleven

On Friday, Anne stood inside the Shadowlands entry and studied the guard dog with a frown.

His gaze was on the desk. His shoulders slumped. He was unshaven and uncombed. In fact, Mr. Super-aware hadn't even noticed her arrival.

Worry poured through her as if someone had left a faucet open.

She walked behind his desk. "Ben." Not wanting to startle an unhappy vet, she waited until her voice registered and his head lifted before setting her hand on his shoulder.

A stressed-out soldier would probably have taut muscles. His weren't. No, his body language read as if he'd checked out.

"What's wrong, Ben?"

"Sorry, Ma'am. I didn't see you." Turning away from her, he made a checkmark on the attendance papers in front of him. "Got you down."

"Good." She pushed aside pity and steeled her voice. "Now answer me. What is wrong, Benjamin."

"Nothing."

She dug her fingernails into his thick deltoid and felt him jolt. "Inadequate response. Try again."

"Fuck." He turned his chair and gazed up at her, his eyes haunted. "Not your business."

"I'm making it my business, subbie. Answer me."

His eyes held defiance for a second, two, then his gaze dropped. "God, Anne."

She waited, watching his endurance disintegrate with her silence.

"It's not..." He swallowed. "My team. My spotter and I were attached to a team. They handled the perimeter. And..." His voice frayed, like a shirt ripping apart at the seams. "My spotter. Mouse. We worked together. For years. He's—he's gone."

Tears burned her eyes. Not only for the loss of good men, but for the almost visible waves of pain from Ben. "I'm sorry, so sorry." She moved close enough to lean her torso against his shoulder, lending him her body's warmth, and then ran her hand through his hair. If only she could stroke his hurt away.

"Thanks," he said and shrugged, as if rejecting her touch and her sympathy.

Her hand paused as she regarded his response, his posture, his averted gaze. This was more than mourning. What else was going on in that head of his?

Unfortunately, it could be anything. He'd been out of the military for years, but emotions weren't logical. And healing marched to its own beat.

Her emotions weren't rational either. She'd planned to avoid him, but now...now all she wanted was to take him into the club and try to help in the way a Domme sometimes could.

To get him out of his head and into "now" time.

"Well, Benjamin, you asked for a scene. I've decided to give you one."

He shook his head. "Ah, no. Thank you, but—"

"I planned it all day long, brought special toys."

Her lie silenced him. He didn't want to do anything right now—at all—and yet, his own submissive nature wouldn't want to let her down.

"Let me call Z and get you relieved." She pulled her cell phone from her bag and moved out of earshot, pleased when three giggly submissives came in the door to claim his attention.

"Anne." Z's smooth voice was unhurried. "Is there a problem?"

"Actually, yes. Have you seen Ben today?"

"No, I haven't been down to the club yet."

As she explained, she kept an eye on Ben. When he forced a smile for the entering members, her heart simply ached.

"I see," Z said.

"Let me have him. However, be aware that if I push him too deep, I'll take him home and he won't return to the desk."

"Understood."

"Can you give me some ideas of what this problem might be?" she asked. "He told me he'd seen you professionally."

"I am sorry, Anne, but…no. Anything he says to me is confidential."

"Of course." She shifted her stance as she tried to figure out how to attack from the flank. "I know you're a veteran. Perhaps you could share what kind of problems soldiers tend to have?"

She heard his chuckle of approval.

"Excellent question, Mistress Anne. PTSD is common, but the symptoms are fairly noticeable if you spend any time with a vet."

In other words, probably not Ben's problem.

"Some feel guilty remaining alive when teammates die. Others feel ashamed about leaving the service, as if they've betrayed their friends. The Special Ops community forges strong friendships as well as a sense of duty."

*Guilt.* That might be it. Her worry increased as the pieces fell into place.

Ben had left the Rangers and then his teammates and best friend had died. He was still alive.

What if her brother Travis took her place on the recovery team one night and was killed picking up a fugitive? Just the thought was a stab through the heart. She'd believe that if she'd been where she belonged, Travis's death wouldn't have happened—or, at least, she'd be there to die with him. She'd feel as if she shouldn't be alive.

Yes, that's what a man like Ben would feel, no matter how crazy.

Logic wasn't a factor in a guilt equation.

"Thank you, Z. I appreciate the quick psychology lesson." Mourning had to run its course, but irrational emotions…well, maybe she could derail him from the *it's-my-fault* track he was on.

"You may take him with you now. I'll guard the desk myself until I can call in Ghost," Z said. "He's lucky to have you, Anne."

*Have me?* "He doesn't—"

But Z had already disconnected.

By the time Ben finished checking people in, Z had arrived. He must have started down the minute she called. "You're relieved, Benjamin."

Ben frowned at him. "But—"

"Let's go, subbie," Anne said. As objections rose in the guard dog's eyes, she pushed her energy outward, bringing her dominance to bear like an invisible battering ram. She held her hand out, pleased when he let her draw him to his feet.

She led him into the main room and toward the back. "As long as I respect your limits, I can do what I want to you. Is that right?"

"What?" The question pulled his gaze away from the passing scenes—the glass cups on a submissive's chest and cock, an exquisite pattern of needles being shaped across a wide back, a Dom using the two-flogger Florentine style.

After a second of processing her question, Ben nodded. "Yes, Ma'am."

A trace of life showed in his face. Not many people could walk through the super-charged ambiance of the Shadowlands and not wake up.

The subtle threat she'd just delivered added to the effect.

She started up the circular staircase leading to the second floor.

He stopped. "Where are you going?"

"We're going to play upstairs in one of the private rooms." Although she'd occasionally used a slave's penis as a leash, today, she only gathered the front of his jeans, belt and all, and pulled him behind her up the stairs.

"I've never been up here." He looked down the long hallway. If a room was in use, a red light glowed above the door.

"After all these years? I'd say it was about time." She glanced in each unoccupied room as they passed. She rejected the ornate Victorian, which would make Ben ill at ease, and then a depressing Goth-styled room. One with a harem decor had potential, but not today. Barbarian—no.

The one she was looking for wasn't where it had been last time. Z's tendency to rearrange and redecorate rooms annoyed the hell out of her.

And there it was.

She led him into the room she'd titled: *Cowboy Central*—although Z called it the Texas room.

Dour Nolan had actually laughed when he saw it.

The walls were paneled with dark wood rather than wallpaper. Cowhide rugs were scattered on the gleaming hardwood floor. An antique chest served as an end table to an oversized black leather armchair. A handwoven Navaho rug in dark-red and black brightened one wall. The other held a mounted buffalo head—and she really, really didn't want to know if it was real or not. A wagon wheel chandelier provided light. Toys were stored in an aged walnut armoire.

Barely loud enough to be heard, country-western music came from the speakers.

She smiled as she saw Ben relax slightly. Big guys tended to prefer rooms without fragile glass and furniture.

When he saw the decorations surrounding the armoire on the far wall, his eyes widened. Welded horseshoes had been turned into hooks to hold a variety of floggers and whips.

She'd noticed how Z enjoyed using implements of pain as artwork.

After setting her toy bag on the chest, she took out some thin Velcro strips. "Strip, then stand under the chains, please." She pointed and watched Ben's shoulders tense as he sighted the two heavy black chains hanging from the dark, exposed ceiling beams.

He silently stripped, still too subdued, still so far into his own head and emotions that he was almost separated from the world.

She could pull him out of that place. But if she didn't effect some change in his thought processes, he'd fall back into his funk afterward.

Her lips pressed together. There were times that being a Domme was like driving up in the mountains. In the dark. On a tiny, curvy road.

Mistakes could be very, very bad.

He trusted her not to screw up his body; he didn't realize she was more worried about his mind.

She tossed one of her subbie blankets over the leather chair and set a bottle of water on the trunk.

As she buckled heavy leather cuffs on his wrists and ankles, a tremor ran through him. Being bound was one of his triggers. One she planned to use—not abuse. "Arms up." She stood on the carved miniature steer footstool to attach his cuff's D-ring to one chain, using a half-inch-wide Velcro strip.

"Pull down," she said.

He gave a slight tug on the restraint and nothing happened.

"Harder."

The Velcro gave with a ripping sound. Just right. He'd know he was restrained—and that he could get free if needed. Silently, she secured that wrist again as well as the other. Once finished, she wrapped his fingers around the chains. "You can hang on for support."

After stepping off the stool, she pushed his feet apart. "Keep your legs wide open for me, Benjamin. I don't want to see them move."

Down on one knee, she ran her hands over his tight calves, the leanly contoured muscles of his thighs, inhaling his masculine musk. His cock was almost flaccid—significant proof of his state of mind.

*Let's see how long that lasts.* She unzipped her leather jacket and skirt. Beneath them, she wore an elastic black tank, a thong with ribbon ties—and thigh-high boots.

His eyes widened.

"I intend to beat you, subbie," she said, keeping her voice husky—

which wasn't a problem. He really did have the sexiest body she'd ever seen. Her usual slaves were classically gorgeous males possessing streamlined, beautifully sculpted musculature. This oversized body in front of her was scarred. With heavy slabs of muscles. With forbidding, blunt features.

The man simply radiated power and strength.

*And he's all mine.*

*For tonight.*

To erase her own tenseness, she went up on tiptoes, arched her back, and reached toward the ceiling.

His pupils dilated slightly.

But the stretching wasn't all for show. This scene wouldn't be a short one, and a good flogging took time and work.

They were both in this for the long haul.

Leaning against him, she rubbed her body over his and let him catch her scent, as she would with a wild animal. Slowly, she ran her hands over his back and ass, waking his skin up with pats and strokes and scrapes of her fingernails.

"I do love this body you've given me to play with," she murmured. "Are you ready for me to start?"

It took a second for him to respond. He still wasn't fully with her. "Uh. Yes, Ma'am. Sure."

He was so not like her Ben, and his palpable despair simply broke her heart.

Taking his face in her hands, she gave him a slow kiss. Not for the scene, not for control—just because she needed to remind him she cared. And that he was alive.


Mistress Anne's lips were a touch of life in what felt like a dead world. Ben knew he was letting her down, but he just…couldn't…get with the program. He felt as if he were trudging through the Everglades, his boots heavy with mud. The muck pulled him downward, the air was too thick, the dense foliage blotted out the sun. There was no escape. He would walk and walk forever and never get out.

Mouse was gone. His friend—

The scent of leather reached him. Softness danced over his shoulders and stroked down his back. He opened his eyes.

The Mistress was teasing a black, multi-strand whip across his shoulders, his chest, his ass. Soft and fragrant. The flicking of the falls across his back was as light as a spring rain.

The strands slapped over his torso and legs in a rhythm that matched the beat of the country music.

Slowly, the slapping sounds grew louder as the blows increased in force. His skin seemed to glow with the heat.

When she stopped, he was almost disappointed, in the same way a person regretted when a massage ended.

She studied him for a minute, and her lips curved up slightly. "Better." Her hand flattened on his chest, and she leaned against him as her tongue ran over his lower lip.

Then she fisted his hair and took his mouth roughly, driving her tongue inside.

His body heated with a rush. She tasted of chocolate and peppermint, like sex and sin, and he breathed her in, feeling as if the sun had shot a ray of sunlight through the darkness.

Her hands held his face in that way she had, so she could look into his eyes. Hers were a clear gray-blue, like the starkly bare sky after a winter rain.

"I'm going to hurt you now, Benjamin. If you move, if you tear loose of your restraints, I'll be disappointed in you."

"I won't, Mistress." The words emerged before he even thought about them.

"Your safeword is red, subbie. Use it if you need to."

"I won't."

Her hands stroked down his chest, riffling his hair. When she pinched his nipples with sharp fingertips, his blood started to race as if someone were cranking open the floodgates.

And then she reached between his legs. She cupped his ball sac in her warm palms, squeezing lightly. And forcefully. She rolled his actual rocks between her fingers, increasing the pressure until he felt sweat breaking out on his skin. Felt his cock stir.

"Such a bad cock, not jumping right up for its Mistress." Her disapproval made him hang his head. Want to apologize.

She slapped his limp dick—*slapped it, for God's sake*—with the tips of her fingers. To the left, to the right, each smack stinging. Shocking.

*Jesus.* He tensed his legs, trying to stay in position as the blows increased to the point of pain.

To his disbelief, his cock filled and rose.

Curling her sure fingers around him, she stroked his dick, up and down. The heady reward lasted far too short a time.

She picked up the flogger.

The first hits landed on his shoulders, worked down his back, avoiding his spine and kidneys. His ass took some serious pounding. And his skin went past the glow to a burn.

After a while, she stopped and slapped his cock.

"Fuck!"

"Silence, subbie," she murmured and smacked his dick again.

He bit back a curse and was rewarded with a long, wet kiss. Jesus, she could kiss. His arms ached to hold her.

He lost track of how many times she went through the cycle. His back and ass felt as if he'd backed into a furnace; his cock stung and throbbed.

His hands gripped the black chains as if he were fused to the metal.

"Time for something new." She smiled at him sweetly and picked up a...thing. An evil, steel, ring-like device filled with a couple of dozen metal studs. It looked like a fucking miniature iron maiden. A mouth with teeth.

His own teeth clamped down on his protest.

She opened the hinged band, closed the damned thing around his shaft, and screwed the studs inward until each steel point barely poked his dick.

Not too bad. He realized he'd frozen in place. Carefully, he exhaled.

And then she reached past his shaft to scrape her fingernail over the sensitive skin between his balls and asshole.

As the searingly sharp pleasure scorched through him, his cock thickened ...and the fucking studs hurt like hell. His hands fisted around the chains as he fought the need to yank the torture device off.

And somehow, the agony only made him harder...which made the pain worse. "*Fuck.*"

Her eyes were bright with pleasure. "That's what I want to hear."

She flogged him again, ruthlessly. Pain upon pain.

And yet, the murky swamp air that had been suffocating him was lightening into a sunlit fog. His cock didn't...quite...hurt, but felt surrounded by a dense heat, as if a wet mouth held him sweetly. Each stroke of the flogger sang across his skin with a heavy liquid pressure like a warm tongue.

He realized...eventually...that she'd stopped.

"What a good Benjamin," she was murmuring, her cool hands stroking over his body, easing the fires.

She kissed him, long and slow, even as he felt her hands on his distant cock, removing the steel ring.

And his shaft billowed with heat, bobbing like a balloon over a bonfire. Pulsing with his heartbeat. The whole room was moving up and down.

His arms were suddenly at his sides. Had he let go of the chains? As he tried to reach up, she laughed—fuck, he could get off just listening to her—"Come here, Benjamin."

With a firm grip, she guided him into a chair. Nice big chair, a soft blanket beneath his trembling legs. He was floating in a cool sea.

"Benjamin." Her hands on his face were sweetness itself. "Look at me, my tiger."

His eyelids were heavy, but she had the most beautiful eyes. He could look into them forever.

When had she sat on his lap? But she was. She'd straddled his legs, her knees bracketing his thighs. If he could have lifted his arms, he'd have held her.

"You remember my brother Travis? He left the Marines because he couldn't cope any longer."

*Her brother.* Yes, he'd met her brother. Somewhere. Nice guy. Ben's skin burned, his cock throbbed so oddly, and her eyes were so, so blue.

"Why did you leave the Rangers, Benjamin?"

He wasn't in anymore, was he? Was discharged. No military career for him. The loss made his eyes prickle, but the fog wrapped around him, kept the grief back. "Got hurt."

"And that's why you didn't go back."

"Nooo." He managed to swallow, and oh, she was stroking his shoulders, his chest. Such little hands to be so powerful. "Not why."

"Why, Ben?"

"Couldn't kill more. Too many. Each one worse. Like a weight. Got jumpy…"


Anne nodded as his voice trailed off. Yes, there was the reason. She ached for him, for his unsolvable dilemma. Because this warrior who was so good at killing had a caring heart that had probably been sliced open with each shot he took.

And then he'd had PTSD to top off the unholy brew.

He'd recovered. In fact, he was the most even-tempered man she'd ever met. But loyalty and duty could create blind spots. "If you'd stayed in, you think you'd have kept your teammates from dying. Is that right?"

His eyes dulled. He nodded slowly.

"Travis wanted to return, but he didn't. He said he'd freeze at the wrong time. Or panic and shoot up his team. How about you?"

His reactions were slow, his mind still in the twilight world of subspace. His gaze had focused somewhere...else.

"What do you see, honey?"

"Rockface freaked. Shot our medic."

"Rockface stayed too long, didn't he?" Anne asked softly. "Maybe he should have gotten out?"

"Yeah."

"Each person hits a point where he can't process anything else. Can't keep up. Then it's time to get out. Or you risk hurting your teammates."

She waited. Waited some more.

Added another fact. "You did the right thing, Ben."

"They're dead."

"And you're alive."

"Should've died with them."

God, what more could she do to help him see?

She gritted her teeth...and picked up the steel cock ring. She set the cold metal against his throat...right over the artery. His mind was slow, his senses messed up. He'd feel the coldness, not how blunt it was.

He'd feel the threat of a knife.

His entire body jerked, his muscles tensing.

The risk nauseated her. "What if you could be with them now, subbie? Do you want that? Or will you fight to live?"

Wide, stunned eyes met hers. And yet...he didn't move.

"I want you alive, Ben. What do you want? Should I let you live?"

After a long, long moment, as her own fears tried to overwhelm her, he nodded.

Pulse pounding in her ears, she sagged in relief. After tossing the ring to the ground, she wrapped her arms around him. "Losing someone hurts, doesn't it?"

"Hurts," he agreed.

"Over there, you fought for me, your family, your friends. To keep us safe."

"Yeah."

"Now you're here. That means your buddies were fighting to keep you safe, too. Weren't they?"

He blinked.

"Mouse would want you to live, Ben. Not to give up. You have to survive to make his sacrifice worth it."

"He died. I should have been there."

"We all die sometime, my tiger. That moment…that place…wasn't yours. Your time will come. Until then, your job is to live as best you can."

He stared at her.

"That's your duty now, Ben."

Should she have taken him deeper?

But he was soaking up what she said, processing it to some extent. His defenses were still down. The guardian of his mind was impaired, so her words were going deep.

She waited.

"He died." His eyes filled.

The grief of a great-souled man who loved deeply was finally surfacing, and her heart broke for him. She pulled him forward, wrapped her arms around him, and laid his head on her shoulder as he shook.

"It hurts, I know," she whispered. Losing someone hurt. There was no pain that comes close.

His arms came around her, pulling her against him so tightly she had trouble finding air.

"Shhh." She held him just as firmly, heart against heart. She would hold him forever if that were what he needed.

But eventually, he moved. Breathed deeper. The energy changed. He was coming out of subspace. Out of despair.

She stroked his back and shoulders gently, easing him into the world. Reality could be difficult. But maybe she could both ease the transition and reinforce the joys of living.

As he lifted his head to look around, she took his right hand.

His golden-brown eyes met hers.

Gliding his hand down her side, she closed his thumb and fingers on the left ribbon of her thong…and pulled. When the bow opened, she brushed his hand over the bared skin. Then she took his left hand and set it on the other bow.

He undid the ribbon all on his own.

Beneath her, a cock that had never gone limp thickened. Lengthened. He'd never even noticed that she'd replaced the steel cage with a condom.

She lifted up slightly and tugged her thong away, then adjusted her position so the head of his cock pressed against her damp entrance.

When he tensed, she stayed…right there…and leaned forward to kiss him.

Anne's soft lips moved over Ben's mouth. But all his attention had focused on one place, on where her hot pussy bobbed against the very tip of his dick. Just the fucking tip.

Engorged again, his erection burned and throbbed—and wanted sex like a motherfucker. She was *teasing* him.

His hands, still at her hips, gripped her thighs, moved her just enough to establish position—and then he yanked her down on his cock, sheathing himself in her to the hilt.

*Fuuuuck.* His abused, sensitive dick felt engulfed in liquid fire. Even more blood surged into his shaft, making her impossibly, painfully tight. His head hit the back of the chair as he shuddered.

And she laughed. *Sadistic Mistress.*

He'd never had anything hurt so much and feel so good at the same time.

Her thigh muscles flexed as she lifted off of him, and the slippery slide of her pussy over his skin almost made his eyes roll back.

*Up, down.*

"I can't..." *last.* He had to. Never leave a man—a woman—behind. Letting her set the rhythm, he moved his hands inward, using his thumbs to bracket her slick clit and rub the sides and top.

Her cunt clenched. Yeah, she liked that.

Hell, so did he. His teeth ground together as he fought against coming. *Hold the line.*

Her clit was protruding, her thighs quivering, her speed increasing.

And she came, arching back in a movement as beautiful as life itself.

He watched in wonder, in awe, and when her eyes opened, the light in them was like the clouds opening to the sun after a storm.

"Come now, Benjamin. You've waited long enough." She braced, hands splayed on his chest as she lifted up and drove down, grinding into him with each pistoning movement.

Sensation flooded him, filled the dry lake to overflowing, burst the dam, and surged through. He came. *Fuck, he came.* Every gripping spasm held molten liquid so hot it vied with his burning cock. Heat everywhere. Pleasure so vast he saw stars exploding in the universe.

Covered in sweat, he looked up into her endlessly deep eyes and saw her dimples. And then her smile.

Yeah. He wanted to live.

He'd faded out on her again. Anne had managed to dress him—she wasn't sure how. Unsure of his balance, she took him down to the first floor in the tiny elevator.

As they crossed the main room, the noise and activity set him to trembling. She stopped to grab a subbie blanket from one of the stands. After wrapping it around him, she leaned into him and let her body heat reassure him. "Benjamin, look at me."

His gaze met hers, eyes still glazed, and he gave her a wry smile. "Sorry, Ma'am. I'll be all right in a minute."

Maybe a bit longer than that. She pulled his arms around her and held him firmly, reminding his body of reality. She felt as well as heard his sigh. Yes, he needed more from her.

She noticed Cullen watching from across the room, his face tight. Undoubtedly worried that the evil Mistress had hurt their guard dog.

She turned her back.

"I'm taking you home with me," she told Ben.

He pulled back and frowned. "I..." His brows drew together and after a second, he said, "Bronx is at home. Can't leave him all night. He'll need to go out."

"Then we'll go to your house."

\* \* \* \*

The dog knocked Anne back a step as Ben let her in the warehouse door.

"Hi, Bronx." Smiling, she knelt to snuggle the retriever. His fur was soft against her face, and his tail whipped her arm with his delight. "You're such a sweetheart."

"Ready to go out, buddy?" Ben asked.

Obviously recognizing the question, Bronx trotted past him while Ben stood in the doorway. Filled with old brick industrial buildings, the streets in the area were evolving into the city's "artsy" district. But this late at night, Bronx would have the street to himself.

As Ben watched his dog, Anne watched the man. Yes, he was back in his skin and functioning well again. He'd be all right.

She walked into the center of the small warehouse and turned in a circle. In the back half, the second floor formed an open loft. The entire front of the building was all windows, clear to the roof. The wood floors were sanded smooth and so well coated that she knew why Bronx had slid into her when they'd arrived.

To her left was an unwalled office space with computer equipment and oversized monitors as well as drafting tables. Green and flowering plants filled the corners and perched on available surfaces, adding a lush element to the industrial ambiance.

And then she saw the pictures. Six feet tall, lining the back wall.

In one, dark thunderclouds brooded over a traditional beach sunset. Evil reddish light angled down to silhouette two innocent children building a sand castle.

Goose bumps rose on Anne's arms.

Another photo showcased a great blue heron in the twilight, its head tilted as it stared back at the viewer.

An alligator basked on a sunny log, seemingly at ease, except for its cold, predatory gaze.

A sunrise photo revealed a very familiar place—Z's personal garden.

Stunned, she bent and read the scrawling signature on the mat. *BL Haugen.* The very *famous* BL Haugen, whose photographs of the war in Iraq had won numerous awards. Who was now renowned as a Florida photographer.

Her gaze lingered on a photograph taken in the Everglades. Ben carried a chainsaw in his Jeep. *"I'm in the wilderness a lot,"* he'd said.

"You took these pictures." Her words came out almost accusatory.

"Mmmhmm." Ben closed the door behind Bronx. "I'm taking him upstairs to feed him."

"Right," she said absently.

She'd thought he was a nice, normal security guard. Okay, sure she'd figured out he was far, far deeper, but he had a whole career she hadn't known about. What kind of an idiot was she?

After she'd looked her fill, she turned and saw that the wall past the stairs held floor-to-ceiling bookshelves. Ben must read. A lot.

Did the man have to keep getting more attractive? As she climbed the stairs to the loft, she surveyed the titles. Lots of mysteries, a smattering of horror, some philosophy and ethics. Books about Florida history and biology.

Halfway up, her legs turned rubbery and she slowed. God, she was tired. A heavy scene left both participants exhausted. After she checked to be sure Ben would be all right, she'd get herself home.

The stairs ended in an open kitchen, dining, and living space. The doors to the rear probably led to a bedroom and bath. A massive plant—an umbrella tree—filled one corner. African violets lined the kitchen island. The man went for greenery. Maybe they helped drive away memories of a desert war?

Ben set down a bowl of dog food for Bronx before smiling at her. "I have water and sodas in the fridge."

"That sounds wonderful." She rummaged inside and found a strawberry sparkling water.

As Ben rinsed out the dog food can and tossed it into recycling, Anne regarded him. He still looked more like a stereotypical street thug than a renowned photographer. "You might have mentioned you take pictures for a living. Why are you a guard at the Shadowlands?"

"Photography is solitary. When I was discharged, my only friends were a couple of vets." He ruffled Bronx's ruff. "Z wanted me to meet people who weren't connected with war. He"—Ben's mouth quirked—"*ordered* me to get a part-time position that put me around people. He didn't care where, even McDonalds, but when I didn't start job hunting, he dumped me on the desk at the club."

This man had gone through hell and staggered out the other side. Battered, mentally and physically, but on his feet. And a few years later, was one of the most confident, caring, amazing men she'd ever known. "I take it Z's unique brand of therapy worked?"

Ben pulled a Coke out of the fridge. "It's difficult to stay depressed at the Shadowlands. People coming in are zinging with excitement." He grinned. "I've had some bad days here and there. Like the first day Jessica showed up. I didn't want to talk with anyone, but Z, damn the bastard, sent her out to sit in the entry. In my space."

"I remember that night." The Masters had enjoyed how Jessica's introduction to the Shadowlands was almost a horror flick cliché: pretty blonde wrecks her car and seeks help at dark, ominous mansion. Rather than vampires, the little innocent had found Masters and slaves, Doms and submissives, sadists and masochists.

Ben grinned. "She was so fucking shocked and cute. Impossible to ignore, although I tried. And then she mustered her courage and marched back in. I figured if a tiny blonde could face down her fears, I damn well should manage."

Z's guard dog was quite a man. Anne leaned into him, snuggled close, and rubbed her cheek on his shoulder. "I'm glad you didn't give up." *Then and now.*

His powerful hands settled on her shoulders, and his voice rumbled through his solid chest. "Me, too."

With a reluctant sigh, she stepped back and gave him a careful study. Eyes clear, color good, posture erect. No trembling. A slight smile. Humor back in place. He was okay. "Now that you're stable, I need to get going."

She leaned in to kiss his cheek.

His arm went around her waist, holding her against him. He set his drink down and pulled her closer, pulled her up so he could kiss her. Long and hard. "Stay."

"Ben—"

His hands closed on her ass. Just like that, desire filled her. Honestly, she shouldn't be this needy after the earlier bout of sex.

Yet her body wanted more. She wanted more. Her voice came out throaty. "How about you give me a tour of the bedroom?"

"Yeah, why don't I do that?" He tugged on her hair. "You going to beat on me?"

Beat on him as if he belonged to her. Was one of her slaves. She stopped. She shouldn't be doing this. She'd told herself not to get involved with him.

"Anne, what is it?"

"You're not..." She huffed out a sigh. "I told you I didn't do relationships. I don't want to hurt you. I shouldn't be here." And yet, she knew...she *knew* it was already too late.

She cared about him.

His chin thrust forward. "You should be here. With me." His expression eased. "Spend the weekend with me, Anne. We'll have fun. If you want, we can forego the D/s stuff." The twitch of his lips clued her in.

"You know I don't set that aside for very long."

"True enough, at least not when sex is involved. But hey, if it makes you feel better, I can try to look pretty." He batted his eyes.

She burst out laughing, took his hand, and led him to the bedroom.

# Chapter Twelve

Anne was a different person outside of the Shadowlands—and still the same, Ben decided. Even after a weekend in her company, he still hadn't figured her out. She had more facets than the diamond earrings she wore—and was more down-to-earth than he'd realized.

With her sprawled over him on his comfortable, suede-covered couch, Ben stroked her back. Earlier they'd argued over the various techniques used in action flicks.

What kind of a sadist hated gory movies?

On the far wall, the television was still playing their mutual pick— *Independence Day.*

Anne had fallen asleep within the first twenty minutes. In his arms. Ben smiled and kissed the top of her head. He was making progress in wearing down her defenses.

Although, he had to admit that he hadn't planned the last battle. Her own soft heart had done her in when she'd seen him grieving. When she'd yanked him off the desk and into a whole new world.

Damn, but she'd dug through his head in a way that made him feel as if she knew him better than anyone ever had. He'd been a mess. Even now, he struggled with the sadness of losing Mouse.

But it was okay to be alive. Anne had forced him to acknowledge that. She'd also taken on his remorse at leaving the service and helped him see that he'd done the right thing.

His guilt for not being there for his team might never fade entirely, but it had decreased. Each person was different in how much he could take. He'd been heartsick at killing others, at the deaths of his teammates, constantly on edge, half-addicted to the adrenaline, half-sick with it. He'd lasted a hell of a lot longer than some; hadn't made it as long as others. Life was like that. He hadn't blamed his buddies who'd quit after one combat tour—why should he blame himself after doing more than that?

She'd helped him understand that.

Quite a woman.

Quite a Domme.

After she'd spent Friday night with him, he'd fed her breakfast the next morning. And with his usual impeccable timing, Z had called to check on him, to tell him to take Saturday night off from the Shadowlands…and that Anne didn't need to come in either.

So Ben had talked her into going to St. Pete's Vinoy Park for the Tampa Bay Blues Festival. *Curtis Salgado. The Bluetones.* The inspiration had been an unexpected win. Who would have guessed she played a saxophone—and loved the blues?

Who would have guessed she would have known his photography work? That had been a hell of a rush.

And today, since she was curious about how photographers worked, she'd been easy to coax into a long hike at Honeymoon Island so he could set up shots with the mangrove backdrop before the afternoon showers. The light right before a storm couldn't be duplicated.

Anne had no trouble keeping up with him—she was certainly in shape—and while he'd been taking pictures, she'd thrilled Bronx by playing fetch with him.

With his toes, Ben rubbed the retriever sacked out at his feet. During an early counseling session, Z had told him to get a big friendly dog. The idea hadn't been appealing in the least. So one day, Z had dropped off a puppy—and left while Ben was still protesting.

Manipulative bastard.

But it'd been impossible to stew at home when the puppy had to be taken for walks. And taught not to eat boots and picture frames. And fed and watered. Difficult to be morose when a game of stick-throwing—or just coming home—would send the furball into a dance of delight.

Although no longer a frisky puppy, Bronx had turned into a damn fine friend.

And Bronx thoroughly approved of Anne.

*Me, too, buddy.*

Ben rubbed his jaw against her silky hair, inhaling the light floral scent. Her skin was so delicate he could see the faint blue lines at her temples and under her eyes. She hadn't worn makeup today. Her eyelashes weren't black, but a dark brown. He wanted to feel that thick fringe brushing against his cheek.

She'd been an excellent companion all weekend—fun to talk with, fun to hike with, pulled her own weight. While he'd packed his photography gear, she'd made the sandwiches they'd taken in a cooler. When he cooked supper, she'd done the clean up.

To his surprise, she'd not stayed in her Domme armor all weekend.

Of course, she'd slip into the role if he pushed her. Or when she felt like messing with his head.

And he totally enjoyed the added zing when she did. *Oh yeah.* When she got that *look* in her gunmetal blue eyes and her voice took on that low tone of command, his blood sizzled and his cock jumped to attention.

Because he was *submissive.* That sure wasn't a term he'd figured would ever apply to him. He gave a half-laugh that roused his woman.

His *Mistress.*

Well, whatever the fuck he called her, she was his.

She blinked up at him, half-irritated, her eyes still foggy with sleep, her mouth too fucking appealing.

By the time he'd kissed the annoyance off her lips, she was awake.

After turning to straddle him, she took his face between her palms. "What were you laughing about?"

"Nothin' important."

"Benjamin." She slid into the Domme mode within one breath. And there his body went, responding with pleasure and arousal...and a heightened urge to make her happy.

*Submissive. Fuck.* "Thinking about dominance and submission. You're a Domme. Not sure I like calling myself a submissive"—and definitely not a slave—"even though I get off on this."

"Ah." She lowered her ass onto his thighs. As her hands flattened on his chest, her gaze stayed on his face. "It's an insulting word in our culture, especially when applied to a guy."

She looked away. Thinking. "All humans—men particularly—strive for power, and in our society, that usually means management positions. CEOs. Presidents. But not everyone enjoys being in command."

"Yeah. I'm more of a loner—photography gives me that." He kissed her palm. "But you like giving the orders. I can see it." She practically glowed when she was in full Mistress mode.

"I do like it. I started topping my last year in the Corps. An older friend in my battalion showed me the ropes, so to speak. Something...clicked...and I knew I'd found what had been missing in my life. "

"You've been a Domme for well over a decade." Or closer to fifteen years. No wonder she seemed so comfortable with who she was.

"Mmmhmm. You know, you're certainly not the only soldier who enjoys being taken under command. In the army, did you want to lead the troops or were you happy to take orders?"

"Being in charge hasn't ever been an overwhelming ambition for me—but I was honored to lead the men when it was my turn in the barrel." And he'd done his damnedest to live up to the responsibility. "At the same time, I don't mind taking orders, as long as my commanding officer is competent."

In all reality, there was a certain ease to operating under a talented leader. And with Anne, he'd found much to admire. She was a truly gifted operator.

Her gaze held understanding. As a Marine, she knew how it worked. "So, rather than 'submissive,' we should have a nice short word for *You can give the orders as long as you don't fuck it up, Sir. Knock yourself out.*"

"When you say it that way, sounds better."

"Maybe not as sexy though." Her hands curved along his jaw, and she kissed him, taking what she wanted. When he tried to put his arms around her, she made a sound that had him lowering his hands to the couch.

*Submissive.* The word sucked, but the feeling of restraining himself and letting her enjoy him was satisfying as hell. He could break her in half within a heartbeat, but the instincts at play said to give her whatever she pleased.

Just her will alone could keep him in place. The dominant animal in a pack wasn't always the biggest one.

He murmured against her lips, "Since I'm the submissive—and this is my quarters—how about I cook you supper? And we'll go to bed early?"

Her throaty laugh made him reconsider the order of events. "You're insatiable."

Only with her. That submissive word was starting to fit better than he'd thought possible. What about the next step? The slave word?

Didn't sound like him. But what would he do to keep this woman in his life?

Who knew—maybe he'd roll that way given the chance. There was only one way to find out. "Insatiable for you pretty much describes it, yeah."

# Chapter Thirteen

On Thursday, Ben parked in one of the two spaces beside Anne's driveway.

Bronx jumped out of the SUV behind him. Tail waving gently, the dog danced across the driveway, checked the air, and headed around the house. Bronx had quickly figured out that Anne usually enjoyed a cup of tea or coffee on her deck so she could watch the sunset. Hearing the saxophone, he stopped to listen. After a moment, he recognized the old tune. "Arthur's Theme" was an unusual mixture of haunting and uplifting.

She was in a fair mood. Anne's body language didn't always reveal her spirits, but her music was a dead giveaway.

As Ben reached the back of the house, he heard his retriever charge across the deck.

"Bronx!" Anne laughed. "Aren't you a pretty boy? Such a smart dog."

Ben grinned. The woman was a sucker for children and animals. "Permission to come aboard?" he called from the foot of the stairs.

"Come on up, Ben."

He climbed up. "You look damn comfortable."

Sitting on a lounge chair, she'd put her sax aside to pet Bronx. Her khaki shorts showed off her long, golden-tan legs. Her sleeveless top was the exact color of her striking eyes—and unbuttoned. Sure, she wore a swimsuit beneath it, but his libido had a Pavlovian switch. A woman—especially this one—with an unbuttoned shirt sent his lust into overdrive.

Bronx was leaning against the chair, collecting as much loving as he could con out of her.

"You're spoiling him, Anne."

"He has beautiful manners. As long as that continues, I'll continue rewarding him."

Ben leaned over and collected a slow kiss. Damn, he loved the way she kissed, the way her fingers gripped his hair, with her other hand fisted in his shirt to pull him closer.

When he finished and straightened, she assessed the muddy scratches on his legs, arms, and hands. Concern edged her voice. "Are you all right?"

"Good enough. My Jeep got stuck in a swampy area. Had to work to get it extricated."

"You look as if you fought your way through the Everglades." She motioned toward the door behind her. "Go grab something to drink— and eat too. I made cookies for the shelter kids and saved a bunch for you."

"Seriously?" Cookies? Yeah, he adored her. A shame the deck was so exposed or he'd have gone down on her right then. "If they have raisins, I'll be your slave for the night."

"Benjamin." One perfectly groomed eyebrow went up. "You'll be that whether or not there are raisins."

Good point. Smiling, he gave her a mock salute and headed for the kitchen before he said something that'd get him in trouble. Or got his treats taken away.

She'd baked chocolate chip cookies on Monday, made carrot cake on Tuesday—Bronx wasn't the only male being spoiled around here.

He grinned. This morning, she'd insisted on jogging an additional mile, complaining that she was gaining weight because of his sweets addiction.

But, far as he was concerned, an extra inch or two on her hips or breasts would be a total turn-on. More to hold; more to play with.

Speaking of playing, he was looking forward to the next few days. This was Ghost's weekend as security guard at the Shadowlands, and Anne was free of dungeon monitor duties. Since Raoul was out of town, Ben had arranged to borrow his sailboat. Hopefully, Anne would be interested in spending a long, leisurely weekend on the water.

The phone rang as he pulled a bottled water from the fridge. "Anne—phone."

"Coming. Answer it, please."

He knew how she answered her phone, never saying her own name. But hearing a man's voice, the caller might think they had the wrong number. So he picked up the receiver and said, "I'm answering for the resident. Please hold."

"What?" After a hesitation, the man demanded, "Let me speak to Anne." Was this one of her brothers? The voice seemed familiar.

"Hold, please."

Followed by Bronx, Anne strode in and accepted the phone with a mouthed *thank you*. "Hello?"

After a pause, she said, "I'm sorry, but that's none of your business." Her brows drew together in irritation.

Someone was going to catch hell. Ben grabbed three cookies and headed out to the deck, whistling for Bronx as he went.

As he stepped outside, he heard her say, "No. I'm not taking you back, Joey."

Ben stopped dead. *Fuck*. It took a second to get himself moving again. He set the cookies on the dark brown wicker end table, dropped into a chair, and put his feet up on the railing.

Like a cockroach, a nasty feeling was crawling into his gut. Joey'd been Anne's last "boy."

Joey got off on being whipped, beaten, his nuts smashed. Her slave had waited on her hand and foot. The young man was slender, ripped, and looked as if he should be modeling men's briefs.

Totally Anne's type. Totally the complete opposite of Ben.

The bottle started to crumple in his grip.

Joey wanted to be her slave again—she could have her pretty boy back.

But she'd said no. Only…she was still talking to the little shit on the phone. How persuasive was he?

How much did she want to have a slave again?

Ben's back teeth ground together. Should he let her know she had an alternate ready and willing to serve?

But he wasn't a slave, dammit. Yeah, he'd pretty much accepted that he fucking loved handing over the reins in the sex arena. The rest of the time? That was negotiable.

He scowled at a soaring frigatebird, its sharp black wings stark against the blue sky.

If she wanted 24/7, then… *Shit*. Could he?

But could he give her up? Go back to empty evenings with no Anne to argue over martial arts tactics or firearms, to wrestle with on the living room floor, to listen to the latest stupid stunt her cousin pulled.

Ben wanted her opinions when he worked on a photograph,

wanted to eat the cookies she saved for him, wanted to see her sneaking Bronx the forbidden tidbits.

He wanted to watch the sunlight on her face in the mornings, to jog beside her on the beach, to enjoy her disapproving frown when he sugared his coffee.

No, he couldn't give her up, not without a fight.

And he wouldn't know if he liked being a "slave" if he didn't try it. Fuck knew, if she went back to Joey, he'd never get that chance.

Anne came out and dropped down in the chair next to him. After a second, she leaned forward and hugged Bronx.

Ben frowned at her unsettled expression. Now that just wouldn't do. He rose, scooped her up, and sat with her in his lap. Soft and warm. Her hip pressed against a part of his body that was rapidly wakening.

"Ben," she said, giving her usual warning when he grabbed her, but she didn't really sound upset.

He inhaled her light, spicy fragrance. She smelled like cinnamon and vanilla—as edible as one of her cookies. "I can't have my mutt getting all the love. You're going to make me jealous."

Immediately, he regretted the words—coming so close after Joey's call. To divert her, he nuzzled the curve between her neck and shoulder and nipped her lightly.

Her squirm made his cock stand at attention. *Reporting for duty, yes, ma'am.*

"What's going on, Ben?" She turned, her hands bracketing his face as she stared into his eyes. "You're different today."

All right. She'd chosen the time and place, although he'd really have preferred to do this when he was buried deep inside her. "I've been thinking. About us. I want to move things up a notch." He grinned. "Let's go to a .44 magnum."

Her head jerked back slightly, and her brows rose.

He traced a finger over the arch of one elegantly curved eyebrow, so different from his bushy straight lines.

With an exasperated huff, she pulled his hand down and frowned at him. "A .44 magnum. You want us to be exclusive."

"Yeah."

"I take slaves, Benjamin. Not lovers."

Why did he see worry and the beginning of grief in her eyes? She started to push back.

His grip clamped on her ass. "I think you care for me, and I very much care for you. So yes, a .44. You're not seeing anyone else, and neither am I. That's exclusive. And I'll be your slave."

"You want to be my slave?" Anne studied his face as if it would reveal the future rather than just his desire. "I'm not sure that would be wise. What does being a slave mean to you?"

"Means I do what you say, try to please you—in bed and out."

"Guard dog," she said softly. "I'm a strict Mistress. Not an easy one. I prefer high protocol—no touching or speaking or sitting without permission. I'll give you chores, ask you to take on duties you might not appreciate."

"I've seen you with your slaves."

She shook her head. "Are you sure, Ben? You're new to the lifestyle. I think you're rushing things."

That phone call said there was a need for hurry.

The thought of losing her was intolerable. What would he do, how much of himself would he sacrifice to keep her by his side? To hear her laughter, to feel her hands on his face, to wake with her in his arms. "I'm sure. I'm not rushing things."

She frowned. "There's a difference between a submissive and a slave. I think the best explanation is that a submissive resembles an employee, whereas a slave is closer to a private in the Marines. A lot of choices are taken away."

He'd been in the service; nothing new there.

"I don't live with my slaves—but they're available to me when I want them."

*They?* Now that was a hard line for him, and this was the time to make that clear. "I want exclusive."

When she nodded, he went further. "My work is separate. And you don't get control over the time that we're not together." He pulled in a lungful of air and committed himself. "Everything else is yours. Yes, Ma'am, this is what I want."

He could see the growing warmth in her eyes, could feel her respect and pleasure. Her chin came up, shoulders straightening as she accepted responsibility for *him*. He knew the feeling—the same one he'd had when a teammate trusted him to take his back.

Knowing he could give her that joy silenced the doubts in his mind.

Anne lay in her bed, her head on his shoulder, her hand on his chest, stroking the crisp hair. His breathing had slowed as sleep caught up to him. His scent mingled with the musky fragrance of sex and the faint clean fragrance of her sheets.

Contentment enfolded her as closely as his arm behind her back nestled her into his side. The sex had been…more than just sex this time. A new element had been added.

She rubbed her cheek on his shoulder. This was why people called it making love.

She'd always cherished the bond between her and her slaves, one made up of affection and concern. It was love, in a way, but the kind of love she held for family.

What she had with Ben was different. And her weapon-based ranking scale was proving to be surprisingly accurate.

She'd called a first date equivalent to a .22. She'd learned to shoot on a sweet little .22 revolver. Easy to handle. Safe with no kickback or surprises. Nicely precise. It had planted small, sedate holes in the target.

But today, this was serious stuff, moving toward…love, and truly felt like firing an S&W .44 in a darkened shooting range. *"I think you care for me, and I very much care for you. So yes, a .44. You're not seeing anyone else, and neither am I. That's exclusive. And I'll be your slave."* The blast of his words had left her ears ringing, eyes blinking against the flame from the muzzle. The shell had ripped appalling holes in what her life had been.

Was she ready for this?

*No.* No, she really wasn't.

But right here in his arms was where she'd ended up, even though she'd fought every step of the way. *Sneaky submissive.* But she wouldn't change a thing about the journey.

Or about Ben.

She hadn't wanted another slave yet, and he sure wasn't the one she would have chosen, and she certainly hadn't planned on letting one be her lover, as well.

Then Ben had maneuvered his way into her life, making changes right and left. He'd brought her Bronx—a furbaby to play with and treat and hug. Every night, Ben had been at her house or her at his. He filled her evenings with laughter and conversation and quiet companionship. Sleeping with him and waking with him had created an intimacy that she hadn't permitted in years.

Maybe because she trusted him more than she'd trusted her slaves. He might not agree with her on everything, but the man's rock-solid character was based on honor, honesty, and loyalty.

She admired him, respected him, liked everything about him, from his body to his easygoing stability.

And the thought of losing him, now that he had hold of her emotions, was terrifying.

Ever since she was a little girl, she'd known…*known*…what it felt like when someone or something tore her love out by the roots. That might be why her few attempts at taking lovers in the service and college hadn't gotten very far. All unknowing, she'd avoided risking that kind of pain.

But now, she would. For Ben.

She curled a little closer, drawing in his scent, hearing his heart's slow thudding. *Please don't let this go wrong.* Please.

# Chapter Fourteen

Anne leaned back in her office chair and studied the computer display. The wind riffled the curtains, carrying the scent of the beach and the pattering of heavy rain. Although near noon, the sky was almost as dark as nighttime. What an excellent day to be inside.

Even better, the weather had been beautiful all weekend for their sail. They'd spent the time picnicking in quiet coves, swimming under the stars, making love…everywhere. And she'd managed to teach Ben more about being a slave, about her requirements, about protocol. By the time they returned to the Shadowlands in a couple of weeks, he'd be comfortable in his role.

He probably wasn't very comfortable today. *Poor Ben.*

Hours before, at dawn, he'd rolled over, seen the incoming storm, and jumped out of bed. Within half-an-hour, he'd headed off to Sawgrass Park.

*BL Haugen.* She'd been both mesmerized and appalled by his Chaos of War series. Now that she knew the photographs hadn't been taken by a photojournalist, but rather by someone truly living the nightmare, she doubted she could view them without crying.

Her photo excursion with him two weeks before had been eye opening. She'd always admired how beautifully BL Haugen used light to evoke emotion. Her favorite photograph of his was of a panther, poised to spring. Behind the cat, black, ominous thunderclouds were piling high into the sky. The scene captured the eternal yet fleeting moment before violence and death.

Last Sunday had shown her how much time, effort, and discarded shots went into achieving one perfect photograph. And the poor guy was out today in the pouring rain.

Well, she'd needed quiet to work on Uzuri's problem.

Sometime later, she heard the carport door open.

"Anne, it's me," Ben called. "Your mom is with me."

Her fingers hesitated over the keyboard. But she had a search running and couldn't shut it down. "Upstairs. I'm in my office."

A door closed. Footsteps thudded on the stairs.

Her mother walked in, carrying a covered bread pan. Ben followed.

Anne sniffed. "Is that banana bread I smell?" The best part of living two houses away from her parents was getting some motherly pampering.

"My daughter always did have a good nose." In pale peach shorts and a matching lacey top, Anne's fine-boned, petite mom smiled up at Ben, looking like a fairy princess next to the big bad wolf.

A couple of days before, she'd dropped by to have Anne set up her new smart phone and had spoken with Ben. Naturally, the guard dog had won her right over. Props to her mother, she'd seen past Ben's intimidating appearance right to his heart. Finding out he was BL Haugen had cemented her approval. Maybe Mom couldn't defend herself against a flea, but she was a superb judge of character. Schoolteachers usually were.

Later, she'd told Anne, "Finally you've found someone who will look after you instead of the reverse."

Anne was still thinking that one over. She'd always felt as if she was the one who needed to protect her slaves, but, of course, her mother had been expecting the guys to guard her daughter. Perhaps that was why Joey, despite his charm and enthusiastic service, hadn't made headway with any of her family. Ben certainly had, at least with her brothers and mother.

Her father would be a different story. Since he still considered her his baby girl—and undoubtedly a virgin—she'd been grateful he and Ben hadn't met during the training exercise.

Spinning her office chair all the way around, she began to smile at Ben—and stared instead.

His pulled-back hair was drenched. Grass stains and mud streaked his clothes and face; his ripped T-shirt showed a long, bloody scrape on the tanned skin beneath.

He'd been hurt.

She started to rise, and then slowly sat again. It wasn't a bad scrape. She just didn't like seeing him in pain or bloody—which seemed funny since she'd dealt out worse injuries to her slaves. "Considering the way you look, I hope you got something worth the work."

His smile was that of a wolf that had downed a plump deer. "Got one that should be perfect for my storm series." His stunning new series was centered on lightning storms.

Anne's mother glanced out the window. "Having been used to the nice, quiet drizzling rains in Washington State, these Florida storms were quite a shock. I swear, sometimes they sound as if Zeus is battling it out in heaven."

"Zeus?" Ben scratched at a streak of mud on his face. "*The War of Zeus.* You might have found a title for my series, Elaine."

"Well. My goodness." Anne's mother almost glowed. "I'm truly honored. Now you'd better take a shower and get out of those wet clothes." She patted his arm and bent to stroke Bronx, who'd obviously been toweled off before coming inside. "Such a sweet dog. I'm glad you've got a pet here, Anne."

Ben tilted his head toward Anne. "Considering how much you love animals, I'm surprised you don't have one of your own."

"I'm never here." Any pet of hers would be lonely when she was working.

Ben gave her a quizzical look. "That doesn't stop people from owning cats or do—"

"She was around ten when she kept a stray kitten for a couple of weeks," her mother interrupted. "Unfortunately, we left on an overseas posting, so she had to give it away. The same happened to an abandoned puppy she'd brought home. She never tried to keep another animal."

Anne's throat constricted. Sammy had been a tiny dog with big, haunted eyes. And so thin. Starving. He'd needed her, and she hadn't been allowed to save him. *"Please, Daddy. Other people take their pets."* He'd refused—perhaps correctly considering the station.

She'd hidden in her room and hadn't spoken to her father for a month after that, had hated him with all of her ten-year-old heart.

"Losing a pet is difficult." Ben's voice stayed level, as if he knew she'd react poorly to open sympathy. "Since your dad was career military, you must have had quite a few moves."

"Oh, we did," her mother said softly. "Oddly enough, I loved relocating; I could teach music anywhere. Sociable Travis thrived. Harrison—well, not much bothers Harrison." Her eyes sad, her mother set a hand on Anne's arm. "But Anne didn't take well to being shifted, and her unhappiness grew worse with each move."

"Yeah?"

Anne felt Ben's gaze, but she looked away. She hadn't forgotten the frustration and anger. The desolation. How she'd screamed and wept and clung to Nessie, her best friend in kindergarten. Her father had finally torn them apart and put Anne in the car. She'd cried herself sick.

And she'd experienced the same devastating sense of loss two years later.

She'd learned. Friends, pets, even favorite belongings were all…transient. *Don't get attached.*

By the third move, she'd stopped crying. Had stopped making best friends. Her mother had tried to help, but Anne had known that no one really understood. Within her loving family, she'd grown closer to her brothers…and felt very alone.

"I didn't realize it then, but I think girls have a more difficult time being displaced," her mother said. "Our friendships are…deeper. Not so easily formed."

*Being the new kid over and over. Watching a popular classmate hand out birthday party invitations to almost the entire class. The girl had wrinkled her nose at Anne, as if she smelled something foul.*

"And even on a base, girls can be cruel to a stranger," her mother finished. She set her hand on Anne's shoulder.

*Being knocked to her knees, her favorite dress torn. Girls could be mean—with no cause other than spotting a small, shy newcomer.*

*One more reason she'd learned to fight.*

"It wasn't that bad." Anne squeezed her mother's hand reassuringly. Mom wouldn't willingly hurt anyone; no one was more caring. But even with love, understanding didn't automatically follow.

A rumble of thunder drew her gaze to the shining streaks of rain slanting downward. Even in darkness, there was beauty.

Ben knew that. Showed that in his pictures. Anne shouldn't forget and perhaps should try to see the positive aspects of her early years. "I had my family," she said finally. "Good schools." Her mind cast about. "Enough to eat."

"That's the best you can say about your childhood? That you got enough to eat? Fu-" He cut off the curse with a glance at her mother.

Moisture gleamed in her mother's eyes. "I'm sorry, Anne."

*Way to put your foot in it, Anne.* "Oh, Mom, there wasn't anything you could have done. Moving is a part of life for military families. I survived—and grew stronger because of it. And because you gave me a beach house, I'm very settled now."

After blinking back tears, her mother finally gave her a wry smile. "You're settled all right. So settled that you smacked Travis for moving one of your chairs." She glanced at Ben. "She doesn't like things changed, so be warned."

He was still regarding her with a deep crease between his heavy brows.

Anne rolled her eyes at him and watched a smile appear in his brown eyes. "Why don't you go cut a few slices of that bread, Mom? As soon as this search is done, I'll be down."

Her mother looked relieved at the change of subject. "Why are you working here and not at the bail company? You said you tried not to bring casework home."

"This is personal. You remember Uzuri? She was over here with a group of women—gave you that department store discount card?"

"The one with marvelous style and an adorable sense of humor?"

"That's her. She's been antsy, and I finally got her to admit she's worried about her ex. She moved here to get away from him. So I'm checking to ensure he's where she left him—a thousand miles away."

"Good for you." Ben's smile warmed her down to her toes.

"Russell and Matt say Anne is absolutely superb at skip tracing," her mother said proudly. "They've never seen anyone as good."

Anne shrugged. "Since I so resented changing my life, I understand how people who are forced to move will react. How they'll cling to old patterns for comfort."

Ben frowned. "Like?"

"Like even if a skip moves to a new city, he'll probably still visit Taco Bell every Friday, if that's what he did before."

"So you took your hard lessons and turned them into useful knowledge. Nice." His respect was gratifying, especially since the talk about her childhood had left her unsettled.

He leaned down and waited until she smiled permission before giving her a light kiss. A comforting kiss. "I'll fix us supper if you promise to share your mom's treat."

"You're such a sugarholic. But I'll take that deal."

As her mother turned to go, Anne frowned, realizing she'd retained some anger that her mother hadn't prevented all the moves. And the trauma. How childish was that? *Man up, Desmarais.* "I love you, Mom."

\* \* \* \*

That night, Ben had his feet up on the coffee table with his laptop in his lap, as he plotted next week's schedule of possible shoots. Across the room, his woman was preparing to go hunt fugitives.

The sound of the waves on the shore came through the open windows. Anne had her soft jazz playlist on the iPod. He was getting used to her music, although he occasionally risked her wrath to play some classical artists—like Willie Nelson or Waylon Jennings.

A so-called slave shouldn't buck his Mistress, but…favorite tunes should be shared, right?

Sharing was part of a relationship, from food to sex to music to…past histories. He'd have to give her a big FAIL there; she was fucking elusive. He'd never met a woman who talked so little about herself.

And it wasn't that she lacked confidence as a Mistress. Hell, she could give the other Masters lessons in self-assurance.

Elaine's visit earlier had shed some light on Anne's past. She'd been ripped away from friends and pets, over and over. The way she'd gone expressionless when the discussion turned to relocating told him that she'd suffered far more than her mother had realized back then.

He shook his head. He'd met some clueless Dominants, but Anne hadn't achieved the title of Shadowlands "Mistress" by lacking sensitivity. If anything, she felt too much.

What were the odds that she was fending off possible future hurt by rigidly controlling both her environment and her lovers?

By guarding her heart.

He had to take her wariness into consideration. *"Make your plans to fit the circumstances,"* Patton had said.

*Can do.* For the environment, he'd be more careful about moving things around or upsetting her routines.

He was already letting her control him. And, at least in the bedroom, he enjoyed the hell out of it.

For her heart's sake, she needed to be certain he was hers. He'd avoid anything that would make her question their longevity—because he damned well intended to be around for a long, long time.

No matter how much she guarded her tender heart, eventually she'd let him in.

# Chapter Fifteen

At the *Tomorrow Is Mine* domestic violence shelter, Anne stood in the group section of the gymnasium. Four of the teenage girls practiced hitting the sand and punching bags. The rest of the dozen had paired up to work on the block-punch technique she'd just taught them. Shouts echoed off the walls, and the acrid smell of teen sweat hung in the air.

From the corner of her eye, she saw the door open.

Beth entered, followed by her Master, Nolan. As always, the discrepancy between them was startling. Nolan was over six feet, and construction work had given him an impressively muscular build. With coal-colored hair and eyes, a scarred face, and a rough expression, his looks ensured people would avoid him.

In contrast, his submissive was short and slender, fair-skinned, red-haired, and soft-voiced.

And she had a very big heart.

Tomorrow Is Mine would have closed if Beth hadn't stepped in with a huge donation. Her abusive ex's death had provided Beth with the money to fund battered women's shelters in Florida and her home state of California.

After that, she'd persuaded several Shadowlands' members—including Anne—to help with the shelter's programs.

Anne crossed the room. "It's good to see you two. Did you come to help teach?"

Nolan shook his head, silent, as usual.

"Can we talk when you're finished here?" Beth asked. Her unreadable face was worrisome. Beth usually showed all her emotions.

"Of course." Anne checked her watch. "The girls have another five minutes. Will that work for you?"

"Sure," Beth said.

"All right then." Anne returned to her class and stopped at the head-high sandbag, hanging from the ceiling rafter. "That kick was excellent, Petra. Can you feel the difference when your power comes from your core?"

The thirteen-year-old girl nodded, her mouth in a line of determination. The canvas-filled bag was taller, wider, and far more threatening than the slim teen—but a dent still showed where her foot had hit. Perfect.

Anne moved to the next girl who was working through block-punch moves with another girl.

Gina was seventeen, pretty, five-ten, and built like an Amazon. She frowned at Anne.

"What's wrong, Gina?"

"No matter what I do, a guy would just flatten me. This is, totally, a waste of time."

*Hmm.* "If you think that, you will definitely lose." Perhaps the staff needed to show more empowered female movies—including some with women fighters. In fighting, the mental attitude was just as important as skill.

Nolan's rough laugh drew the attention of the girls. He and Beth had moved close enough to hear Gina's comment. Two of the newer teens backed away from him, but the rest continued practicing, having seen the big contractor working on the buildings.

Annoyed at the interruption, Anne set her hands on her hips. "Something funny, Nolan?"

"These girls ever seen you fight?"

Anne frowned. Actually, they hadn't. She demonstrated techniques, but actual fighting? *No.* And she caught Nolan's point. The girls needed the bone-deep belief that a woman *could* effectively use her fists and defend herself.

"Do you think it would help if Anne and I sparred?" Beth asked.

Nolan smiled down at his submissive. "Sugar, you've come a long way, but she'd flatten you." His black gaze hit Anne. "Fight *me.*"

Gasps and whispered protests ran around the room, warming Anne's heart. Her students cared about her.

Although it was pretty insulting the way they assumed she'd lose.

"You're on. Let's go for medium impact." After handing Gina her watch, Anne led the way to the area covered with thick floor mats and sank into a ready stance.

Nolan stripped off his belt and wedding ring, removed his boots and socks. Face impassive, he attacked immediately. A right toward her face—slightly wide—testing her readiness. She slapped it aside and followed with a solar plexus punch with just enough power to make a point.

She ducked under his return backhand, thumped his ribs, and continued turning, using the momentum as a foot sweep.

He rolled to his feet and pressed her ruthlessly this time with a one-two-three punch flurry that she blocked as she stepped forward. One of the girls gasped.

Inside his guard, she shoved him back—to open his stance—and set her knee against his balls gently.

He froze and let out a laugh. His muttered, "Mistress," was for her ears only.

She smiled and lifted her voice. "What happens when my knee hits your balls?"

He played along and groaned, hands covering his crotch. She gripped his thick hair and yanked his head down far enough to show how easily his face could meet her knee.

Turning toward her class, she said, "If you can, always just get away. If you have to fight and you get a man down, then it's smart to incapacitate him, giving yourself time to escape. Have you watched movies where the woman drops the bad guy—but he tackles her before she reaches the door?"

Hands lifted everywhere.

"Exactly. Deliver that extra kick so he stays put." Feeling Nolan move, she spun in time to block his left, then used the block-punch movement she'd just taught them. Her fist hit his gut solidly enough she heard his grunt.

She ducked his follow-up, punched back, and delivered a carefully pulled strike toward his throat.

To her surprise, he hammed it up—so not Nolan—and fell, hands to his throat.

She mimed a kick to his knee. "Knees are wonderful targets. Now, I know he won't get up any time soon."

Two girls were cheering; the rest were silent. Anne checked them. Some were a bit pale. Most had intent expressions as they absorbed the lesson.

With a faint smile, Nolan propped himself up on an elbow. "Have you let them see how hard you can punch?"

Again, she hadn't.

After a second, she realized she'd worried that the munchkins had already witnessed too much violence. But, he was right. They needed to know that women could hand it out as well as take it.

She leaned over, offered Nolan a hand, and yanked him to his feet. At the sandbag, she delivered a few light taps to gauge the distance, then worked through solid one-two punches before moving on to snap and roundhouse combinations that would destroy a man's knee before breaking his neck. She finished with a powerhouse back-kick that would have wrapped the poor bastard's liver around his fractured spine.

As she turned, all the girls were whistling and shouting.

*Well. Good enough.* Her gaze met Gina's.

With tears in her eyes, the girl gave Anne a firm nod. She was in.

"All right then. Class dismissed."

Anne followed Beth and Nolan into the inner courtyard. Encircled by buildings containing dorms, the dining hall, laundry, classrooms, and meeting rooms, the grassy center held a playground and scattered picnic tables.

Beth and Nolan chose a corner table.

"What's up?" Anne sat down across from them.

"It's Gretel." Beth pushed her hair back and leaned against Nolan. "Her husband located her yesterday."

Hell. *Hell.* Fury rose so fast Anne felt her control waver. After suffering years of abuse, Gretel'd walked out when her husband destroyed the *Happy 50th Birthday, Mom* cake her daughter had baked.

Having her children and grandchildren in Tampa, she'd stubbornly refused to relocate, hoping a restraining order would deter her husband. She'd stayed at the shelter a month—and the children had pined when the kindhearted grandmother moved to her new place.

With an effort, Anne shoved her anger down. "Is she all right?"

"She'll be fine," Nolan said. "The bastard was drunk."

"He spotted her in a mall parking lot and attacked. She was caught by surprise," Beth said.

"He nailed her in the face. Knocked her down. Busted a couple of ribs. Even on her back, she kept her wits and kicked at his legs." Nolan gave a nod of respect. "He stepped back, and she hosed him down with the pepper spray attached to her key ring."

"The police arrested him," Beth added.

Anne frowned as she realized her friend was shivering. "Beth—"

Nolan was already wrapping an arm around his submissive, pulling her in close. "Anne, Gretel said to tell you that, thanks to your lessons, she survived."

"He's in jail now." Beth's voice sounded strained. "How long will he stay there? Guys like that don't stop." As her gaze dropped to her hands, her shoulders hunched as if to protect herself. Anne could see she was fleeing inward to memories of her own abuse. To the scars she still carried.

"Beth," Nolan growled.

*God, Beth.* Anne's eyes prickled with tears as she reached across the table and took Beth's trembling hand. *Fucking men.* "I swear, Nolan, I like you, and still, there are days I want to go out and geld every male in every town in all the world."

Buried and suffocating in brutal memories, Beth heard Nolan, but it was Anne's voice—icy cold, yet filled with rage—that sliced through her fears and ignited a fire to burn away the past.

Hauling in a deep breath, Beth leaned into her Master, who'd proven over and over that he could be trusted. Her gaze met Anne's furious eyes, and she offered, "I have pruning shears. And branch loppers as well."

Nolan snorted a laugh. "That's my girl." Relief as well as pride roughened his deep voice.

"I'm okay," Beth said to both of them, heartened by their concern.

"You're far more than that." Anne squeezed Beth's hand, a fierce look on her face. The Domme was fully as protective as Nolan. If anyone threatened a woman here, her friend would fight shoulder-to-shoulder with the Masters.

And Beth would darn well join them, even if she were shaking in her sneakers.

The opening of the door to the admissions building drew her attention, and she watched as a shelter advocate stepped out, followed by a woman in her thirties.

"This is the commons area," the advocate said, waving at the grassy yard.

The new woman was limping, exhaustion and pain evident with every step. Her face was black and blue; her neck and arms displayed small, round scars.

Deliberate cigarette burns. Beth knew, all too well, how that felt.

Two boys, about six years and four years, followed the women.

As the advocate moved toward the center of the courtyard, the youngest boy stopped and sat down with his back against the wall.

Beth frowned. The mother—if that's what she was—never looked around to check on her sons. The advocate was fairly new, so might be forgiven, but someone should watch the children. How could a mother not notice her littlest wasn't right there?

The older boy saw his brother and abandoned the tour as well.

Poor babies. Beth shook her head. At least she hadn't suffered abuse until she was an adult. How horrible to discover violence so, so young.

On the same wavelength, Anne started to rise.

"I'll take care of them." Beth grinned at her. "I've learned to carry bribes." Using Nolan's knee as leverage, she pushed to her feet. Slowly, she walked toward the children.

They were so little. Faded shorts and ripped shirts revealed toothpick-thin arms and legs. Their hair was dirty and tangled. And bruises marked cheeks and jaws, arms and legs.

With Beth's approach, they hunched as if trying to disappear into the wall like mini-turtles.

"Hey." Stopping at a non-threatening distance, Beth sat on the grass. Cross-legged. *See, I can't quickly chase after you if you need to escape.* "I'm Beth. You guys look thirsty. Want some apple juice?"

Without waiting for an answer, she pulled two small bottles out of her bag. After tugging off the insulated sleeves, she opened the tops. The containers were still nice and cold, although the ice was gone. She offered one bottle.

After a long hesitation, the oldest took it. Watching her warily, he took a sip...and his face lit up.

"It's good," he whispered to his brother who carefully, like a terrified puppy, accepted the other bottle. They both drank thirstily. Every few seconds, their big brown eyes would turn to check on their mother.

"Should I try to guess your names?" Beth asked, smiling slightly. "Maybe John? Or Adam?"

"Uh-uh," the youngest said.

"Oh dear. Um, Greg? Horace? David? William?" Each name got shakes of the head—and less tensed muscles.

"I'm bad at guessing names," she admitted, scrunching her face up. "Peter Pan? Clark Kent? Ironman?"

Giggling, the littlest couldn't hold back any longer. "He's Grant. I'm Connor."

"Oooh, those are nice names." The boys were adorable. An ache tugged at her heart. Thanks to the damage she'd suffered during her marriage, she'd never carry a baby...and, oh God, she really wanted children. "Grant and Connor, it's nice to meet you."

"Sugar." Nolan's Texas-accented voice came from behind her—although she'd known he was approaching from the way the children had molded themselves to the wall. "We need to get going."

She glanced at her watch and winced. "Right." As the boys watched Nolan with ill-concealed terror, she leaned forward and whispered, "He's my Ironman. He saved me from the bad guy, and now he keeps me safe, and he won't let anyone hurt me. That's what heroes do, you know?"

Their eyes got wider. Some—not all—of their fear disappeared to be replaced with awe.

"I'll see you guys next time I'm here," Beth promised and let Nolan lift her to her feet. "Nolan, this is Grant and Connor."

Nolan nodded gravely. "Men. Good to meet you."

As Beth walked through the door, she heard Grant whisper in wonder, "He called us *men*."

# Chapter Sixteen

Carrying a small basket, Ben opened the front door. As Bronx led the way into the house, Ben grinned, his spirits soaring. Anne's Escape was parked in the low carport, so she was home. The past couple of weeks—since their relationship had upgraded to .44 magnum level—had been a revelation. He'd never known that a woman could fill a man's life so completely.

Make him so happy.

They were good together. He knew it. Cooking, lifting weights, sparring and wrestling, jogging on the beach, watching the news—even if he was relegated to the floor sometimes—reading quietly. Everything was more fun with her beside him.

Even the slavery shit was mostly cool. Anne was slowly teaching him what she required from him and he was improving—although she rather disapproved that his massages inevitably led to a hearty round of fucking. He'd tried to explain that when she went all Mistress on his ass, he got turned the hell on. Not his fault she was so damned sexy, right?

And not having to scramble for condoms meant they could fuck anywhere. And did.

As Ben followed Bronx through the kitchen, he glanced at the spotless counters. Having been through basic, he didn't have any problem with cleaning. He preferred things tidy himself, although she did have a penchant to over clean.

And he was getting pretty good at the personal care stuff now that she'd abandoned having him do her toenails or whatever the hell that procedure was called. Painting walls was a piece of cake, but with his big hands, trying to paint a toenail the size of a pea had turned into a complete clusterfuck.

He'd found out Anne could giggle like a little girl.

He grinned at the memory. Damn, she was cute sometimes.

In her Mistress role, she was taking things slow. Taking care with him. Like the way they weren't scening in the Shadowlands, although they'd both worked last weekend.

At first, he'd wondered if she were ashamed to be seen with him, but instead, she'd noticed he wasn't quite…comfortable…with being a slave in public. He felt as if he'd let her down, but seems his reaction wasn't unusual. She said she was happy keeping things private, for now.

Her concern for his feelings and health kept surprising him. Hey, he was supposed to be doing everything for her.

So, to have her change plans because he was a sensitive pussy was…fucking amazing.

Besides, he liked the bubble they'd created—one with just the two of them inside. Especially since gossip about the Mistress and security guard was undoubtedly running rampant through the small-town-like Shadowlands community. Hell, after the vets' group meeting last week, Z had told Ben to call if he had questions or wanted to talk.

*Questions? Sure. Want to talk? Nope.*

Tail wagging frantically, Bronx impatiently waited as Ben slid the back screen door open.

There she was. Amazing how the sight of one special person really *could* make a man's heart skip a beat.

Sitting on the decking, Anne was facing the railing. Thick, dark brown rope dangled from the top rail. The strands held knots here and there and terminated in coils in her lap. Red wooden beads were piled off to one side.

She turned at the sound of Bronx's charge across the deck and spotted Ben. "You're home!"

He fucking loved the way her eyes lit.

She pushed the rope out of her lap to hug Bronx. "You guys got done early."

After Bronx had curled up next to her, Ben set the basket beside her, went down on one knee, and patiently waited for her to indicate she wanted a kiss. She always wanted a kiss—he knew that—but he tried to be an obedient slave.

Pissed him off sometimes when he wanted to scoop her up for a long hug.

Her brows drew together and rather than giving him permission, she touched his face with her fingertips. When her fingers lingered on his forehead, he realized he was frowning.

"Benjamin. I get the impression that"—she was speaking as carefully as he might navigate a Baghdad street, uncertain what trash-filled pile might contain explosives—"perhaps, serving as a slave isn't what you really want. This might not be a good—"

"No." He interrupted before she could finish. "No, Mistress, I'm where I belong." In her home, at her side, in her heart. Maybe parts of the service chaffed like wearing an undersized jockstrap, but being with her was fucking more than he'd ever imagined.

The emerging sorrow in her eyes could break his heart. "I've had slaves, my tiger. I think you're uncomfortable."

"Some, yeah." He took her hand to stop her. "I'm new to this, and being a slave wasn't how I saw myself. But this is where I want to be."

She looked down at his fingers that had swallowed hers. Dammit, if he let her think, she'd talk herself into letting him go.

While her keen gaze wasn't on his face, he pushed with all the determination that years of missions could generate. "I'm *happy* as your slave. This is what I want."

When she put her other hand on top of his and looked up, he knew she'd accepted what he said. Mostly. A tiny furrow still creased her brow. "I'm not sure, tiger. True slaves are driven to both relinquish control and to serve. It's a need and a joy for them—and painful when they can't. But, with you, I don't see—"

"I've been having flashbacks," he interrupted quickly. Who knew that a history of PTSD would come in handy? But it made a hell of an excuse. "They've left me on edge. That's what you're seeing."

"Oh, no." She released his hand and took his face between her palms. "You're supposed to tell me these things. How else can I help?"

"Yes, Ma'am," he said softly. Thank fuck, she'd bought it.

As he eased down to sit beside her, he flattened his guilt under a heavy boot. Yeah, he was struggling, but that was his problem. He'd get his act together, and this would all work out fine. No need for her to stress about his struggles or cut the ties and set him free for his own fucking good. That's how she'd see it. She looked after him better than he did himself.

As her lips met his and she leaned into him, he reveled in the feeling of being cherished.

Coming home to her was…was what every soldier in the world dreamed about. All those long, lonely nights overseas had taught him to treasure these moments. Yeah, this was what it was all about.

Soft lips, caring heart. He sighed when she pulled back.

She lifted the basket next to her and looked into it. "Caramels?"

"Happy May Day, Anne—Mistress."

She looked surprised, then delighted. "What a perfect choice. For the last few days, I've had caramel cravings." After tearing the wrapper off, she popped one in her mouth.

Her low hum of delight made him hard. Hell, everything about her made him hard...which meant he spent a lot of time semi-aroused.

Couldn't be healthy.

Then again, he'd never had so much sex in his life, so maybe everything balanced out.

When she picked up another candy, he glanced at the railing. "What's with the rope? Are you planning some colorful kind of bondage?"

Her smoky laugh reminded him of the low notes on her saxophone.

"Bondage?" She ran her hand down the knotted rope. "Only if you're into stringing up foliage. Actually, this was supposed to be a surprise for you."

Carefully, she threaded one cord through a bead and knotted three cords beneath it.

Why did that look familiar? Foliage... He grinned. "It's for hanging plants. *Macramé*?"

"Mmmhmm. You have all that open space at the warehouse and more than enough greenery. The spider plants and vines would look stunning if hung up in the high corners."

He needed a minute to move past the realization that she'd thought of him and spent a lot of time to create something just for him. Damn.

Yeah, this was where he belonged.

"Ben?"

"Sorry. Got distracted." He visualized his warehouse space. "You're right. Hanging plants will look fantastic. Thank you." And he did have a shitload of foliage. He'd picked up a few plants to study the light on the leaves and kept buying when they made his barren, stark warehouse feel more like a home and less like a barracks or desert.

Could be he'd gone overboard.

Maybe he should bring some here, if she had space. He glanced around and saw...nothing. "Why don't you have any plants?"

"I don't, do I?" She looked around blankly, as if expecting to see greenery. "I suppose I never thought about getting any."

Just as she never thought about owning a cat or dog? Yet the woman adored Bronx and spent hours working with the shelter children and babysitting Z's baby.

Apparently, even brilliant Mistresses had blind spots in their own lives.

Without waiting for fucking permission, he leaned his back against the railing, lifted her, and settled her on his lap.

"Benjamin." Her voice held a warning.

Having lost contact, Bronx rose and curled up against Anne's legs. Again.

"Anne." He ran his fingers through her hair. "It's time to let your childhood go. Time to realize you've got a huge need to care for things. People and animals. Even plants."

"I don't—"

"You were a kid. And you lost pets you loved. Were torn away from your buddies."

Hell, he could see the grief in her eyes.

"It fucked you up." He wasn't a Dom to create a scene and heal a person's soul. He could only blurt out what he thought. But aside from a blind spot or two, Anne was one of the most intelligent and rational people he knew. No matter how badly stated, she'd think about his words.

Her gaze dropped to where Bronx had settled against her calves.

"You're trying to keep from getting hurt again. I get that. Trouble is, you're not allowing anyone or anything into your life." He tightened his arms around her, wishing he could fend off any heartache to her forever. But that wasn't life. "You showed me that the proper response to the gift of life is to live it."

She was perfectly still, head bowed. Anne never bowed her head.

Fear dried his mouth, shattered what he'd planned to say.

But when the silence continued, he rubbed his cheek on the top of her head. Fuck, he knew how she felt, wanting to dodge pain…since right now, the thought of losing her was a blade to his throat.

And then he knew what else he should say—because, pain or not, he'd never regret a moment he spent with her. "People and animals and plants will leave you, but"—he pulled in a slow breath—"the joy of having them, for however long, is worth the sorrow."

Muscle by muscle, she relaxed against him. Thinking.

Thinking was good.

Eventually, she pulled in her own deep breath and looked up at him. "You're right." Her smile was rueful. "I hadn't realized how odd it was to never even consider owning a pet until Mom mentioned it last week. But to avoid plants as well? That's just warped. I guess I really am afraid of being hurt again."

"Yeah." He understood why. Under her cool front of indifference, Anne had the most caring heart in the world. Her parents couldn't have known how much she'd suffer with each loss or they'd have been more careful.

She reminded him of a glass knife. Unbelievably sharp, yet frighteningly vulnerable to being shattered. And she brought out every protective instinct he had.

But, as with his teammates, he couldn't fight her battles. She'd have to evaluate the risks and decide whether or not to advance.

He kissed her lips and felt them tremble. "Seems as if being aware is the highest hurdle. And you'd already started to change. Bronx and I are here, after all."

Hearing his name, Bronx sat up...in case someone felt the need to administer a few pats.

Anne never turned the furball away—and didn't now, even as she blinked back tears. Although she poured out her warmth to children and animals, she was more cautious with women—and damned careful with men.

But not with Ben. Not any longer. Her trust was one of the finest victories he'd ever achieved.

With an effort, he relaxed his hold. "While you play with the ropes, how about I make us some supper?"

"Actually, I have chicken marinating." She smiled and he saw the Domme slide into place. "I'll cook; you're assigned cleanup."

Not exactly a hardship. She cooked far better than he did. "Yes, Ma'am."

In the living room, he studied the white and pale blue color scheme. Seemed to him as if African violets would look just fine in here.


A couple of hours later, Anne walked out on her deck while Ben cleaned the kitchen. He pretended to hate scrubbing pots and was grumbling away. Unfortunately for him, she knew he was simply putting on a show. Really, the man had it easy. Unlike him, she washed up as she cooked.

In contrast, he could make a complete disaster out of a kitchen.

She smiled. She actually found it satisfying to create order from chaos. Cleaning up didn't bother her at all...although she'd never shared that information with her slaves.

Her fingers ran over her saxophone as the peace of the twilight washed over her. The setting sun was a brilliant yellow line on the horizon. Resembling miniature rockets, black skimmers flew just above the gilded breakers.

The tide was coming in, and the waves made shushing sounds on the sandy beach.

Lifting her sax, she wetted the reed and tested a wandering set of notes. With one hip on the railing, she let her internal playlist scroll and found herself playing "As Time Goes By." Like a soft rain, the notes spilled over her deck and joined with the evening. A slow song, but not sad. It reminded her that the fundamentals of life, living and loving and dying, held the same from generation to generation.

That life could change for the better.

She was changing, as was her world. Or maybe she should call it *growing*, rather than changing.

As the tune went into the chorus, she heard Ben say something to Bronx in the kitchen. The dog whined an answer, and Ben's big laugh rumbled out.

He was quite a guy. He'd been so careful with her this afternoon. Not pushing, but not stopping before he'd made his point.

Sometimes his internal strength was a bit disconcerting. All her slaves had wanted her in charge, wanted her to take control of everything. But Ben didn't need her guidance.

At the same time, he wouldn't fall apart if she showed any weakness, and because of that, she could relax around him.

But his obstinate need to be tough—to hide any weakness—was a problem. She should have noticed he was having flashbacks. But now she knew, and she could lead him to talk about his past. She'd pamper him up, keep him close, and ensure he got his sleep. He said he slept better at her house. With her.

He liked being with her. The realization was...amazing. Overwhelming.

She felt the same and more. He'd filled her life. Warmed it.

With a slow flourish, she ended the song and started another. One that had been growing in her heart over the past week, with the knowledge, the worry, the awe. "When I Fall in Love." The music flowed, the ache of her soul merging with the notes.

She'd wanted to run. To push him away. And she hadn't.

*Ben, I love you.*

The knowledge was terrifying and wonderful. For a little while yet, she'd savor the gift, and then she'd share.

Light washed out over the deck, and he stood there, filling the doorway as completely as he did her heart. "I was listening to you play."

His golden-brown eyes held hers as he slowly smiled. "Mistress, may this submissive haul you off to bed?"

# Chapter Seventeen

The next day, Anne let herself into Z and Jessica's private gardens and ran up the steps to the third story. She tapped on the door.

Jessica called, "It's open. Come in."

The door was unlocked?

It was. Frowning, Anne walked through the kitchen, dropped her folder on the dining room table, and entered the living room.

Z had redecorated a while back. The décor was still traditional—of course—with high ceilings, arched windows, and a bronze and etched glass chandelier. The cappuccino-colored walls, lightened with white crown molding and trim, created an inviting, intimate look. The carpeting had been replaced by a richly shaded Oriental rug over a gleaming hardwood floor.

Jessica was nursing Sophia on the suede-cushioned, dark leather couch. Gabi sat in a matching chair nearby.

"Jessica…" Anne stared down at the petite blonde. "You may live in the country, but you really should keep your doors locked."

Gabi snorted. "Same lecture I gave her. But we knew it was you. We saw you when you opened the garden gate, and Jessica unlocked the door remotely." She pointed to a small monitor standing on the end table.

Anne eyed it. "Is this new?"

"A friend of Z's from San Francisco stopped by." Jessica grimaced at the device. "Simon not only gave Z hell for the lack of security up here in the living quarters, but he also summoned one of his employees to install it. He called it a baby present."

"Phooey." Anne sank into a chair. "You just took all the fun out of my scold."

"Aww. Poor Mistress," Gabi said.

"You're lucky I only beat on males—with occasional exceptions," Anne said mildly. When the subbie didn't look worried, Anne shook her head. There was a downside to being friends with submissives.

Given the choice, she'd take friends any day.

When Jessica continued to scowl at the monitor, Anne asked, "Aren't you happy about the security?"

"Oh, I'm glad it's safer for Sophia, but all the alarms and buttons make me nervous. I have to remember to turn the alarm off before I open a door and reset it when I leave, and blah, blah, blah." Jessica rolled her eyes. "Z wanted to install one when I first moved in until I said I'd move back out if he did. But with Sophia here, he insisted."

"Of course he did." No one was more protective than Z. "I should put one into my place, actually. Being on a cul-de-sac with only family around gives an illusion of safety that isn't really valid."

"We have a system. I'm all in favor of extra security," Gabi said.

"You would be, oh, FBI person," Jessica said, then smiled down at her baby, who'd fallen asleep. "And for you, babykins, I'll put up with it." After arranging her clothing, she burped Sophia and rose, heading toward the nursery.

"Uh-uh," Anne held her arms out. "I brought over those background checks that Z wanted. The price is a baby snuggle."

With a laugh, Jessica handed her daughter over.

Anne gathered the baby close. So adorable. Below her rosebud mouth, a little milk bubble decorated her chin.

Jessica walked into the kitchen, calling back, "You know, since the background checks were Z's request, the payment should come from him."

"You're such an accountant. The last time I looked, this child was half your Master's, so I'll just hold Z's half. Would that be the left side?" Anne nuzzled Sophia's left cheek, inhaling the sweet infant scent.

"You should be a lawyer." Jessica returned with a sparkling water, which she set at Anne's elbow before dropping onto the couch.

"You're looking good, Mommy," Gabi said. "Not nearly as tired as a few weeks ago."

"That diapered mini-Domme there is sleeping longer at a time. Finally." Jessica frowned. "I'm back to normal, but Z can't seem to see that."

"What's he not letting you do?" Gabi asked.

"Letting isn't the issue. It's what he's not...um, doing." Jessica flushed.

Gabi looked confused, but Jessica's reddened cheeks told Anne what Z wasn't...doing. "Isn't it a little early to start having sex?"

"Ooooh, *sex*," Gabi said, enlightened.

"Well, the midwife said the date when we could resume 'marital relations' is variable. Basically, I have to wait at least four weeks, *and* until I feel ready *and* until the spotting stops. That's all good. But the OB doctor"—Jessica rolled her eyes—"said six weeks *period*, and it's only a little over five. Of course, Z's listening to the dude with the big credentials."

"Hey, he'd go the conservative route. He's crazy protective about you, even if it means he goes without," Gabi said. "I'm impressed. Who ever heard of a guy turning down sex, especially since it's probably been a while?"

"More than a while." Jessica crossed her arms over her chest and pouted. "I miss sex. I miss being held. And I miss the Dominant/submissive stuff too. He's depriving me of *everything*."

Z *was* very protective of his submissive, and a few more days of abstinence shouldn't matter that much. "It's just another week," Anne said gently. "Then you can have it all back."

"I guess. Maybe." Jessica shook her head. "But I'm getting so mad at him that by the time the week is over, I might tell him to go fuck himself."

Rocking Sophia, Anne regarded her friend more closely. Not at ease. Muscles tight, mouth compressed, lips trembling at the same time her fists were clenched. Someone's emotions were all over the map.

"Ouch. Hormonal much, girlfriend?" Gabi switched seats to sit beside Jessica and wrap an arm around her shoulders.

Jessica's eyes filled. "I really am. But I need him. And the intimacy. It's more than sex between us and...I need it."

"But he's worried he might hurt you." Anne pursed her lips, considering. She thought of her feelings when she and Ben made love—because love was what it felt like these days. If he ever refused her, whether for her own good or not, she'd feel horribly rejected.

To have two differing medical opinions was maddening; however, the midwife's criteria seemed more sensible than some arbitrary number set in stone.

Maybe she could tell Z that Jessica was especially vulnerable right now? "Let me talk with him and—"

"No!" Jessica shook her head vehemently. "If he fucks me because you tell him to, then that's like...like making love to me is a medicine he has to take. A chore."

Anne huffed a laugh. "Somehow, I doubt he'd see it that way."

"But I would." Jessica's shoulders slumped. "He must just not want me enough. I won't have you telling him he has to make love to me."

Oh, this was not good at all. Friends could never convince a woman that her husband still found her appealing.

"Anne, you're the pro at getting guys to do what you want them to do. Maybe if you give Jessica some advice?" Gabi asked, her arm around Jessica. "Seduction 101?"

Manipulating Z. For his own good. Considering how often he butted into all the members' affairs—for their own good—the idea was fairly irresistible. Her lips curved up. "He'll be home for supper soon?"

Jessica nodded.

"And Sophia will sleep for a couple of hours? Or at least, not need any food for a while?"

Another nod. Jessica's eyes brightened.

"Since I don't start work until later this evening, I can babysit the imp." As if that would be a hardship. "We'll rock and read in one of the second floor rooms."

"You'll get bored," Jessica protested.

"I always have a book in my bag. Just give me the diaper bag, and you'll have two baby-free hours."

"That'd be great," Jessica said. Then her face clouded. "But he still won't—"

"Now this is what I think you should do… Consider it a win-win, since even if he doesn't cooperate, you'll get off."

\* \* \* \*

"Jessica?" Zachary called quietly, not wanting to wake the baby—or his wife—if they were sleeping.

He tossed his cell phone on a folder on the dining room table and went in search.

The living room was empty.

Zachary pushed open the door to the master bedroom and heard soft music. The curtains were drawn, and the only light came from the scented candles around the room.

Jessica stood at the foot of the bed, wearing a black waist cincher with garters, dark fishnet stockings, heels…and nothing else.

All the blood in his body surged into his cock.

Her shining blonde hair, even longer than when he'd first met her, tumbled over her bare shoulders and down her back, begging for a man's hand. *His* hand.

She glanced over her shoulder at him. "Oh. Hey."

Her waist flared into her beautifully full hips, setting her round, white ass on display. His fingers curved, already feeling the smooth skin against his palm. He had to clear his throat before he could speak. "There's a week yet to go."

She sniffed. "That's according to the male doctor who doesn't have any children. Because he doesn't have any girl parts. My midwife, who I talked to today, has cleared me for sex since I'm no longer spotting."

"Indeed." Anticipation revved Zachary's pulse even as he kept his tone even. He had in his possession two differing medical opinions. Both sources—MD and midwife—were respected authorities. Much as he wanted his wife, he wouldn't risk hurting her.

She'd been hurt enough. His memories of her labor were far too clear, and, no matter how unreasonable, he felt as guilty as if he'd caused the appalling pain. Odd how he could watch a sadist work over a masochist without a worry, but to see his wife—his submissive—hurting so badly that she'd screamed had shaken him to the bone. He shook his head at the memory.

"I see," she snapped. "Well, no problem, *Master.* Since you won't let me play with your cock, I found one of my own."

From the bed, she picked up a...dildo. And a vibrator.

"Jessica." His voice came out a growl.

"Don't worry; I checked," she said. "When I called Fay, she said I could keep myself as happy as I wanted." Holding his gaze, she flipped the vibrator on, held it against her clit, and...moaned.

At his sudden rise of lust, the entire bedroom blurred out of existence for a second.

Damned if he—

His phone rang from the dining room.

Jessica waved a hand at him. "Go. I don't need you."

Even though he knew her words were based in her own anger, they still hurt. He hesitated, considered ignoring the phone call. He couldn't. "I have a patient being admitted to the hospital, pet. I have to hand him off properly and give a report. I'll be back in a few minutes."

She snapped *"fine"* in a tone that meant it was anything but fine.

His body shouted a protest as he left the room.

It only took two minutes to give the admitting physician a rundown.

Calling the obstetrician and pinning him down took more time.

But, when Zachary told him that Jessica was no longer spotting and that the midwife had okayed intercourse, the doctor gave his go-ahead as well.

"Excellent. Thank you." As Zachary turned the phone off, he had to reach down and adjust his straining cock. It'd probably been a couple of decades since he'd gone for more than a week without sex. He missed touching and holding. Missed the way Jessica would yield under his hands. The way sex with her was an affirmation of joy. Of love.

He glanced at the baby monitor as he entered the bedroom. No noise from there; Sophia must be asleep.

And the only sound in the room was the vibrator humming away.

His stubborn little wife hadn't been bluffing. Eyes closed, she had her hands on her pussy as she lay on the bed with her legs spread. The dildo rested on her stomach. Her fingers were slick as she played with herself, applying the vibrator at intervals to make herself last.

He watched for a minute. He'd never seen anything as purely seductive as his wife making love to herself. He'd loved her round body before she was pregnant. When she was pregnant. And now as well. If anything, his desire for her had only grown.

"Jessica."

Her eyes popped open.

"I called the doctor. He—"

"He can go to hell." Her face was turning the clear red of an infuriated blonde.

"Kitten, the doctor said—"

"I don't give a damn. I don't give a damn about anything *you* say either, you-you asshole Dom." She picked up the dildo and threw it violently. At him.

The toy stung his palm as he caught it.

"Now shove it up your ass," she hissed like the kitten he called her.

As he walked over to the bed, he could feel her anger beating at him. And then it was washed away by her sense of loss…her feeling that she'd gone too far with her words and actions. That she'd destroyed what they had. That she'd lost him.

Losing him would never happen.

Her belief that mere words could break them apart showed his failure as a Dom. "That's enough, kitten."

She sat up on the bed and glared at him.

Her hair was loose and made a convenient leash when wrapped around his hand. He used it to tilt her head back so he could take her mouth and silence further insults.

After a second of struggle, she…surrendered. So completely that he felt his chest squeeze with the sweet ache. Her lips were warm and soft and giving.

Still gripping her hair, he lifted her hands, one by one, to suck on the fingers, taking in the tantalizing musky taste.

As he kissed her again, her arms came around his neck, and he could feel her other emotions disappear under a growing urgency.

The bullet vibrator still buzzed away beside her, he realized. And it would be a shame to waste available resources. So, before he did anything else, he'd remove the sexual frustration that had caused her emotional storm—and also take the opportunity to remind her that her orgasms came at his discretion.

When he placed the vibrator in her palm, despair filled her eyes…until his hand covered hers and moved the toy to her pussy.

When the vibrations struck her clit, her body tensed.

*Very nice.* Taking his time, holding her in place by her hair, he kissed her, even as he controlled her hand, directing the bullet to one side of her clit, then the other.

As she started to pant, her hips rose to meet the stimulus.

"I love you, Jessica," he murmured.

"I love y—"

He moved her hand to set the vibrator on the very top of her clit and…pressed down.

Her neck arched. "Aaaaah."

Although he'd never forgotten how stunning she was when she came, each time still stopped his heart.


As her pulse slowed, Jessica opened her eyes…and met Z's gray ones.

He'd released her hair. He wasn't smiling. And he was studying her in a way that sent her pulse skyrocketing again.

She swallowed. "What?"

"What, indeed." His voice was low. Ominous. Sorrowful. "As I recall, you threw a dildo at me." His lips quirked. "You called me names without having the excuse of being in labor."

Still fully dressed, he sat on the edge of the bed. "In addition, you tried to manipulate me into doing what you wanted, rather than what I thought was right."

Uh-oh. Anne had warned her about his probable reaction. *"Very few men can resist seeing a woman taking pleasure into her own hands. The difference here is that, once Z is thinking, he'll completely understand that you were topping from the bottom. You might not like what follows."*

She might have been all right if she'd done what Anne had suggested. The trouble was, she'd gone further. Had snarked at him. Then lost her temper and yelled at him. And thrown a toy at him.

Unable to meet his eyes, she dropped her gaze.

She'd tried to push him into having sex—and she knew full well he didn't want to. Might never want to again. Who would, after all? Tears filled her eyes. She was such a cow and—

"What in the world are you thinking?" With a hand on her chest, he pushed her onto her back. When she fought to sit back up, he bracketed her wrists with his right hand and pinned her arms above her head.

"Stop it!" She struggled. "Don't. I don't want to—"

"Jessica. Stop." The command in his deep, rich voice halted her completely. Cupping her chin in his hand, he ran his thumb over her wet cheek.

Blinking back more tears, she stared up at him. Whatever was wrong with her? Throwing fits because she didn't get her way? And blaming Z? He'd only been trying to protect her. Had deprived himself as well.

And, as his submissive, she'd given the reins into his hands. This was hardly submitting to him. "I'm sorry," she whispered.

"As am I," he said in a level voice. "First, you should know that I called the doctor—and he agreed that we could resume sexual relations at this point."

She closed her eyes for a second as humiliation swept through her. He'd tried to tell her, and she'd yelled and thrown things. *Marvelously mature, girl.*

Without a doubt, he was annoyed.

"Now that you can no longer pelt me with sex toys," he said in a dry voice, "perhaps we can speak reasonably."

Uh-oh. She had a bad feeling about—

"I can understand your anger. But, kitten," his voice went gentle, "what made you cry?"

"Nothing."

His brows drew together. Lying was a crash and burn offense in Master Z's opinion.

"I mean, I was just frustrated."

His gaze didn't waver. He obviously didn't believe her.

This was intolerable. The tears started again as her defenses fell. "I-

I know you don't want me anymore, and I felt—"

"What?" As he gazed down at her, unhappiness lined his face.

Misery filled her. Now she'd made him feel bad, and he'd done nothing wrong. This was all her fault.

"Kitten," he said softly. "I don't think there has been a moment since we met that I haven't wanted you. I know you didn't appreciate the way you looked carrying a baby, but I thought we'd gotten past that."

Oh God, why did she have to be so insecure? "You did; we did." Because during those months of pregnancy, she'd seen herself in his eyes, seen how beautiful she was with his child growing within her. How much in awe he felt. "But, now..." She bit her lip, unable to continue.

With his hand against her cheek, he tilted her face up. His warmth seeped into her; his control sapped her resistance. "Tell me."

"I'm not carrying a baby, and I'm huge and...and saggy and—"

He shook his head ruefully, then took her hand and set it on his groin. On his very, very, very thick erection. "Does that feel as if I don't want you?"

Heat swept through her as she caressed him. She wanted him inside her, wanted—

His gaze met hers and oh, boy, he was still in Master-space. "How long have you been worrying about this?" he asked, way too softly.

She swallowed with difficulty. "Since..." Since the day she saw her stomach in the mirror after Sophia was born. "A while now."

"I. See." Slowly, he lifted her hands and secured them above her head again. His strong fingers easily held both her wrists. "Did we have an agreement that you would tell me when you were feeling insecure?"

"Yes," she whispered. "But you were pulling away." Her anger flared back to life. "You weren't even holding me at night."

"True. I wasn't." He actually chuckled. "Jessica, I've needed you so badly that I feared I'd take you in my sleep."

Z didn't lie. Z never lied. A heady cocktail of warmth and relief seeped into her veins. He hadn't been trying to move away from her.

With a half-smile, he caressed her cheek. "All right. This gives us a place to start."

*Start.* Start didn't sound good. "What do you mean?" Marrying a psychologist had been a really bad move. What had she been thinking?

"We'll keep talking about your worries. I daresay the long period without any intimacy made your fears worse than they might have been."

She could only nod.

"However, I want a daily report from you for the next, say, month."

When she started to scowl, his eyes darkened and turned her willpower into mush. "But, I don't like journaling."

"I know, pet. We'll work something out. Perhaps a spreadsheet. Color-coordinated, with a rating system. How you feel about your body. How you think I see you. A scale of one-to-ten. With notes on the side."

*Hmm. This is do-able.* She could total the results and average them weekly and do a graph to track if…

His eyes had lit with amusement.

"You're laughing at me."

"Actually, I'm in love with you," he said softly. "And glad to have my Jessica back."

"Oh." How much more could she love him?

His kiss started gentle and turned forceful enough that she could see he really was holding himself back. And wasn't that a rush? She pulled at his hands, wanting to touch him.

He released her, but straightened out of her reach. Gripping her upper arms, he sat her up on the bed.

She looked at him, confused. "What's wrong?"

Rather than answering, he opened his bedside stand and withdrew a…a mini-flogger with seven inch falls.

*Oh no.* Sure, the tiny flogger looked all innocuous, but it didn't feel so innocent on tender bits…like a pussy.

"What's that for? Am I being punished?" she protested.

"Before everything can flow smoothly, we have some clearing away to do—think of it like a blockage in a riverbed." He handed her the flogger and rolled his right sleeve up past his elbow before holding his arm toward her, forearm bared.

"What are you doing?" She pulled back.

"Since I'm not going to let you anywhere near my cock with a flogger, I want you to hit my arm. You will continue until you've given me a nice set of welts."

Her heart dropped right into her stomach, and not in a good way. "No." *No, no, no.* "M-Master, I can't."

"You can and will. Hopefully, next time, I'll hear the words you aren't saying. Or you will trust me enough to say them. I failed you as your Master," he said gravely.

"You didn't," she whispered.

In answer, he tapped his forearm. "Now, please."

Her first attempt barely stroked his skin and earned her an unyielding look.

Her second wasn't much better.

His lips curved slightly. "We'll continue this all night, if need be, pet."

The sense of his strength wrapping around her made her eyes fill. "I love you, Master."

"I know, kitten." He glanced at his arm and lifted his eyebrows.

She hit him. At the cruel sound of the strands slapping skin, she cringed.

"Harder."

So to get it over, she did three more as forcefully as she could.

"More—just like that."

By the time she'd struck him another three times, she was crying.

"Go on."

Her eyes were blinded by tears, but nothing could shut out the slap of the strands against skin.

Finally, finally, he caught her wrist and tugged the flogger from her hand. His strong arms enfolded her as he pulled her to his rock-hard chest.

She turned into him, burying her face against his shoulder, crying so violently she almost couldn't breathe. She'd hit him; *hurt* him.

"All done. You did well, little one." He was wrapped around her, his cheek on her head, rocking her gently. Making her world right again.

*Never, never make me do that again.* And yet, even as she soaked his shirt with her tears, she realized her anger at how he'd listened to the doctor instead of her had dissolved.

Slowly, her crying eased into shuddering breaths.

He kissed the top of her head and straightened. But when he finger combed her hair out of her wet face, she saw the horrible red welts running up his forearm and started to cry again.

"Poor pet." He pulled her back into his arms. After a minute, she noticed he was laughing...and fondling her breast.

She pushed him back. "Z!"

An eyebrow rose—unaccompanied by a smile.

She sputtered. "I mean, "Master, you-you—"

"That does sound nice. I think I'll forego gagging you, so you may beg me freely."

"Beg? For what?"

"For mercy. It's your turn to be punished, kitten."

Oh God, he was fully in Dom-space. Under his gray gaze, a dark desire seeped into her blood, and her nipples spiked into throbbing peaks.

His hands were merciless as he flattened her on her back and secured her wrists to the headboard. He positioned a cushion under her hips and bound her knees widely apart, using the mid-bed straps. Close to the end of the bed, her pussy was tilted up…and open. Air touched her folds, emphasizing how damp she was.

As if to point that out, he bent and circled a finger around her entrance and over her clit, which still hummed from her orgasm.

"Nice and aroused. Unfortunately, being wet will make your punishment worse, I'm afraid," he said in a serious tone.

"Punishment—there?" Using that damn flogger? "You wouldn't."

The set of his jaw said her protests would be ignored. He picked up the short leather flogger. "Jessica, look at me." The caress in his deeply resonant voice overlaid a steely edge.

Her gaze lifted to his.

"I love you, my spitfire. I love you enough to give you the sex you want—and the control you need."

And with that, he flicked the strands hard over the inside of her left leg and the right.

Her legs jerked as the burn bit into the delicate skin, and she yelped.

He ran his hand over the light red marks, his tender touch at odds with the pain. Cupping her chin with one hand, his eyes trapped hers. "Jessica, this is going to hurt. It's punishment, not pleasure. I want you to accept the pain silently."

Her eyes filled with tears—and relief. No anger showed in his expression, just determination. He wouldn't let anyone or anything break what they had together.

If he'd let her provoke him into behaving as she wanted, she'd be in control. And she didn't want that any more than he did. "I'm sorry," she whispered.

"I know, little one. As am I." After kissing her tenderly, he stepped back.

When he lifted the flogger, she saw the welts she'd left on him. She gritted her teeth. She'd be silent and take her part of the punishment that they both shared.

And then, he continued. With infinite care, he flogged her inner thighs, moving in painful increments from above the knee straps toward her groin.

*Ouch, ouch, ouch.*

He'd pause long enough for the sting to register, for her to pull in a breath through her nose, and…for her to anticipate the next blow.

Her hands were clenched and a few tears slid down her cheeks. But she hadn't made a sound.

He set the flogger down. "You did very well, kitten, for this part. I'm proud of you." The approval in his voice started to loosen the knot of guilt.

As he sat on the end of the bed between her burning thighs, he examined the marks. "Nice and pink. We should make sure your pussy matches your legs, shouldn't we?"

"God, no. No, no, no." Her throat clogged with a mix of lust and utter fear. Her legs tried to close—but no one did bondage better than Master Z. She couldn't move an inch.

The bone-deep knowledge that he could do what he wanted turned her to jelly.

The finger exploring her folds slid inside with a betrayingly wet sound. The sheer pleasure of his intimate touch made her moan.

He didn't smile—but the corners of his eyes crinkled. Then, oh God, he bent and he teased his tongue over her clit. Already sensitive, the nub of nerves flared to life as his tongue flicked it, then rubbed lightly…in direct contrast to how he'd wielded the flogger.

His finger inside her increased to two, moving in slowly rotating thrusts.

Her muscles started to tighten as the need to come amplified. She whimpered, tried to move, couldn't.

Pulling back, he rose. "Since your punishment isn't over, you should have a diversion for the next round." Opening the drawer, he pulled out the toy she loved and hated in equal parts—the vibrating anal plug.

"Nooooo."

Ignoring her, he lubed it and set the plug at her back entrance. When her rim puckered in refusal, he lightly slapped her sore thigh. "Push back, Jessica."

She'd never been able to defy him when he used that low, commanding tone. Not ever. Her muscles loosened.

The plug slid into place with a slight plop, and her anus closed around the narrow part before the wide flange. His warm palm pressed against her buttocks. "Your body is mine, Jessica. Is it not?"

*His.*

And he'd deliberately taken possession of her most private area to reinforce that reality. His gray eyes held hers with the inflexibility of forged iron.

The melting sensation in her belly wasn't new, but somehow the entire bed seemed to be sinking into the floor. She was his. *Forever.* "Yes, Master," she whispered.

"Very good."

He flicked the switch and rose.

Vibrations started, exciting her asshole and pussy, sending sparkling desire all along her nerve endings. Her hips tried to lift again, and she moaned when nothing moved.

As he observed her, his lips curved in a faint smile. "You're so beautiful."

When he looked at her with such warmth in his eyes, she felt beautiful. And cherished. Staring up at him, vulnerable and open, she smiled her love back.

"That's my submissive," he murmured. He bent and fondled her breasts into aching mounds...and how wonderful was it to have his hands on her again. Gripping her hair with his free hand, he kissed her, long and slow.

When he lifted his head, she was ready for—

"Let's finish this. Brace yourself, pet." He picked up the pussy flogger.

*Oh God, no.* Her body squirmed as if she could wiggle off the top of the bed—and his lips twitched.

To her dismay, he started at her knees again, delivering stinging hits to the inside of her thighs. The blows weren't as powerful this time, but oh, she was already sore. The strikes inched up her legs.

She knew he wouldn't stop when he reached the apex.

Her muscles clenched when the flogger neared her pussy. Yet, somehow, her clit was throbbing with need. And that stupid anal plug kept vibrating, sending her arousal higher.

The falls hit barely below her pussy on one side, then the other. Then he flicked the strands upward against her left labia. The sudden nipping shock made her gasp. She struggled to bring her knees together even as he delivered the next blow to the right folds.

Her arms were completely tied, her legs open, there was no way to avoid whatever he wanted to do. His compassionate...unyielding...gaze met hers as she jerked at the restraints.

The flogger struck her folds, avoiding her clit. Again and again, the merciless leather strands flicked her until the entire area burned. The pain was bearable and yet too, too much.

"You'll discuss problems with me openly. Honestly." He punctuated the statement with a harder flick, and she fought unsuccessfully to remain still.

"Yes, Master." Tears filled her eyes from the pain, from the knowledge she'd angered him, from the sheer need to have him hold her.

The next blow came down on her mound—high on the plumpness—as he created a ring of burning flesh.

In the center was her clit.

The exquisitely sensitive nub felt as if it was cringing—yet was engorged with blood, throbbing and anticipating the pain.

Master Z watched her squirm and pull at the restraints. "No, you can't get free, Jessica. You'll take what I want to give you." The rich timbre of his voice stroked over her, another restraint in its own way, making her see and feel exactly how exposed she was. How helpless.

And how much he enjoyed it.

Two more blows hit her mound, ruthlessly, bathing her in liquid heat that was almost pain. Was past pain.

He bent and licked over her clit, sending her, almost, almost into a climax. All the stinging, the vibrations, everything coalesced deep within. Her skin slickened with sweat.

Then he straightened. The flogger impacted against her folds from beneath, her mound from above, and back again. Folds, mound. A pause that seemed interminable as her pulse surged in her ears.

He moved. And the cruel strands struck her clit.

Right. On. Her. *Clit.*

Pain blasted upward, stealing her air with the shock. Her center clamped down…and fireworks exploded inside her. Her back arched as pleasure ricocheted through every nerve in her core before reverberating outward in waves of sheer sensation. Her insides contracted and spasmed, tightening around the vibrating plug in her ass and increasing in intensity. *Oh, oh, oh.*

"Look at me, Jessica."

She managed to open her eyes.

His dark eyes held hers as his callused, powerful hand covered her pussy, holding in the burn and the pleasure…sending her over again. "This pussy is mine, pet. Do you think you can remember that?"

She barely heard him through the roar of her pulse. Gasping for air, she could only nod.

"Very good." He opened his trousers, set a knee on the bed, set his cock at her entrance, and pressed past her slick, swollen tissues. With her ass already occupied, the shaft penetrating her pussy seemed impossibly huge as he took her. Steadily. Inescapably.

"Oooooh, God." Her body wouldn't stop coming as she stretched around him. His thickness increased the sensations from the anal plug until his cock seemed to be vibrating as well. Her whole lower half spasmed with exquisite pleasure.

He was deep within her, his muscular body pressing down on hers, one arm beside her shoulder, the other cupping her cheek so he could watch her. "You feel very, very good, Jessica," he said softly—and no lie was in his words or his gaze. He still wanted her.

The knowledge was heady. Wonderful. Sending her spiraling on a fountain of joy.

She wanted to hold him, to feel him, to be anchored before she floated away. She tugged at the ties holding her arms above her head. "Please, Master, can I touch you?"

His stern face softened, and he reached up and released her wrist cuffs with one hand.

Her arms went around his shoulders. Oh, she'd missed touching him, missed his weight on her. Stroking his back, she felt his iron muscles bunch and loosen as he moved.

*More.* She wiggled her restrained knees and looked up with an unspoken appeal.

His grin flashed, almost too fast for her to see. "No, little one. You'll stay spread and open and will deny me nothing."

Just his words made her clench inside.

Deliberately, he increased his pace, his thick shaft driving deep with each thrust.

His rhythm was ruthlessly compelling, and she felt her body gathering again into a sweetly rolling orgasm.

"That's my kitten." He gripped her face, holding her for a possessive and penetrating kiss, taking her mouth as he took her below. Under her fingers, his muscles tightened and then he drove deep, deep, and she could feel the spasming of his cock in the most intimate of sharing.

His gray eyes had never left hers. "I love you, Jessica. Never doubt it."

"I love you, Master," she whispered, holding him closer and letting herself drift.

Sometime later, she realized he'd cleaned her up, released her, and was now settling her on top of him. With firm hands, he molded her close, so not the slightest barrier came between them.

She could hear the slow thuds of his heart; her breathing rose and fell with his; his masculine scent surrounded her. And she gave a tiny sigh of perfect content.

In all the universe, this was her happy place.


Two hours had almost passed, so Anne was unsurprised to hear footsteps in the hallway outside the room she'd chosen. She looked up from her book.

Z walked through the door, wearing his usual black jeans and black shirt with the sleeves rolled up. His hair was damp from a shower, and his eyes were heavy-lidded with satisfaction.

Jessica had won the day.

He studied Anne silently, his face unreadable. "My submissive doesn't have a devious bone in her body," he said finally. "I didn't test her loyalty by asking, but I would guess the advice came from you or Gabi."

*Oh. Damn.* Meddling in another Dom's affairs was considered ill mannered. Aiding a submissive to manipulate her Master? Especially when the Master was Z?

Hanging offense.

Admittedly, she'd hoped Z wouldn't figure out she'd given Jessica more than babysitting services, but she'd known the possible consequences if he did. "I gave her the suggestion."

His gaze stayed on her. "You had a reason. Might I know it?"

He knew her well, knew meddling wasn't her style. "This is something you should discuss with your submissive."

A corner of his mouth lifted. "We did. But your interference is between you and me, Dominant to Dominant. Explain, please."

"Her talks with you had proven unsuccessful." After a second, Anne added diplomatically, "Actually, I didn't think waiting another week was unreasonable to be certain of safety."

He nodded.

"However, after giving birth, women aren't especially reasonable. She said she needed not only the sex, but also the intimacy and the power exchange that came with it. It appeared her frustration was rapidly turning to anger. Toward you."

Z rubbed his face. "I understand. In this case, I appreciate the…intervention…although you might have simply spoken to me instead."

"I offered. She refused that idea. Vehemently. You may ask her about it."

"I will." He walked over and picked up his daughter, snuggling her close with a kiss to her fuzzy head.

Arms empty, Anne felt the slow slide of envy.

Taking his extended hand, she let him pull her to her feet. After handing him Sophia's diaper bag, she scooped up her purse.

At the door, she hesitated. "Are we good?"

"We are. Thank you for your care, Anne." Laughter lit his steel-gray eyes. "I'm glad to see the Mistress hasn't lost her touch—your advice was quite effective."

"Good to know." As they parted ways, Z back upstairs and Anne to the outside, she decided she'd have to check Ben's reaction if he saw his Mistress taking her pleasure into her own hands.

# Chapter Eighteen

"Day's over. Head on in," Ben shouted from Raoul's patio.

Groans came from the dozen teenage boys on the beach.

"Here you go, Bronx." A boy pitched the Frisbee into the waves. "Get it one last time."

Bronx barked happily and charged into the surf.

"These are good children." Raoul joined Ben at the railing. "I'm glad they could all make it here."

Slowly, reluctantly, the boys started up the steps toward the house. Sunburned, sandy, scruffy. Some had more tats than clothes. More piercings than money. A few of them looked as if they'd murder their grandmothers and rob a 7-11 on the way home.

Yet, as Bronx pranced out of the water, Frisbee held high, every single boy cheered. Each gave the dog pats and scratches as he trotted past them on the steps.

Ben accepted the Frisbee and ruffled the dog's ears. "Thanks, Bronx. You did good today, buddy."

If there were therapy dogs for unhappy teenagers, Bronx would be a natural. Even the quietest kid blossomed under the retriever's attentions, and the dog had become an essential member of the group soon after Marcus recruited Ben.

The original bunch had been kids in Marcus's martial arts club. The sensei there had offered some at-risk teens free lessons, hoping the discipline of karate would benefit them. Marcus started the outings, partly for fun, partly to acquaint them with various careers. Then his friends had stepped in. Now, some of the kids worked for Andrea's cleaning business, some in Beth's landscaping company.

Somewhere along the way, Ben had been roped in. A few months ago, he'd taken a handful to an art gallery and later on a photo expedition.

Last month, the boys had visited Raoul's offices to learn about civil engineering…and to design bridges on the high-tech software.

Today'd been simply to have a good time.

Ben had enjoyed himself as well. Kids were fun—all of them, from the terrifyingly small ones like Z's Sophia to this batch of rabble-rousers. He wanted children of his own, someday. Didn't matter how many as long as the number started at two.

Anne didn't even want pets in her life.

No, that was inaccurate. She was changing. And fuck knew, she loved children. As with plants and pets, she'd just never thought about having her own.

How far could he push her before hitting a wall?

"Y'all fetch your bags, grab water, and line up at the door," Marcus ordered from the living room. He counted off boys as Raoul tossed them bottles of water.

"Thanks, Raoul." "Thanks, Ben." "It was great." The chorus of farewells and gratitude continued as the teens headed out the front door and to the rented mini-bus. Undoubtedly, they'd party all the way back to Tampa.

"Thank you for hosting the invasion, Raoul." Marcus stopped in the door to keep an eye on the bus.

"It was a pleasure, my friend, and an honor. Here—one for you." Raoul tossed over a bottled water.

Marcus caught it. As Raoul headed into the kitchen, Marcus turned to Ben. "Thank you for—"

"Don't even start on that gratitude shit, Atherton." Snorting a laugh, Ben nudged the lawyer out the door. "You know I have as much fun as they do."

As Marcus jogged to the bus, Ben raised his hand to the boys and got back a burst of whistles and cheers.

And that was that. He glanced at the clock and winced. Time to get a move on.

Kim was in the kitchen. "Hey, Ben. Raoul went out to the patio. He said his ears were ringing."

"Got that." Noise and boys—inseparable. "Do you have an old towel I can use on Bronx? He's covered in sand, and we're driving to the Everglades after this."

"Of course. I'll bring one out."

When Ben went out the French doors to the back, he found Raoul at a table in the shade.

Off to one side, Bronx was lapping water from a wide, foot-high, terra-cotta fountain.

Hell of a fancy pet-waterer. Something so pretty would look just about right on Anne's deck. Maybe in a ceramic blue.

Ben looked around. "Where's your dog?"

Raoul grinned and pointed under the table to where Kim's dog was sprawled out, dead to the world.

"Poor bastard," Ben said. "It's a lot of work to protect and serve—and play—all at the same time."

"He takes his guard dog duties quite seriously," Raoul agreed. At a rocky point in their relationship, he and Kim had broken up. Worried about her being alone, he'd bought the highly trained German shepherd for her.

Today, although the dog played on the beach with the group, Ari had remained vigilant. Any time someone approached Kim, the dog'd charge up the stairs to the patio…just in case.

Who knew when some skinny fifteen-year-old might go berserk and lay a hand on his mistress, right?

"If you are not in a hurry, please, join me for a beer before you leave." Raoul motioned to a seat across the table. "I'd like to talk to you."

Some problem with the boys? The drive could wait a bit. "Sure." As Ben sat, Kim appeared with a towel.

"Thanks, Kim." When Ben whistled, Bronx trotted over to get wiped down.

Kim turned to Raoul. "Drinks, Master?"

"That would be good, *gatita*, thank you. Dos Equis, I think, for Ben." He leaned back in his chair and studied her. "Wine for you, if you wish. I think you have more than earned it today."

Under her Dom's appreciative smile, Kim flushed a pretty red and simply glowed.

His voice lowered, and he murmured something to her.

Feeling as if he were intruding, Ben concentrated on de-sanding his dog, then waved him under the table to join Ari for a nap.

As Bronx flattened out with a soft sigh, Kim returned from the house with a tray. She handed an opened Stump Knocker to Raoul, a Dos Equis to Ben, and took the glass of red wine for herself.

"I sampled your Brooklyn Lager at the Shadowlands," Raoul said. "Dos Equis is as close to it as I have on hand."

"Good choice." Fuck knew he didn't want Raoul's favorite beer—the stuff was so malty it was almost black. He raised his bottle to both his hosts. "Thanks."

Nodding in reply, Kim picked up a chair cushion, placed it on the ground, and with her drink in hand, gracefully settled at her Master's feet.

As a slave would.

Ben frowned. Was that behavior what Anne expected of him? Even with guests present? If that was what she wanted, he'd do his best...but the idea made his skin crawl.

"This way you look..." Raoul drank some of his beer and set the bottle on the table. "This is what I wish to speak of."

"You don't like the way I look?" What the fuck? Helping with the boys required good looks?

"No, no. You are frowning because my *sumisita* is here. At my feet." When Raoul laid his hand on her shoulder, Kim rubbed her cheek against his wrist.

Ben straightened as the Dom's intention became clear. Anne would be the topic of discussion. How could he politely refuse? "Listen—"

"My friend, I do not usually interfere in business not my own, but you are new to the lifestyle. I am...concerned...you might be in over your head. As I am familiar with Master/slave relationships, perhaps I can answer some questions?"

Was every Shadowlands Master going to butt into his affairs?

Ben took a drink, stalling for time. Because, maybe, Raoul had a point.

Over the last few days, Anne had kept him close. Because he'd...lied...to her, she was worried about him. He couldn't object. Hell, even more than the sex, he got off on their long talks. She'd served as a Marine. Been deployed. She *got* what he was talking about.

Trouble was, she was his Mistress. He was her slave. And that...power exchange...never let up.

He was starting to wonder if he really could do that shit. Forever.

But some people could. He put his beer on the table and studied Kim.

She'd set the wine beside her and was still. As calm and peaceful as a person deep in meditation, yet she held herself ready for whatever Raoul wanted her to do.

She was a slave.

Was Ben willing to go as far as she had? His gut was saying no. "She do that all the time?" Ben nodded at Kim.

"Actually, no." Raoul stroked her hair. "And yes. She enjoys the calmness of high protocol after events. And I wanted you to observe formal Master/slave dynamics in a home setting."

"But normally you don't do this…stuff. Sitting at your feet and not talking?" Anne got off on the formal protocol shit though.

"Kimberly is always under my command, Ben," Raoul said gently. "At home, the rules are loosened for comfort, so she is free to speak, to sit, to dress as she wishes…unless I wish otherwise. I often wish otherwise. This is because, as with electricity, when the power between two poles is not equal, a sizzle is created."

A sizzle, huh? Well, he and Anne enjoyed an excellent sizzle in the bedroom. But elsewhere?

Kim sat with her eyes closed, and as her Master petted her like a cat, her contentment was obvious.

Ben wasn't sure he'd be as damned content.

Drifting, Kim tilted her head under her Master's touch, feeling like the *gatita*　little kitten—that Master R often called her.

His big hands were powerful. Deadly. And ever so gentle with her.

His callused fingers trailed over her cheek and down to tug her collar slightly, letting her know she could rest against him.

She counted on that. Her Master was her anchor. Whether the ocean was peaceful or stormy, he was there for her. Although he'd reluctantly taken her as a slave to help bring down a human trafficking ring, neither of them had been willing to separate afterward. Master/slave was what worked for them both.

But now…now she was making him unhappy because he wanted to marry her.

Considering she was his slave, marrying him should be a no-brainer, right? But after a childhood of watching her mother suffer within matrimonial bonds, marriage looked too much like a trap. Being a wife was far scarier than being a slave.

But with Raoul, she was learning she could handle scary.

Sometime last month, he'd bought her a ring—a gorgeous, heart-stopping ring that she'd discovered by accident. Obviously not wanting to pressure her, he'd tucked it away in his dresser drawer. He was patiently waiting until she was ready.

No one had ever known her and loved her as well as her Master.

She shifted to lean against his leg, letting him take some of her weight as the men talked.

Ben sounded unhappy.

The Shadowlands' security guard had scared her the first time she'd seen him. She'd thought he resembled some medieval torturer. But he'd been so pleased that Master R had found himself a woman that she couldn't remain afraid. Ben had a big heart.

And, according to the gossip making the rounds, he was Anne's new slave.

Raoul had been a Master for years, was a power within the local Master/slave community, and he'd watched Ben's relationship with obvious worry.

Poor Ben didn't look comfortable at the topic of discussion—but that wouldn't stop her determined Master.

"My first concern is that Anne is a sadist, but I do not think you are a masochist," Master R said.

"I'm not. But, you know, she's not as sadistic as you think." Ben drank more of his beer. "She told me she didn't need the hard-core shit any longer. I think, maybe, she was working out her anger toward men. And everyone says her slaves were masochists—and more than willing."

Kim glanced up under her lashes.

"Has she changed?" Raoul thought for a minute. "You are right, I think. Her scenes truly have lightened over the last year."

Ben nodded.

"As to working out her anger? As a sadist, Anne never stepped over the line. And she wouldn't be the first or last Dom to find relief from life's frustrations in a scene." Master R tugged Kim's hair. "Submissives do the same. A good spanking serves as an excellent overflow valve."

Kim suppressed a laugh. She certainly couldn't disagree. Her Master somehow knew just when she needed that kind of release.

Ben's gaze was on her, she realized, but he apparently wasn't sure if he was allowed to talk with her.

She glanced up at her Master and got a nod. "What do you want to know, Ben?" she asked.

"Do you like it? Being a...slave?"

She no longer flinched at the sound of the word, although Master R still called her *sumisita*—Spanish for little slave. "I like what Master R and I have together, but *slavery* means different things to different people. Everyone arranges matters to suit themselves. Master R doesn't want my money; other Doms might want more control. I retain an hour every night that is all mine for girly pampering or just reading a book, and it keeps me from feeling trapped. Other slaves might not need that." Because others might not have been kidnapped and brutalized and truly enslaved.

Ben leaned forward, forearms on thighs as he listened.

"Sometimes I resent my service and having to answer to his every whim."

When she grinned up at Master R, the warmth in his dark chocolate eyes still possessed the power to make her melt.

"But the annoyance of being at his beck and call is equivalent to having to get up in the morning for a job or having to take a vitamin—just another of life's little chores you do to get to the good stuff. Because serving him"—she felt her throat clog—"having his hands cupped around my life and being able to tend his needs and desires in turn simply...fills...me. I would be a dry ocean bed without him."

Master R's fingers tightened on her shoulder. His voice was low. Deep. "*Tesoro mío.*"

Her eyes closed as she drew in the happiness. Because to serve a Master who considered her his treasure was all her joy.

When she opened her eyes, she saw Ben had seen and heard and understood.

And his eyes held grief. "I don't feel that way. Not..."

Master R said, "Each relationship is different, Ben. Not every submissive wants to give up as much power as Kimberly. Not every Master or Mistress wants to bear such responsibility for another adult. There is no one true way—you have to talk until you find what will satisfy you both."

"Yeah," Ben muttered. "That's not as easy as it sounds."

After staring at his beer for a minute, he finished it off and rose, snapping his fingers for Bronx. "I need to get moving before I lose the light. Thanks for the beer—and the information."

Master R walked him to the door, and Kim heard them saying good-bye, then footsteps returning.

Her Master took his chair again.

Although she kept her eyes down, she could feel his gaze on her, like the warmth of the sun, penetrating through skin and bone.

"*Sumisita*, I want you without clothes right now." With the command, his Spanish-tinged baritone had taken on an added smoothness. One that sent shivers across her skin.

She rose and slowly...provocatively...removed her clothing. When she unhooked her bra, she arched her back to push her breasts out. As her shorts slid off, she tilted a hip to enhance her curves. When she was finished, only her sapphire-studded choker remained, and she touched the tiny heart-shaped padlock on it. He held the key to her collar even as he held the key to her heart.

Following her movements, his eyes lingered on her collar and darkened to almost black. When he pulled her between his parted legs, his jeans rubbed against her bare thighs. The feeling of being naked in front of a fully dressed man made the inequality between them so much more potent.

And as he'd said—added to the sizzle.

She stood, everything she was open and receptive and glorying in the truth that she was his...to tease. To touch. To take.

His gaze moved over her in appreciation and pleasure. Leaning forward, he curved his hands over her bottom, squeezing, separating, stroking, before moving to her hips, and upward. He cupped and weighed her breasts in his callused palms.

Need rolled up and over her, heating each breath she took of the sultry air.

"You did well with answering Ben." His brows lowered. "I'm afraid of how this is going to end for him."

"Why?" Kim's toes curled as his thumbs circled her nipples. "Um. He loves her—that's pretty plain."

"Yes. But do you remember when we didn't think we could be together? Because our needs weren't in equilibrium?"

Just the memory of that miserable time made her spirits droop. "But we got past that."

"Only because we did want essentially the same thing. And because we love each other." He pulled her down into his lap, taking her mouth more possessively than normal, as if to drive away the memory of their days of loneliness.

Oh, she loved him so much. She snuggled closer, tangling her hand in his thick hair. Although some Masters didn't let their slaves touch unless given permission, he never minded and rarely took that privilege away from her. He liked her hands on him.

He lifted his head, smiling down at her, palming her breast again, simply enjoying her body.

Poor Ben. If what he and Anne had built was similar to her relationship with Master R, then its loss would devastate him. Couldn't Anne back off a bit? How could she not see how important she was to him? But women... Kim sighed. Women were obstinate when it came to guarding their hurts. Their hearts.

And maybe Kim should be studying her own life instead. Because, spit in the surf, how totally over-fearful was she being about getting married?

Raoul wasn't anything like her father. Married or not, he'd never take her for granted. Never grind her down to serve his ego. She'd not only be loved, she'd be cherished.

Maybe it was time to rethink her own cowardly stance.

"I think Anne and Ben can work it out," she said, turning her thoughts back to her friends.

"I see something of my marriage when I look at them. My ex-wife was not submissive. She wanted pain. I wanted a slave. Our needs were at cross-purposes, making us both unhappy."

That was an understatement. From everything Kim'd heard, Raoul's breakup with his wife had nearly destroyed him. Her compassionate Master wouldn't want Ben to make a similar mistake.

He continued, "Anne's slaves never live with her. When they're with her, they're slaves, not friends. I think Ben wants to be her lover and her companion, not merely her slave. What do you think, *gatita?*"

He stilled his hands, holding her waist, letting her have the space to think.

Ben's dilemma was so close to what she'd gone through with Raoul. Her heart broke for him because she could relate to his pain. "Maybe they're not swimming in the same current—not yet—but surely, they can get there if they try. He really cares for her."

"I agree. But does Anne feel the same? Will she put in the effort?" Raoul kissed Kim's fingertips. "The Mistress is a good person. As a Domme, she is strong and careful and responsible. But I'm not sure she possesses the heart of a lover to give to our friend."

Kim bit her lip. She hated disagreeing with him, but he only saw Anne at the Shadowlands or the occasional party. He hadn't seen her with Jessica's baby or at the battered women's shelter with the children. "I think she has more of a heart than you give her credit for."

He smiled, his gaze soft. "I know who has more of a heart than her little body should hold. You are a generous friend, *sumisita.*"

He didn't believe her.

She frowned. "You'll let them work things out though, right?" Doms were notoriously protective, and if Raoul worried that Ben'd get hurt, he would step in.

"I will." His white teeth flashed in his darkly tanned face. "I'd hate to have Ben smash my face into the pavement."

"As if he could. I've seen you fight."

"I'm good, but Ben was an Army Ranger, and he hasn't lost those skills."

*Whoa.* She hadn't known that one. *Go, Ben.*

Then, smiling to herself, she wiggled her ass right on top of Master R's solid erection. "In that case, you'd better behave. It would be a shame if some manly bits got squished."

He choked, then tucked a finger under her collar to restrain her while he kissed her mercilessly.

Desire was a rising tide within her.

Lifting his head, he murmured, "Someone is being a naughty *gatita*, no?"

She was too breathless to answer.

"Perhaps I shall see to your needs now…in case I am incapacitated in the future." Chuckling, he rose, tossed her over his shoulder, and administered a stinging swat to her bare bottom that set every single nerve to blazing.

He was so strong, he didn't seem to even notice her weight. He made her feel little.

And precious.

As she rubbed her cheek against his back, Kim ran a hand under his belt to squeeze his muscular ass—and earned herself another swat on her butt.

Oh, he was in the mood to spank her and she knew it, or she wouldn't have teased him. In her turn, the anticipation of his incredibly hard palm on her naked skin was making her really, really hot. With no effort at all, he'd reduce her to a whimpering mess.

And then he'd pin her down or tie her up…and take her rough and fast.

She squirmed, wanting to be there now.

After that…

He'd murmur to her in Spanish, his voice like the rocking waves in the ocean, and she'd wrap around him, her anchor, her love, and float there in contentment.

But then…maybe then would be a good time to rummage through his dresser drawer and find the engagement ring he'd bought her.

# Chapter Nineteen

Late Sunday afternoon, Anne followed the hostess through the Chinese restaurant in downtown St. Pete.

Ben's call an hour before had come as a surprise, since he'd left for the Everglades yesterday after spending the day with Marcus's boys. He hadn't planned to be back until late tonight.

*"My sisters and brother-in-law are here from New York. Camille got a special deal to come down for a long weekend and decided to surprise me. I came back early to take them to the Dali Museum, and now we're going to get something to eat. If you're off work, can you join us? Be nice to let them meet you."* His voice had dropped. *"And I've missed you."*

She understood. She'd missed him last night, more than she found comfortable.

Happily, her skip assignment for today had turned out to be more absent-minded than criminal and had been an easy recovery. She was free to join them.

What was annoying was the amount of anxiety simmering inside her. Since when had she been worried about meeting anyone?

The Chinese restaurant smelled like garlic and ginger, and Anne's stomach growled as she crossed the room. She'd skipped breakfast—eating early hadn't appealed—and had a granola bar for lunch. Now, she was starving.

The red-and-gold Oriental décor barely registered as she approached the far end. Ben sat at a round table with three women about Anne's age and one black-haired man.

Both men rose. Ben was a good six inches taller than his brother-in-law, and, as always, Anne's heart lifted at the sight of him. His white, short-sleeved shirt set off his wide shoulders and dark tan, and his jeans cupped his ass delightfully. He'd worn his caramel-colored hair loose over his shoulders, tempting her to perform ill-mannered public displays of affection.

When she stepped close and smiled in permission to touch, Ben put an arm around her waist. "Anne, here are my sisters and brother-in-law." He motioned toward a tall honey-blonde in a pale green blouse and white capris. "Camille and her husband Leon manage a boutique tourist agency."

"Which is how we managed to score this trip." Camille's wide smile was totally Ben's. "It's wonderful to meet you."

"Pleased to meet you." Leon had a faint lilting Cajun accent.

"And you," Anne said, meaning it. Ben had told her a few stories of this sister. He was very proud of her.

"My sister, Deanna," Ben said.

The striking platinum blonde in an emerald tank top nodded with no warmth. "Anne."

Before Anne could respond, Ben nodded at the last woman seated to his left. "Sheena is a friend of Deanna's."

"Oh, and surely yours as well, Ben," the brunette said in a throaty voice and touched the back of his hand. Her hand lingered on his as she gave Anne an insincere smile. "Deanna had raved about her big brother for years, so I was delighted to finally spend time with him last Christmas." The subtext was obvious. She and Ben had done more than "spend time."

"We had so much fun," Deanna agreed. "Remember that day we went sledding?"

"Oh, such a day." Sheena caressed Ben's hand and gazed up at him with big eyes. "I'd have broken my neck if you hadn't caught me at the top of the hill."

The woman had probably flung herself into his arms. *Charming.* Anne glanced at her chair—the empty one to Ben's right—and Ben moved to hold it for her.

*Deal with this, Sheena.* Anne edged her chair to the right toward Deanna.

After sitting, Ben scooted close enough to brush his leg against Anne's. She'd expected his move. Her slave had very assertive behavior, yet she could hardly reprimand him for claiming gestures she enjoyed.

Even better, he now was far enough away from *Sheena-the-slut* that her irritating, touchy-feely maneuvers would be blazingly obvious.

Leon noted the distance between Sheena and her prey, and the corners of his mouth tipped up. "So, Anne, Ben tells us you're a bounty hunter. What's that like?"

"I'm afraid what I do isn't as exciting as what's shown on television. Technically, in Florida, the job is called fugitive recovery, because an agent isn't independent, but employed by a bail bond company. Mostly I do paperwork, computer searching, knocking on doors, and diplomacy. Occasionally, we see some action."

"Action. I can't imagine why a woman would want to put herself in danger." Although Sheena's eyelashes held enough mascara to resemble hairy tarantula legs, she still managed to look up at Ben through them. "Men are so much stronger."

"They are?" Anne ran her hand over Ben's biceps and gasped. "Oh, *my*. How strong you are! Who knew?"

Ben, Leon, and Camille broke out laughing. Unfortunately, Deanna's glare was a match for Sheena's. *Naughty Anne*. Not good to piss off relatives.

*Time to defuse the situation.* "Actually, Sheena, I like the action and the satisfaction of tossing the bad guys back in jail." As Ben put his arm over the back of her chair, Anne turned to her right, put on her company smile, and asked Deanna, "What do you do for a living?"

"I-I'm between jobs at the moment," Deanna said.

The arm behind Anne tensed. "Seriously? You lost the sales position at the clothing store?" Ben growled. "Then why are you here instead of searching for another?"

"Ben." Deanna snapped. A second later, she managed a pitiful-me expression, complete with teary eyes. "I should have stayed home. It's just, I was s-so upset. I only wanted to get away."

Anne turned to check out Ben's response.

His expression was soft. "Now, Dee-dee, it'll be all right," he said gently.

Anne barely refrained from rolling her eyes. As a Domme, she'd seen far more skillful performances, but Deanna's wasn't bad. She definitely had her big brother fooled.

To top it off, Deanna added the tried-and-true lip quiver. "No, it won't be all right. I can't pay my rent and"—she half-sobbed—"Sheena was wonderful and lent me money for food, but I can't ask her for more."

"Of course not," Ben said.

Anne had to smother a growl. During their time together, Ben had already received a couple of phone calls from this sister, hitting him up for money.

But…to pull this crap in front of other people and put Ben on the spot? That was purely manipulative. He obviously had no clue he was being played. Not surprising. Family could do that to a person.

Anne bit her lip. It wasn't her money, wasn't her family. As Sam would say, she didn't have a dog in this fight.

Yet…she did. When Ben had given her his submission, he'd become hers to protect, even from his own family if needed. So be it.

"Asking for and giving money between family members is tricky, isn't it?" Anne said brightly to the table at large. "Last week, my friend Linda cried after she said no to her grown son. She was heartbroken to have to refuse him, especially when a little money would help. But she says her parental goal is for her son to be independent, and if she constantly rescues him, he won't exert the effort—or learn enough diplomacy—to keep a job."

Ben looked down at Anne, his brows together. "Did Sam agree?"

The gray-haired sadist had certainly had an opinion. "He thinks enabling a person like that is as detrimental as abuse." Anne half-smiled. "He told Linda to envision the future. If she died in a car wreck tomorrow, would her adult son survive without her?"

Ben was silent.

Anne carefully didn't look at Deanna, but the waves of fury coming from that direction were almost palpable. "Leon, have you run into such situations in your family?"

"*Mais*, yeah. Cajuns have big families. An' whoever has money gets hit on by them that don't." He eyed Ben. "You ever watched a mama dog when she decides the pups are old enough? They try to suckle, an' she just walks away. Sometimes she'll have to nip the ones that won't take a hint, otherwise some puppies'd be happy to suck the tit forever, yeah?"

"Jesus *Christ*." Deanne glared at Anne. "Who the hell do you think you are? This is between me and my brother. You—you just want to get your claws into his money and—"

"I don't need Ben's money, but it *is* my job to shield him." She heard his startled grunt. After his time in the Shadowlands, had he missed learning that Mistresses as well as Masters protected their slaves? "How old are you, anyway?"

"She's thirty-one." Camille turned angry eyes on her sister. "Mimi said you told your manager to fuck off because he instructed you to work with middle-class customers as well as the rich ones. God, Dee. Mimi stuck her neck out to get you that job. Now, she's in trouble with her boss for recommending you."

Deanna slumped. Her expression indicated she blamed everyone except herself.

To Anne's relief, Ben slid his arm across her shoulders and pulled her close. "Thank you, Ma'am," he whispered into her ear. Then he looked around her at his sister. "It hurts to think I've helped you turn into a fuck-up, Dee-dee, but I guess I have. Camille and I already know that if we lose our jobs, we don't eat. Or we end up homeless. So we behave accordingly. Time for you to learn the nasty facts of life, sis."

"But, Ben." Sheena scooted her chair near enough to lay her hand on Ben's forearm. "She's your sister. She loves you because you have a big heart." And then the woman actually leaned against him and stroked him.

Fury crackled across Anne's nerves. So much for being tolerant. She didn't share her slaves. She certainly didn't share Ben. *Never.*

Anne picked up an unopened chopstick packet, slapped it on her palm to check the sting factor—*very nice*—then sharply smacked the back of Sheena's trespassing hand.

Sheena jerked her hand away. "Hey!"

Anne gave her the stare that kept men on their knees and silent.

Sheena's face paled, but she still...stupidly...tried to speak. "Listen, you—"

"Maybe your wimpy friends put up with you touching and hanging on their men, but I don't. Hands off." She twisted to put her hand on Ben's stomach in her own claiming gesture. Why be subtle? *"Mine."*

Across the table, she heard muffled laughter from Leon and Camille. But Deanna was scowling. *Way to make friends, Anne.*

"Ben, she hit me." Sheena looked up at him with wide eyes. "Are you going to let her do that?"

Ben laughed. "Gotta say, I find it really hot when a woman says, '*Mine.*' What do you think, Leon?"

Leon smiled at his wife. "My Camille destroys poachers verbally. But that physical stuff? Whoa, that's hot. I'm gonna buy you some chopsticks, *bebe.*"

"Sheena should be glad you didn't have a whip at hand," Ben murmured to Anne.

As his gaze held hers, heat sizzled through her blood stream. And just south of her fingertips, his jeans bulged. The man really had enjoyed seeing her go all Domme on Sheena's ass.

After that interlude, both Sheena and Deanna concentrated on their food, while the rest of them talked.

"It seems that all of you have moved out of the city. Didn't you like growing up in the Bronx?" Anne asked Camille.

"The South Bronx isn't the best neighborhood. But after our father died, Mom couldn't make enough to support all four of us. She tried—God, she really tried." Camille exchanged a sorrowful look with Ben.

The way his shoulders tensed, as if he blamed himself, hurt Anne's heart.

When she took his hand, his big fingers closed tightly around hers. "Considering the children she raised, I'd say your mom did a fine job, even if money was tight."

Camille gave her a grateful look. "She did, against all odds. Ben, especially, had a rough time since he was under pressure to join a gang. He was working part time, going to school, and trying to protect Deanna and me. And we were so broke, he..."

Camille stopped suddenly and gave her brother a repentant look.

Anne frowned. Something had happened. She'd have to ask Ben later.

Being Ben, he let it all spill out. "We were short on money, and I got talked into a scheme to rob a liquor store. But...Mom's morals held up. I couldn't do it and backed out two days before. Pissed off the guys involved, and they jumped me after school. I got messed up pretty good." He gave her a half-grin and rubbed his nose.

The nose that had been broken.

He hadn't been an adult—had been in high school. She wondered how many other broken bones he'd suffered.

He continued, "In the hospital, a cop took my report and then came back the next day just to talk. To help me figure out a better path. So I enlisted and skipped the last of my senior year. With my pay, Mom and the girls moved into a safer neighborhood."

He'd ended up helping them after all.

Anne hoped his mother had known how wonderfully she'd succeeded in her task—she'd raised an exceptional man.

At the end of the meal, Anne rose. "Excuse me, please. I need to visit the ladies' room before I head home."

Ben turned, located the restrooms, studied the intervening tables, and apparently decided no zombies or madmen would leap up and attack her. "All right."

She shook her head in amusement. Her father and brothers possessed that same instinct to protect. So did she. It was difficult to be offended.

Still...

With her fingernails, she pinched his neck in warning and

murmured, "So good of you to give me permission."

He met her gaze and grinned unrepentantly.

*Oh honestly.* He wasn't a brat. Exactly. In the bedroom, he was superbly obedient. But the rest of the time? Not so much.

Unsettled, she walked to the restroom.

In all reality, he wasn't deliberately defiant. He simply didn't look to her for instruction or permission. While her other slaves had wanted her oversight, her direction, she was beginning to see that Ben…didn't.

But if that were true… Her chest felt as if she'd strapped on her body armor too tightly, restricting her lungs. With an effort, she pushed away her growing anxiety. Not the time. Not the place.

A few minutes later, while Anne was combing her hair, Camille entered. Instead of using the facilities, she leaned a hip on the wall. "I'm glad I caught you alone. I wanted to apologize for Sheena and Deanna. And to thank you."

"Thank me for what?"

"Growing up in the South Bronx wasn't easy. Ben tried to take care of us all, but he had no one watching out for him. Not since he was nine. Not until now." Camille scowled. "I just wish you hadn't had to protect him from his own sister."

"Deanna might have blundered onto a wrong path, but Ben won't be misled again," Anne said. "I can see she has a lot going for her, and once she realizes her future is up to her, I think she'll do fine. And probably be happier for it."

"I think you're right. And as for Sheena"—Camille rolled her eyes—"honestly, who does stuff like that? But Ben sure does attract some winners. Either money-grubbers latch onto him or he finds himself these obnoxious women who act as if they're too good for him."

Not unusual. Submissives searching for dominant partners could easily end up with control freaks. In Ben's case, he wound up with bitches.

Camille moved away and paused at the door to say, "I'm really glad he found you."

"Me, too."

*At least I'm not a bitch.* Hopefully. And she loved him with all her heart.

But was she good for him?

Sometimes he seemed totally content with what they had together. But sometimes she wasn't sure he really was happy, even though he said he was. Even though he insisted being her slave was what he wanted.

222 / Cherise Sinclair

Was she not meeting some of his needs in return? Was he sharing everything with her?

She bit her lip. If she had to, she'd go the intrusive route and plan a scene that would have him spilling every little secret he had. Or she could make him write a journal.

But, this was Ben… She didn't want to trespass all over his privacy.

So, maybe next weekend, after their scene, during the aftercare and the warm glow, she'd press him to share. It was their special time. Surely then, she'd find out what was wrong.

# Chapter Twenty

Anne slowly drove down a street of squalid apartment buildings.

The Tomorrow Is Mine manager hadn't wanted Anne to go after the woman, but when told the police would provide an escort to the shelter, Sue Ellen had panicked.

The thought of the police sometimes had that effect. Involving law enforcement meant the abuser would probably be arrested. Some women couldn't face that—they just wanted to run.

If Sue Ellen became too frightened, she might abandon her escape. So Anne would go get her. Unfortunately, the woman sounded pretty injured. Carrying her infant son, she wouldn't be able to walk very far.

*Damn men.*

Anne spotted the small 24-hour market chosen for the meeting place. Had Sue Ellen made it?

Yes, there was a woman leaning against a wall as if she'd fall if she didn't have the support. A baby was in her arms.

Any threats? Anne did a quick, but thorough, scan of the sidewalk and street. Two women chatted by a car. A teenager rolled by on a skateboard.

Good enough.

Anne parked and left the Escape running as she approached the woman slowly. "Are you Sue Ellen?"

The woman's eyes went wide as a startled rabbit. "I—" Her mouth closed as her paranoia bloomed.

"My name is Anne and I'm from Tomorrow Is Mine. You spoke with the shelter manager, Amy, and she sent me."

The terrified woman took a minute to process the information before saying in a hoarse, Southern-accented voice, "Ah'm Sue Ellen. And thank you for coming for me."

Dark bruises marked her throat. Her bastard husband must have choked her.

Anne throttled her anger and motioned to the SUV. "You're very welcome. Now, let's get you off the street." Because, damn, this was a small neighborhood. Everyone probably knew everyone.

"Yes'm." Sue Ellen followed and put her child into the car seat in the back. When she reached for the straps, a groan escaped her.

"Let me, honey." When Sue Ellen stepped back, Anne strapped the little boy in, crooning to him. He watched her warily. Not much older than Sophia, he had soft brown hair and pale skin. A bruise mottled one cheek.

As Sue Ellen slid into the front seat, a huge man walked out of the market and spotted them.

"Sue Ellen. What are you doing here?"

*Oh, damn.* Anne slammed the door and ran around the vehicle to jump in the driver's side. Before her door had even shut, she stomped the gas. Not enough to squeal the tires…but damned fast.

As adrenaline danced in her veins, she checked the rearview mirror. Thick build, brutish features, the man resembled an ogre…and he was staring after them. "Is that your husband?"

"My husband's brother." Sue Ellen tried to turn and flinched at the movement. "He's exactly like Billy. His wife divorced him last year and moved out of state. I should've gone with her." She stared down at her hands. Bruises mottled the back of one in the shape of a heel. "I was too pregnant and too scared."

"But you're here now, and you'll have help," Anne said in a soothing voice. She'd misjudged Sue Ellen on the phone. This woman wasn't about to go back to her husband. Probably the bruise on the baby's face had strengthened her resolve. It was amazing how many women would finally act when their children were in danger.

"Billy will come after me," Sue Ellen said, a tremor in her voice. "He won't give up. And he has a lot of friends."

"The shelter's address isn't listed anywhere. And there are safeguards."

Hopefully, the brother hadn't been quick enough to read the SUV's license plate, but even then, no problem. Although the Ford Escape was Anne's, since she drove it for fugitive apprehensions, her registration papers used the bail office as the address of record. Her own residence and phone number were unlisted.

Anne reached over and patted the woman's leg. "You and your little boy are going to be fine."

"We got away." Sue Ellen's chin lifted. "Me and my baby'll start a new life. From scratch, but that's all right. We're free to make our own way."

Tears stung Anne's eyes. The woman had left behind everything. But rather than dwelling on her loss, she'd set her sights on building something new.

That truly was courage. In the light of this shining example, could Anne be any less brave?

Ben was her man, her submissive. It was her job to provide what he needed. To do that, she had to be brave enough to dig deep and hear what he had to say.

# Chapter Twenty-One

On Saturday, Ben followed Mistress Anne up the Shadowlands spiral staircase, admiring the stiletto boots that barely showed under the rear of her black skirt. In the front, her skirt split almost to her crotch, giving tantalizing glimpses of her lightly tanned thighs.

Her black stretchy tank was his favorite—tight enough she went without a bra and her cleavage was emphasized by the sheer black lace around the neckline. Her outfit looked even sexier now that she'd removed the gold-trimmed vest she'd worn as a dungeon monitor.

How did she manage to look like a wet dream and still deliver that gut-clenching sense of menace?

Even Ghost, who was manning the security guard desk tonight, had given her a respectful look.

Ben reached the top and followed her down a quiet hall. Downstairs was where all the action was, right? "Why upstairs?" he wondered under his breath. Did she not want to be seen with him? Aside from not being her normal choice, he wasn't a particularly good slave either.

Although he hadn't spoken loudly, she answered. "Because you shouldn't have to deal with the discomfort of scening in public on top of the nasty things that I want to do to you."

*Jesus.* His jeans were way too fucking uncomfortable now.

She stopped at a door and let him open it for her—a habit he liked. She might be magnificently dominant and one of the deadliest women he knew, but she enjoyed letting him behave like a gentleman.

Wasn't there an old saying about the perfect woman being a lady in public and a whore in the bedroom?

Anne was a lady in public and a ballbuster—literally—in private.

With a smile, she trailed her hand over his bare chest as she walked past. "And, since I don't indulge myself for all to see, the privacy is for me as well."

*Indulge.* Refined language that meant he'd get to go down on her or fuck her.

A private room had advantages without a doubt.

He closed the door behind him and checked out the surroundings. Sure wasn't the western room they'd used before, but more like the clichéd "harem" décor seen in old black-and-white movies.

Of course, the Shadowlands took the theme to a whole new level.

Opulent. Lavish. Darkly erotic.

Showcased in the center was a mahogany-fretworked canopy. Its golden draperies half-concealed a wide lounge.

Ben looked up. The ceiling was painted maroon and stenciled with elaborate designs. Under his bare feet was a silky Oriental carpet in golds and reds. *Amazing.* The whole room sang of carnal heat—and his blood was picking up the tune.

At the door, Anne turned a dial, dimming the brass-and-amber candelabra lights on the metal-trimmed dresser.

As Ben checked out the X-shaped St. Andrew's cross in one corner, his image in the ornate mirror on the wall duplicated his movements. Great—he could watch himself getting his ass beat.

He eyed Anne. "So...am I the sultan or the eunuch, Ma'am?"

"Well, Benjamin, let's check." She reached between his legs, fondled his solid erection, and cupped his balls.

The surprise was a shot of hi-test octane to his spine.

"Mmm." Her appreciative hum made his chest expand. "You're definitely not a eunuch. I do believe all your equipment is functioning nicely."

His blood pressure rose. If she kept stroking him like that, he'd show her every function he had.

Then she gave his testicles a toe-curling squeeze and moved away to set her toy bag on an ebonized-wood Moroccan chest. "Strip off the jeans, please, Benjamin. Then lie down on the chaise longue there."

"No restraints, Ma'am?" He could try the bondage shit. He would. For her.

"Not this time." As she pulled two floggers and a short, ugly black whip from her bag, her half-smile was...worrisome. "I don't think you'll move a muscle after I begin."

His feet halted at that. In fact, his gas pedal was stuck on empty until she jerked her chin at the chaise.

Fuck, she was going to mess with him all right.

Yet, as he walked across the room and drew in slow, deep breaths, his mind eased into acceptance, sliding down into a quiet place that was both erotic as hell and almost meditative. The combination was unsettling. She'd hurt him in a way that wasn't…quite…pain, dealing out sensations that'd transmuted inside him into something new. Something fucking carnal.

Sometimes the burn was that of an intense workout, one where his muscles were pumped and screaming to stop. He loved a good exercise rush—but working out never gave him a hard-on like this.

Or made him want to put his arms around the weights and kiss them senseless, to drive himself into—

"*Ben.*"

"Right. Sorry, Mistress." Stripping didn't take long since all he'd worn were jeans. He set them to one side and stretched out on the unusual furniture. Fairly comfortable. Wide enough for his shoulders. Even had an armrest on the right side.

A man had to wonder what'd happened to the second armrest.

At the St. Andrew's cross, Anne was setting up her instruments of pain and pleasure. Then she dipped into her toy bag one more time, removing a pair of scissors, a towel, and a small brush and comb.

"You going to cut my hair?"

Both of her dimples showed. "That depends on your answer."

He liked his hair, but… *Man up, Haugen.* "If my long hair bothers you, go ahead, Ma'am. Wouldn't be the first time I've had short hair."

Her laugh was low. "I wasn't talking about the hair on your head, guard dog."

*Oh shit.* He managed not to cover up his package. Barely. "You want to shave my dick?"

"Actually, yes." Her smile widened. "You see, Benjamin"—she sat on the lounge beside him—"I object to having hair in my face, which means you lose out on nice long blowjobs, which I enjoy giving."

She'd suck his dick? And like it? He inhaled slowly. "I thought Dominants weren't into offering BJ's."

Puzzlement drew her brows together before she shook her head. "I'm sorry, Ben. You've been part of the Shadowlands so long, I sometimes forget you've been stuck out in the entry. You're right to a degree. Some Doms believe going down on their submissive decreases their power." She took his hand and sucked on one finger.

His cock did a victory dance.

"Some Dommes think that, done right, the person giving head is the one in control."

His cock sure as hell agreed. "Is that why you grab my hair when I go down on you? To make sure I know who's in charge?"

"You've very perceptive."

And he sure wasn't missing the point of the discussion. She'd give him a blowjob if he lost his curlies. He looked at her soft lips…imagined them elsewhere…and couldn't come up with the hint of an argument. "I'm in, Ma'am. Whatever you want."

"Very good. Thank you, Ben." She slapped his leg lightly. "Open up, now."

As he spread his legs, he frowned. "No razor?"

"I'm content with trimmed hair, and we won't risk irritated skin." After putting a towel between his thighs, she picked up the dauntingly pointed scissors. "I trust you can keep from moving?"

He could feel his balls shriveling. "Oh yeah, Ma'am."

As Anne cut his curly hair to an even half-inch, her concentration—and competence—was damned reassuring.

After a minute, he relaxed, listened to the low, exotic Moroccan music and drew in the sandalwood-scented air. Z didn't miss a trick, did he?

Each time Anne moved his cock and balls with her soft hands, Ben felt like a pampered sultan being tended by one of his harem girls.

Of course, if he shared that with the Mistress, he'd end up a eunuch.

"There. You look lovely. And even bigger," she said.

He glanced down. The shortening of the forest made his dick appear another inch or two longer. "Want to…ah…check your work, Ma'am? Make sure it's short enough."

Yeah, her laugh went right to his cock.

"Sorry, Benjamin, but you have to earn a blowjob. Tonight, if you take everything I give you, I'll suck you most of the way off—and let you finish by taking me as roughly as you want."

*Totally* his fantasy. His breath wedged in his chest. "That's a hell of an incentive."

She pointed to the St. Andrew's cross. "Then get over there, grab the pegs, and hang on."

As he crossed the room, his dick registered the added wind factor, but then his brain got caught up in other thoughts. Like she planned to beat on him. Hard.

Anticipation made his blood churn…and his mouth dry. His hands closed around the pegs, and he braced.

The first blows of her flogger were nothing as she teased the falls over his skin, tickling and stroking. Mild hand swats were a pleasant punctuation.

Then the strands hit more forcefully. Not a problem. He liked her thumpy floggers. They reminded him of a light artillery barrage.

But when she upped the game and started to really nail him, his shoulders and back and ass began to sting. His skin tightened, the sensation changing from a light to a nasty sunburn.

Yet, his cock persistently pointed toward the ceiling.

The entire room began to feel like the Grand Bazaar under a hot noon sun, and he broke out in a sweat.

"That was the easy stuff, Benjamin," she said quietly. "Now your test begins."

*Easy? Fuck.* He'd thought she'd be about ready to finish. "Yes, Ma'am."

"Bend and spread your cheeks."

"What?" His glutes tensed, and he turned. Anal? "I told you I wouldn't—"

"Your restriction was because"—she tilted her head and quoted him—"'*I don't know you well enough for whips or anal shit.*' I'd say that's changed."

Well, hell.

She smiled slightly, reading his acceptance. "Your ass is mine, my tiger. But—if it helps, I'm not going to don a fake cock and pound you with it."

"There's a relief."

His sarcasm got him a swift slap of the flogger, far too close to his balls.

He barely bit back a bark of concern. After a second, he bowed his head; he'd been out of line. "Sorry, Ma'am."

She stepped nearer and put her palm on his cheek. "I know this worries you. But I'm going to use a small anal plug. We'll talk about it afterward. If it's truly a problem after you try it, I'll respect your wishes."

He let out the lungful of air he'd held. Couldn't get much fairer than that—aside from not doing it at all. But, she probably knew her way around a man's body better than he did, even if he lived in one.

And hey, he had a blowjob waiting at the end of this. "Go for it, Ma'am."

She rocked up and gave him a long, luscious, appreciative kiss. "You're a brave man, Haugen."

*Rangers lead the way.*

Yet, her words, *"You're a brave man,"* sent a slow slide of satisfaction through him. As he turned, he wondered if the Mistress realized she never called him *boy* as she had with her slaves. Her previous slaves.

Bending, he gripped his ass cheeks and opened. *Prostate exam, here we go.*

Cool liquid drizzled over his crack. Something pressed against his backhole.

*Fuck.*

"Push back against it, my tiger. It'll go in easier."

Gritting his teeth hard enough to bust a mouthful of molars, he obeyed and felt the damn thing slide in. He'd glimpsed it as he'd turned—the size of a fat man's thumb—so why did it feel big as a fucking fist?

*Burning. Stretching.* Finally, it settled into position with a plop. He had a plug in his ass.

"Thank you for taking that, Benjamin. Taking it for me," she said softly, her hands caressing his hips and thighs. "It means a lot to me."

He exhaled. The feeling of her gentle hands on his skin and the sheer...ownership...of her claiming that forbidden place sent a heated warmth through him.

He was hers. That was right. The way it should be.

Did she realize possessiveness went both ways?

"Stand and hold the pegs again," she instructed.

As he straightened, he had to grit his teeth. The damn invader sat in his backhole like he'd—

She reached around him and gripped his cock with her slicked fingers.

*Oh shit, yeah.* His hands clenched the pegs convulsively.

Her breasts were against his back, her hips against his ass. Her firm fingers slid up and down his dick, over and over. And then she moved a hand down between their bodies and wiggled the ass plug.

Every single fucking nerve back there wakened with a roar. "Fuck!" As the urgent, needy throbbing consumed his entire groin area, he almost came right then and there.

"Yes, I rather thought you might enjoy this."

She waggled it again.

He made an indescribable noise as he fought back his release.

She laughed. *Fucking sadist.*

Her fingers pumped his shaft, then gripped his balls, squeezing mercilessly enough to turn his shortened curlies gray—and yet, the damn thing in his ass made her every sadistic action feel like shiny-bright pleasure.

She stepped back and picked up the other flogger, the vicious one that stung like hell. Even as she started, his cock was pulsing in time with his ass and balls in a carnal concerto. And the stinging blows from the flogger were amping up the volume.

Every stroke seemed to hit in rhythm with his pulse—and the throbbing of his dick. More and more...and as his brain filled with smoke, the world slid sideways until each blow was a hot splash of sensation sliding down his back right to his straining shaft.

"Don't you just look pretty, all glassy-eyed."

He realized she'd turned him around. Had put her hands on his face.

Her eyes were bright, sunlight through a gray sky. Pink flushed her high cheekbones. Her hair had escaped the braid to create fine tendrils over her temples and neck. Her shoulders and arms were pumped up...and he could see her bunched nipples beneath her elastic tank.

"Fuck, you're beautiful," he said. Thought he said. Wasn't sure.

Her eyes half closed, and her voice came out a low murmur. "You're something, Benjamin." She caressed his cheek and kissed him so sweetly, so fucking lovingly that his heart did a slow somersault.

Damn, he loved her.

But then she moved back. "Drink this, and we'll move on to other things." She curled his fingers around the bottle and helped him hold it.

His head wasn't...quite...in the game, but his body was demanding those *other things*. Was screaming, *sex, sex, sex*, with every pulsation of his cock, every throb of his asshole. He wanted to go down on her, to taste her sweetness, inhale her musk, run his tongue over—

She pinched his arm. "*Drink*, Benjamin."

As he gulped the cool liquid, his head cleared. Slightly.

But seeing her strip right down to naked yanked his mind into sharp focus. She even released her hair and left it loose the way he liked it. *Oh yeah.*

When she stepped to the lounge and crooked her fingers, he was right there with her, first sitting, then letting her push him onto his back.

In this position, the fucking anal plug felt bigger. Dammit.

Yet, the discomfort disappeared when Anne bent and gave him his first treat—a long, slow kiss.

Sometimes she kissed like a Domme—controlling and teasing— and sometimes she was all soft, generous woman. Damned if he didn't savor both. Today, he got the sweet as if to provide a contrast to the sadistic, flogger-wielding Mistress.

Still kissing him, she sat on the lounge. When she lifted her head, he expected her to cut to the chase. Instead, she nuzzled his cheek.

Then his jaw. His neck. So very gentle, and he realized she was kissing each white scar. So sweetly.

He closed his eyes and relaxed into the sensations—despite the increasing demands of his dick. Warm lips, then she gave him a sharp bite at the base of his neck.

He'd have a mark there in the morning—but compared to the way his back burned and his cock throbbed, the pain barely registered. "Ow," he murmured and heard her chuckle.

Trailed by the cool silk of her hair, her lips moseyed down his body, over his collarbone, and down to tease his nipples. She kissed his belly. And moved down. When she reached his hips, his heart rammed into overdrive.

Wet and slick, her tongue licked up his cock and traced a single vein's twisted path from base to helmet before trailing back down again. Each exhalation bathed him with a puff of warmth. She was going to kill him.

When she slid him into her hot, hot mouth, he had to fist the cushion to keep from losing all control.

Even as she engulfed him in heat, her tongue roamed over him, around him. The skin of his cock felt too fucking tight, the pressure growing, even as she took him deeper.

Ever so slowly, she lifted her head, sliding upward, her lips squeezing his shaft like a narrow fist.

When she sucked on the tip, small explosions lit the area behind his eyes.

"Breathe, Benjamin. If you come, I'll be displeased. I want you to finish in me."

She'd promised him rough sex. A blowjob and rough sex—birthday and Christmas combined.

Although…he might not live that long.

Her hands curled around his balls, rolling the nuts, even as she sucked his cock in, hard and fast, right down into her throat. Then out again. Bobbing up and down. She let him go and sent a puff of cool air over his wet skin—and she tugged on his balls.

His hips rose at the jolt of sensation.

Her teeth nipped a trail down his shaft, sending sharp zings up his spine, then she bathed him in heat when she took him back in her mouth.

The pleasure was purely fucking enormous.

She worked him, giving generously, taking him deeper than anyone ever had. Abandoning his rocks, her hand slid down to toy with the anal plug until the entire area from cock to anus merged into one sensitive nerve, shrieking for release.

Pressure built, searing in intensity, drawing his balls upward.

Even as he approached the point of no return, she wrapped her fingers around the base of his dick and squeezed. Backing him off.

He let out a groan of both relief and serious fucking frustration and met her amused...and very heated gaze.

His cock throbbed, the plug throbbed; he needed to come, but damned if he'd give up one moment of his chance to enjoy her with no restraints. With an effort, he cleared his throat. "Thank you, Ma'am. My turn? Please?"

She angled her head in agreement. "Your turn."


Before Anne's next heartbeat, her *slave* was off the lounge and on her like a savage. One second she was sitting; the next, she was flat on her back.

"Finally," he growled, running his callused hands up and down, from her hips to her shoulders, from her pussy to her breasts.

Zeroing right in, he licked and kissed one breast before moving to the other, leaving a hot throbbing in his wake. His lips were firm, his tongue wet—and her breasts already felt overly sensitive and swollen. She must have put on weight; no more sharing his sweets.

When he drew one nipple into his mouth and sucked strongly, she closed her eyes under the inferno of desire. He was rough, his usual *I'm-a-big-man* restraint shattered by how deep he'd gone into subspace—and his ravenousness hit her like a hammerblow.

Feeling her control sliding away, she put her arms around him, pulled him down, and opened her legs.

Burning tiger's eyes met hers with raw determination. "You said as I want."

She had.

Rather than taking her, he firmly set her hands onto the cushions...and moved down her body. A nip on her stomach was soothed by the caress of his tongue.

When he nuzzled her mound, the muscles drew taut in her belly.

His breath stroked her pussy with a waft of warm air before he licked slowly over her clit with unerring precision.

The full, hot sensation lit every nerve in her lower half, and she moaned.

His head rose, and his cautious, tawny eyes regarded her for long seconds.

She could see the moment he decided she wasn't taking back her gift—that he really could do as he wished.

He forcefully pushed her legs apart. Curling his big hands under her ass, he ran his thumbs up and separated her labia. Opened her widely. A second later, he began to…feast. His tongue was everywhere, tracing her folds, dipping in, teasing her clit, sending pleasure rioting around her system.

He sucked her, licked her. As the clawing need grew within her, her hips rose, demanding more.

"Uh-uh." He lifted, propping himself up with a hand on her pelvis and holding her down in the process. Slowly, ever so slowly, he slid a thick finger in her pussy.

Lovely new nerves wakened to life under the slow stretch and friction. *More. Need more.* She reached for his hair…then pulled her hands back. This was his reward—and she sure couldn't complain of his skills.

When he added another finger, the sensuous slide of his thrusting made her breathing hitch. And then his tongue lashed her clit, top and side, as he plunged his fingers in and out in a demanding rhythm.

Up, up, everything tightened inside her. The tension built, and her legs trembled, her muscles turned taut.

His laugh rumbled against her skin and then his lips closed tightly around her clit and he sucked. Sucked *hard.*

Her breathing stopped completely as the pressure peaked and then an upsurge of sensation rolled over her, through her—drowning her in pleasure.

Wave after wave.

Even as she gasped for air, he flipped her onto her hands and knees, and came down on her. One iron arm curved around her waist as he fit himself to her entrance.

"Brace yourself, Mistress. I'm so fucking going to take you."

"Be—"

He slammed into her.

She was so swollen that his penetration shocked her with the force of a blow. He felt huge, filling her to the point of pain—and yet his second violent thrust pitched her right over into an unstoppable, shocking orgasm. Her head swam as the blinding release shuddered up her center.

"Fuck, woman, yes." His low, harsh voice rumbled against her like a landslide. Pressed deep within her, he palmed her breasts and pulled on her nipples, drawing out the waves impossibly.

*God.* Her fingers curled around the lounge frame. Her arms gave out, dropping her head to the cushions as her whole body sang with delight.

"Anne." At the strained sound, she realized he'd held himself in check. Worrying about her.

From somewhere, she managed one tiny breath. "*Take* me, Benjamin. Hard."

"Thank fucking Christ." His hands seized her hips as he pulled out fast, and then he hauled her back onto his cock. Growling his pleasure, he controlled her, pushing her off his shaft and yanking her on in a rhythmic impalement. Again and again. The slapping sounds of flesh on flesh echoed in the room along with the wet noises and his grunts of enjoyment.

With each breath, she drew in the scents of sex, his clean, earthy aftershave, and tantalizing musk.

His fingers gripped her hips fiercely enough to bruise, adding the kind of erotic pain she'd given him, like a high note in the song that was sex.

And then he drove painfully deep, holding there as his thick shaft pulsed. His guttural groan was born in the depths of the earth.

God, she loved him.

He stayed still a moment, frozen in place, as the tides of pleasure flowed between them.

With a low sigh, he curved his arms around her and rolled them onto their sides, her back to his chest. Her head rested on his arm and his other hand settled over her breast. Still intimately deep inside her, he shaped himself as closely to her as he could.

He kissed her hair, rumbling something unintelligible, and then simply held her as if she was the most precious thing he had.

Her hand covered his, holding him to her, feeling his warmth all along her back, feeling the strength in his arms.

No one had ever held her like this.

With tears burning her eyes, she lifted his hand and kissed his fingers. *I love you, love you, love you so, so much.*

The rush of emotion was overwhelming.

Terrifying. Where were they going with this? She breathed out slowly. This was the time she was supposed to talk with him and find out what was bothering him. To learn how to make things better for him.

He curved his hand under her cheek; his thumb stroked her lips.

How did women handle such emotions? A tremor shook her as her happiness mingled with the fear of losing him.

Already, he was so inextricably connected to her that they were practically living together. She'd never allowed her slaves to become such a daily part of her life. If nothing else, she'd withdrawn from them before and during her period, because, Lord knew, she turned into a bit of a grump. Although Ben hadn't ever compl—

Between one breath and the next, her head got light. A roaring in her ears drowned out the music.

*Her period.*

How long since she had a period? Her heart started to thud painfully.

For sure, she'd menstruated on St. Patrick's Day in March. Harrison had thrown a party, but she'd been flowing so heavily she'd foregone wearing her favorite white slacks.

Had she had one since? Being on birth control pills, she was always on time. She visualized the packet...she was days into the blank pills. *Days late.* Dismay seized her.

*No...no.* The lateness must be due to stress. Or something. Anything.

She'd made a sound for Ben's arms tightened. "Anne? Was I too rough?"

Rough? She tried a laugh and succeeded. He hadn't been too forceful, but perhaps too potent? *Oh God.* "No. No, you were amazing. Wonderful." She rubbed her cheek on his palm, feeling the structure of her life start to shred.

Pushing her worries away was similar to rolling a boulder uphill, but she managed. She'd figure out what was...going on...later. Ben *had* been amazing. And she'd taken him pretty deep during the flogging. He needed her full attention and some pampering.

Her own concerns would have to wait.


As Anne led the way out of the private rooms upstairs, Ben's back burned from the flogger. His asshole was tender, although the plug was gone. He shook his head. He'd hated having to admit that the anal jobbie had ignited every fucking nerve he had.

The good Mistress had known exactly what it would do.

He'd come so violently, it was a wonder his head hadn't blown off.

Anne stopped at the head of the spiral stairs and tucked an arm around his waist. "Are you all right, my tiger?" Her heavy-lidded eyes assessed him, tallying his resources in the way he'd done with his team before taking them into enemy territory.

Although she was unusually quiet, her smile showed her pleasure in him. She'd enjoyed getting him off and didn't hesitate to let him know.

"I'm more than good." He tucked a loose strand of hair behind her ear. Her hair was still damp from her shower—which she'd needed. She'd come as hard as he had, another thing he loved about her. No pretenses, no bullshit. She liked sex and wasn't afraid to show it.

Smiling, he put an arm around her shoulders, needing her close. He'd never felt so much for a woman before, as if more than his body and emotions were bound to her.

"So. Did you enjoy your rough sex or...?" She lifted an eyebrow.

Or did he prefer her in charge? "I liked grabbing and taking over— as a change of pace." He grinned. "I'm a guy; we live to hammer things. But..." The notion of her not ruling in the bedroom, not giving him orders in her throaty voice, not putting her stilettoed heel on his chest or even his balls, made him uncomfortable. As if he'd dropped his compass and GPS unit and had no stars with which to navigate. "I'm yours to command, Ma'am, and I prefer it that way."

"I'm pleased as well."

"And thank you, Mistress, for the treat today." He kissed the top of her head and murmured, "All of the treats."

Her smile held tenderness and enough caring that his heart seemed to expand within the confines of his ribcage. And yet...her eyes were vulnerable. Almost confused. His protective instincts surged to the fore.

"What's wrong?" He started to step back.

She didn't answer, just pulled his head down and took his mouth right there on the stairs. Her kiss was so abso-fucking-loving, her Mistress rep might well be endangered.

Or enhanced.

Fuck, he didn't think he could fall for her further, but apparently so.

When she released him, he didn't straighten, but smiled into her eyes. "I could use a drink if the Mistress would permit?"

"Of course. Let's see what Cullen can round up."

Something else he enjoyed. She didn't deny him something just to be bitchy. Although she sure pushed that protocol shit.

The trouble was she didn't change when she left the Shadowlands or the bedroom. When the sex was over and done, she still held the reins, and he wasn't so sure he liked that.

Out in the field, when in reach of the enemy, he'd always wanted the chain of command clear. Wanted no questions as to who was in charge. But back at base or on leave? *No.*

"Uzuri," Anne said as they walked past the trainee. "Can you bring us drinks, please? A beer for Ben, water for me. And some of the less messy finger foods?"

"Of course, Mistress Anne."

As Uzuri glided toward the bar, Ben lifted his eyebrows. "No alcohol for you, Ma'am?"

"Since you hit subspace, I'm designated driver," she said quietly. "And I'm tired enough that alcohol wouldn't be wise." One dimple dented her cheek. "You have so many muscles that it takes a long time to flog them all."

She knew just how to make a man feel fucking pumped up.

As he chuckled, he noticed a raised hand near the center of the room at the same time she did.

Galen was motioning for them to join him.

Anne nodded and headed that direction, her arm around Ben's waist as if she wanted to be sure he was with her. Or didn't trust him to walk in a straight line.

As they passed through the room, she greeted various members. Ben caught a wave from Rainie, spotted Z and Cullen watching from the bar, and smiled at Linda, who sat with her Dom, Sam.

Beth stopped Anne with news that the latest addition to the shelter was doing well, although her abusive husband and all his cohorts were raising a ruckus with the woman's family and friends as they hunted for her.

Damn good thing the shelter was well hidden.

Galen and Vance rose as they approached. "Anne. Can you join us?" Galen asked. "I had a question about skip tracing."

"Of course."

The men resumed their chairs with their submissive Sally kneeling on the floor between them.

Anne took the chair across from them.

Ben figured he was probably supposed to go to his knees too. As he hesitated, he noticed Raoul nearby, supervising a scene with Kim kneeling beside him.

"Benjamin," Anne murmured and glanced at her feet.

As he settled there, he decided he was good with the position. *Here.* In many ways, the Shadowlands felt like an erotic war zone with the same kind of power shifts, and aside from his knees expressing their annoyance, he liked kneeling for her.

Liked her hand in his hair.

When she shifted to trap him between her legs, he felt only satisfaction.

He turned so he could slide an arm around her hips. Her split skirt had fallen open, and he pressed a kiss to her inner thigh, inhaling the fragrance of freshly clean skin and the lotion she used on her legs.

Instant turn-on since these scents marked his favorite erotic path. Starting here, he could travel upward and reach journey's end. Or the beginning. He kissed an inch higher and caught the scent of her delicate musk.

When he tried for another inch, the Mistress smacked the back of his head and gave him a reprimanding look.

He could only grin. After any scene when she'd combined pain and pleasure, he'd noticed the strangest contentment, as if the bond between them would grow to encompass more than just hearts and souls. "Sorry, Ma'am."

She huffed a laugh. "Such a bad subbie." As she stroked his hair, he tilted his cheek into her hand as Bronx would. Hell, he'd be happy to be her pet.

*Here, at least.*

What did she think, though? What did she want? She was so bloody reserved. Fucking honest, yes, but getting past her defenses was akin to assaulting a medieval castle.

They needed to talk. Soon. But right now, his head was still on the fuzzy side. Discussions could wait. With a sigh, Ben contented himself with being close.

After a minute, he realized Raoul was watching them and frowning. Probably because he saw one well-used guy wearing only jeans, hair loose, with a bite mark on his neck. In contrast, Anne was perfectly made up and clean.

It undoubtedly looked as if she'd worked him over good without breaking a sweat. Without getting involved in the least.

He laughed silently. She looked so put together because she'd popped into the shower and cleaned up. In fact, she'd given him a half-smile as she did so, saying, *"I have to uphold the honor of all Mistresses everywhere."*

He could have joined her, but his legs had felt like over-stretched rubberbands. And when she'd run her hands over his damp chest and said she'd enjoy showing off her sweaty submissive, he'd have denied her nothing.

Uzuri returned with their drinks.

Anne took the beer—a Brooklyn Lager—put it into Ben's hand and accepted the water. "Thank you, Uzuri."

As Anne fed him the food, taking only a few bites for herself, she, Galen, and Vance discussed search techniques, software she preferred for skip tracing, and tricks used in changing identities.

In a comfortable haze, Ben drank his beer. At some point, he realized he was leaning with all his weight against her legs—strong woman—while her fingertips traced patterns on his shoulders.

Yeah, he liked right where he was. And he'd think about the rest when his head was on straight.

# Chapter Twenty-Two

Anne stood in her bathroom the next morning, counting off seconds as she watched the strip from the pregnancy kit.

Misery burned in her gut when she thought of the way she'd left Ben earlier.

He'd still been half-asleep when she'd slid out of his bed, kissed him, and told him she needed some quiet "alone" time. And that she'd see him on Monday.

*"What the fuck?"* he'd said. Waking completely, he'd tried to grab her hand, but she stepped away and firmed her resolve. Pulled on her Domme armor.

"Tomorrow, Benjamin," she'd said firmly. The unhappiness in his eyes had hurt her heart. "I'll see you on Monday."

She hadn't had any excuses to offer him…because she'd wanted to do this test first. No need to worry him if she was completely off base.

Biting her lip, her stomach in knots, she watched the colors shift on the *are-you-or-aren't-you* strip. Even before the final second, she knew the result.

Oh, she really, really was.

*Pregnant.*

No question at all about those colors. Her legs shook as she crossed her bedroom and sank down on the fainting couch. It was a well-named piece of furniture.

For long minutes, she just sat there. Stunned stupid.

Outside her bedroom window, a gull screeched its laugh.

"I'm missing the humor in this, bird." How in the world could she be pregnant? She was on birth control. She never missed a pill. Ever.

Then realization hit like a body slam. *Ever*...except that time when she got a stomach bug and puked her guts out. Three days' worth of throwing up. Three days of no pills.

Ben was the only man she'd been with then. But, dammit, he'd worn a condom.

*Except...*

As dismay filled her, she dropped her head into her hands. That first time they'd been together, he'd entered her and yanked back out in a hurry. After sheathing himself, he'd continued, and neither of them had thought much about it. After all, they were both tested at the Shadowlands...and she was on the pill.

*Just shoot me now.*

But surely she'd had a period after that. Back in April, right? Her lips pressed together. Actually, she hadn't experienced more than a few cramps and some spotting—enough to make her think she'd had one.

How far along was she then? She frowned. Z's Sophia was born at the end of March and that was when she and Ben had first had sex. This was May.

She was six weeks pregnant? *No way.*

*Way.* Her hand cupped her stomach as she gulped.

No wonder she'd been unable to summon any appetite for breakfast over the past week and had made up for the lack by eating like gangbusters later in the day. She was pregnant.

*I'm going to have a baby.*

As exhilaration swept through her, the room seemed to brighten. And then anxiety slid cold fingers up her spine. Because this was wrong. She wasn't married. Wasn't prepared.

A rueful laugh escaped. Here she'd been terrified of change and carefully guarded her structured life. Looked as if structure had flown right out the window.

She was going to be a single mother. This was just...impossible. She swallowed hard. How could she tell Ben? Or her family?

Daddy would have a cow.

Mom would... Later today, she'd planned to visit her mother to wish her Happy Mother's Day. Now there was irony. *"Happy Grandmother's Day, Mom."*

But Mom would deal. And after the shock was over, she'd be wonderful.

What about work? Anne closed her hands on the cushion and stared at the wall. Stared at the image of her, heavy with child, chasing after a fugitive. Her job was not a good...fit...for a pregnant woman.

Oh God, what a total mess.

She'd have to quit before she got to that point.

Because the only other option was to terminate the pregnancy. Everything inside her rejected the idea. *My baby. And Ben's. Ours.* Warmth filled her as she thought of what the combination of genes might produce. Norwegian and French—nice mixture.

How was she going to tell Ben? She pushed to her feet and walked out onto the balcony. The morning was foggy and still. Grayness covered the world, blurred the shore, erased the horizon. Invisible waves hissed on the beach.

"Ben, my dear. You're going to be a father." She leaned her forearms on the railing and imagined his reaction.

He wouldn't be furious. And he liked children.

The problem was their relationship. Because he was uncomfortable with being her slave. Her hand rubbed her sternum, trying to ease the ache beneath it.

He wasn't happy.

He'd told her he was doing good. That he loved being her slave, but…did he? Really? He'd reassured her enough earlier that she'd overlooked the signs—because she hadn't wanted to see them. Because she was a coward.

In bed, they had no problems whatsoever. The rest of the time…he was struggling.

If she told him that she was pregnant, he'd turn protective and demand to marry her. Insist on taking care of her. He'd stay.

But…she swallowed against the thickness growing in her throat. She didn't want him if he married her just for the baby. She'd seen parents who'd remained together for a child's sake, and all the child saw was dislike and coldness. Not love.

Better to be separate.

A chilled sea breeze whipped at her clothes and blew her hair into her face. She pushed the damp strands away, feeling the worries piling up. They were so new, she and Ben. Too new to make decisions like this.

He should be able to choose her—just her—without the pressure of a baby or her family's expectations or his own principles.

She loved him. Oh God, she really did. She wanted to be with him forever. Needed him in her life. But love meant she also wanted the best for him.

She mustn't mess up his life with her wants and wishes.

He'd never said he loved her.

Well, she hadn't told him either. Fair was fair. She frowned, trying to think of why it seemed worse that he hadn't. Maybe because Ben didn't hold things back, so if he did love her, he would have said so. For a Dominant to say it first—when she wasn't certain of her submissive—felt like coercion.

Did he love her?

She wasn't...sure. She blinked quickly against the prickling in her eyes. He acted as if he did, but this was Ben, who always cared for the people he'd taken on and who found joy in looking after his family and his Domme.

Even if he did love her, they hadn't proven they could live together, had they?

No, they hadn't.

She looked down at her stomach. "Sorry, baby. But you need to keep quiet for a bit longer. Your daddy should have a chance to decide if he can stand *me* before he has to deal with an *us*.

What if he couldn't?

Far behind the clouds, the sun remained hidden. The thick fog dampened her skin, engulfing her in mist. She couldn't see anything— let alone what was coming.

Everything in her wanted to share, to tell Ben, her family, everyone. To rejoice.

But...not yet. *Be fair, Anne. Give the man time.* Surely she could stay in control and simply take each moment as it came.

Maybe, maybe it would all work out.

*Please, God, let it work out.*

# Chapter Twenty-Three

As the sun glimmered its last rays on the horizon, Ben walked through Anne's house, filled with dread. Even as his heart rose in anticipation of seeing her, the rest of him was tense as hell because he just knew this was going to turn into a clusterfuck. His stomach felt like he'd lunched on ground glass instead of McD's.

When she'd hauled ass out of his bed on Sunday and said she needed a break from him, she'd given him no other fucking explanation. As if he didn't deserve to know anything. As if he wasn't anything more than a slave. As if he had no right to anything more than a command.

He'd known then that Raoul was correct. He had to man up and tell her the slavery shit wasn't working.

He'd gotten his head around the appropriately diplomatic words and had been ready to talk with her on Monday.

And then one of his Ranger buddies had returned Stateside and needed support, so he'd spent Monday and most of today there. The diplomatic words had disappeared from his brain. So had his courage. He was tired, dammit.

Maybe he should delay the "discussion" until tomorrow?

He walked onto Anne's deck to see her on the long swing, talking on the phone. Her saxophone leaned against her legs.

"I'm so glad you called," Anne was saying. She looked up and her smile wavered when she saw him. Tears had turned her eyes a rainy gray as she swiped the phone to off.

Concerned, he sat beside her and took her hand.

Automatically, she frowned at their hands and glanced at the deck. She wanted him to kneel.

Although his gut clenched, he stayed where he was. "Problems? Bad news?"

"No. Happy news. Kim agreed to marry Raoul. They're engaged."

So the little slave was going to be a wife as well. *Good job, Raoul.* "Andrea and Cullen are engaged, too." The Shadowlands' Masters were falling fast. "So, more weddings this summer?"

"I'm afraid not. Kim's wedding will probably be in Georgia, where her mother is. And Andrea's grandmother wants a Catholic ceremony with all the trimmings, which takes months to schedule and plan."

"I'm surprised Cullen was willing to wait."

"Cullen knows better than to take on Andrea's *abuela.*" Anne grinned. "She's a pint-sized, Hispanic version of Z's mother."

Shit, he wouldn't take her on either. "So no weddings any time soon. But Kim's engagement is good news, right? Why the tears?" He touched Anne's wet cheek, feeling a pull at his heart. Had he ever seen her cry before?

She rubbed at her face. "Happy tears. Kim suffered so many horrors, and…she kept dodging Raoul about getting married. Her father treated her mother like a slave, so she saw marriage as servitude without the love."

Anne's lips pressed together. "Children shouldn't be given bad models. It messes with their heads."

She sounded pretty vehement, but she'd probably seen some screwed-up examples of dysfunction at the shelter. "I guess."

"How was your day?" Anne asked.

"Good enough. I didn't get rained on, at least."

She tilted her head. "Then what's wrong?" She was studying his face. Such a Domme. Sometimes she rivaled Z with her mind-reading ability.

So much for avoiding the discussion. And, yeah, he'd been procrastinating for long enough. He lifted her hand. "When I sat down on the swing and took your hand, you frowned. How come?" He already knew the answer.

"You know why, Benjamin. Because my slaves kneel and touch me only when given permission." Her gaze met his directly. Unapologetically.

His mouth felt dry. "Yeah. That's what I figured." He ran his free hand through his hair, tempted to yank at it. *Fuck.*

"Those protocols bother you." She regarded him narrowly. "You were all right at first, but rather than growing comfortable with them, you're having problems."

He nodded. "Listen, Anne."

"Who?" Her expression flashed cool.

His mistake. But see, that was another problem. Her name *was* Anne. "Mistress, I'm not a slave. Not even a full-time submissive. I'm totally down with the D/s stuff in the bedroom, but not the rest of the time. I don't need you making all my decisions for me. I'm not a child."

"But…" Her voice shook. "You said this was what you *wanted*. And then, later, when I asked you about being uncomfortable, you said it was just PTSD. Was that the truth?"

*Fuck.* "No."

She flinched.

"I'm sorry, Anne. I fucked up. I was buying time. I thought I just needed more time. But it's not working for me."

Her face should have been unreadable, but he could see the dismay in her eyes. "I've never had a slave who resented doing those little things. Who didn't want to serve me."

God, he'd hurt her. He'd known this would go south; he had fuck-all talent with communicating. "I don't want to give up on us, but I don't…I can't act like I don't have a brain in my head." His jaw was so tight the words emerged sounding angry.

She looked as if he'd slapped her. "I don't treat you like that." As she pulled her cold, cold hand from his, her face went totally blank. She was pulling away from him. Shutting down.

Shutting him out.

And hell, she didn't treat him as if he were stupid. That'd been wrong. "Anne." *Shit.* "Mistress, I didn't mean—"

"Stop." She held up her hand—and it was trembling.

*God. Damn.*

"I…" She took a slow, controlled breath. "Well. I should have realized you hadn't been honest with me." Her voice was thin but her words calm. "I'd rather she'd thrown things at him. "I need some time to think about this. Perhaps you do, as well. How about we"—she drew in another measured breath—"step back for a couple of days and then talk again." The way she attempted a smile hurt him deep inside. "Renegotiate."

They'd fallen into patterns, so taking a break was smart. Why did it feel as if she were cutting him loose? But she'd said renegotiate, and he'd totally sprung this on her. Fuck him, he shouldn't have lied to her before.

"Okay, renegotiate." He took her small hand between his. Cold little fingers. Motionless.

What had he done?

He took his own slow breath. "I'll be down in the Everglades for the next few days so how about we meet at the Shadowlands? I return Saturday, and we're both off club duties for the weekend. Hopefully we can seal what we decide with a scene?"

His hopes almost died until she finally nodded. "Saturday."

Good. They'd talk. And then have a scene and sex—because they never had problems communicating when they got physical. "Until then." *Please don't give up, Anne.*

As he walked out, he could only wonder if he'd just destroyed what he'd been looking for all his life.


Anne heard him walk off the deck and back into her house, and each heavy footstep felt as if it crushed a piece of her aching heart into dust. A minute later, the front door opened and shut.

Even as desolation filled her, she didn't move. If she moved, she'd...break.

Her mind was stuck on an eternal repeat, seeing him leaving, over and over. Seeing his big, rough face, the scar on his jaw, the way one hair in his left eyebrow never stayed straight, how his nose had a bump from when he'd broken it.

He was gone. She'd let him walk out. Hadn't...acted. Tears trickled down her cheeks. She could hear the *splat, splat* of each drop.

*I'm going to have your baby, Ben.*

*I love you, Ben.*

*Don't leave me. Please.*

*I'll change.*

The words she hadn't spoken choked her.

He shouldn't have lied to her before. But—she should have been able to tell. Should have seen through his lie sooner. He had his needs, and she'd ignored them.

The knowledge formed a heavy pool of misery under her heart. She'd been a lousy Mistress. A thoughtless lover.

She'd never had a real lover before, though. And, she had to say, this learn-on-the-job training was just miserable.

The darkness gathered around the house, encroaching on the deck, wiping out the beach, the Gulf, the horizon.

Surrounded by the night, she watched the stars appear. The moon rose, its pale light hitting the black waves and splintering into pieces.

He was gone.

With cold fingers, Anne picked up her saxophone and played.

Played songs for the ocean, songs for the stars, songs for the moon that moved across the sky and started to sink into the west.

How long had she been out here? After a minute, Anne realized the tune she'd wandered into was Whitney Houston's "I Will Always Love You."

*Oh, honestly.* She shook her head roughly. *How embarrassingly sappy.* Hauling in a breath, she scrubbed the tears from her cheeks.

*Enough.*

This pitiful behavior wasn't to be borne. Maybe the baby had messed up her emotions, but who was in charge here—her or an unborn infant?

*Pull it together, Anne.*

After a hot shower, she fed herself, ignoring her queasiness. She had a baby to nurture…and how amazing was that?

At sunrise, she made herself walk the beach so the brisk morning breeze could chase the stupor from her brain.

And then she sat down in her living room and tried for some logical thinking. When a few tears appeared, she blamed her hormones and moved on.

*Think, Anne.*

But she kept getting stuck in one place. He didn't want her as his Mistress.

She hadn't been good enough to keep him. Wasn't ever good enough, was she? She let everyone down.

As she heard the internal words, she shook her head vigorously and growled at herself. That was childishly stupid thinking. She was a good Mistress—and human. She'd been at fault in not seeing that her routine made him uncomfortable. In not realizing he was forcing himself into the slave mold because he desired her.

He'd lied to her because of his own fears.

They'd both messed up.

*Oh, Ben.*

Why had he told her he wanted to be her slave? Whatever had possessed him? She'd known he was almost vanilla. Had cautioned him because he was so new to the lifestyle. Told him he was rushing things.

Her eyes welled with tears. Her memory of that day was so clear, the joy she'd felt so brilliant. *"I'll be your slave."*

And because she remembered so well, she also recalled what had happened before. How Ben had handed her the phone.

Joey'd been on the line.

She froze as the puzzle came together. *Oh. Damn.*

After a long moment, she rubbed her hands over her face gently. Her skin felt fragile, as if a sudden movement might cause pieces to fall away.

Joey'd asked to be her slave again, and Ben had heard enough to worry.

She sighed, seeing how events had created the inevitability of this day. Because Ben wasn't the sort of man who'd allow someone to poach his woman. If he'd been with her longer or understood more about the lifestyle, he'd have known he didn't want a 24/7 submissive or slave relationship.

But Joey had forced his hand.

She'd been so stunned—*"Yes, Ma'am, this is what I want"*—and so filled with happiness, that she hadn't questioned his motivation.

Then, as she tumbled into loving him, she'd seen only what she wanted to see. Love might be blind, but it was also deaf, dumb, and stupid.

She pressed her lips together. Her heedlessness had hurt them both.

Now what should she do?

A half-laugh escaped. The person she'd normally ask for guidance would be *Ben*. She rubbed her chest where the aching mass of bruised heart muscle hadn't stopped throbbing. He knew her. He'd have given her solid advice because he liked her the way she was.

With him, she'd been able to relax and not stay "on" all the time.

Was that because he didn't *need* her to always be strong and invulnerable.

He was smart. Easygoing. Deadly. Competent. A survivor of the worst New York could throw at him and war, as well. He didn't need her to make his decisions.

She blew out a breath, feeling like an idiot. Caught up in the way she always did things, she'd tried to make every choice for her, for him, for them.

He didn't need her to be in charge.

What about her? Could she cope with a relationship where she wasn't in control all the time?

Rather than an instant "no," she heard only silence. As if the answer was...*maybe*. How odd.

The thought of having a relationship where she wasn't always in charge was almost as exhilarating as frightening. She'd had a couple of days like that, right? Their first weekend together, she'd only taken charge in the bedroom. The rest of the time, she'd kicked back and not even tried. She hadn't wanted more control. Hadn't missed it.

*But, but, but*...she'd *never* accepted a non-slave.

She huffed out a laugh. She'd *never* had houseplants either. With a sigh, she eyed the tiny African violet on the coffee table. A gift from Ben. As were the giant schefflera that stood in a corner of the room and the pothos vine trailing down from the top of the china hutch. Instead of being annoyed at a slave's presumptuousness, she'd been touched. Pleased.

Quite honestly, she loved the "life" the plants brought to her home. She enjoyed caring for them.

She *was* changing. And perhaps she didn't require as much control as she had required in the past. Could that be possible?

Ben had shown he could adapt to whatever life threw at him. In that respect, he'd done far better than she had.

He was gone, but they'd talk on the weekend. She stared at the African violet, the tiny purple flowers a symbol of hope—because she was glad it was in her home. Because it showed that she had changed.

Linda had told her, *"The earth is all about change. The seasons move from summer to winter. The continental plates push up mountains that the weather slowly grinds back down. On this planet, in this universe, nothing stands still."*

Ben had been brave enough to try to be her slave. It was her turn.

On Saturday, she'd ask him for another chance. She'd be his Mistress only in the bedroom—and his lover full time.

# Chapter Twenty-Four

Late Friday afternoon, Anne arrived at *The Brothers Bail Bonds* and crossed the parking lot. Her feet were dragging as they had after her first three days in boot camp. Her eyes burned from lack of sleep. In fact, she was completely, purely exhausted.

Over the last few days, she'd examined her past, trying to see how much of her need for control was due to experiences she'd had and what was integral to her personality. Her uglier memories had given her some emotional moments.

And her guilt kept growing that she hadn't seen how Ben must have been suffering.

To top off her woes, being lonely was…horrible. Ben's absence filled her home, stabbing her whenever she tripped over something they'd done together.

Since they'd done almost everything together, the pain had been nearly constant.

The kitchen was too silent without Ben's laughter and teasing, even his messes. And the key to her house still lay where he'd left it on the island.

But her miniscule baby needed food, whether or not its mama had to force herself to swallow. And, somehow her realization she was pregnant had summoned the nausea that went with it. Skipping breakfast no longer held it at bay.

In the evenings, Ben wasn't on his side of the couch or at her feet or anywhere in the house. Last night, when his favorite program came on, she'd cried.

At night, in bed, when she rolled over, no one was there. And she'd cried.

Damn hormones.

Damn Ben.

Damn Anne for being so blind to his needs.

Despite her exhaustion, she was relieved to be at work. Yesterday had been her day off, giving her all day to mope. For the first time, she'd regretted her flexible hours.

With a shake of her shoulders, she lifted her chin and opened the back door to the building. She'd come in early to type up the team briefing about the fugitive they'd go after later that night. Funny how much she was looking forward to the diversion.

This morning had started bad. Although she hadn't puked her guts out before breakfast—as Jessica had done during her pregnancy—the nausea that had swept over her had turned her hot, then cold, and had her gulping and panting like a fish out of water.

Tomorrow night, she'd see Ben.

Just the thought made her quivery and hopeful and despairing. She'd even tried calling him last night, but no answer. He was out in the middle of some swamp—she knew that—but she'd still felt...rejected.

Such an insecure girly feeling.

But tomorrow, they'd talk. She'd see if he wanted to try again and keep the D/s power exchange to the bedroom. She'd ask him to be patient with her as she worked to break her constant Domme habits.

She'd tell him she missed him so, so much.

That she still forgot and put water down for Bronx every morning.

That the plants he'd given her were still alive.

*Come home, Ben.*

Tears didn't belong in a bail bond agency. She blinked and bit her lip, letting the pain force them back. And then she walked down the hall toward the recovery agents' room.

Matt's office door was open. The desk photo showed him with his latest grandchild—such an adorable baby.

Anne sighed. Wanting to avoid Z, she'd canceled her usual visit with Jessica and Sophia. The Shadowlands' owner could read a person almost as if he possessed mind-reading abilities—and she knew he'd take one look at her and know she was pregnant.

No matter how much she'd love to share the news, Ben deserved to be the first to hear.

Besides...confessing to Z that she'd managed to get knocked up? Talk about the walk of shame.

Half smiling, she strolled into the room. Panels divided the perimeter of the room into cubicles, all open to the conference area in the center.

In one corner, Aaron was at his desk, typing a report.

Her cousin Robert stood in Anne's cubicle. He dropped a paper on her desk and spotted her. "Why if it isn't Mz. Desmarais."

She should have stayed in bed today. "Robert. Did you have something for me?"

His smirk gave her a bad feeling. "Left you an update."

An update on what? Anne set her folder down. The paper Robert had brought was her list of agents for the team tonight. Under the team leader designation, her name had been crossed off and Robert's substituted.

In fact, she wasn't on the list at all.

The anger that flared across her nerves was out of proportion to the problem. *Just hormones. I can deal.* She throttled her temper back and kept her voice even. "Robert, that's not funny."

His smile grew. "I didn't make the changes. Uncle Matt did. He said you can have today off and then work the desk on Monday."

Desk time meant answering calls, visiting the jail, taking down information from felons, and skip tracing. It was the same scut labor she'd done in her college days when she'd worked part time here.

Maybe she could stand to do the desk, but what about her team? Robert was incompetent enough as a team member. Having him in charge would be a disaster.

"That's my team," she said evenly. "I built it."

"Actually, they work for my father and Matt, not you. And they'd rather be led by someone else. Not a fucking—"

"Robert," Aaron snapped. "Watch your mouth."

Anne looked across the room. "What do the others think about this?"

"People are fucking pissed." Aaron's jaw was tight. "Nobody asked our preferences. But, as he pointed out, Russell and Matt own the company. The rest of us take orders."

So, Robert had gotten his way.

Anne forced her fingers open. *Stay calm.* Her first reaction was to tell him and the uncles to shove their job where the sun didn't shine. But she had more control than that. And it was stupid to walk out of a job before finding another—if that's what she decided to do. Although just the thought of having to search for a new position right now was disheartening.

Think of that later. Of more concern was her team. The rodent was liable to get one of her people killed.

"I'll talk with Matt and Russell," she told Aaron.

"They're not here." Robert grinned widely and winced before continuing. "Besides, they—"

"What happened to your face?" she interrupted. A scrape marked his jaw, one lip was swollen and split, and his right eye was partially black.

He took a step back, eyed her, then puffed up like a toad. "None of your fucking business, bitch. Or maybe it is, considering the kind of assholes who show up at the office looking for you."

"Ben was here?" If Robert had bad-mouthed her, the guard dog wouldn't think twice about backhanding him.

He flushed. "Yeah. Ben."

Had he targeted her tiger with his filthy insults?

He'd better *not* have. Anger surged higher. What had he said to her man? If he'd made Ben feel bad, she'd… "At least I associate with *men* and not dickless wonders like you."

When Robert's hands closed into fists, she smiled and crooked her fingers in a *come-here-boy* gesture.

He stopped.

*Right.* The rodent didn't fight, just manipulated people. With a sniff of disgust, she picked up her folder with the extra research she'd put in.

"Aaron, I'll leave Matt a message that I'll talk with him on Monday." She gave him a serious look. "You all be careful. It's dangerous having an unreliable team member."

Ignoring the sputter from Robert, Aaron dipped his head. "I hear you."

# Chapter Twenty-Five

Saturday night, Anne sat at her parents' overcrowded table, trying to act festive and worrying about what would happen later when she met Ben at the Shadowlands.

Would he listen to her? Want to try again?

*Breathe.*

Unfortunately, the inhalation carried the fishy smell of red snapper—her father's favorite dish—and her stomach turned over.

*Wonderful.* She took a careful sip of Sprite and fought for calm under the barrage of piercingly loud voices around the table.

Since this was her father's birthday dinner, her uncles and their families were present. When they'd arrived, she'd greeted them with a cool politeness. Uncle Matt had looked guilty and still couldn't meet her gaze. Naturally, Uncle Russell and Robert acted as if nothing was wrong,

But she was all for a detente with the relatives tonight since her emotions were already on a rollercoaster ride.

Every time she thought about Ben, she wanted to cry.

Every time she looked at her uncles, she wanted to throw something at them. And subscribe them to *Ms. Magazine.*

Every time Robert leered at her breasts, she wanted to beat him into a gory heap.

And that just wasn't worth it...because the smell of the blood would probably make her throw up.

Her snort drew Travis's attention, and he bumped his shoulder against hers. "What's got you so quiet, sis?"

She shrugged. This wasn't the time or place to indulge in a

complaint fest.

Seated across the table, her cousin overheard. "She's pouting because I run the recovery team now and she's off completely. Or maybe it's something else. You on the rag, cuz?"

Her mother gasped at his coarse insult.

"Shut your mouth, Robert," Travis snapped.

Touching her brother's arm, Anne shook her head. Rancorous discussions didn't belong at a birthday dinner, and her mother'd put in long hours on the party.

"Tell you what," Robert announced. "The guys were fucking happy to finally having a man leading them."

The rodent wasn't going to shut up.

Harrison growled, "Jesus, you're so full of—"

"This discussion is more appropriately conducted at the office, not at a celebration," Anne interrupted before things could get out of hand. "I'll discuss this on Monday with the owners."

"Thank you, darling," her mother said, looking relieved.

Her father frowned. "What the hell is—"

"No need to wait." Robert said. "About everyone here has been involved with the company at one time or another. I bet they're interested in how you're always trying to shove your way into running everything."

She eyed the rat. "I didn't have to shove my way anywhere. I built that team from scratch and ran it because I have the education, experience, and skills to do so." Still hoping to salvage the dinner, she didn't add, "*all of which you lack.*"

Harrison growled, "Exactly."

Perhaps her cousin had heard the part she left out. He glared. "You don't have anything that I—"

"Enough." Her *What-the-Fuck* Meter zoomed past orange and into red. "You took the team because you can't stand taking directions from a woman. You're not a leader because you're better, but because you went crying to your daddy—which you do whenever you don't get your way. I realize it's difficult to man up when your equipment is the size of peanuts, but do give it a try."

Robert turned purple.

Travis inhaled beer, making appalling sounds on her right. Most of the relatives were roaring with laughter.

Not all.

Her father leaned forward and raised his voice over the noise. "Russell, you've removed Anne from fugitive recovery?"

"Since Robert is *quite* capable of leading the team, I decided to make the change." Russell's florid complexion was heightened; his jowls quivered with anger. "I've never been comfortable sending a woman into combat, so to speak."

Anne choked her response back. Why fight to remain as team leader when her pregnancy would sideline her soon anyway? But, she'd worked her hardest for her uncles and to make her team the best. Being booted out...

It *hurt*.

Robert gave her father a sincere look. "A woman is far too liable to get herself killed. And a wanna-be cop doesn't have what it takes."

"A what?" her mother asked in surprise. "She's not—"

"Robert has his head up his ass," Harrison interrupted, frowning at Matt. "If you don't recall, you and Russell hired her so she could bring in her law enforcement experience and train your agents. The team was her idea and creation. And she's why you have the highest recovery percentages in Florida—and the lowest insurance rates."

"That may be, but recovering skips is still no place for a woman," Matt said.

She'd known Uncle Matt had qualms, but he was the one who'd recruited her. Now—because of Robert—he'd changed his mind. The betrayal was another small ping of pain in a growing avalanche.

When Travis started to speak, Anne shook her head at him. No point.

What a disaster. She needed to get their attention and quiet this mess. This was her father's birthday party, not a venue for a verbal brawl. She held up her hand. "Uncle M—"

"I must say, I'm relieved. I never wanted my girl working recovery and endangering her life for a few extra bucks. It's just not safe." The words came from the head of the table.

From her father.

She turned to look at him, feeling as if he'd picked up the knife sitting beside his plate and plunged it into her heart.

Robert could manipulate his father into anything—because his father believed his child could do anything.

Her father was the opposite.

She'd tried all her life to be competent—outstanding—in any task, especially the ones traditionally assigned to men. She'd succeeded.

But her father, the one who should have believed in her and supported her, didn't.

Her eyes stung with unshed tears. She pushed her chair back.

"Anne, no," Harrison whispered.

She felt Travis grip her arm and shook him free.

"You win, Dad." Shoulders back, chin up, she faced her father. "You've made it clear over and over that you don't think I can be as good at anything as your sons."

Her father's face went blank. "Anne—"

"Darling." Her mother's face was white. "He doesn't—"

"He does, Mom. It's fine. I get it." Her voice didn't betray the echoing emptiness inside. Her gaze turned to Russell. "You win too. I quit as of this moment." She glanced at Travis. "Please pick up my things for me."

Face set, he nodded.

Finally, she looked at Robert. "You are a slimy turd not worth scraping off my stiletto, let alone speaking to. So fair warning. If you ever address me again for any reason, you'll wake up in a hospital bed, pissing blood for a month."

Silence accompanied her as she walked out.

* * * *

In the Shadowlands, Ben leaned against a black leather couch and idly watched a chain station scene. In a dark-red suit, the Domme was wielding a cane on a gray-haired submissive. Her husband, actually, as Ben recalled. She was whacking him in time with the Aboriginal-sounding drums of Massive Attack's "Inertia Creeps." His groans provided an interesting counterpoint to the lead singer's whispers.

The Domme stopped to observe her sub.

The man kept trying to look over his shoulder. As the seconds passed without a blow, he continued to tense.

"Take a deep breath now," she ordered in a light, sweet voice.

The guy didn't listen.

*Bad move, bro,* Ben said to him silently.

And yep…

The Domme moved the cane and lightly swatted her beloved's ball sac.

The man's yelp pulled in air—and focused his attention on his Mistress, where it belonged.

*Ouch.* Ben shook his head, recalling how a whack in the jewels felt. Poor fucker. Why were Dommes so fascinated with a guy's junk?

Not that he was complaining. The results were—he watched the guy shake with the need to come—like *that.*

"You are not working security this evening?" The Spanish-accented voice came from Ben's right. Raoul glanced at the scene. "Are you taking notes for Mistress Anne?"

Just the sound of her name upped his pulse as if an RPG had hit nearby—and made his chest ache. Dammit, he missed her.

Raoul's brows drew together. "*'Mano*, are you all right?"

"Don't know yet." Ben turned away from the action. "I told her I'm not cut out to be a slave."

"It was what she needed to know, yes?" Raoul studied him. "What was her response?"

"She asked for time to think." Not even the beauty of the Everglades had been able to keep his mind from Anne. The slow sway of the royal palms reminded him of her grace. High clouds in a sunlit sky made him remember how her eyes lightened when she was happy.

But now the time had come to hear her answer, and he was worried shitless. "She'll tell me tonight what she decided."

Raoul's jaw tightened, and Ben could see he wasn't optimistic.

"You know something I don't?" Ben asked.

"Only that when slaves have requested more from her   to receive more attention and time or to live with her—she would pull away, match them with Dommes who would satisfy their needs, and find herself someone new."

*Great.* Being replaced would be even worse than being dumped. A lead ball settled in Ben's gut.

Raoul moved his shoulders. "Although for you, she might, perhaps…change."

*Change. And Anne. Right.* Ben tried to shrug. "It'll fall out as it will."

"Life does do that," Raoul agreed gently. "Will you… Can I—"

"I'll be fucking fine." Because Anne had forced him to see that life was meant to be lived. "She should be here by now."

\* \* \* \*

Why in the world had she exploded at her father and uncles? Anne shook her head as she walked into the Shadowlands clubroom. Her body, even her skin, felt fragile, like a hollowed-out egg that the slightest bump would crack.

Of course, the confrontations with her father and her uncles had been long overdue. She hadn't said anything she hadn't thought for a long time. It had been…maybe…a bit freeing to express herself.

But for the rodent Robert to set off the fire and make her burn her bridges so thoroughly? That stung.

Whatever had happened to her control? Her temper never flamed out of hand like that. She didn't yell, didn't scream, didn't cry. But now, rather than properly stored inside, her emotions clung to her fingertips, shaking loose with any minor upset.

And then she knew. Hormones caused mood swings. Tears...*and* anger.

A corner of her mouth lifted even as she scowled down at her belly and the cause of her wayward emotions. *You and I need to talk about your effect on me. Soon.*

Her hand ran over her stomach—still flat—and gave it a pat. She was going to have a *baby*. *A real baby*. Her eyes instantly prickled with happy tears.

*Oh, honestly.* She hauled in an exasperated breath. At this rate, she'd start bawling during cat food commercials.

A sudden scream drew her back to reality.

On a nearby bondage table, a petite submissive had started to struggle frantically, sobbing, and screaming. "N-n-no! Asparagus! V-vinegar. Please, no more. Apricots. Stop. God, please stop!"

Someone had just discovered she hated needle play—and apparently couldn't remember her safeword.

Anne took a step in that direction.

"Easy, pet. Your safeword was artichoke, but I understand anyway. We're stopping right now." The sadist Edward was trying not to laugh. He noticed Anne and winked before telling the submissive, "I'm going to take the needles out nice and slow. Take a breath."

Good Dom. Anne shook her head. There were several advantages to the stoplight safeword system. "Red" was short enough to gasp out between screams. Submissives rarely forgot the word. And everyone in the lifestyle knew the meaning.

Turning away, she pulled in a slow breath and wished she had a safeword for her talk with Ben.

Was he here yet?

She should have asked the new gray-haired security guy, but her voice had disappeared when she saw him. He...wasn't Ben. Apparently her subconscious had expected her guard dog to be at the desk.

Well, she'd start looking in the usual place. As she headed for the bar, she glanced at the scenes.

A male submissive was bent over with his neck and wrists secured in the wooden stocks. A spreader bar kept his legs far enough apart to display a straining cock.

The spider web held two female slaves restrained side-by-side to get easily caned by their Master.

A young man was doing self-suspension, with a couple of people sitting nearby to assist if needed.

She nodded at Marcus, who was setting up a St. Andrew's cross. Nolan was taking over the adjacent cross while Beth and Gabi waited on their knees. The two Masters probably had something devious planned. Maybe she could bring Ben back to watch...if he agreed.

She'd see him soon. Her Ben. Like a cold tidal wave, anxiety washed over her, sending her heart to thudding.

*No, no, relax.* It would be all right. It *would*. People in relationships...negotiated. Worked things out. Took turns—and it was her turn to try it his way.

*Please be willing to try, Ben.*

The thought of losing him created a jagged ache in her chest. Firmly, she pushed the feeling away.

If only she didn't feel so...alone.

She'd fought with her family. Had no job. Was pregnant. Now, maybe she'd lose Ben too.

She stopped, took a breath, and remembered she had a spine. Yes, it was scary to imagine being on her own with a little one depending on her for everything. But she was an independent, smart, caring adult. She wouldn't let her baby down.

And she mustn't allow her weakness to push Ben into something he didn't want. He should be able to walk away from her if that was what he needed.

Would he want that? As she approached the bar, her emotions were an unsettled stew of misery rather than frothy anticipation.

"Anne," Cullen greeted. "Drink?"

A waft of perfume from the subbie area tipped her stomach into nausea and kept her from sitting. "No, thank you."

Before he could answer, a thudding noise caught his attention.

A submissive roped down on the bar top—a bar ornament—was thumping one foot on the gleaming wood.

Since the knotwork looked like Nolan's, the sub had probably annoyed the *you-will-be-respectful* Master and gotten herself tied to the bar. She was positioned on forearms and knees, her hair fastened to an iron rung. Ropes secured her widely separated lower legs to the bar. Nipple clamps attached to another rung pulled her chest low and onto one end of the miniature seesaw. A vibrator was bound to the teeter-totter's other end...and positioned against the sub's clit.

From her flushed color, the sub had recently orgasmed and was struggling to get the vibrator away from her undoubtedly sensitive clit. But for the vibrator end of the seesaw to drop, the submissive had to raise her chest. She tried—and wailed as the movement pulled on her nipple clamps.

It was a superb example of predicament bondage.

After adding more restraints so the sub couldn't kick his bar, Cullen patted her ass and rejoined his submissive Andrea in mixing drinks.

Would Ben like predicament bondage and being in a no-win situation? Anne considered. Perhaps she'd set up something that would make him choose between his balls being squeezed or an anal plug? They had so many things that would be fun to explore. Some of her slaves had loved predica—

"Mistress Anne."

She glanced over.

Joey stood at her elbow. "Please, Mistress Anne." His desperate voice held a vulnerability that called to her Domme spirit.

As she'd taught him, he gracefully went to his knees. His chain harness pressed into his chest, showcasing his pectoral muscles beautifully.

"Joey. How are you doing?"

"Mistress." His head bent, his voice wavered, and yet he maintained his perfect posture with his gaze on the floor, his hands open on his thighs. "Mistress, I miss you so much. Please take me back."

The plea caught her in a place that had been aching since Ben had said he didn't want to serve her.

She bent and lifted Joey's chin and saw the utter surrender in his eyes. Saw the hope that she'd exert her will and hurt him, that she'd force him to accept everything she wanted to give, that she'd push him beyond what he thought he could take.

His shiver under her touch brought back the past and memories of how he'd cleaned her house and cooked for her. While they watched television, he'd sit at her feet...in the position Ben found objectionable.

But she didn't need a slave at her feet. Didn't need complete control of someone all the time. Ben had helped her see how she'd changed.

Even if she couldn't have Ben, she wouldn't go back to the way she'd been.

As the warmth of Joey's breath bathed her hand, she realized she'd been staring at him for…for a while. Loosening her grip, she gave him a slight smile. "Joey, I—"

"See you found your boy."

Still bent over Joey, Anne looked up into Ben's eyes.

Ben had thought getting gut-shot was the worst pain in the universe.

He'd been wrong. His entire chest felt sliced through with shrapnel, every shard targeting his heart.

But he'd had plenty of experience in staying upright despite hurting like hell.

Jesus, he might've known Anne would go back to her pretty boys. To her obedient, fawning slaves. Why would she want a man like him? One who'd put limits on her and told her he wasn't a slave.

But she could've talked to him before kicking him to the curb.

"Ben." She straightened.

At least she'd taken her hand off the pretty boy. When she had bent and stared into the bastard's eyes for—for fucking ever—he'd come close to ripping the little shit away from her.

She held out her hand—the same hand that had touched her *slave.* "I'm not—"

"No." Ben stepped away. Then he mentally took out his K-bar and sliced through the hold she had on him. His life. His heart. "Don't see any need to talk this to death. You were right. I'm vanilla, and I don't need this kink shit. Thanks for the taste."

The shocked pain in her eyes couldn't have been greater if he'd gutted her.

He found no satisfaction in the thought at all.

As he walked out of the Shadowlands, his chest hurt so badly he looked down at his shirt, half expecting to see it covered in blood.

*But…no.* Anne stared after Ben. He hadn't even given her a chance to speak. To explain. Anything. With a cruelty unlike him, he'd delivered his decision with sledge-hammer effectiveness—and had broken her fragile hopes into tiny fragments.

She could feel her lips trembling, how her skin had gone cold, and somehow couldn't pull her gaze from the direction he'd taken. From where he'd disappeared.

He hadn't even looked back. *Please. No.*

"Mistress." Joey's voice recalled her. Blinking, she looked down at him, and his expression turned to concern.

That wouldn't do. She was the Domme. Supposed to be in control of herself. Able to support those who were weaker.

It took all her strength to bulldoze the damage under enough to move. She had to swallow several times before her voice could get past the rawness. "Joey, I'm not taking on any slaves right now."

The floor was shaking under her feet; no, the trembling came from deep inside her.

"Oh, but Mistress." His voice broke. "I-I need…" Desolation filled his eyes before he looked down.

Disgusted with herself, she straightened her shoulders and pushed her self-pity and ego away. She was a Mistress of the Shadowlands; this was a submissive who needed help. "Do you want me to find you a new Mistress?"

His gaze lifted, hope lighting his face. "Really?"

She managed to curve her lips up. "I'm sure I can find a Domme who is more of a sadist than me. I should have done better for you, pet."

He bent and kissed her boot. "Oh, thank you. Thank you."

"Give me a few days to make some inquiries, and I'll get back to you."

Quivering with happiness, he rose and backed away. Then hesitated, and his brow furrowed as he looked at her.

She motioned with her hand. *Off with you.*

He complied. He knew better than to linger if she indicated otherwise.

*Ben* would have ignored her wishes, would have talked to her and comforted her, no matter what she said she wanted. The thought brought another stab of agony as she looked around, hoping against hope he'd changed his mind.

No tall man topped the crowd, broad shoulders taking up more than his share of the space.

He'd left. Just walked out without talking to her. Without even giving her a chance to work it out. Why? After pushing himself into her life, he just…gave up?

The savage ball of pain in her chest continued to grow, pressing against her ribs, cutting off her breathing. One hand over her heart, the other over her baby, Anne struggled for the next breath.

"What was that about?" Raoul appeared in front of her. "What hap—"

Cullen stalked from behind the bar. "What happened was she ripped his heart right out of his chest." His eyes were chill. Unhappy. "That man trusted you. Was doing his damnedest to serve you, and you go right back to your previous slave and—"

"I what?" Anne stiffened. "Tell me, *Master* Cullen, have you touched another submissive since Andrea became yours?" Her gaze went to the bar ornament and back to him.

"That's different. I wasn't hitting on her. Andrea knows that."

"I wasn't either," she said softly. God, God, she couldn't take this. Tears kept filling her eyes, and the struggle to blink them back pissed her off.

It all pissed her off. As anger battered her defenses into broken fragments, she knew the damn hormones were messing with her.

And yet…wasn't Cullen supposed to be her friend too? And Raoul, as well. She'd held his hand when his ex had almost gutted him. Didn't they know her character at all?

She couldn't survive losing more friends, more family, more… But she already had, it seemed.

From a place deep in her soul, she found her Mistress gear and strapped it on like a weapons belt.

"Anne." Even as Raoul stepped forward, his hand out, she shot him a stare that made him stop.

"You needn't worry about your guard dog." Her voice came out calm and cold. *Dead.* "Or protect the vulnerable submissives from the dishonorable—cheating—Mistress."

Cullen flinched. "That's not—"

"Tell Z to cancel my membership," she told him.

He took a step back. *"What?"*

In the moment that shock held the Masters pinned, she made her escape. Not running, but quickly.

Because Mistresses didn't walk through the Shadowlands crying.

# Chapter Twenty-Six

On Wednesday, after four days in the swamps, Ben parked his Jeep at the curb of his warehouse and hauled his weary carcass out. His sweaty, filthy, rain-sodden clothes dragged at him.

His spirits felt as if they were trailing behind him on the ground. He was a fucking mess.

How could he be so damned angry with Anne and yet miss her so damned much? Every time he thought about that night at the Shadowlands, his head pounded with pain, like the inside of an artillery shelling.

He couldn't forget how her hand had cupped the little shit's chin. How Joey had knelt at her feet, the scrawny bastard, while she looked at him. And *looked* at him.

Ben's back teeth ground together with an ugly sound. If he hadn't shown up, would they still be there in that position?

Jesus *fuck*. Even after seeing that, he still wanted her. His idiot heart *yearned*. Made him want to enlist again, just to get out of the country. To keep from showing up at her doorstep some night.

"C'mon, buddy."

Bronx jumped out, clearing the way so Ben could snag his pack.

He'd just got the warehouse door open when a voice came from behind him.

"Where've you been?"

Ben spun. Even as he started to drop his pack and charge, he recognized Anne's brother, Travis. Not a mugger.

Travis had jumped back, empty palms facing out. "Sorry, guy. I thought you'd seen me."

Ben pushed air through his teeth. "S'okay. I'm tired, and you took me by surprise." Tired wasn't the word for it. After the clusterfuck, he'd headed back to the Everglades—although abandoning the field hadn't helped worth shit. He'd still reached for Anne every time he turned over at night. Still noted things to share with her at dinner.

Only now there was no one in his bed. No leisurely evening chats.

Somewhere along the line, his mission had become as fucked up as a soup sandwich.

And he needed fluids before he dealt with the brother.

"C'mon." Leaving the door open behind him, he went in and up the stairs. After guzzling half a bottle of cold water, he felt his brain click on.

Travis was pacing back and forth, all tensed up.

"What the fuck are you doing here?" Ben asked. Nothing came to mind except disaster.

"It's Anne."

Ben got in his face and barely kept from hauling him up by the shirtfront. "What about her? Is she all right?"

Travis's expression tightened. "She's not been here?"

"No. I haven't seen her since Saturday night."

"Saturday. Jesus, where could she be?"

Ben glanced at the clock. Late afternoon. "Probably headed in to work."

"You really haven't seen her, have you? Saturday's when she got into it with our uncles and Dad. And when she quit the agency."

Ben's hand stopped halfway to his mouth. Quit? On Saturday, Anne had planned to attend her father's birthday dinner. She hadn't worked that day.

Then again, a family event meant the uncles and asshole cousin had probably been there. "Robert gave her grief?"

"Worse than that. Seems he talked Uncle Russell into giving him Anne's leader slot and removing her from the team. She tried to maintain her cool at the party, but then our fucking father said he was glad she was off the team. He didn't want his girl being in danger."

Jesus, that'd be akin to tossing a match into a gas tank. "She blew?"

"Oh, fuck yes." Looking exhausted, Travis scrubbed his face with his hand. "She's not picking up her phone. She's not been home."

"Maybe she's home and not answering the doorbell?"

"Her car's gone."

"Hell." Like a slow-building avalanche, his worry grew, burying everything before it. Had she gone through that crap right before coming to the Shadowlands? Anne loved her father. Loved her job. The bastards had gutted her.

And then he'd taken a good long swipe at her himself. Yeah, maybe she'd chosen the little shit and didn't want a non-slave, but Ben hadn't needed to be an asshole about it.

"I'm not liking the look on your face," Travis said quietly. "What do you know that I don't? Do you know where—"

"I saw her after your supper." Worry clawed at him. "Not since. We're not together anymore."

"You…" Travis's face darkened with anger. "What'd you do? After what she'd been through, you—"

"I didn't know. And *she* broke up with *me*, okay?" She hadn't said anything about her job. Her family. He hadn't given her a chance. *Fuck.*

Travis's glare slowly died. "Sorry. She's my little sister, you know?"

Ben could sympathize. The guy was as protective as Ben—and Anne wouldn't have been an easy little sister to shield. Still wasn't. "I have two younger sisters. I get you."

Travis's lips twisted into wry acknowledgment. "I don't suppose you have any idea where she might've gone?"

Ben shook his head. "You still fill in at the bail bond agency. Can't you track her down?"

"Yeah, well, she knows exactly how to prevent someone from doing that. Even worse, with her gone, my uncles don't have anyone, including me, who can do more than a standard trace. She's the one with the talent."

"Dumb fucks, pushing her into quitting."

"They're starting to figure that out." Travis pulled out his wallet and set a business card on the counter. "If you can think of where she might be, no matter how unlikely, I'd appreciate a call." A muscle in his cheek jumped. "When she was little, she'd hide in her room when she was hurt, but she's not home. Or anywhere. She's never just…left."

Ben straightened, feeling the need to go search for her himself. Only she wasn't his problem now, was she? They weren't together. At all. She'd dumped him for the little shit.

Travis was still waiting and Ben scowled. Yeah, she'd kicked him to the curb, but not until after he'd said he couldn't take the heat. Total goatfuck. And she'd lost her job and fought with her dad.

He sighed. No one knew better than him how all her toughness sheltered a frighteningly tender heart. *Dammit, Anne, dammit. Where are you?*

"I'll call you if I figure something out." Ben stuck his hand out. "If you'll promise to let me know if you find her first."

Travis took his hand. "You're going to hunt, too?"

"Fuck, yeah."

# Chapter Twenty-Seven

Trying to keep her mind empty, Anne closed her eyes and let the masseur work the knots out of her shoulders.

Almost a week had gone by as she'd lounged by the pleasantly energetic Atlantic coast, sampled every spa treatment, ignored the alcohol, and indulged in rich desserts. Could a baby be born addicted to caramel?

In between eating and swimming and reading...she moped.

Days had passed, yet her family dinner, then Shadowlands blowup, seemed to have happened last night. She still felt as though she'd just driven across Florida and checked into a St. Augustine hotel.

She'd run away. Hadn't even packed her phone. No orderly retreat for her—she'd totally fled the field of battle.

Then again, she always had when it came to emotional upheavals. During confrontations, she'd go nose to nose. But afterward...she'd hide out until her emotions settled.

She was getting there. Soon. Really. As soon as she could breathe without hurting, she'd return to her life.

But...she could still see the pain in Ben's eyes. Hear his anger. *"Thanks for the taste."* Her fingers curled into—

"Stop that. Relax," the masseur murmured. His low voice was as even as a river stone with the edges sanded smooth. Nothing like Ben's rough voice with the faint New York bite.

*I want Ben.* When her eyes prickled with tears, she inhaled through her nose, fighting them back.

The masseur sighed, covered her up, and rubbed her shoulder lightly. "Rest and when you're ready, pull on the robe and enjoy the steam room. I'll leave a glass of water outside the room for you. Drink it all."

"Thank you, Marc. Nice massage."

He huffed. "Hardly. You kept undoing my efforts." His gaze roamed over her face. "It's tough to move on from the past sometimes. I'd be happy to help with that as well."

The offer was polite and careful. And she wasn't interested in the least. "You're very kind. But I'm returning home tomorrow."

He tilted his head in acceptance. "In that case, I'll simply say, it's been a pleasure."

"For me, as well."

An hour later, lacking any motivation to do…anything…she lingered on the deck outside the hotel restaurant. Her supper dishes had been cleared away, and the cheerful waitress had brought her a cup of herb tea.

Past the lush tropical landscaping was a long expanse of white sandy beach. Waves rolled in, high and foamy, with a grumbling roar never heard on the Gulf. The Atlantic Ocean was so much bigger, so much more powerful. Like the difference between the masseur and Ben.

*No. Not going there.*

She rested her bare foot on the adjacent chair and studied her pedicure. Her toenails were dark blue with tiny glittering stars, like a night sky.

During her days here, her body had been refreshed, pampered, and decorated. Physically, she felt well enough she had trouble believing she was pregnant. Well, except when she lay down on a massage table and realized her breasts were uncomfortably larger and more tender. Or when some scent would make her want to heave. Or when an emotion would yank her along like a riptide.

Yes, she was positively pregnant. And her time for mindless moping must come to an end. She needed to make some decisions about her life. A whole lot of decisions, actually.

She wiggled her toes, creating mayhem in the starry skies. Good at that, wasn't she? If someone had paid her, she couldn't have managed to sabotage her careful, comfortable life better than what she'd accomplished last weekend.

As Ben would say, *"Bravo Zulu, Anne."*

Ben. What should she do about him? Would he even speak to her? The memory of his unforgiving expression was accompanied by his cruel words, *"Don't see any need to talk this to death. You were right. I'm vanilla, and I don't need this kink shit. Thanks for the taste."*

He was done with her. Done.

As anguish expanded from her chest throughout her entire body, she froze, trying to breathe despite the pain. Trying not to burst into tears.

After a few seconds, a few lifetimes, the agony receded, leaving aching emptiness behind. She let out a breath and picked up her tea. *Right.* She did have to think about Ben, but…this wasn't the place. She needed to wait until she had her home around her.

She took a sip and forced herself to swallow.

No matter what she decided, she had to tell him about the baby. He was the father. She didn't want child support, but…but being Ben, he'd insist on providing it. And he'd want to be part of the baby's life.

That would hurt. And yet—she rested her hand on her stomach— whether girl or boy, the child could only be better for having an example of the finest of men.

For her baby's sake, she would manage to cope with seeing Ben, and he'd do the same.

She pulled in a breath and blinked back tears. Why did life have to be so painful?

*Onward, Anne.* Next up, the Shadowlands.

Unable to swallow any longer, she set the tea down with a thump.

"Miss." The man standing beside her table had gleaming white hair. Dressed in all white, he leaned on a black cane. His blue eyes were faded, yet observant. "I fear I am interrupting, but child, is there anything I can do to help?"

"I'm sorry?" She frowned, not following. Had she dropped something or—

"I've never seen anyone outside a hospital look so in agony. Would you permit me to help if I can?" The question brought more pain and yet—a sweetness accompanied it.

The world still contained wonderful people. She held out her hand. Her voice came out husky with unconquered tears. "A recent loss." *So many losses.* "But time will take care of it, I'm sure." *Never.* "Thank you for your concern."

Much like the masseur, Marc, the senior tilted his head in acknowledgment and gave her fingers a squeeze. "All right then, missy. You take good care now."

"And you."

He had helped after all, boosting her up and out of her grief. Reminded of the balance of life, she blessed the stranger, and then set her mind to considering that night at the Shadowlands, Cullen and

Raoul, and her behavior.

Not good. No matter what they'd said, she herself had overreacted and lost her temper. She couldn't exactly blame them for doing the same.

If necessary, a talk would see things right between them. But, maybe even that wouldn't be needed. She wasn't in the Shadowlands any longer.

And she didn't plan to reinstate her membership. Ben worked there, and...for both their sakes, she'd keep a distance. And, in all reality, it would be a long, long time before she opened up to accepting a submissive again, even for lightweight play.

But she'd miss seeing her friends there. Not only the Masters and Mistresses, but also the submissive women, Jessica, Beth, Kim...all of them. She'd always had casual friends, but this group had become more. They were an important part of her life.

Just another change she hadn't noticed sneaking up on her.

Her mouth firmed. The Shadowlands was out, but she wouldn't lose her girlfriends. She'd never willingly left a friend behind. Not when she was a child and dragged away by her father. Not now. Maybe they'd find it awkward to be friends with both her and Ben, but they'd manage, because loyalty was one of their finest qualities.

Next subject to fret about: her occupation.

She smiled. The job topic wasn't nearly as painful. Wasn't that nice?

Leaning her head back on the chair, she considered her options.

First possibility. She was a very, very good skip tracer and team leader, and Robert truly was incompetent. The uncles might well reconsider and want her back.

Second possibility. She could pursue other jobs. If she tightened her belt—uh, bad phrasing. She patted her stomach. *Sorry, baby.* If she pinched her pennies, she could take her time finding a new position. She'd banked most of her wages so her savings account was healthy. Her beach house had been a gift, so she had no rent or mortgage to pay each month. *Thanks, Mom.*

The only trouble with her home was living so close to her father. Unfortunately, moving away for a few years would hurt her mother.

Besides, her love for him hadn't died. Dad was a total archaic butthead about equality and about seeing her as she was, but he loved her too. Somehow they'd make up.

But he needed to make the first move. Damn straight.

There, she had some plans made.

Tomorrow, she'd check out of the hotel and return home. It was time to put things right and deal with the changes that she would set in motion.

And then there was the biggest change of all.

With a half-smile, she laid her hand on her stomach. *I'm carrying Ben's baby.*

\* \* \* \*

Since Travis's visit yesterday, Ben had searched for Anne without results. Called the bail bond company. Checked the shelter. Used the Shadowlands membership list to check with her girlfriends…and the little shit, as well.

He'd come up empty.

At his monthly veteran's group meeting, he lingered behind the others. "Talk to you for a minute, Z?"

"Of course. Help yourself to a beer; water for me, please." Z squeezed his shoulder and walked out to say good night to the rest.

Ben grabbed a beer and water, took a seat at the iron-and-oak table, and…stewed. Where the fuck could the woman have gone? Surely she'd have checked in.

Gaze on Ben, Z crossed the lanai and sat across from him. "What's worrying you?"

Before he could answer, the door on the third floor landing opened. Jessica came down the stairs with Sophia asleep in her arms and spotted Ben. "Oops, sorry. I thought everyone had left." She turned to go.

"Nah, Jessica," Ben said. "No secrets here. I wanted to talk about Anne. Need to share some information and get some advice."

"Okay. If you're sure."

"Here, little one." Z rose and held a chair for her, before touching the baby's cheek with gentle fingers.

Envy—and grief—filled Ben's heart. With losing Anne, hopes had died that he hadn't even known he'd created.

"Go on, Benjamin," Z prompted, resuming his seat.

"All right. Last weekend in the Shadowlands, Anne and I planned to discuss our relationship."

Z nodded, unsurprised.

"We didn't." Ben sipped his drink, unsure how much to say. "I saw her back with Joey and lost my temper. Told her I was done."

Jessica's eyes widened, but she didn't say anything.

"That seems unlike you." Gaze on Ben, Z pulled Jessica closer and put his arm under the baby for added support.

"Maybe. But we'd been…" Ben rubbed his unshaven face. "I'd told her a few days before that I wasn't a slave. She wanted to think about it. We were going to talk that night."

"Ah." Z eyed him. "She said she was taking Joey back instead?"

"I didn't give her a chance to talk—but yeah, that's about right. Only now I think I might have fucked up."

Jessica's snort sounded like a sneeze.

Ben glanced at her. "You got something to add, blondie?"

"She wouldn't go back to Joey. He's a heavy masochist and she…well, she's not that sadistic any longer. She told me that." Jessica shook her head. "Could you have misread the situation?"

When Ben had called, Joey hadn't had a clue where Anne was. Had seemed surprised that anyone thought he would.

*Did I pull the trigger without taking in all the details?* He scowled at the table. No problem to bring up the image burned into his brain. Anne bending down to Joey, his chin cupped in her hand, looking into his face…for fucking ever.

But that was all Ben had seen, really. A long look. Had his own insecurity made him read more into the body language? "Maybe I…was hasty."

"If you made a mistake, you'll talk to her, whether she wants to or not, even if you have to tackle her at her workplace," Z said with no doubt in his voice. "I can't imagine you doing less."

"Roger that."

Z lifted his eyebrows, silently asking what advice he wanted.

"There's more information you need to know." Ben felt his gut clench. "Earlier that night, she'd fought with her family and then quit her job, too."

"Nooo." Jessica shook her head. "She loves her job. And her family."

"Yeah. And that's the problem. No one—family or friends—has seen her since she left the Shadowlands that night. Have you?" He looked at Z.

"I haven't heard from her, no." Z gazed at the darkness outside the lanai. "She's strong, but her heart leaves her vulnerable. How many blows can she take before breaking?"

A delayed realization dumped guilt on Ben's shoulders. If she hadn't taken Joey back, then…one of those blows could have come from him. What the fuck had he done?

"And Cullen said…" Jessica pressed her hand to her mouth, tears in her eyes. "That's not fair; she's had too much."

"Shhh, little one." Z lifted his wife and daughter into his lap, pulling them close.

"What did Cullen say?" Ben asked.

Z shook his head. "Cullen apparently thought the same thing you did, that she'd left you for Joey. He was angry on your behalf."

"Jesus, I don't need help." Had Cullen come down on her when she was hurting and pissed off? "Is that where she is? In jail for leaving bloody chunks of a dick-headed, dumbass Master all over the bar top?"

"Benjamin." Z's voice was dry. "Before Anne returns, you might work on the respectful language considered appropriate for a submissive."

As long as she returned, he might do that.

Z stroked Jessica's hair. "I wish Anne *had* reacted with violence. Instead, she quit."

"Quit what?"

The lines beside Z's mouth deepened. "She terminated her membership. And, yes, I've tried to reach her with no success."

*She quit the Shadowlands?* The sinking feeling in Ben's chest was new, as if his heart had bottomed out. What the fuck was she thinking, cutting every tie she had? Was she crazy?

No, but she had a hell of a temper when she actually let it loose.

She'd worked her ass off to be an outstanding fugitive recovery agent and Mistress. To have everything she'd built questioned by idiots like her uncles and father. And Cullen. Hell, he couldn't blame her for blowing her stack.

Travis said she tended to retreat when wounded. But she wouldn't stay away from her family and friends. Not long. "She'll be back to her friends—and the Shadowlands—when she's ready. Anne doesn't lack courage."

If she was all right.

She had to be all right. "When she returns..." Ben hesitated. "Z, I've seen you step in when things get fucked up. Will you help out?"

"No," Z said gravely.

Both Ben and Jessica stared at him.

"Benjamin, you have all the talent and determination required to see this through. Whether you two part ways or not, I know you'll support her until she's steady again." Z's smile was fleeting. "Whether she wants you to or not."

"She won't," Ben muttered. But, dammit, if she needed help, he'd see she got it. And she'd take that help, like it or not.

Although, it'd be easier on him to simply kill everyone who'd hurt her. He'd start with her cousin. Meantime, he had to find her. "I'm going to have Ghost take over the desk this weekend. Okay with you?"

Z nodded. "Of course."

Ben finished off his beer and rose. "Sorry to have cut into your evening, Jessica. I'll get out of your way now."

"I'm glad you came by," she said. "I'll talk to the other Shadowkittens and try to give you some ideas."

"Thanks." As he let himself out, he saw her turn and bury her head against Z's chest.

Anne had done that too, taken comfort from Ben. Had made him feel needed and powerful, as if he could keep the world from harming his woman.

Fuck, he missed her.

# Chapter Twenty-Eight

"You'll get calls from them, Joey," Anne said into her house phone. The two Dommes she'd spoken with earlier were sadists. And both were open to taking on a new slave.

"Thank you so much, Mistress Anne." He was so thrilled he sounded almost breathless.

"You're very welcome. You take care—"

"Are you going to be at the Shadowlands tonight?" he asked before she could say good-bye. "It's Saturday. And you weren't there last night."

Actually, she'd planned to be home last night, but the small matter of the SUV's cracked radiator had kept her in St. Augustine an extra day.

Not that she'd have gone to the club anyway. She wasn't a member any longer. "No, I'm planning a nice, quiet evening at home. I'll sit on the deck and watch the storm coming in."

"Ugh," he said.

She smiled, imagining his shiver. He hated storms. If he were smart, he wouldn't share that information with a new sadistic Mistress. "Good night, Joey."

Anne set the phone down and frowned at the blinking message machine. She had a myriad of calls.

But…she'd endured enough phone time for now, especially since the messages were from her family and maybe some of the Shadowlands members, including—she winced—Z. She'd already listened to two messages from Travis and Harrison. With each punch of the play button, she'd held her breath, hoping the caller was Ben, and then suffered through the pain when the voice hadn't been his.

She couldn't take more right now.

\* \* \* \*

In the deepening twilight, under the rumbling sound of thunder, Anne heard someone walking the stone path that ran beside her house. Her heart leaped. *Ben?*

From her sprawling position on the lounge chair, she pushed up on one elbow.

The tops of three heads showed, coming around the front of her high deck. Not Ben. *Women.* She exhaled in a sad little huff.

She recognized her visitors just from their hair. Sleek hair so black it glinted blue—Kim. Thick, wavy blonde hair—Jessica. Gleaming black with crinkles—Uzuri.

The Shadowkittens were here to…to what? She frowned as they came up her steps.

"Hey," Jessica called. "Will visitors be forced to walk the plank, Ma'am."

Anne's lips curved…slightly. "This isn't a ship; it's a deck. But come on up. I'll decide about the plank after hearing what crimes you've committed recently."

Only Uzuri looked worried. Kim actually laughed.

Anne felt like pouting. Her rep as an evil Mistress had just plain gone to hell. Then again, that was what happened with good friends, wasn't it? "To what do I owe the honor of this visit today? And how did you know I'd be here?"

No one knew she'd be here. Well, aside from Joey. Come to think of it, at one time, he'd been the token male submissive in the Shadowkittens. "Joey called you," Anne said flatly.

The three exchanged glances, silently electing Jessica as spokesperson.

"Everyone was worried when you disappeared." As the gusting wind whipped at her clothes, Jessica perched on a chair, her hair gathered in one hand.

Kim said, "Raoul and Cullen are really upset with themselves. Cullen says he stuck his foot in his mouth. Again. He's trying to think of ways to apologize."

"No apology necessary." Anne felt the pang of loss as she added, "I'm not liable to see them anyway."

"No!" Uzuri pushed past Kim, and suddenly Anne had a

submissive kneeling at her feet. "Please, Ma'am, don't let a quarrel change your life for the worse."

The memory of Ben kneeling…right there…stabbed into her heart.

"It's more than a quarrel." She'd thought she'd moved beyond their betrayal, but…it still hurt. "They thought I was dishonest and cheating on Ben."

"Anne." Kim's soft voice held the sweet stubbornness that Raoul adored. "They were just guys rallying to defend their bro. We women do it all the time. And Raoul realized even before you walked away that Ben wasn't the only person in your relationship who was hurting."

Anne blinked. Replayed the conversation. Yes, Cullen had been protective of Ben. And they hadn't heard any of what she and Joey had said, had just seen her with him, and how Ben had stormed away. They'd jumped to conclusions.

Stupid, true, but hey, *males*, right? Apparently, they'd bought into the cold-hearted Mistress image she'd created.

The ugly coil of pain in her chest unwound. "They rallied, and I lost my temper." She helped Uzuri back to her feet.

"Actually, I thought you held it together pretty well," Jessica said and settled further into the chair as Kim took the one beside her. "I'd say you had just about the worst evening known to womankind. Your job, your family, and then the club."

*True.* Anne observed them for a moment. "How do you know about my evening?"

"Oh, girl." Uzuri sat on the swing. "The Shadowlands is even gossipier than the little town where I grew up. Your brother talked with Ben, who talked with Z who told him what Cullen and Raoul had said."

"I called Joey," Kim said, "and he added in the rest."

Travis had told Ben what had happened? Head spinning, Anne held up her hand. "I got the picture."

"Ben's worried about you," Jessica said.

Would it matter? He cared about people. Just because he'd broken it off with her wouldn't make him stop caring.

Someone should let him know she was fine. Kind of fine. "Did someone inform him that I was home and all right?"

"No. We wanted to talk with you first." Jessica gave her a soft smile. "You might be a Mistress, but you're also in our gang. And a woman needs her posse around her when things go bad."

Jessica's affection lapped over and into the empty recesses of Anne's heart. She had good friends. A look at the other two women showed they felt the same, even before Jessica added, "Everyone wanted to come, but we were afraid you'd feel invaded."

"When Sally lost out, boy, you should have heard the swearing. And Olivia said she's going to beat our asses at the club for not letting her come." Kim's lips tilted up. "See how much we love you?"

And here she'd been feeling bereft. "Thank you. Thank you all."

"Right. So—do you have a blender?" Uzuri picked up the brown grocery sack at her feet. "We can't share disastrous relationship stories without alcohol."

They'd have to do the drinking for her, but okay. Laughing, Anne rose and led the way inside.

* * * *

Watching the black clouds cover the sky, Ben pulled his phone out of his rear pocket and answered without checking the display. "Yo."

"Ben? Travis."

Ben froze. "News?"

"Yeah. Lights are on at her place."

"Did you stop by?" Ben asked.

"No, Harrison's wife noticed and called me. Dad and I are in Tampa and heading there now, so if you want to see her before us, this is your chance."

Ben smiled. *Good man.* "Copy that. Thanks."

"No thanks needed. Just be aware that if you don't make her happy, I'll break your neck."

If he fucked this up, he'd welcome an early demise.

* * * *

As Uzuri concocted daiquiris with the fresh strawberries she'd brought, Anne took charge of adding rum to each drink.

A salt-laden, wet wind gusted through the screen of the open deck door to announce the storm's arrival. A minute later, rain pattered on her deck and grew into a noisy drumming. "You got here just in time," Anne raised her voice to be heard. "It's turning into a mess out there."

Kim wrinkled her nose. "No driving in that until it calms down a bit." She accepted her glass.

*No driving, period.* Smiling, Anne handed over the other two rum-heavy drinks. If her friends tried to get behind a wheel after they'd been drinking, they discover what a hardass Domme she really was.

She picked up her rumless drink, heaved a sigh, and plopped in three extra strawberries to make up for the absence of alcohol.

After using the remote to start her moody playlist, she settled into her favorite armchair. Over the low strains of Enya, rain slapped against the night-darkened window.

Cross-legged on the couch, Jessica leaned toward Anne. "I saw Ben on Thursday. He looked really wrecked about you two not being together."

Anne blinked at the straightforward approach and then narrowed her eyes. "Aren't you supposed to build up to grilling someone about their relationship? You know, be gentle with vulnerable, upset friends?"

"You're right. God, Jessica, were you raised on the docks?" Kim shook her head and smiled sweetly at Anne. "Don't you just love how pretty the weather is today?"

Anne glanced out the arched windows to the white-capped waves slamming into her beach. Over the black ocean, lightning created stark ribbons of jagged light. The sound of the palm trees whipping in the wind could barely be heard under the thunder.

Uzuri followed her gaze and—giggling—told Kim, "You're an idiot."

Kim scowled. "I like this kind of weather, although it's better when I have Raoul to wrap around."

"See? That's what I'm saying. Anne needs her giant, studly teddy bear." Jessica nodded. "Are you going to take him back? Give the poor man a break?"

*Take him back? He broke up with me.*

"Maybe she wants younger—or doesn't want a huge guy," Uzuri said.

The other two gave her looks of disbelief.

Uzuri lifted her chin. "Hey, some of us prefer normal men. Besides, those pretty boys of hers were gorgeous and built *and* in their guy prime."

"You have an excellent point." Kim raised her glass to her friend. "Joey's butt? Work of art."

"This is true," Jessica said with due consideration. "And yet, maybe Anne got fond of that big build. There are a lot of pluses to older and bigger. More muscles. More experience. Bigger…masculine attributes."

Kim hummed. "Larger masculine attributes can't be discounted lightly.

"It's actually a detriment, in my opinion, unless the male in question knows how to wield it." Uzuri sniffed. "And everything else as well."

Anne swung a leg over the arm of her chair. If she stayed silent, these three might settle all her concerns.

Unfortunately, all three turned to look at her expectantly.

"Ben can definitely wield all his weapons superbly." Oh, he could. "And I did get fond of his build—as well as his masculine attributes." Time to actually share, not something at which she was experienced. "But he doesn't want to be a slave. He's more of a sexual submissive." Final confession. "And I hate to change." She hadn't moved fast enough.

When Kim nodded, obviously unsurprised about Ben, Anne asked, "You knew?"

"He'd talked with Raoul. And Raoul was worried about you two. He wasn't sure you'd accept a sexual submissive rather than a slave."

Raoul'd been worried? Anne tried to remember. After Ben had dumped her and left, Raoul had come over. Frowning. Had his expression held more concern than disapproval? She sighed. Unsettled emotions really could mess up a person's ability to read body language.

"I hear you on wanting things to stay the same," Uzuri said. "But when I. . had to move to Florida, I learned change can be good. Open new worlds, new possibilities." She smiled at the others. "Bring new friends."

"You don't really want your life to remain the same forever, do you?" Jessica's smile was soft. "I've seen you with Sophia. You want one of your own."

"I do." Anne sighed. She *had* wanted a child—and now, here she was. Pregnant. It almost made her feel guilty, as if her yearning had resulted in her pregnancy. "I'd like a baby—no matter how much my life would be altered."

"I might eventually, too, but we're not ready," Kim admitted. "I'm still getting over the trauma of consenting to be married."

Uzuri snickered. "Anyone else would worry more about that collar he locked around her neck."

"Beth wants a baby too." Jessica grinned. "Can you see Nolan's face if he has to convert his customized, hand-crafted dungeon into a kid's playroom?"

Anne had seen his expression when he'd held Kari's Zane. The big Master wouldn't have any trouble clearing his life out for a child.

"Babies undeniably transform your life." Uzuri raised her brows at Jessica. "I know it's early days, but did Sophia muddle yours up at all? Is Master Z still your Master?"

Anne smothered a smile. Z had certainly looked like a Master on the day Jessica had taken Anne's advice.

Catching the twitch of Anne's lips, Jessica turned red. After clearing her throat, she smiled at Uzuri. "I don't think anyone could take the Master out of Z. But our relationship's gone through some changes. We've had a couple of fights."

"Really?" Kim leaned forward.

"Like the day that I got too tired. Well, we both were, really. Sophia was fussing, and the phone was ringing, and Z didn't answer it. He was on his cell, but I didn't know that and thought he was being lazy, and I blew up into a total hissy fit."

"Oh my God, you took on Master Z?" Uzuri looked terrified enough to have Anne frowning.

Dammit, they really needed to work on some of those fears. No, Anne wasn't a member of the Shadowlands any longer. Well, she'd give Z a heads-up. And...and she'd do some digging as a *friend* instead.

"I wasn't thinking of Masters or submitting or anything," Jessica said. "I was just...I simply lost it." She scowled. "But it was *Master Z* who spanked me, and it sure wasn't an erotic spanking, but mean and merciless. I cried my eyes out. Would you believe he said I needed the release?"

When Anne laughed—because Z'd obviously been right—Jessica wrinkled her nose. "I'd rather have had a different kind of release, right? But afterward, he held me and cuddled me. When Sophia started fussing again, he put me to bed and told me if I didn't go to sleep, he'd spank me again."

Uzuri gave a contented sigh. "Okay. You had me worried for a minute there."

Kim frowned. "Aside from you yelling at him, that's not much of a change."

"Right. That's what *hasn't* changed; he still takes total charge when he feels protective. When it comes to Sophia and the house, then I make most of the decisions. We decide a lot together, and if we don't agree, the final say is his, and I prefer that. It's...comforting."

Anne thought Z had a good handle on balancing everything. And Jessica's contentment bore that out. Interesting. Was this what Ben wanted?

"That's what I had planned to try with Ben," she admitted. All three gazes snapped to her. "Move the D/s more into the bedroom. Not make Ben twist himself to be a slave."

"Ben would be good at juggling everything, I think. Outside the bedroom, he'd insist on protecting you and supporting you," Kim said.

"And then hand you the whip in the bedroom," Jessica added.

"I wish." Anne's drink tasted like hopelessness. "That was what I'd wanted, but Ben said he's vanilla. He thanked me for the *taste of kink*, as if he wanted to spit at what was left in his mouth."

"That was that night at the Shadowlands? And you believed him?" Uzuri looked at her in disbelief. "You're a Domme—you're supposed to read us better."

Jessica laughed. "Pfft, even mind-reading Dominants screw it up when their own emotions get involved. And that night, she wasn't operating on all burners." She glanced over. "Sorry, Anne."

"It's the truth." Anne hesitated as her anxiety and hope fought a battle. "What did I miss?"

Uzuri frowned. "I was in the subbie section, watching. You were bending over Joey, holding his chin all sweet and Mistressy, and just…*looking* at him. A long time. And Ben saw that, and his face totally changed—like mad and jealous and hurt. He thought you went back to Joey."

Anne held up a hand as the memory seared through her, clear as crystal now. "He said that. *'See you found your boy.'* I thought he meant I'd found Joey to talk with. But he thought I chose Joey, rather than him. And then he…unleashed."

"Like a typical hurt guy," Jessica said.

"Yes, like a wounded man, he not only picked up his cards, but kicked over the table as well," Uzuri agreed.

"He lied about what he wants, Anne," Kim said. "He's not a slave, but he's not vanilla either. He told Raoul that."

"Hey, I saw him after one of your scenes. He looked past content and well into blissful. It's obvious he's into that part of submission." Jessica smiled.

*"Blissful."* And didn't that lovely description make Anne feel good?

Kim nodded. "You two need to talk. I think you belong together."

Their expressions held such conviction that Anne's eyes burned with tears. She'd avoided thinking about Ben and what to do. Maybe this was why—because her memory was all mixed up with pain and lost hopes.

But these women were her…her posse…as Jessica had said. They wouldn't steer her wrong. "All right. I'll—"

The sound of ripping drew Anne's attention toward the deck.

A hand reached through a long gash in the screen door and unlatched the lock. A huge man slid the door open and stepped in.

Anne shot to her feet. "Who—" She stopped at the sight of his face.

Although a panty hose over his head flattened his features, the rage came through clearly. "More 'n one bitch here, bro." He waved the knife toward them.

More men crowded through the door—all masked. An armed robbery?

Adrenaline dried Anne's mouth.

Uzuri squeaked with fear.

Her heart kicking against her ribs, Anne faced the men, sliding into a non-offensive stance that still prepared her for battle.

"What do you want?" Anne counted five men. Too many to fight successfully. *Damn.* Her stomach twisted to the point of nausea.

From the corner of her eye, she saw Kim take a grip on a lamp.

Jessica retreated behind a chair, holding the phone in her hands out of sight. Hopefully she'd hit mute when dialing 9-1-1.

To keep the men's attention from Jessica, Anne backed toward the kitchen. "What do you want?" she repeated in a calm voice. The longer they could avoid violence the better.

Five men. 9-1-1 might be too late.

The man in the forefront had a bulky body the size of Ben's, an oversized head, and a snarl like a vicious pit bull. "Where'd you hide my wife and my son, you cunt?"

Oh, bad. Home invasions were rampant in Tampa, but this wasn't an attempted burglary. *"My wife."* This was an abuser trying to find his victim. The knot in Anne's belly tightened. The masks had given her hope—but these guys couldn't afford to leave witnesses behind.

*My baby.* Anne started to cover her stomach, then forced her arms to hang loose. Never draw attention to a vulnerability. *I'm not pregnant. No, not me.*

Fear dried her mouth. The storm and accompanying accidents would slow the arrival of the police. How long could she stall? "Who's your wife?"

"Sue Ellen. Now where the *fuck* is she?" He swung his arm and knocked a lamp into the wall.

Hand against her mouth, Uzuri gave a thin scream.

Sue Ellen. The woman had been choked, and her son had displayed a fist-sized bruise on his baby cheek. *"Billy will come after me,"* she'd said.

"I'm so sorry." Meeting Billy's raging eyes, Anne spread her hands out helplessly. "I don't know who that is. As a bounty hunter, I meet a lot of people every day."

"Bitch, you took her to some fucked-up place for women. You're trying to hide her—hide her from me, her legal husband," he said.

A man who also rivaled Ben for height and muscles moved forward. His mask had smashed his broad features, but Anne recognized the build of the ogre-like brother-in-law who'd seen her with Sue Ellen.

His gaze took her in. "That's her, brother."

Billy took a step forward. "You fucking—"

"Don't got time to fuck around." The brother grabbed Uzuri's hair and slapped her so violently her head jerked back.

Tears filled her eyes as she struggled in his grip.

He grinned at Anne, feeding off Uzuri's whimpers. "Tell us the address or we fuck up your girlies." He held up his hand again, and Uzuri cringed.

"Stop." Shoving down fury, Anne made her voice waver. It wasn't difficult with the waves of fear chilling her blood. "I'll tell. P-please, don't hurt us."

"Sounds more like it." Another of the men approached Anne. Faded shirt. Dark tan. The sickening sweet smell of chewing tobacco couldn't overwhelm the stench of his sweat. "Gimme the fuckin' address."

Ogre shoved Uzuri away. She landed on her hands and knees, crying and shaking.

Anne's jaw clenched. These good ol' boys who thought spousal abuse was their God-given right still might not be stupid enough to take her word for the address.

She didn't have much choice though. Hoping against hope, she rattled off a made-up number on a large St. Pete street.

*Now leave us here and go check it out.*

\* \* \* \*

*Goddamned rain. Goddamned flooding.* Ben finally reached Clearwater Island, navigated through streets tangled with branches and debris, swerved around the inevitable fender-benders, and slowly trailed another car into Anne's cul-de-sac. To his surprise, two beat-up pickups were parked on the street on each side of her driveway.

Was she having a party?

Annoyingly enough, the car in front of him turned into her drive. *Fuck.* The detour he'd been forced to take getting out of St. Pete had given Travis and Anne's father time to arrive.

Hell with it, he was still going to see her.

Recognizing the location, Bronx whined. He wanted his Anne.

*So do I.* He ruffled Bronx's fur. "You have to wait, buddy. Anne and I have things to settle before you jump in."

He closed the door and flinched at the streak of lightning followed by the crack of thunder. After a slow breath, he crossed to Travis. "I got held up."

"I figured. The roads are a mess." Travis nodded toward his father, who walked around the car. "Dad, this is Ben Haugen. Ben, my father, Stephan Desmarais."

Desmarais was about six feet, dark haired, with the lean build of his sons and a military bearing. "Good to meet you." He shook Ben's hand before his mouth firmed in a determined line. "I realize you're probably here to see my daughter. I want to talk to her first."

Ben set his feet. "We all have reasons to see her. I figure the choice of who she speaks with first is hers. Not mine. Not yours. I'll accompany you to the door."

Travis coughed, as if covering a laugh.

Anne's father wasn't laughing, and his glare was worthy of note. Not that Ben would change his mind, but it was a pretty good glare.

Anne's was better.

\* \* \* \*

Terror and rage mixed in an unholy brew as Anne watched the men spread out in the room, far too close to her friends.

Her very vulnerable friends. Jessica had a new baby. Kim and Uzuri had already suffered at the hands of abusive men.

Starting the fight now wouldn't help anything. *Wait...*

The guy with a bushy brown beard pulled out a phone and tapped in the address Anne had provided.

Anne's heart sank. Didn't it just figure one of them would know how to check a map app? As his comrades waited for the bearded one's results, she moved closer to her friends.

*Wait...*

Beard shook his head and snapped out, "No such address. She lied."

"You fuckin' cunt." Billy started toward Anne.

"Brother. No. That one's got to be able to talk." Ogre glanced at the red-shirted man and pointed to Jessica. "Cut that bitch."

"No," Anne cried. "Wait—"

Red Shirt yanked out a knife from his belt sheath and grabbed for

Jessica.

Even as Anne charged across the room, Jessica jumped sideways, out of reach.

Kim threw the lamp.

The metal base struck the side of his head and knocked him back a step.

"Fuckin' bitch." Chewing-Tobacco lunged at Kim. She dodged but tripped over a side table and landed on her side on the floor.

*Knife first.* "You!" Anne shouted at Red Shirt. Skidding to a stop, she pivoted. Powered with all her anger, her sidekick smashed into the man's leg. The crunch of a knee bending in a direction it wasn't designed for was accompanied by his shriek. The knife hit the floor; then he did.

Ogre backhanded her.

Pain exploded in her cheek.

*Falling.*

Her head slammed into the floor.

\* \* \* \*

"What the fuck was that?" Travis asked from the stoop of Anne's front door.

Ben knew. *A man in agony.* He hadn't heard that since Iraq.

Shoving Travis aside, he tried the door handle. Locked.

Why the hell had he given her key back? He sprinted toward the back. If necessary, he could bust through the deck's sliding glass door.

Pounding footsteps sounded behind him as he rounded the side of the house, went up the steps three at a time, and across the rain-drenched deck.

Both glass and screen doors stood open and the inside was chaos.

Fighting filled the room. Men with hose over their heads. One rolled on the floor, holding his leg. The rest... Where was Anne?

Ben's rage erupted. The bastards had attacked women. A slight brunette—*Kim*—punched a bearded guy with her tiny fist forcefully enough to stop him—and then Jessica hit him over the head with an end table.

Anne was on the ground.

*Shit!*

A puny-ass punch thumped into Ben's ribs, and he shoved the attacker over the couch and headed toward—

Anne scrambled to her feet, unsteady, staggering clumsily away from a fucking big bastard, shaking her head. The man swung at her.

"No," Ben roared.

She dodged and whirled, her leg rising, rising, and the top of her bare foot smashed into the man's temple. He went down.

Two men remained. One turned toward her.

"*Assholes.*" Ben charged the short bastard standing in the way of his goal. He buried his fist in the man's gut and followed with a right hook to the jaw that broke everything moveable and ensured the bastard'd be sucking his food through a straw for a long time to come.

The bearded, lamp-victim staggered to his feet and charged Jessica. Travis and Stephan intercepted.

Ben turned his sights on the last one. Even bigger than Ben and bulky. *Fine target.* Ben swung.

The man sidestepped far enough that Ben's punch caught only his ribs. With a grunt, asshole absorbed the blow and counter-punched with a meaty fist.

Ben slapped his arm to one side.

"Billy!" With a livid bruise marring her cheek, Anne stared at the asshole. Her expression was purely furious, her temper white hot. And she wasn't ready to quit.

Ben almost…almost took the guy out, but pulled his punch at the last minute.

*Hell.*

Some men gave their women flowers to apologize.

If her temper was riled, Anne was liable to return a bouquet, aiming it right at his head. But there were other ways to ask forgiveness.

Like a Billy present. Still wanting to kill the asshole, Ben grabbed his collar, tossed him into a wall to keep him busy, and called, "I'm sorry for what I said, Ma'am."

Diverted, Anne turned her steel-gray gaze to Ben.

"Can I make it up to you?" He caught the bastard on the rebound and shoved him toward her. "A treat?"

"What?" She dodged the staggering asshole and kicked his legs out from under him.

Billy landed, and the house shook.

"What are you doing here, Benjamin?" When Billy lunged to his feet, Anne punched him in the chin and propelled him back toward Ben.

"Apologizing. I fucked up…thought you'd gone back to your pretty boy." Just thinking about the little shit added a bit of emphasis when Ben backhanded the dazed asshole across the face. He pushed him to Anne.

She muttered something about her posse being right. After ducking under Billy's wild swing, she side-kicked him in the gut and returned him to Ben. "You idiot, I love you. Why would I want Joey?"

The words…the *words*…paralyzed Ben completely. *Love?* She loved him? The thrill ran up his spine, sending rockets exploding in the air, making his ears ring.

Something thumped his belly, and he realized the asshole had hit him. Forgetting even to reprimand him, Ben snorted in disgust and tossed him to Anne. "Me, too. You. We need to talk."

"I agree. It's time." She took out the man with a blazing jab-jab to the stomach, and a left hook to the jaw, followed by a right cross.

"Bravo Zulu, Ma'am," *Well done.*

"Shit, that was pretty, sis." Travis smiled at her before frowning at Ben. "You could have let me play too, dickhead."

"Your sister's house; your sister's toys."

"You cowardly bastard, you shoved him at my little girl?" Anne's father was red with anger. "And you…" He shouldered aside his son, who'd apparently blocked him from participating. "You're no better."

"Hey, they were having a talk," Travis said so virtuously there should've been a halo over his head. "Mom said not to interrupt serious discussions."

"Don't look now, Stephan, but she's not a little girl." With pride, Ben watched Anne—*my woman*—help Uzuri stand.

Sirens sounded, growing in intensity.

Off to one side, Travis was still arguing with Stephan.

Ben grabbed some duct tape from the kitchen drawer and started to immobilize the bad guys, leaving the obviously incapacitated one for last. He'd bet his last dollar that the guy—still moaning over his visibly destroyed knee—was Anne's work.

"Jessica, are you all right?" Anne called as she helped the trembling Uzuri into a chair. "Can you let the police in?"

"I'm good." Blondie shoved her hair out of her face, scowled at the bearded idiot on the floor, and thumped him in the ribs with her little foot. "And I'd be delighted."

"You?" Anne glanced at Kim with eyebrows raised.

She got a firm nod back. "I'm fine." Kim picked up an overturned, metal-based lamp and whacked the same poor bastard with it before setting it on an end table.

Ben chuckled. The Shadowkittens had some wicked keen claws.

Anne heard him and turned. And approached.

His heart rate increased. He straightened and set a foot on the half-secured bad guy.

She flattened her hand on Ben's chest. Her knuckles were reddened, the creases between the fingers showing broken blood vessels. His woman had hit hard. He'd have to get her an ice pack.

She went up on tiptoes to kiss him lightly. "You've earned a reward for sharing the treat."

"Not much I won't do to earn a reward," he murmured. Fuck, he wanted her. Wanted to kneel at her feet, to be ordered to service her, to taste her, to breathe her in.

To feel her hands in his hair as she led the way…and took him with her.

Her hand hadn't moved from his chest, and she studied him for a second, then her lips curved. "After the garbage is taken away, we'll talk. Then…"

*Then. Yeah.* "Works for me."

With hope budding in her heart, Anne turned to deal with the tasks awaiting her. *Bad guys, cops, friends, family. And Ben. Ben most of all.*

Uzuri first. But even as she headed that way, Kim pulled the little submissive out of the chair, saying, "While Anne talks with the police, why don't we clean up the mess?"

"Okay," Uzuri whispered, but she didn't move.

Guilt ran through Anne. Those men had been after her, not Uzuri. The vulnerable woman shouldn't have had to endure the resurrection of past traumas.

Anne put an arm around her waist. "Uzuri."

Her velvety-brown eyes dropped.

With a finger under the subbie's chin, Anne tilted her face up. Her beautiful brown skin was marred by a bloody scrape along her jaw and a cut lip, making Anne want to start another brawl. "How are you doing, honey?"

"That's just it. I didn't *do anything.*" Shame showed on Uzuri's face. "Didn't fight back. Just…took it."

Ah, so that was what was wrong. Anne shoved her welling pity to one side; it wouldn't benefit the young woman. "You're right. You were no help at all in the fight."

Tears filled Uzuri's eyes at the merciless statement.

Anne ignored Kim's gasp and kept her grip on Uzuri's chin, holding her gaze. "And that means next time you'll need to do better.

You're going to take self-defense classes, even if you're scared."

Uzuri blinked. "But—"

"That's an order, sub," Anne said softly, adding a thread of ice. "Am I clear?"

Uzuri was still trembling, but resolve firmed her mouth and filled her eyes. "Yes, Ma'am. I will."

"That's what I want to hear." Anne squeezed her waist. "You're stronger than you think; you just need the tools to prove it." *And I'll be on your ass to make sure you do.* "Now, can you help clean this place up while I deal with the cops?"

Given a command, Uzuri pulled herself together. Relief eased her expression. "Yes, Ma'am."

Obviously recognizing the Domme's technique, Kim winked, gave a mock martial arts bow. "Let's get some bags and pitch everything that's broken."

As the two headed for the kitchen, Anne turned to her next task.

"Anne." Her father pulled free of Travis's restraining grip. "What the hell was going on?"

*Oh, honestly.* So much for making amends any time soon. She gave him a disgusted stare. "I can't believe you called Ben a coward for being nice enough to let me finish a fight."

His mouth dropped open. "You're my *daughter.* I—"

"We've had this talk before." Anne was through with his crap. "Go home to Mom. Maybe she enjoys being treated like a precious figurine that will break if you look at it too roughly—although I'd say she's stronger than you give her credit for."

When she heard Ben's rumbled laugh, Anne glanced his way. He was looking at the kitchen—where her mother stood, hands on hips, staring at her oblivious husband.

"You don't understand," her father protested, his back to the kitchen.

"Oh, I do, all too well. My parents raised me to be strong and competent. Deadly, even. It's a shame my father still thinks his thirty-five-year-old daughter belongs in a playpen." She waved her hand at the good ol' boys littering her living room. "Three of those on the ground are mine."

Her father didn't move. He just stood there, looking more unsettled than she'd ever seen him. "I'm sorry, Anne."

An apology? The surprise held her in place. He looked...sad.

Her heart urged her to tell him it was all okay. But it wasn't. And she rather doubted that his beliefs had really changed. Firming her resolve, she stepped into a Domme mindset. He might be hurting, but remorse was an excellent learning tool. "For what are you sorry? Exactly?"

"I never meant for you to feel less valued. I love you, Anne. Love you fully as much as the boys." The lines on his face deepened. "But, baby, I can't stand you doing something that might get you hurt. Killed."

Before Anne could throw him out of her house, a delicate growl came from the kitchen.

He turned.

Her mother stalked forward. She punched her beloved husband in the stomach fiercely enough to make him grunt.

Anne's mouth dropped open.

"You hypocrite," her mother actually shouted. "When I objected to Travis and Harrison playing football, taking karate, and *enlisting*, you said, '*Suck it up, Elaine. Be tough.*' You said a good parent let her children fly from the nest and cheered them on, wherever their hearts led them. You told *me* I was a coward."

"But...But—"

"Who's the coward *here*?" Her mother punched him again—even harder.

Near the door, Travis was laughing his fool head off.

With hand over mouth, Ben was muffling his amusement in deference to her father.

"Elaine," her father protested.

Her pint-sized mom ignored him and turned to give Anne a gentle hug. "What are the damages, darling?" It was the same question she'd asked her boys when they returned from sports and wars.

Anne blinked back tears. "I'm fine," she whispered.

Her mother stepped back and frowned at the bruise on Anne's face. "Put some ice on that, dear." Her gaze swept over the bodies littering the floor. "Outstanding job. I always knew you could handle yourself as well as the boys."

"Thanks, Mom."

Her mother turned. "Stephan, we're going home now. To talk."

He looked as if she'd invited him to his own execution.

Anne's sense of humor finally kicked in. "Sounds good. Dad, if and when Mom forgives you, so will I."

When he opened his mouth to object, she gave him the icy stare that had silenced submissives for years and waved her fingers toward the door. "Dismissed."

Her mother winked at her as they left.

Anne turned to Travis.

"Jesus, sis, remind me not to piss you off. My balls just shriveled up."

She sighed. "I really don't want to hear my brother talking about his testicles, thank you very much."

When Ben snorted, she smiled, then pointed at the intruders. "Can you and Travis finish securing the bad guys while I jump through the formalities?"

"My pleasure."

She studied him for a minute. Strong. Brave. He didn't need to throw his weight around to prove he had courage. He knew he did. He knew who he was and was comfortable with the knowledge.

So he could let her be who she was.

How could she do anything less?

And he'd shared his bad guy with her. Actually been delighted to share.

She had a feeling they'd be just fine sharing other things.

Like a baby.

Like a life.

The cops entered the room—one glanced around and started calling in an ambulance. The other was in the doorway, talking with Jessica.

Raoul pushed past him and into the living room.

Kim shook her head at him. "You're late."

He stared at the rough-looking men on the floor for a second. "Are you hurt, *gatita*?" He looked Kim over carefully, searching for damage.

"I'm fine."

"Home invasion?"

"An abuser looking for the battered women's shelter," Kim said.

Fury darkened his expression, yet he drew her into his arms very, very gently. His gaze took in the graze on Uzuri's jaw, checked over Jessica, then lingered on Anne's cheek. "Are you all right?"

"Minor damage to everyone. And Kim did very well. She has an excellent punch, in fact."

Kim beamed.

"But battles bring back..." Anne let her voice trail off, but he'd caught her meaning. The violence could well resurrect nightmares from his submissive's past.

He nodded his understanding.

Anne looked at her friend. "Kim, I'm so sorry."

"For what?" Kim asked.

"It was my activities with the shelter that endangered you." Although she couldn't figure out how the bastards had found her home.

Raoul shook his head. "We all volunteer there, Anne. We know the dangers."

"It's not your fault," Kim said. "And I'm really, really glad we were here."

Anne felt a chill at that thought. She truly would have been in trouble if she'd been alone. After a second, she smiled. "In that case, I very much appreciate the visit, the advice, the help with the...trash"— she glanced at the men being handcuffed by the officers—"and the cleaning up after."

Kim pulled free of her Master and gave Anne a gentle squeeze. Jessica and Uzuri both came to claim hugs as well.

*My posse.* "Thank you all," she whispered as tears prickled her eyes.

After another set of hugs, the women headed out. Hands waving in the air, Kim and Jessica were comparing their fighting techniques and teasing Uzuri about how she'd have to catch up.

Raoul still stood in the center of the room.

Anne frowned. "How did you get here so quickly?"

"I was already on the island. I asked to be their designated driver so I could speak with you afterward."

"Raoul..."

"My friend, please forgive me for last Saturday," he said softly. "My worries caused me—"

"I know," she broke in. "You were right to worry. I wasn't paying enough attention." She remembered how Raoul's ex-wife had blindsided him. How he'd blamed himself for not seeing what was in front of his face. "You realized that, didn't you?"

"I had told him to talk with you." His mouth flattened into a line. "That night at the club—"

"You did nothing wrong. And it's done," she said. "Thank you for being there for Ben."

"Is it done?" His lips twitched. "You realize if I don't inform Z that you're returning, you'll have him on your doorstep within an hour...if not sooner."

She raised her eyes to the ceiling, asking the universe for patience.

Ben appeared and drew her against his side, so solid and warm that she wrapped her arms around his waist to pull him closer.

Raoul's gaze went soft.

Ben kissed the top of her head and said to Raoul, "You tell Z if he interrupts my time with Anne, I'll teach Uzuri how to booby-trap every piece of equipment in the Shadowlands."

"Now that is a very effective threat." Raoul gave him a respectful nod. "I'll let him know."

"Ms. Desmarais? If I could get some information from you?" More police as well as paramedics had arrived.

"Of course." With Ben at her side, she gave Raoul a kiss on the cheek and turned to give her report.

# Chapter Twenty-Nine

An hour later, the house was quiet, thank fuck. Raoul had left with the women, promising the Mistress that Uzuri would spend the night at his house.

The cops had left.

Travis had left.

Ben was alone with Anne. About damn time.

After grabbing drinks from the fridge, he entered the living room and looked around. Despite being upset, Anne's friends had done a fine job of cleaning.

Anne was finally still. At the end, she'd been exhausted, running on nerves, and hadn't sat until he'd brought Bronx in. Then she'd dropped down onto the couch to hug the ecstatic dog.

The woman had so much love to share.

Bronx was still sprawled over her lap as if he couldn't stand to let her out of touching range.

Ben knew the feeling. Good thing there was enough room for another person on the couch. After handing over the sparkling water, he sat down and pulled her close.

At one time, he'd have taken the liberty of lifting her onto his lap.

Times changed. The sense of loss filled him again. Damn but he'd missed holding her. She felt like a part of him, like the sun in his sky. "Ready to talk?"

Her shoulders curved inward slightly, as if she wasn't sure she could bear what he might say.

He felt the same. She could break him far too easily.

Stalling, he took a drink of his cold lager for reassurance. She hadn't thrown out his beer. And she'd said she loved him. His voice came out hoarse. "Where should we start?"

She met his gaze with her level, honest eyes. "I'm sorry, Ben."

She wasn't going to give them a chance, was she? She didn't think love was enough to overcome the differences? Heart sinking, he bit back his protest.

After a moment, he managed to clear his throat. "I am, too. I'd hoped you'd give us a chance."

Her brows drew together and then she shook her head and half laughed. "We're good at miscommunication, aren't we?" Her shoulder rubbed against his chest as she took his hand, her grip firm and warm. "What I meant is that I'm sorry you misunderstood that business with Joey. Uzuri said you thought I was taking Joey back because I was staring at him."

"I…yeah."

"That wasn't what was happening. Actually, I'd totally zoned out and was thinking about you."

His brain was having trouble keeping up.

"I've already found Joey a couple of Dommes who will suit him better."

Jessica had been right. Damn. Ben felt as if he'd been pushing a boulder uphill and reached the top without realizing. After a few thousand seconds, he caught up. "I'm sorry I jumped to conclusions." He stared at the window, out at the black water, seeing the faint rim of white on the waves like a touch of hope.

But he needed to clear away the past first. He took her hand. "You weren't even tempted to go back to Joey?"

"Not even. Our needs don't mesh any longer, although I didn't want to admit how much I'd—"

"Changed?"

She made a tiny growl. "There's that word again. You know how I feel about change."

He snorted. "Pretty much how most people feel about necrophilia."

She gave a startled laugh and leaned into him more fully. *Fuck, yeah.* He released her hand and lifted her onto his lap. Bronx gave him a disgruntled look

But this was where she belonged. She fit perfectly in his arms.

"But yes, as my anger at men died, so did my enjoyment of hurting them." Her hand curved around his jaw firmly enough to give him a surge of pleasure. "I'm still quite, quite fond of domination, though."

"I never doubted that for a moment, Ma'am." He considered her confession—because that was what it sounded like. He grinned, remembering how she'd said once that her anger had started with God for not making her male, expanded to her father, brothers, uncles, grew to include the government for not allowing women in combat, and on and on. "So, you took out your annoyance on those poor helpless slaves?"

Her frown stopped just short of a scowl. "So it seems. I'm not happy that I used them that way."

Raoul hadn't thought her motivation was unusual. He shrugged. "Seems as if everyone has a shitload of reasons for doing what they do—from getting up in the morning to pounding on someone. You never dished out anything that the slaves didn't love and beg for."

"Until you."

He pulled her closer, kissing the curve between her shoulder and neck. "I've liked everything you've done to me."

"Just not full time."

"Not full time." His arms tightened. "Anne, I'm sorry I jumped to conclusions. I should've given you a chance to explain."

"This is very true." Tears shimmered in her eyes before she blinked them away. Her tone turned judicious. "I'm afraid I'll need to punish you for that. Bear it in mind as we talk."

The way his cock shot to full arousal, it was liable to sprain something.


The lovely bulge beneath Anne made her want to smile. Made her want to start some action right then and there. But their conversation wasn't over, and burying problems hadn't worked well for them.

She indulged herself for just a tiny second, nuzzling his neck to inhale the lingering fragrance of his earthy aftershave and his own underlying, totally masculine scent.

His arms tightened...and the erection beneath her thickened.

*Oops.* She cleared her throat. "I believe it's time to move into thinking about you and me and how you asked to keep the D/s within a sexual context."

Every muscle on his body tensed.

Her realization of the depth of his need was glorious and humbling.

"Anne, if I thought I could take the full time, I—"

"I think it'll work," she said quickly. "I want to try."

His arms turned to steel bars around her as he rasped, "What?"

"Disgusting as the word is, I've changed. I don't need to control everything and everyone any longer. I suppose the need for full-time domination arose from my own fears." She rubbed her cheek against his shoulder and barely resisted a nibble. "But I'm still totally a sexual Dominant."

He huffed a laugh. "I'm good with that."

"It might be nice to live with someone who isn't a slave. You like me as more than a Mistress—as Anne. I can relax with you."

She lifted up far enough to capture his lips, those firm knowledgeable lips. God, she'd missed kissing him, missed the way he could make her feel both delicate and powerful, like the time she'd ridden a Clydesdale, knowing the huge horse could easily kill her if it had wanted.

After a minute or more, she sat back. Holding his gaze, she ventured even further out of her comfort zone. "Would...would you like to move in?"

His answer came instantly. "Hell, yes. I love you, Anne."

Her breath halted as her heart swelled until it took up all the room there was in her chest. He'd said it.

"Ben." The word was barely audible, and she had to blink back tears. Damn hormones.

His big hand stroked her cheek. "Since we got all that settled, now can I beg the Mistress to take me to the bedroom and punish me?"

"I suppose I can fit you into my busy schedule." She had a second of grief for the knowledge that she didn't have a schedule any longer, or a job at all. Then she pushed her worries aside under the rising tide of desire.

She stood and pulled him to his feet. As she led him up the stairs, electricity flickered along her nerves like heat lightning.

Clothes dropped behind her. Behind him.

Feeling the stickiness of sweat and blood on her skin, she veered into the bathroom.

He stepped into her marble shower with her. She'd taught him how to bathe her, and he took over the task now, massaging her scalp and neck, shampooing and rinsing her hair.

His oversized hands were surprisingly gentle as he washed her body, kissing every battle mark. He traced over the painful bruises on her face and hip as well as the ones on her arms showing the blows she'd blocked.

The way his face darkened made her heart melt. He'd accepted that she could care for herself—and now she could see his protectiveness as a gift.

When he finished, she took the soap from his hand and did the same for him. His wet hair tangled, brushing against his thickly muscular shoulders.

Her hands moved down. Had she ever met anyone with such a gorgeous back? She traced her fingers across the hills and valleys of each muscle.

She kissed his neck, inhaling the clean scent. Under the light mat of chest hair, his pectoral muscles turned taut under her touch. His nipples were tiny points. When she stroked and counted the ridges on his abdomen, one ridge at a time—*eight*—she heard his teeth grinding together.

Eventually, she reached his cock and the very neatly trimmed hair around it. Such diligence should be rewarded. "Very nice, Benjamin." She ran a finger around the base.

He made a pleasingly guttural sound.

And her need soared. "I've heard this part of the body must be kept very, very clean. I'll do my best." First, she soaped the straining erection, enjoying the slippery silkiness and how it tried to bob within her grip.

His balls, with their slight furriness, felt heavy and potent in her palms. She snorted. Very potent, actually.

"I think I'm clean, Mistress," he muttered, bracing a hand on the wall.

Her clit was throbbing with its own demands, and her core ached to be filled with him. But more than that, her heart wanted his arms around her, his mouth on hers. She wanted to breathe him in, to burrow against his strength, to hold him and comfort him in return.

But not yet. Mistresses were stronger than that. And she had a...need...to push him.

"Ma'am," he growled.

"Almost, my tiger. You're almost clean enough." She picked up her exfoliation mitt from the low bench and applied it to his shaft, gently at first, then slightly more vigorously, until he groaned as he struggled for control.

*Lovely.* Her body was humming with need, the hot shower cooler than the blaze of her skin.

In the bed, she had him stretch out, his poor reddened cock standing straight as a flagpole. "You want me to climb on, don't you?" she asked, smearing the pre-cum on the head.

Oh, the joys of having the control in her hands, to have the fun of teasing and taunting the guard dog.

And how she loved him. Unable to resist, she bent to take his lips. He gave to her so freely, even as his hands rubbed her shoulders, stroked her arms, fondled her breasts.

When she lifted her head, his glowing eyes were the color of old amber. "More, please."

"Don't worry, my tiger. I'm going to give you more." She opened her bedside table. The first thing to come out was the lube.

He tensed slightly.

"I have a desire to possess all of my domain." She chose a toy he hadn't experienced before. It formed a long curve, made up of a combination of cock and ball rings that terminated in an anal plug.

Tonight, as their previous behaviors were being altered, she needed to prove to herself that here in bed, he was happy as her submissive. "Bend your knees Benjamin."

She loved the rush of color into his face, the conflict in his gaze. She could almost read the battles going on in his mind. He hated having anything in his ass, even as he craved how powerfully he got off with anal play. And the act of being penetrated was both humiliating— which he hated—and submissive, which he desired.

But when it came down to it, he'd do as she requested because he was hers. He loved to please her. Did he have any idea how much she felt the same?

He hadn't moved. "Bend." Gripping his cock, she tugged a warning.

His muscled legs lifted.

"Very good." Smiling, she applied cool lube to his asshole in preparation. Then she started attaching the device. Modified to her specifications—with him in mind—the stretchy ring fastened around the base of his cock.

His shaft seemed to enjoy the attention.

Farther down the curve was the adjustable ring that wrapped around high on his ball sac, forcing his heavy testicles downward. Preventing them from drawing up against his groin. His gaze was on her face, so hot, so intent...with a lovely edge of worry.

The front half of the device was for the cock and balls. The rest of the arc was all about the prostate and made of firmer material.

Right after the ball ring was a vibrating bump that would press against the taint—the outer prostate area located between his balls and anus.

He made a faint sound when the vibrations hit there.

And for the grand finale... With a wicked smile, she slowly eased the anal plug in. Longer than two inches, the rounded end was perfectly designed to stimulate the prostate from the inside.

"Fuck." His head lifted from the bed, the cords in his neck straining.

*Perfect.* If a cock could be considered similar to a clitoris, she figured the prostate was much like a woman's G-spot.

"Please tell me you're planning to climb on and ride," he gritted.

"Soon, guard dog, soon." She'd like nothing better.

But if she could get him off without ejaculating, he'd be able to come again. Multiple orgasms for her tiger—it seemed the least she could do.

First, she'd rev him up a bit further.

She pumped some lotion from the bottle on the bedside stand and rubbed it into her arms. "A woman should keep her skin moisturized for the enjoyment of her man."

His eyes on her were hot enough to sear.

Another pump. She lotioned her shoulders.

"Seems as if the man should help out—since all that soft skin is for him," he offered.

"That does sound logical," she agreed amiably.

"*Yes.*" He tried to sit up and froze as everything she'd put on him pulled and tugged. With a growl, he continued out of the bed, moving carefully.

Excitement simmered within her as she looked at him. His body was tense from head to toes, already well stimulated. He certainly wasn't thinking of anything except the moment...and her.

She took his place on the bed and opened her legs, letting him kneel between them. His hands were huge and hot, the lotion disconcertingly cool as he stroked it down over her front before returning to concentrate on her nipples.

And another gift of pregnancy, she was not only slightly larger, but also very sensitive. He grinned when she squirmed under his usual pressure, then lightened his touch. "I get the impression you're as turned on as I am, Mistress."

His hair brushed her breasts as he spread the lotion over her stomach, following with kisses.

He reached her mound.

*Oh. Yes.*

His tongue found her clit, circled. When he started to use his fingers, she ordered, "Tongue and lips only, please," and gripped his hair to enforce her will.

The vibration of his laugh teased her nerve endings. He ran his tongue over her clit, wiggled it against the sides, descended to circle and probe her entrance, then returned to suck lightly.

His hips rocked slightly as the stimulation to his prostate began to provoke a reaction.

When his hand moved toward his cock, she laughed. "Take hold of me, please."

With a huff of surprise, he snatched his hand away. Brow furrowed with concentration, he gripped her hips and gave her his full attention. Sucking and licking. Such a beautifully hot tongue—and he was uncannily clever at reading her reactions.

Because he loved her.

And God, she loved him. Her hand stroked his head before she fisted his hair again, making him laugh.

Heat grew inside her, the gathering of pressure focused high and in her clit, tightening, tightening.

As it did, she could feel his grip on her hips become painful as his own climax approached.

And then he closed his mouth over her clit and sucked, flickering his tongue over the top between each vigorous pull. The ribbons of sensation flowing through her system gathered into a tight, colorful ball. More…

Between one breath and another, she exploded, her core pulsing and sending bright streams of pleasure surging outward.

His breath was hot on her pussy, the whine of his own approaching climax almost audible, as she clasped his hair. "Benjamin, look at me."

His head lifted, his eyes dark with lust.

She held his gaze, fingertips of one hand stroking his cheek.


The scent of her cinnamon lotion, of her juices, filled him with every breath. Her hand in his hair clamped down almost painfully as she stroked his face sweetly.

And that fucking thing she'd put on him hummed and vibrated against an incredibly sensitive place on his groin.

Her clear blue-gray eyes were the most beautiful eyes in the universe, all framed by those thick, dark lashes, and she watched him as the pressure built at the base of his spine and in his cock and low inside him, somewhere deep in his core. Tighter and tighter.

He stared into her eyes, unable to look away, held by her hand, her voice, her eyes.

"Come, Benjamin," she said softly. "Let it happen."

And fuck, fuck, fuck, it did. The climax was nothing he'd ever felt before, shaking his body, an impossible brilliant orgasm that somehow happened without him shooting his wad.

His back arched, pulling his hair against her grip. And then it was over. His heart was hammering, fit to destroy him.

Her gaze dropped to his groin.

She smiled. "Let's see if you can still perform, guard dog."

Seriously? He looked down. His impossibly erect dick was straining toward her. He pulled in a breath. The fucking vibrations were still hitting him and each time he moved, the rings on his cock and his balls tugged and dragged like squeezing fingers.

*Perform.* Her pussy was wet and slick and her legs were open and...

She was going to kill him dead.

He lifted his gaze to see if she realized what would happen if she let him loose to...

Her eyes were soft and the look in them hit his heart like a Ma Deuce round, knocking him back, filling his chest as her love went singing through every cell in his body.

"I love you," he grated.

Her eyes filled with tears, shocking him, terrifying him.

"Anne."

And then she'd blinked them away. "I love you, too. But if you don't take me right now, I'll still beat your ass."

"Now there's the Mistress I adore," he muttered—and sheathed himself in her wet heat with one forceful thrust.

She gasped.

A second later, his cock felt as if it'd been submerged in a boiling tub of sheer fucking pleasure.

*"Fuuuuck!"* His roar echoed off the walls. Her and that damned abrasive bath mitt. He fought for control as the vibrating devil's device started bringing him back up.

And she was laughing.

Sweat slicked his chest and back. His entire lower half was one massive exposed nerve. His dick burned with each movement in her incredibly tight, hot cunt—and all he could think about was how much he'd missed her husky laugh.

He grinned at her and palmed her breasts. How could anything be so soft and firm at the same time? "You're an evil Mistress."

Every laugh contracted her cunt around him. "Move, Benjamin," she suggested.

"Fucking happy to oblige." He planted an arm beside her shoulder and lifted her ass with his other hand, surging in even deeper.

Her right leg wrapped around his waist, her left around his hips, and her arms clasped his shoulders.

He felt surrounded with her scent, her strength, her body.

"Let go, my tiger," she whispered. "I don't break."

He knew that. No matter what life handed her, she didn't break.

She'd be beside him as they moved forward, supporting him as he guarded her in turn. Yeah, they were going to make it.

Growling, he held her hips to him and pulled out, pressed in. God, the feeling of wet heat was too fucking much. With a low groan, he totally lost control, hammering into her, hard and fast.

As his cock swelled further, the ring at the base grew tighter, keeping the pressure inside him rising and rising. Jesus, he needed to come. The other ring pulled his balls downward. The thing in his ass zinged with every movement, the vibrations behind his junk kept shifting with every thrust.

*Fuck.*

Her trembling legs gripped him as she reached her own moment. Her body arched backward, and he felt her cunt squeezing him in spasms as she came. Sheer beauty.

Shaking, he held himself back, reveling in the sight. She was so fucking gorgeous when she climaxed.

As she sagged back on the bed, her eyes opened, almost completely blue, and clear as after a tropical storm. Her smile said it was his turn.

Yeah, he loved her.

He let the sensations engulf him as he thrust hard, harder, harder, pressing deep.

And then she tilted her hips and deliberately squeezed her pussy around him—and nothing in the world could have kept him from shooting off.

Jesus, he could feel the molten heat flooding from his rocks, the pleasure searing as it worked past the ring on his balls that forced it to travel so fucking, fucking far, all the way to his cock, through his cock, and blazing out in violent, ball-squeezing glory until his entire body was shuddering and each separate cell sang with his climax.

\* \* \* \*

Sometime later, Anne lay with her head on Ben's shoulder, tucked against his side, still shimmering with pleasure. The man had incredible control.

How she loved him.

And now…she needed to muster her courage. With a sigh of effort, she moved up onto one elbow. The moonlight shone through the balcony doors, illuminating the bed like a fairy tale. Lighting the stern, tanned face of her prince.

At her movement, he opened his eyes. His lips twitched. "Mistress, if you want more, you're going to have a dead body in this bed."

She laughed and loved the way a grin transformed his features. "You're safe, guard dog." With one finger, she traced over his thick eyebrows, the lines beside his eyes. There was the bump where his nose had been broken. His lower lip was slightly fuller than the top. A scar made a thin line on his right jaw. "Ben, are you truly comfortable with being submissive in the bedroom?"

Under her fingers, his brows drew together. "You still worried about that?" He took her hand and kissed the fingertips. "Been looking for this all my life and not knowing what was missing. My Mistress reigns in the bedroom, and that's just the way I want it."

Well, that was firm enough.

He ran his hand through her hair, pushing the long strands out of her face. His brows drew together. "What's wrong, Anne?"

She flattened her hand on his chest, feeling the slow thud of his heart under the thick pectorals. Her pulse had increased as fear slowly unraveled her assumed composure. "I need to talk with you about something else."

"Shoot."

"Let's discuss children," she said in an even voice. Hopefully, he wouldn't notice her hand was trembling.

He blinked. "You move fast, Mistress." His lips curved as he ran his hand down her waist, over her hip, to squeeze her ass. "Guess that's one way to keep us equal. You rule the bedroom. Outside of it, I'll keep you barefoot and pregnant."

"You might well get punished for making jokes like that." Her lips curved. *The oaf.*

He grinned, then sobered. "Anne, I love you. I'll give you as many babies as you want if that's what you're asking."

She could only stare at him. His statement was…more…than she'd dreamed of.

"Mistress, this is when you say the words back," he prompted. And his gaze deepened, his grip on her growing painful. "I love you, Anne," he said slowly again.

Of course he'd worry, what with her saying they had to talk. His insecurity snapped her out of her paralysis and gave her the right path.

Still on one elbow, she stroked his cheek, feeling the dense bone structure like an outward representation of his solid character. She indulged herself with a slow, sweet kiss before whispering, "I love you, Benjamin. More than I can possibly tell you…but I'll keep trying."

The rising moon lit his face, showed the warmth in his amber eyes.

Oh, she really, really did love him.

The next sentence required all her courage.

"As to giving me babies?" She took his hand and flattened it on her stomach. "You already did that."

Fuck, she was cute sometimes. Ben grinned at his woman. "Right."

She didn't laugh.

"What?" The import of her words circled inside his head, buzzing faintly, like an insect that couldn't quite be seen. No, no fucking way could she mean…

She was still holding his hand on her belly.

His voice came out higher, not his at all. Maybe one of those rings had emasculated him. "A baby?"

"Mmmhmm. I'm pregnant." She sighed. "This wasn't exactly in my plans."

"But, you're on the pill." He stopped, knowing he was stuttering.

"That first day we were together? I'd spent the previous three days sick with the stomach flu. Throwing up everything, including my pills."

That was the night he'd started to fuck her without a condom. His fault. "God, I'm sorry, Anne."

"Not all your fault. Not all mine." Her hand was still over his. "I'm going to call this the forces of the universe coming together to create a child."

*A baby.*

A little tiny life like…like Sophia.

A baby.

*His* baby.

He'd be a father. The thoughts spun in his head, a whirlwind of shock and…sheer glory.

"Jesus, Anne." He pulled her down, wrapped his arms around her, tried to express how he felt with his embrace. He laid his cheek on the top of her head. "We're going to have a *baby*."

Her laugh was soft. No, she wasn't angry with him. Wasn't unhappy about the baby. She'd had time to get past the shock.

He remembered how she'd held Sophia. How she'd talked to the child at the shelter. How she snuggled with Bronx. Her big heart would easily expand to loving another.

And him? He already loved it—whoever the little one turned out to be. *My child.* "We need to get married."

Her shoulders shook with her laugh. "And now who's moving fast?"

"But...she...he can't be born without my name. We have to get married. Tomorrow."

Silence.

He sighed. "All right. Too fast. You want to live together first?"

"I think that might be wise."

"Got it." He pulled her closer, if that was even possible. Fuck, he loved this woman. "We'll get married in two weeks then."

She smacked the top of his head with her open palm.

*Fine. A month.*

# Chapter Thirty

Anne leaned against the railing of her deck. The day after the storm held a gloriously blue sky and sparkly clean, brine-scented air. Downed palm fronds and piles of seaweed littered the beach, creating challenging obstacles for Harrison's children as they chased Bronx.

Her niece and nephew thought Ben's dog was a marvelous toy. Anne knew that Bronx thought exactly the same thing about human children.

Sipping after-dinner wine, Harrison and his wife had positioned themselves near the edge of the deck where they could keep an eye on their offspring.

Both chowing down on seconds of Anne's chocolate cake, Ben and Travis sat at the adjacent table with her mom and dad.

Her family was a unit, once again.

After talking—and making love—through the night and Sunday morning, she and Ben had invited them over for a Memorial Day gathering.

The late afternoon barbecue would be the perfect venue in which to make her announcement...which she hadn't managed yet, much to Ben's amusement.

Well, honestly, she just hadn't found the right time to introduce a whole new topic of dissension. She studied the group around the table.

Her mother was her usual bubbly self.

Her father...well, Anne had accepted his apology. And what an apology it'd been.

She smiled, thinking of how her parents had arrived last and walked onto the deck. She'd risen, worried at the tentative look on their faces.

She'd thought the small box her father carried was candy, his traditional get-out-of-the-doghouse offering for her mother. But, oh, it hadn't been...

After setting the box on the table, he turned to Anne, lines carved deeply into his hard face. "I'm sorry. Sorry for not seeing you as more than my baby. Sorry I treated you and your brothers differently, that I didn't support you and recognize how much you've achieved. You deserved better from me." His eyes gleamed with moisture. "I really am very proud of you."

She could only stare. How many years had she longed to hear him say that? "Really?" she whispered.

Her mother smiled...and her father's firm, make-it-so nod said he meant every word.

"Oh, Dad." Her eyes blurred with tears as she threw herself into his arms.

His hug hadn't changed...and she realized Ben's embrace conveyed the very same sense of safety and strength.

When Anne stepped back, her mother patted his arm in approval. "Well done, dear. And?"

"Ah." He cleared his throat and his lips curved slightly. "Your mother and I are sorry about...when you were little."

She gave him a puzzled look. Where did this come from? "When I was little?"

"I should have been more understanding, made things easier for you. The relocations weren't good for you. So..." At a loss, he slid the box across the table toward her.

Still confused, she set her hand on it. "Oh, Dad. Mom." They were sorry she hadn't dealt well with moving? "You couldn't have changed any—"

The box...*bounced.* Tilted. "What in the world?"

When she pulled the tape off and raised the lid, a tiny furball emerged.

Ears pricked, the tiger-striped kitten looked up at Anne and gave a pitiful mew.

"Oh, honey." Pink nose, golden eyes, so adorable. Anne lifted it against her chest and a little fuzzy head rubbed her neck. When the purrs began, her heart was lost.

Now she glanced at the exhausted kitten asleep in Travis's lap. Quite an apology gift—and from the way her mother had winked at Ben, she knew exactly who'd had a hand in the choice. Sneaky guard dog.

After that, the gathering had been a decided success.

Unfortunately, the peace was going to be short-lived. Anne sighed. She couldn't stall the announcement much longer.

Feet dragging, she walked over to her man.

Travis tucked an arm around her hips as she stood between him and Ben. "Thanks for having the barbecue, sis, to give us a chance to get back together."

"Can't have the family fighting," she said lightly.

"Some families can. I'm glad you've got a healthy chunk of sweetness under all that tough." He squeezed her, and his voice roughened. "I missed you, sis. Missed listening to your sax in the evenings."

She frowned. "You told me you could hardly hear me."

"Get real. I'm next door." He grinned. "If I'd told you I was listening, you'd stop."

Her smack on the back of his head cut short his laugh.

"You deal with her, Ben," he said, rubbing his head. "She's too mean for me."

"I'll do that." Ben pulled her down onto his lap.

When she narrowed her eyes at his presumption, he gave her the same look back. *Ah, right.* She'd asked him to remind her when she relapsed into Mistress habits—and warned him that if he failed, she'd punish him with an oversized anal plug.

"Sorry, my tiger." She leaned her head against his shoulder and relaxed, knowing his strength wouldn't fail her.

A corner of his mouth tipped up.

She lifted his hand, kissed the scarred knuckles, and whispered, "I love you."

"Anne." His almost inaudible voice held enough warmth to rival the sun. With one finger, he pushed her hair back and murmured into her ear, "You just gave me a hard-on that's fucking uncomfortable. Thanks."

She broke out laughing.

When she turned around, she realized everyone had gone silent.

Travis and her mother and Harrison's wife were smiling in approval, Harrison was giving Ben a considering stare, and her father was frowning darkly.

Well, that frown would turn even blacker with her news.

"I haven't heard you laugh like that in a while." Travis lifted his fork with a big bite of the cake. "Must say that I appreciate how there are always desserts around since Ben's been here."

Anne gave him an assessing look. "Is that why you've stopped by so often in the past month?"

"Hell, yeah." Travis grinned at Ben. "Thanks, man."

"Anne." Her father inclined his head toward several men rounding the corner of her deck. "You have company."

Those weren't just men; they were Masters. Anne shot Ben a glance.

He gave her a rueful shrug. Undoubtedly, the guard dog had reported in to Z—as had everyone else. And the Masters never postponed dealing with problems.

Anne rose and smacked his head in exactly the same way she had her brother—and received an identical laugh.

"May we come up?" Z called.

Honestly, why did everyone act as if her deck was a ship and required naval courtesy? "Of course. Join us." She glanced around. "Mom and Dad, these are old friends of mine. Zachary Grayson, Cullen O'Keefe, Galen Kouros, Dan Sawyer." She accompanied the introductions with casual gestures indicating which man was which.

And wasn't this awkward, considering she wasn't about to tell her family in what context she knew the guys. "Gentlemen, my parents, Stephan and Elaine Desmarais. And my sister-in-law and brothers, Alison, Harrison, and Travis."

With brows drawn, her father noted the chin lifts Ben received from his friends.

With his effortless charm, Z acknowledged the introductions before moving right into the reason for the visit. "Our apologies for the interruption, Anne, but we wanted to determine that you were unharmed, to report on your belligerent visitors, and to interfere with your future."

Kitten held in one arm, Travis took a step forward. "Are the assholes still in jail?"

Z's smile went thin. "The man's wife had already filed a complaint of domestic violence. Add last night with armed break-in, assault and battery with a deadly weapon—he and his cohorts won't see freedom any time soon."

"Excellent," Anne said. Nonetheless, she and Ben would install a security system.

"My turn." Cullen's repentant gaze met hers. "You're one of the finest we have—and we've been friends for years. I fucked up, and all I can do is hope you'll take pity on me and forgive me."

*Oh honestly.* An exasperated laugh escaped. Trust Cullen to tackle an apology right out in front of everyone. "Of course, I forgive you. I overreacted as well."

Cullen's deep laugh boomed out. "You did, love, but I lit the match. I'm sorry, Anne." He rubbed a bruise on his jaw. "Ben made it clear I was out of line."

Ben had punched his oldest friend in the Shadowlands? At Anne's startled glance, he shrugged, totally unconcerned.

Yes, he really had.

"I told you he was more your guard dog than mine," Z said quietly.

What had she taken on? But all she felt was delight that her child would have such a marvelous protector—much as her father and brothers had been for her.

However, Ben was a man who could and would step back and let his baby fly when the time came. She squeezed his hand and watched his smile warm.

"Still friends?" Cullen asked her softly, holding his arms out.

"Oh fine." She took the step forward and hugged him.

He gave a huge sigh of relief. "I really am sorry, Anne."

"You really are forgiven."

"Told you she had more fun going on than we knew about," she heard Travis tell Harrison.

Ben had joined Z and was saying he planned to quit. "I know you prefer your staff to be"—he saw her family was in earshot—"focused only on the job." Because Z preferred vanilla guards.

But Ben enjoyed being the club's security guard. Anne moved forward to interrupt.

"Anne," Cullen said. "Z and I will get out of your hair. *And* we'll see you this weekend." He crossed his arms over his chest and gave her an unyielding stare.

She could go back to the Shadowlands, she realized. Go to her other home. Her vision went blurry with tears.

"No, no, don't do that, sweetie. Damn." Cullen yanked her in his arms again. "You're breaking my heart here."

*Stupid, stupid hormones.*

But leaving the Shadowlands had hurt. It really had.

He tipped her face up and used his thumbs to wipe the tears from her face, and his obvious dismay mended the aching wound in her soul.

She pulled in a breath. "I'm fine. Be off with you—and I'll see you next weekend."

"That-a-girl." He grinned at her warning growl. After nodding to her family and giving Ben a chin lift, he asked, "Ready to go, Z?"

Z didn't answer, his gaze on Anne. With narrowed eyes, he was studying her like a Dom, like a Master of Masters, taking in the dampness of her cheeks, how her hand had settled on her low belly, her shirt that was a bit tighter because of her fuller breasts.

After a second, his dark gray eyes warmed. He'd figured it out.

But, with his usual tact, he simply returned to his conversation. "Benjamin, I think you'll find yourself...busier ...in the future. I'll increase Ghost's hours and leave it up to the two of you how you wish to cover the position."

Ben nodded. "Works for me. For us both."

Anne exchanged a glance with him, smiling, as she remembered the last time they'd scened together at the club. How hot it had been. Now they could continue. After all, Kari and Dan had a child and still enjoyed an occasional night at the Shadowlands for kink and loving.

Z turned and touched her cheek lightly. "Anne." He said nothing more, but somehow managed to convey his affection and concern—and approval.

After smiling at Ben, he joined Cullen and they headed off the deck.

"Who were they?" her father was asking her mother. "And why did—"

Galen moved forward. "My turn."

"Turn for what?" Anne regarded him.

Black hair, black eyes, olive complexion. He hadn't lost any of his intensity when he'd gone from being an FBI special agent to owning his own company. Maybe because his organization specialized in finding missing things—children, documents, people, secrets. Sally, the wife and submissive he shared with his partner Vance, adored tracking down money.

"His turn to talk to you," Dan explained with a scowl. "He won the toss. He gets to go first."

"Oh, well, of course." Seriously, how did men function with all that testosterone tripping them up?

Galen nodded to the empty table on the other side of the deck, distant enough that her family couldn't eavesdrop without being too obvious.

She glanced at her parents, "Can you—"

Her mother shooed her off with a gesture. "We're fine. They drove all this way to speak with you. Go ahead, dear."

"Thanks, Mom." When she checked Ben, he simply smiled and stayed beside her brother.

As soon as she took a seat across from the two Doms, Galen leaned forward and fixed her with his dark gaze. "I have a proposal for you."

"What kind—"

"Come and work for me."

"*What?*" Too many surprises in one day, in one month. If this kept up, her baby was going to be born hooked on adrenaline.

Not waiting for her to recover, Galen continued. His new company was inundated with contracts to find missing people: runaways, wives, husbands, stolen children, embezzlers...everything. And she had a reputation as being the best skip tracer in the business. She could write her own ticket—work full time or part time, set her own hours—and he'd pay her three times what she'd earned at the bail bond company.

"Problems?" Ben was suddenly beside her. He rested a hand on her shoulder in concern. He'd probably seen the shock in her face.

"Actually, no." Galen's offer would solve her employment problem. Much as she'd loved the active part of bail bond pickups, she couldn't put her unborn child at risk. "Galen offered me a position with his company. No travel. No danger. My own hours."

Ben squatted beside her. "You know I can support us both while...uh, for a while. There's no rush to find a job."

"Damn you, Haugen." Galen's annoyance turned his New England accent even crisper than normal. "Don't listen to him, Anne. You'd be bored within a week. If we—"

A hum interrupted him. With an annoyed sound, he pulled out his cell phone, checked the display, and answered. "Right. Yes. Going on right now. You want a turn?"

Anne frowned.

"Since we're in a bidding war for your services, Anne, here's another contender." Galen was laughing as he set his cell on the table between them. "You're on speaker, bro," he said to the phone, "so watch your language. Go."

"What's going on?" Anne asked.

"Anne, you're there. Good." The voice from the phone was Vance's, Galen's partner who still worked for the FBI. "You'd be wasted working for Galen. You have the skills we need in the FBI. Let's talk about it."

She bit her lip to keep from breaking down. After feeling as if she wasn't valued at all, now she had two job offers at once.

"The FBI?" she heard her mother say.

Looking up, she realized her family had ignored politeness and blatantly moved close enough to eavesdrop. She should have known.

They were totally snoopy. And interfering. And loving.

She firmed her voice. "Thank you, Vance. Much as I appreciate the work you Feebies do, I'm a little too settled to want to move around. I'm afraid the FBI isn't for me. But thank you."

"Well, I'm disappointed. If you ever change your mind, I want to know."

"Excellent decision, Anne," Galen said loudly enough for Vance to hear.

"Asshole. You win this one, bro," Vance answered. "I hope you realize what a prize you got. See you in a bit."

"In case Sally didn't tell you, you're cooking tonight." Galen closed the phone over his co-husband's curse.

Dan grinned at Galen, then fixed Anne with an intent gaze. "My turn." He leaned forward. "Don't you think it's time to return to law enforcement, where you belong? We have an opening—and I know you'll find my station more to your liking than the archaic one where you started."

She smiled at him. He'd been after her for years to rejoin the force.

To the police, fugitive recovery was a necessary evil, but not held in high respect. And in all reality, many of the agents were wanna-be cops who'd not scored a law enforcement job. She was the rarity that went the other direction.

Wasn't it nice to be wanted? She squeezed Ben's hand before telling Dan, "I'm afraid that wouldn't work. I'm looking for something part time."

Ben's exhalation of relief was audible. He wouldn't stand in her way, but he'd worry his heart out if she worked law enforcement. Just as she would if he chose that career, actually.

Dan sighed. "Fine." He glanced at Galen. "Might you contract her out to present skip tracing workshops at my station?"

Galen's gaze met hers. "Are you accepting my offer?"

"Assuming the contracts and all that look good, yes. I'd be delighted to work for you."

"Wicked good." He offered his hand, and they sealed the deal with a handshake. "We're all set." He turned to Dan. "We'll map something out to get you access to her expertise."

"Anne!"

The familiar voice had her turning to see her two uncles walking up the steps.

Way to ruin a fine day.

She fixed an accusing stare on her father. He'd obviously told his brothers that she was home and having a party.

When he held his hands out in a "What could I do?" gesture, Anne's mother glared at him as well.

From the way the two incoming resembled Anne's father, Ben figured they were the asshole uncles from the bail bond company. Fighting back irritation and amusement, he squeezed Anne's thigh and said in a low voice, "Got a feeling your dad's going to be sleeping on the couch again tonight. Want me to dispose of the trash for you, Mistress?"

Amusement replaced her frozen expression, and she gave him a light kiss. "I can handle my uncles and I love you."

That was definitely his win. Rising, he took a position where he could guard her six.

"Now, Elaine, don't be mad at Stephan," said the gray-haired uncle. "Anne, we asked him if we could come by and apologize."

With a Mistress's self-possession, Anne folded her hands in her lap. "All right, Uncle Matt. Go ahead." Head tilted, she waited for her apology.

She'd put them right on the spot.

Biting back a laugh, Ben saw Travis and Harrison doing the same.

Matt gaped for a second and glanced at the other. "Russell, tell her."

"Right." Russell ran his hand over his shiny bald pate. "We want you to come back, niece. We'll let you take over the team again."

"We need you," Matt said. "No one is as good as you are at skip tracing."

"Anyone in the business in Florida knows she's the best." Openly amused, Galen butted in. His nosy submissive undoubtedly kept him up on Shadowlands' gossip—including Anne's fight with her uncles. "Which is why I hired her the minute she was free."

"What… You did what?" Russell's face reddened. "Who the hell are you?"

"I'm a man who appreciates talent and will pay well for the privilege of having Anne in my company," Galen said smoothly. "Even better, I got here before the Feds made their offer."

"Feds?"

At the nasal voice, Ben spotted Anne's asshole cousin Robert.

Harrison straightened.

Scowling, Travis handed the kitten to Anne's mother. The party was going downhill fast.

And yet, Anne still sat, cool and composed. There were times he appreciated that Mistress armor of hers.

"She's a police force dropout." Joining his father, Robert asked Galen, "Did she tell you the FBI wanted her? And you believed her?"

"Actually, my ex-partner at the bureau, Special Agent Buchanan, made the offer and is pretty steamed she turned him down." Galen had a wolfish grin. "I win."

"Don't know your source of information, boy, but she's not a dropout," Dan said. "She quit the force. A lot of us have been trying to get her to return to us, where she belongs." As Detective Sawyer leaned back in his chair, his jacket fell open enough to allow everyone a good long look at his holstered weapon.

That silenced the cousin fairly well.

Ben met Dan's gaze and saw both amusement—and impatience. The cop had a low tolerance for assholes.

"Anne," Matt whined. "You really took a job elsewhere?"

"Yes." Anne tilted her head. "Gentlemen," she said coldly, "if you don't wish to offer that apology, please remove yourselves from my property."

Russell puffed up. "We did—"

"Actually, you did not. I didn't hear any phrase containing the words *forgive* or *sorry*." Anne's father folded his arms over his chest. "My gi—Anne built you the finest team in Florida, and you handed her crew over to your incompetent kid. That showed disrespect to Anne—and wasn't fair to your agents either."

"Uncle Stephan, the guys wanted me. Not her," Robert yelled.

"Sure, they did," Travis said sarcastically. "Two of the wimpy part-timers wanted a male—not particularly you. The rest wanted the person who melded them into a team and who kept them safe. Not the cowardly asshole who botched the last three apprehensions with his grandstanding, who almost got Aaron killed, and who got Michael winged."

Anne was on her feet. "Travis, is—"

She'd gone pale. Damn, she shouldn't have to deal with this crap. Ben put his arm around her and felt her tremble.

"He's okay, sis. They all are. But it only took three times with dumbass here and the men are jumping ship."

"The team is yours if you come back, Anne." Matt directed a stern stare at Robert's father, who stayed silent.

"Thank you, but no," Anne said firmly.

Ben cheered silently. She didn't need those fuck-ups. Galen would value her.

She continued, "I won't be back. Perhaps if you remove Robert—completely—and make Aaron the team leader, you might keep your agents."

Matt's shoulders slumped. "I understand. We'll give Aaron the job."

"You'll what?" Robert shouted. "You'll listen to that cunt?"

Ben growled.

Anne's upraised hand held Ben in place. She frowned. "Ben, did you ever visit the bail bond office to see me?"

"No. Never been there."

When her gaze turned to Robert, the asshole turned white.

"I couldn't figure out how the bastards last night got my address," she said. "But a week ago, someone beat you up. You said it was Ben."

Robert took a step back at the menace in Anne's voice.

She leaned both hands on the table and fixed him with a cold stare. "I think those guys came into the office, slapped you around, and you told them where I lived. And you never even warned me."

"I never..." Robert sputtered, eyes shifting sideways. Every single person on the deck could see his guilt.

As fury roared through Ben, he moved forward. Paused. It was Anne's right to tear apart the chickenshit. But *damn*. "Anne. *Please?*"

She smiled and patted her stomach. "Feel free to tend to these little chores for me...for a while. Don't kill him."

"Fuck, I love you." Ben advanced on the asshole, swung from his hip—and, obediently, pulled his punch. Barely.

Robert flew halfway across the deck.

Arms crossed over his chest, Ben waited for dumbass to rise. Instead, he lay there, flat on his back. Eventually he put a hand on his jaw.

The cheers meant nothing compared to Anne's soft, "Excellent work, my tiger."

"Okay, I want to know something." Stephan scowled at his daughter, not quite belligerently, but obviously annoyed. "Last night, you yelled at me for expecting Ben to defend you. Said you could do it yourself. So why is it different today?" He waved at Robert.

"Well, actually, last night I didn't have any choice as to fighting," Anne said, "and once I started, I kind of lost my temper. Ben knew I needed to release some anger."

Ben shrugged at her father. "Her home. Her toys."

"After I calmed down, I realized I shouldn't have…indulged." She gave Ben a wry look because when he'd understood how she'd risked herself and the baby, he'd given her hell. "So today Ben got to deal with the problem."

With a smile, Ben took her hand, silently letting her know that he was available to deal with all her little problems. Any time. Any place.

Travis stared. "Since when do you not *indulge?* You've been knocking guys into next week from the time you were ten."

*Oh yeah?* It'd be entertaining to hear some of those stories. Maybe if he gave Travis enough alcohol…

"My indulging days are over for…oh, another seven months or so. Until after the baby is born." Anne set her hand on her stomach and smiled.

As the uproar broke out, she leaned into Ben, fisted his hair, and demonstrated that her *indulging* would be in a whole different arena.

With satisfaction, Ben pulled her closer and gave her everything she demanded, knowing his heart and mind and soul were safe in her very capable, loving hands.

The mission had been a long one and filled with peril, but somehow—*some-fucking-how*—he had won for himself the love of the Mistress of the Shadowlands.

*Well done, Haugen. Bravo Zulu.*

~ The End ~

Sign up for the 1001 Dark Nights Newsletter
and be entered to win a Tiffany Lock necklace.

There's a contest every quarter!

Go to www.1001DarkNights.com to subscribe.

As a bonus, all subscribers will receive a free
1001 Dark Nights story
*The First Night*
by Lexi Blake & M.J. Rose

Turn the page for a full list of the
1001 Dark Nights fabulous novellas...

# 1001 Dark Nights

Welcome to 1001 Dark Nights... a collection of novellas that are breathtakingly sexy and magically romantic. Some are paranormal, some are erotic. Each and every one is compelling and page turning.

Inspired by the exotic tales of The Arabian Nights, 1001 Dark Nights features *New York Times* and *USA Today* bestselling authors.

In the original, Scheherazade desperately attempts to entertain her husband, the King of Persia, with nightly stories so that he will postpone her execution.

In our versions, month after month, each of our fabulous authors puts a unique spin on the premise and creates a tale that a new Scheherazade tells long into the dark, dark night.

WICKED WOLF by Carrie Ann Ryan
A Redwood Pack Novella

WHEN IRISH EYES ARE HAUNTING by Heather Graham
A Krewe of Hunters Novella

EASY WITH YOU by Kristen Proby
A With Me In Seattle Novella

MASTER OF FREEDOM by Cherise Sinclair
A Mountain Masters Novella

CARESS OF PLEASURE by Julie Kenner
A Dark Pleasures Novella

ADORED by Lexi Blake
A Masters and Mercenaries Novella

HADES by Larissa Ione
A Demonica Novella

RAVAGED by Elisabeth Naughton
An Eternal Guardians Novella

DREAM OF YOU by Jennifer L. Armentrout
A Wait For You Novella

STRIPPED DOWN by Lorelei James
A Blacktop Cowboys ® Novella

RAGE/KILLIAN by Alexandra Ivy/Laura Wright
Bayou Heat Novellas

DRAGON KING by Donna Grant
A Dark Kings Novella

PURE WICKED by Shayla Black
A Wicked Lovers Novella

HARD AS STEEL by Laura Kaye
A Hard Ink/Raven Riders Crossover

STROKE OF MIDNIGHT by Lara Adrian
A Midnight Breed Novella

ALL HALLOWS EVE by Heather Graham
A Krewe of Hunters Novella

KISS THE FLAME by Christopher Rice
A Desire Exchange Novella

DARING HER LOVE by Melissa Foster
A Bradens Novella

TEASED by Rebecca Zanetti
A Dark Protectors Novella

THE PROMISE OF SURRENDER by Liliana Hart
A MacKenzie Family Novella

FOREVER WICKED by Shayla Black
A Wicked Lovers Novella

CRIMSON TWILIGHT by Heather Graham
A Krewe of Hunters Novella

CAPTURED IN SURRENDER by Liliana Hart
A MacKenzie Family Novella

SILENT BITE: A SCANGUARDS WEDDING by Tina Folsom
A Scanguards Vampire Novella

DUNGEON GAMES by Lexi Blake
A Masters and Mercenaries Novella

AZAGOTH by Larissa Ione
A Demonica Novella

NEED YOU NOW by Lisa Renee Jones
A Shattered Promises Series Prelude

SHOW ME, BABY by Cherise Sinclair
A Masters of the Shadowlands Novella

ROPED IN by Lorelei James
A Blacktop Cowboys ® Novella

TEMPTED BY MIDNIGHT by Lara Adrian
A Midnight Breed Novella

THE FLAME by Christopher Rice
A Desire Exchange Novella

CARESS OF DARKNESS by Julie Kenner
A Dark Pleasures Novella


*Also from Evil Eye Concepts:*

TAME ME by J. Kenner
A Stark International Novella

THE SURRENDER GATE By Christopher Rice
A Desire Exchange Novel

SERVICING THE TARGET By Cherise Sinclair
A Masters of the Shadowlands Novel

# About Cherise Sinclair

Authors often say their characters argue with them. Unfortunately, since Cherise Sinclair's heroes are Doms, she never, ever wins.

A *USA Today* bestselling author, she's renowned for writing heart-wrenching romances with laugh-out-loud dialogue, devastating Dominants, and absolutely sizzling sex. And did I mention the BDSM? Her awards include a National Leather Award, *Romantic Times* Reviewer's Choice nomination, and Best Author of the Year from the Goodreads BDSM group.

Fledglings having flown the nest, Cherise, her beloved husband, and one fussy feline live in the Pacific Northwest where nothing is cozier than a rainy day spent writing.

Search out Cherise in the following places:

Website: http://www.CheriseSinclair.com

Facebook: https://www.facebook.com/CheriseSinclairAuthor

Goodreads: http://www.goodreads.com/author/show/2882485.Cherise_Sinclair

Pinterest: http://www.pinterest.com/cherisesinclair/

Sent only on the day of a new release, Cherise's newsletters contain freebies, excerpts, upcoming events, and articles. Sign up here: http://eepurl.com/bpKan

**If you enjoyed the Shadowlands, you might also enjoy Cherise Sinclair's Mountain Masters & Dark Haven series. Here is an excerpt from book 1: Master of the Mountain**

Brande at Book Junkie says: *"I loved it! Every word, every page, every moment until the end! So that is my review in a nutshell... OK I can do better than that, but seriously a melt your panties right off, intriguing love story that forces you to turn the pages until the wee hours of the night just to get to the end! How about that!"*

~ ~ ~ ~ ~ Blurb ~ ~ ~ ~ ~

When Rebecca's boyfriend talks her into vacationing at a mountain lodge with his swing club, she quickly learns she's not cut out for playing musical beds. Now she has nowhere to sleep. Logan, the lodge owner, finds her freezing on the porch. After hauling her inside, he warms her in his own bed, and there the experienced Dom discovers that Rebecca might not be a swinger…but she is definitely a submissive.

~ ~ ~ ~ ~ Excerpt ~ ~ ~ ~ ~

The sun was high overhead and unseasonably hot by the time the trail descended, leaving the pines behind. He led the group across a grass- and wildflower-filled meadow to the tiny mountain lake, clear and blue and damned cold. Granite slabs poked up through the wildflowers, glimmering in the sun. With yells of delight, people dropped their backpacks and stripped.

Logan enjoyed the show of bare asses and breasts as the swingers splashed into the water like a herd of lemmings, screaming at the cold. As he leaned on a boulder, he noticed one person still completely dressed with wide eyes and open mouth. The city girl. Considering she and Matt bunked together, Rebecca couldn't be a virgin, but from her reaction, she was pretty innocent when it came to kink.

"C'mon, babe," her boyfriend yelled, already buck naked in the lake. "The water's great." Not waiting for her response, he waded out deeper, heading for a blonde who looked as if she had substituted bouncy breasts for cheerleading pom-poms.

Rebecca glanced from the water to the trail, back to the water, where Matt wrestled with Ashley, and back to the trail again.

Logan could see the exact moment she decided to leave. He walked over to block her way.

"Excuse me," she said politely.

"No."

Red surged into her cheeks, and her eyes narrowed as she glared at him. Red-gold hair. Freckles. Big bones. Looked like she had Irish ancestry and the temper to go with it. Stepping sideways to block her again, Logan tucked his thumbs into his front pockets and waited for the explosion.

"Listen, Mr. Hunt --"

"It's Logan," he interrupted and tried not to grin as her mouth compressed.

"Whatever. I'm going back to my cabin. Please move your... Please move."

"Sorry, sugar, but no one hikes alone. That's one safety rule I take seriously." He glanced at the swingers. "I can't leave them, and you can't walk alone, so you're stuck here."

Her eyes closed, and he saw the iron control she exerted over her emotions.

The Dom in him wondered how quickly he could break through that control to the woman underneath. Tie her up, tease her a bit, and watch her struggle not to give in to her need and... Hell, talk about inappropriate thoughts.

He pulled in a breath to cool off. No use. It was blistering hot, and not just from his visions of steamy sex. Nothing like global warming in the mountains. He frowned when he noted her damp face and the sweat soaking her long-sleeved, heavy shirt. Not good. The woman needed to get her temperature down.

At the far end of the meadow, the forest would provide shade. He could send her there to sit and cool off, but she'd be out of sight, and from the obstinate set of that pretty, pink mouth, she'd head right back down the trail in spite of his orders.

Shoulders straight, chin up, feet planted. Definitely a rebellious one, the type that brought his dominant nature to the fore. He'd love to give her an order and have her disobey, so he could enjoy the hell out of paddling that soft ass. But she wasn't his to discipline, more's the pity, since a woman like this was wasted on that pretty boy.

And he'd gotten sidetracked.

With a sigh, he returned to the problem at hand. She needed to stay here where he could keep an eye on her, and she needed to cool off.

"Even if you don't strip down completely, at least take some clothes off and wade in the water," he said. "You're getting overheated."

"Thank you, but I'm fine," she said stiffly.

"No, you're not." When he stepped closer, he felt the warmth radiating off her body. Being from San Francisco, she wouldn't be accustomed to the dryness or the heat. "Either strip down, little rebel, or I'll toss you in with your clothes on."

Her mouth dropped open.

He wouldn't, would he? Rebecca stared up at the implacable, cold eyes, seeing the man's utter self-confidence. Definitely not bluffing.

Well, he could be as stern as he wanted. Damned if she'd take her clothing off and display her chunky, scarred legs. She shook her head, backing away. If she needed to, she'd run.

Faster than she could blink, he grabbed her arm.

She tugged and got nowhere. "Listen, you can't --"

With one hand, he unbuttoned her heavy shirt, not at all hindered by her efforts to shove his hand away. After a minute, her shirt flapped open, revealing her bra and her pudgy stomach. "Damn you!"

She glanced at the lake, hoping for Matt to rescue her, and froze. He was kissing the oh-so-perky Ashley, and not just a peck on the lips but a full clinch and deep-throating tongues. Rebecca stared as shock swept through her, followed by a wave of humiliation. He... As her breath hitched, she tore her gaze away, blinking against the welling tears. Why had she ever come here?

"Oh, sugar, don't do that now." Logan pulled her up against his chest, ignoring her weak protest. His arms held her against chest muscles hard as the granite outcroppings, and he turned so she couldn't see the lake. Silently, he stroked a hand down her back while she tried to pull herself together.

Matthew and Ashley would have sex. Soon. Somehow she hadn't quite understood the whole concept of swinging and what her gut-level reaction would be. But she could take it now that she realized...what would happen. After drawing in a shaky breath, she firmed her lips. Fine.

And if Logan insisted she strip to bra and panties, that was fine too. So what if these people saw her giant thighs and ugly scars. She'd never see any of them again. Ever.

For a second, she let herself enjoy the surprising comfort of Logan's arms. Then she pushed away.

He let her take a step back and then grasped her upper arms, keeping her in place as he studied her face.

She flushed and looked away. God, how embarrassing. She had melted down in front of a total stranger, showing him exactly how insecure she was. But he'd been nice, and she owed him. "Thank you for…uh…the shoulder."

With a finger, he turned her face back to him. "I like holding you, Rebecca. Come to me anytime you need a shoulder." A crease appeared in his cheek. He ran his finger across the skin at the top of her lacy bra, his finger slightly rough, sending unexpected tingles through her. "You think I can talk you out of this too?"

On behalf of 1001 Dark Nights,
Liz Berry and M.J. Rose would like to thank ~

Steve Berry
Doug Scofield
Kim Guidroz
Jillian Stein
InkSlinger PR
Dan Slater
Asha Hossain
Chris Graham
Pamela Jamison
Jessica Johns
Dylan Stockton
Richard Blake
BookTrib After Dark
and Simon Lipskar